FALSE SECURITY

Angie Martin

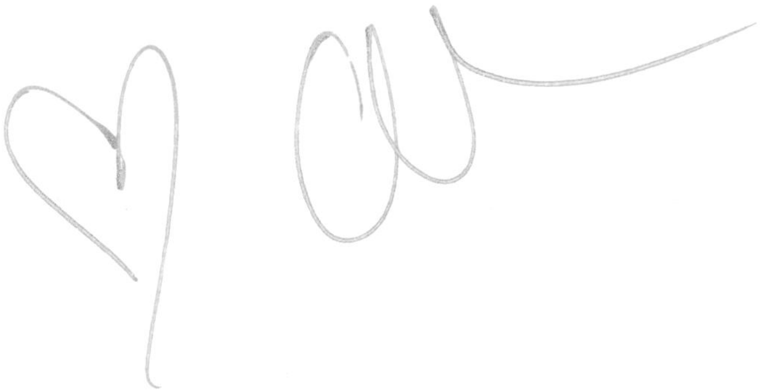

This edition published by Angie Martin for CreateSpace
Text © Angie Martin 2013
ISBN-13: 978-1511677431
ISBN-10: 1511677430
© Angie Martin 2004
ISBN: 978-1301378739

This book is a work of fiction. Any references to historical events, real people, or real places are used fictitiously. Other names, characters, places, and events are products of the author's imagination, and any resemblance to actual events or places or person, living or dead, is entirely coincidental.

Cover Art by: Book Cover Machine

To learn more about author Angie Martin,
please visit her website at www.angiemartinbooks.com

This work of fiction contains adult situations that may not be suitable for children under eighteen years of age. Recommended for mature audiences only.

Also by Angie Martin

Novels

Conduit
The Boys Club

Poetry Collections

the three o'clock in the morning sessions

Dedication

For Kailar and Christian: dreams are designed to come true.

Acknowledgement

Thank you to my wonderful husband, for putting up with me while in the writing zone. Thank you to my mother for your continuing love and support. Thanks to all my awesome beta readers, especially Becky Golba for all your hard work. A very special thank you to Andrea Denning, for all your support, and for all the memories: you'll always be my favorite character.

Prologue

She ran.

Jumping over fallen branches, avoiding small craters embedded in the black forest floor, she pushed her way through the dense woods. Trees hiding in the dark recesses of night jumped out and scratched her arms with their sharp fingernails. Though the forest seemed to prevent her from moving forward, she couldn't stop running. To stop could mean death. Or worse.

She stepped in a hole not large enough for her shoe and fire blazed in her ankle. The pain seared up her leg and she lost her footing. Her black duffel bag flew off her arm and into the dirt and leaves. Her back crashed against the damp ground and her teeth came down on her bottom lip to stop herself from crying out. She rolled to her side and her elbow raked a rock as she grabbed for her ankle.

No matter how sprained her ankle or broken her body, she needed to keep moving. She turned onto her stomach and forced herself to her knees. She gave a half-hearted attempt to stand up, but only managed to fall forward onto her hands. Her fingers lifted to her cheek and dirt smudged across her skin, mixing with the tears she tried to wipe away.

A disjointed voice stirred in her mind. The same voice had plagued her since the beginning of her journey. *Go back*, it tempted. *You can go back right now and everything will be fine. You will never get away with this.*

But she had to get away with it, despite what the voice told her. No sane person would return to hell.

She pushed herself to her knees again, but hesitated at the sound of an unseen owl. The night creatures of the forest lurked all around and she had to move fast to avoid any unpleasant encounters. She extracted a penlight from her pocket and illuminated her watch. Too late to go back. She had been gone for a few hours. They were already searching for her.

Reaching back into her pocket, she pulled out a compass and read the needle under the glow of the penlight. Facing east and still on course, she clicked off the penlight and stared into the vast forest in front of her. She ignored the steady throb in her ankle and the raw, burning pain in her back and coaxed herself to her feet. She tucked the penlight and compass back into her pocket, and used her long, black sleeves to dry the remaining tears on her face.

She closed her eyes and steadied her breathing. In the shadows of her mind, fingers danced over the ivory keys of a grand piano. The beautiful melody wrenched her soul. Her eyes flew open, erasing the picture from her head, but not the song. Raising her eyes to the sky, she said a silent prayer.

She ran.

Part One

Chapter One

"What happened to my office?"

Mark Jacobson looked up from his paperwork. His older brother, Greg, stood in the doorway clenching a bottle of Pepto-Bismol in his fist. "It's my office, too," Mark said.

Greg stepped into the room and looked around. "What did you do in here?" he asked. "I only left for two weeks."

Mark glanced at the new file cabinet resting in the corner. On top, a shuddering black fan paused before rotating in the opposite direction. The noisy fan did little to rid the air of fumes from the fresh coat of off-white paint on the walls.

He looked back at Greg. "I couldn't take the chipped paint and rusty file cabinet another day."

Greg leaned against the edge of the desk and fought the child safety lid on the bottle. "All I wanted was to come back to my office the way I left it, but you couldn't resist using my absence as a chance to paint, could you?" He tilted the bottle and took a large swallow.

"Two weeks on a beach in Florida and you're complaining already," Mark said. "If this is the way you come back from vacation, you're not allowed to go anymore. I hope Anna had a better time than you."

Greg wiped pink residue off his lips with the back of his hand. "Anna's pregnant."

Mark jumped out of his chair. "That's great!"

Greg grunted, and stared at the wall.

"Aren't you excited? You've been trying for a year now."

"Fifteen months and I'm excited, but I'm also scared out of my mind and sick. Very, very sick. Maybe we didn't think this through all the way when we said we wanted kids." He threw his hands up. "And she wants two more after this one!"

Mark smiled at his brother. Though rooted in childhood experiences with their father, Greg's physical features exacerbated his concerns for fatherhood. A string of freckles and the red of too much Florida sun traveled across his crooked nose, while blond kisses of sun tried to hide his lifeless, brown hair. With blue eyes deep-seated in his long face, Greg could be mistaken for their father, a similarity Greg abhorred.

Ten years separated the brothers in age, so Greg had taken the brunt of their father's disdain for children, which grew after their mother's suicide. Their father never laid a hand on either boy, not even for the occasional well-deserved spanking. Their mother handled all the discipline in the house, as well as the minimal amount of love afforded them. When home, their father managed to speak only a few words to either Greg or Mark. His truck-driving career had him on the road more days than not, but when physically present at home with his family, the rest of him remained on the road until the day he never came home again.

The emotional absence of their father left its toll on Greg, who took on a paternal role after Mark's birth. Mark tried once again to assure Greg the resemblance to their father stopped with his physical similarities. "You'll be a great dad. You did a wonderful job raising me."

Greg glared at him. "Oh, yes," he said, waving his hand around the renovated office. "I did a great job with my brother, the neat freak."

Mark frowned, but did not take the comments to heart. Greg's mind focused on Anna and their unborn child, and not on Mark's hard work. "I thought the office looked good," he mumbled.

"You don't like the office, Greg?" James McCormick shuffled through the door, clenching a greasy fast food bag at his side. In need of a tailor's artful hands, his work uniform of black pants and a red shirt hung off his tall, wiry frame. Even his head appeared oversized in comparison to his body, as if it belonged to another person. "Mark and I did a great job painting the office last weekend," James said. "No spills or anything."

Greg groaned and took another large gulp of the antacid. "I don't like things changing when I'm gone. It's too disconcerting for an old man who's fixed in his ways."

"It didn't change that much," James said. He tossed the fast food bag on the desk in front of Mark. "You owe me $4.89. I drank your soda on the way here, so I took a couple bucks off the bill for you."

Mark wondered for the hundredth time why he ever bothered asking James to bring him dinner.

James scratched at his Irish red goatee, a stark contrast to his messy mop of curly, brown hair. "By the way, Sarah wants me to tell you she's here."

Mark's eyes lit up and his breath caught in his throat. "Sarah's here or *she's* here?"

"*She's* here."

Greg's brow furrowed with confusion. "Who's here?"

Mark combed his fingers through his disheveled hair. "How do I look?" He drew the front of his shirt up to his nose and sniffed, grateful to find the scent of his cologne still lingering after a long day at work.

"I guess you look okay," Greg said.

Mark shot out the office door and into the bookstore. He slowed his pace at the first row of books and smiled at a passing customer. He swung a hard right at the self-help section and turned left at the romance novels.

His heart raced at the sight of her standing in the mystery section. Bending over to see a title on one of the lower shelves, her chestnut hair cascaded over her shoulders. He maneuvered his way around another row of books so he could approach her from behind.

"Something I can help you with, ma'am?" he asked.

Rachel Thomas whirled around, one hand on her chest and the other clasping a book. A relieved smile crept over her lips. "You scared me."

"Oh hi, Rachel," he said, feigning surprise. "I didn't know it was you. How are you today?"

"I'm good. I came in to find another book." She held up the book for him to see.

"You finished the other one already? You just bought it yesterday."

"It was hard to put it down."

"Glad to hear it. Are you looking for anything in particular this evening, or do you want something similar to the last one?"

She wrinkled her nose. "I'm getting kind of tired of the cheesy, Hollywood endings."

"Yeah, happy endings always bring me down," he said. He reached out and took the book from her. Studying the title, he said, "Then you won't like this one. In fact, it's not a good book to begin with, let alone one to satisfy your sophisticated tastes in literature."

Rachel laughed. "Then I'm glad you came along to save me from a horrific night of reading."

"Anything for my favorite customer." He moved beside her and replaced the book on the shelf. He scanned the titles until he found the one he wanted. Pulling it off the shelf, he glanced at the back and handed her the book. "This one should do it. The author has a similar style to the last one you read, but the ending should appease your ill will toward all the innocent characters. It's also the start of a four book series, so if you like it, then you'll be busy for at least four days at your reading rate."

Rachel laughed again and pink crept into her cheeks. "Thanks, Mark," she said and started toward the register.

He fell into step beside her. "Aren't you going to read the back and make sure it's what you want?"

Rachel glanced at him with a beautiful, yet timid smile. "The last several books you've recommended have been great. I don't think I'll have any problems with this one."

"Good to know I've been able to help."

Sarah Landers, his store manager, stood behind the counter, writing up the work schedule for the next two weeks. She pushed her glasses up on her nose and continued with the schedule. Mark approached from the center aisle so he could get her attention. When she looked up, Mark caught her eye and gave her a signal with his expression to shoo her away.

Sarah looked off in another direction. "I'll be right there, sir," she called to an unseen customer. She scurried away from the register, her long ponytail bouncing against the back of her neck. Over the past two weeks, Mark made sure Sarah knew to give him every opportunity alone with Rachel, even if it meant making up excuses to leave the area.

Mark rang up the sale and took the ten-dollar bill Rachel offered while keeping her engaged in small talk. He stalled by opening a roll of pennies, despite having more than enough change in the register to give her.

After placing the change in her open hand, he squashed his jumping nerves. "I'd like to hear more of your thoughts on the last book. Maybe I could buy you a cup of coffee after I get out of here tonight."

Her smile faded, and she fumbled with transferring the change from her hand to her purse. "I, uh…" She picked up the book from the counter. "I don't think I should."

"Oh, I'm sorry," he said. "I didn't realize you have a boyfriend."

"I'm not seeing anyone," she said, "but I don't think it's such a good idea to have coffee with you." She gave him a weak smile, her wide emerald eyes warm and sincere. "I'm sorry."

He stared at her as she walked away. The ding of the bell on the front door rang out, driving her rejection home.

"Great," he said under his breath. He probably managed to lose one of their regular customers along with a little bit of pride.

Mark never flirted with customers, but he couldn't ignore the initial spark when he met Rachel, and their chemistry intensified every time she walked into the store. He frowned and sauntered back to his office. The attraction must have been one-sided.

James reclined in a chair next to Greg, feet propped up on Mark's desk. "I can't believe Greg knocked Anna up," he said. He swiped a pen off the desk and inserted the barrel end into his mouth.

"Anna's my wife," Greg said. "You can't call it knocking her up." He scowled at James, who chewed on the pen like it was his last meal. "Throw the pen away after you're done eating it, please."

James shrugged. "Of course." Turning to Mark, he said, "So, how'd it go?"

Mark walked around the desk and collapsed into his chair. "I bombed," he said, dropping his elbows to the desk. He slumped over and his chin landed in his hands.

"Why didn't you ask her out?" Greg asked.

"I did ask her. She turned me down." Mark grabbed the Pepto-Bismol bottle and removed the lid. He grimaced as the chalky liquid coursed down his throat.

"James says she moved to town a few weeks ago," Greg said. "How come it's taken you so long to ask her out? Usually, you're done with them by now."

James spoke before Mark could answer. "I told you already. He's acting weird like that."

Mark held his breath and tried to remain patient with James's attempt to bait him. For the past two weeks, James taunted him almost to the point of humiliation because in Mark's eyes, only one female now resided in all of Wichita, the largest city in Kansas.

"He hasn't gone out with any girl since *she* came along," James continued. "He even broke off his date with the chick that works at the deli over there." He pulled his feet off the desk and stood up. He returned the gnarled pen to the desk organizer.

"That's not like Mark at all," Greg said.

"See? I told you. Weird."

"Are you guys done discussing my life?" Mark asked.

"Yeah." James moved toward the door. "I'm late for work so pay me tomorrow for your dinner. I'm glad I got to see you fall on your face for once." His laughter trailed behind him.

Greg glared at Mark. "He's your friend."

"He grows on you."

"Yeah, all that vagueness. Did you really break off your date with the chick that works at the deli over there?" he asked, his tone imitating James.

Mark chuckled and leaned back in his chair. "Yes, I did. Now James has to get me sandwiches from there so I can avoid her."

Greg rolled his eyes. "Any particular reason why you didn't go out with her?"

"This girl, Rachel, walked into the store two weeks ago, the same day you left for Florida. I greeted her like I would any other customer. She smiled at me and I swear my heart stopped. She's got these incredible green eyes that kind of grabbed me." Mark paused and narrowed his eyes at Greg. "Why are you looking at me so strange?"

Greg placed his hand over his smile. "I'm sorry. Keep going."

"She comes in every couple days and buys a new book. She's nice, intelligent, and not to mention, beautiful. Anyway, to answer your question, after I met Rachel, Lisa didn't seem worth my time anymore."

"Poor Lisa. Why did it take you so long to ask out Rachel?"

"I don't know. It's like I freeze up every time I see her. I've never had that problem before. It's crazy."

"You've become a monk over some girl who won't go out with you? James is right. You are acting weird."

Mark ignored him. "Why don't you go home and spend some time with Anna? I don't know why you came in at all."

"Because I'm scheduled to close the store tonight."

Mark noticed Greg's tired eyes. "I'll stay and close up the store for you."

"That's unselfish of you."

"It's not like I have anything better to do now. Besides, it's your first day back from vacation. Go relax and unwind before you have to come in tomorrow morning and deal with real life again."

Greg started for the door. "You know, Mark, I think the office looks great."

Satisfaction zinged through Mark and he smiled. "I appreciate it. Now get out of here."

Chapter Two

Mark locked the front doors of the bookstore after his long day. Time had dragged its feet against his ego from the second Rachel gave him the brush-off. He'd been so sure she would say yes. Girls never said no.

He flipped a switch and darkness claimed the store. His eyes adjusted, and he moved through the shadowed rows of books to a door with a red and white "Employees Only" sign. He entered the storage room and maneuvered around the racks containing books and supplies. Searching for anything out of place, he glanced at the shelves and stopped to straighten up the cleaning supplies.

Mark placed a hand over his mouth and yawned. The past two weeks, he had worked twice as hard to make up for Greg's absence. Mark's body never missed an opportunity to remind him of its limitations, but the frequent visits of their newest patron kept him going.

Mark shook the thought out of his head. At twenty-nine, he reveled in his bachelor status. Greg nagged him to settle down, reminding him he couldn't chase women for the rest of his life, but Mark never listened.

Commitment didn't scare him. Anna turned Greg's life around for the better, and Mark dove into the role of best man at their wedding. Yet, when Greg tossed the garter belt, Mark thrust his hands into his pockets. Standing in a crowd of men cheered on by zealous girlfriends with weddings twinkling in their eyes, Mark stepped away from the action.

Mark relished his perfect life, and he controlled everything the world threw at him. He had no boss looming over him, no landlord collecting rent, and no significant other monitoring him. He needed nothing else to keep him happy.

Though Rachel declined to have a cup of coffee with him, he shouldn't have asked in the first place. Out of all the women in the world, she had the potential to bring complications into his otherwise uncomplicated life.

The silver lining of the rejection cloud bringing him comfort, Mark activated the security alarm and opened the back door. The chilly night greeted him, and he regretted not grabbing a jacket at home that morning. The automatic door lock on the backdoor engaged itself, and he took a few steps outside into the cool night air. He froze in mid-step.

Rachel Thomas stood in front of his old Chevy pickup truck.

Positive she would disappear, he closed his eyes. When he reopened them, she shoved her hands into the pockets of a form-fitting black jacket and smiled. Under the glow of the parking lot lights, a crisp May breeze moved her hair around her shoulders. Moistening his lips, he started toward her.

"I assumed this was your truck," she said.

"You assumed correctly." His hyperactive nerves made his voice sound foreign. "What are you doing here?"

"I've been thinking about it, and I'd like to have that cup of coffee with you. That is, if it's not too late to take you up on your offer."

Mark smiled. "I'd love to have a cup of coffee. I know this great place on 21st Street—"

"I live right over there," she said, pointing to the neighborhood behind the store, "and I have a coffee maker."

"That sounds fine, too." Not seeing another vehicle with his truck in the parking lot, he asked, "Did you walk here?"

"Yes."

"Then let me drive you home."

Following her directions, he steered his pickup through a sleepy neighborhood and into the driveway of a light blue house with white trim. The sidewalk led past a willow tree threatening to overtake the lawn. On the front porch, the wind pushed a wooden swing along to the tempo of rustling leaves. Each creak of the swing invited them to sit and enjoy its relaxing movements.

Rachel pulled a set of keys out of her jacket pocket. Mark's curiosity grew with each of the three deadbolts she unlocked, all requiring different keys. After they entered the house, she relocked the deadbolts along with two chain locks.

"You do know you're in Wichita, Kansas, right?" Mark asked. "We have our share of incidents, but it's not the crime capital of the world, especially not this neighborhood."

"We rent this place from an elderly woman," Rachel said. "She probably feels safer having so many locks. Oh, and the house came furnished and decorated as is."

Mark followed her into the living room and realized why she made the last statement. The avocado green couch resembled one his parents owned during his youth, and the blue and orange plaid recliner complemented the orange walls. "It's very colorful," he said. They walked up two steps of shag carpet into a kitchen with yellow countertops, accented by daisy wallpaper.

"I don't quite know what to think about the house, but Danielle loves it."

"Is Danielle your roommate?" Mark asked.

"She's more like a sister to me than a roommate."

Not hearing any other noise in the house, Mark asked, "Is she here?"

"She's out at some club, getting into trouble, I'm sure."

"I take it you don't approve."

"It's not like I don't approve of her going, but clubs and bars aren't for me. I would rather be at home reading than in a club sitting at a corner table, sober enough to know most of the people dancing look like complete fools."

Mark chuckled. "That's a good way of looking at it."

"Danielle's a good girl, though. She doesn't go there to drink or pick up guys. She only wants to get out and dance for a few hours. It's her release from the stress of life." She opened a cabinet beside the sink and removed a coffee can and a box of filters. Turning to Mark, she said, "There's a catch to this whole coffee thing."

"What?"

A corner of her mouth turned upward. "I have no idea how to make coffee."

"You have a coffee maker and you don't know how to make coffee?"

"Danielle always makes it. I never paid attention before. All I know is you add water and hot coffee magically appears from nowhere."

"This particular coffee maker is much easier to operate than you think," he said. Taking the box of filters and can of coffee grounds from her hands, he explained his actions while he worked. "You put four scoops of grounds into the filter, then pour water into the top. That pushes the hot water from the reservoir through the filter and gives you instant, hot coffee." As soon as he stopped speaking, the first drops of coffee fell into the carafe.

"I'll never remember that. Kitchen appliances and I don't get along." Rachel wrinkled her nose. "I guess it's the kitchen in general that doesn't like me."

He laughed with her. "Any other catches I should know about?" he asked.

"Nothing comes to mind." Rachel leaned against the counter and crossed her arms. Her mouth twisted into a crooked smile. "Why don't you tell me something about yourself? I only know you own a bookstore and you have great taste in mystery novels."

"I wondered about that. How do you know I'm not some deranged, psychotic lunatic?"

"Outside of being able to tell you're not one, ask me what I do when I'm not in your bookstore."

"What do you do when you're not in my bookstore?"

"I volunteer at a domestic violence shelter, where I teach self-defense."

"So if I was psychotic—"

"You'd probably end up in the hospital with any number of contusions and broken bones."

He raised a brow. "Good thing I'm not psychotic. Now, I know you're new in town, but you never said where you're from."

"Danielle and I moved here from Indianapolis, but I'm originally from California." She pulled two mugs off the tree on the counter and handed them to him. "Are you from here?"

"Born and raised." He filled the cups with coffee. "It might be a little strong. Do you take it black?"

"Yes." She accepted the cup from him and sipped the coffee. "It's good," she said and sat down at the table. "Much better than Danielle's coffee. She makes it so weak, and then loads it up with cream and sugar."

Mark grabbed the handle of his mug. The backs of his fingers grazed the hot ceramic, and the heat from the coffee burned into his skin. He juggled the hot mug and chose a chair adjacent to her. The fragrant steam of the coffee wafted into his nostrils, and the liquid warmed its way down his throat.

"Why did you move to Kansas?" he asked. "Do you have family in the area?"

Rachel set her mug down on the table. Tucking her hair behind her ears, she said, "I don't have any family. My parents both died when I was young and I have no brothers or sisters."

"I'm sorry to hear that."

"It was quite some time ago. They were in a car accident. A drunk driver ran them off the road."

"That's terrible," Mark said. "You don't have any aunts, uncles, or grandparents?"

"Both of my parents were only children and my grandparents passed before I was born. The death of my parents left me an orphan."

"Did you go live with a foster family?"

"I didn't have much of a choice since I didn't have anyone else. Does your family live here?"

"Greg and his wife, Anna, are the only family I have. Mom died when I was ten and Dad had his heart attack a year later. Greg was twenty-one when Dad died, so he assumed responsibility for me. I was lucky to have him."

"Sounds like it. I was also ten when my parents died, so I know how hard it is. Your parents didn't have family, either?"

"They did and I imagine they're still alive somewhere, but I never knew them outside of a few scattered photographs. I think both my parents were the proverbial black sheep." Not wanting to scare her off with the dark conversation, he changed the subject. "What does your roommate do for a living?"

"She waitresses at some restaurant by the mall. Dos Amigos or something like that. All I know is she brings home delicious enchiladas for me. She also volunteers part-time at the shelter on her days off."

"I don't mean to pry, but if you volunteer at the shelter, and your roommate is a waitress who also does volunteer work, how do you guys live?"

Rachel shifted in her chair, and Mark worried he pushed the conversation too far with the personal questions. "I'm sorry," he said. "I shouldn't ask you things like that."

"It's okay," Rachel said. She moistened her lips. "My parents left me a trust fund, which allows me the freedom to do volunteer work instead of sitting in a cubicle all day."

"Ah, so you were a rich kid, huh?"

Rachel laughed. "I guess so. I don't really think of it like that, though."

"If I grew up with someone else making my coffee, I wouldn't know how to make it, either," Mark said. "I take it you had maids, gardeners, and at least one cook."

"All of the above," Rachel said. "In a way it was bad because I never learned how to cook. Danielle can't cook, either, so unless she's making boxed macaroni and cheese, our meals consist of 'Welcome to Greasy Burger, can I take your order?' It's a far cry from having a personal chef."

"Well, you are in the company of a pretty good cook. Maybe I can remind you how wonderful real food can be."

Her smile grew, and her eyes sparkled. "Maybe."

Chapter Three

Rachel couldn't erase the smile from her face and butterflies danced in her stomach without thought of ever stopping. Talking to Mark seemed so natural, and she found herself unable to keep her eyes off him. She didn't know which attribute drew her in the most: the wisps of dark hair falling around his brow, the intensity of his bluish-grey eyes, or his sensual, wide mouth. It all came together and brought her insides to life.

Though men had approached her before, most deemed her off limits after speaking to her for a few minutes. If they didn't, she excelled at alienating them. She also ignored Danielle's attempts to persuade her to date. She avoided luxuries like dreaming, dating, and love.

But Mark was so far removed from any man she had ever known. Around him, she didn't feel so trapped or caged, and her reservations disappeared. She looked forward to going to his store, to talking with him, to seeing his face. She devoured the words in every book she bought to have an excuse to go back to his store and interact with him. With Mark, laughter came easy and smiling came easier. She missed those rarities in her life.

His intrusion into her life unnerved her. She had devoted too much time and energy to constructing the fortress around her world. The well-fortified walls had no visible entrance, yet Mark somehow broke through her defenses. She had not intended for this to happen.

Rachel glanced at her watch, prompting Mark to do the same. Two hours had flown by without consulting her. Their chairs had moved closer to each other during their conversation, and Rachel battled the urge to push her chair away from him.

"I didn't realize it was so late," he said. "As much as I don't want to, I should get going. I have to open the store tomorrow morning."

"I have to get up early, too."

He didn't move.

Her heart picked up speed and her breathing shallowed. She tried to look away, but his eyes held hers captive. Without thinking, she reached out and touched his lips with her fingers. She closed her eyes as he took her hand and kissed her fingertips.

A slight tremor rattled her body, and she withdrew her arm. The spell broken, she picked at a small chip in the handle of her mug, aware of Mark's scrutinizing gaze. She stammered and tried to find some nonsensical excuse for her actions.

She turned toward the sound of the deadbolts unlocking on the front door. "Danielle's home," she said, trying not to sound relieved at the interruption. "I'd better go let her in."

Danielle banged on the door and yelled Rachel's name. A touch of panic latched onto Rachel, and she froze for a moment.

"Is she okay?" Mark asked.

Rachel realized the cause of Danielle's behavior, and her eyes widened. "Your truck is out front," she said. She rushed through the living room and tore the chains off the front door.

Danielle Palmer stood on the porch, wearing black pants and a black spaghetti strap top under a light black jacket. Large, golden curls bordered the frightened look on her face, and she held a can of mace in her hand.

"What are you doing?" Rachel whispered. "Put that away!"

Danielle returned the mace to her purse and stepped through the door. "I thought they… wait a second. Whose truck is parked outside?" she asked. Her mouth dropped when Mark entered the foyer. "Oh, wow." She straightened her posture and extended her hand. "I'm Danielle Palmer."

He shook her hand. "Mark Jacobson. Nice to meet you."

"Same here."

"Danielle, Mark and his brother own the bookstore on the corner," Rachel said. "You know, the one I get my books from."

"Oh," Danielle said, drawing out the word as if making a connection. To Mark, she said, "I apologize for all the commotion. I didn't know Rachel had company tonight. I've been on edge since our last home was broken into. That's why we have so many locks on our door."

A puzzled expression crossed Mark's face. "I thought the lady you rent the house from put on the locks."

"She did," Rachel said, "but Danielle wanted to keep them because of the break-in."

Danielle put her hand on Rachel's arm. "You know, Rach, I think I'll head back out. I'm a bit hungry and I'm sure there's a drive thru open somewhere."

"You don't have to go on my account," Mark said. "I was getting ready to leave."

"I'm sorry," Danielle said, her energetic voice deflated. "I didn't mean to make you leave."

"You didn't, don't worry," Mark said.

"Oh good. Then I guess I'll see you around soon," she said. She raised her eyebrows and directed her last words at Rachel. "At least I hope I do."

After Danielle walked into the living room, Rachel smiled at Mark, as if the simple gesture could explain her best friend to him. She turned and led him outside into the night air, which had chilled even more while they stayed warm inside. She wrapped her arms around herself and stepped down from the porch.

"I'm sorry about Danielle," she said when they reached his truck. "She gets paranoid at the littlest things. She must have gotten scared because she didn't recognize your truck and didn't know you were coming over tonight."

"I'd be a little paranoid myself if my house had a recent break-in."

Rachel bit down on her bottom lip and wrung her hands in front of her waist. "You know, earlier, I didn't…" She took a deep breath and tried again. "Well, I didn't mean, you know—"

"You are so damn cute when you're nervous," Mark said.

She pursed her lips and dropped her hands to her sides. "I'm not nervous. I… I don't know what happened earlier, and I'm sorry. I didn't mean anything by it."

"Yes, you did."

Embarrassed, Rachel laughed and looked away from him. He laid his hand on her face, and she lifted her eyes. His thumb traced her lips. She didn't want this, didn't need this, but she couldn't help herself. Mark lowered his head, and she smiled when his lips touched hers.

Chapter Four

After Rachel closed the front door and replaced the locks, Danielle ambushed her. "There was a man in our house." The words gushed out of her like an excited child on Christmas morning.

"I'm aware of that," Rachel said. She moved around Danielle and down the hall.

"You had a man in our house," Danielle said.

Rachel entered the living room and walked toward the kitchen, with Danielle on her heels. "And you keep repeating this because?" she asked.

"Because there was a man. In this house. You have to tell me everything."

"There's not a whole lot to tell. He asked me to go for coffee when I was at the bookstore earlier. I turned him down at first, but then I changed my mind."

"Come on," Danielle said. "I want to hear every little detail."

"We talked and drank coffee." Rachel placed the coffee mugs in the sink and filled them with hot water.

"And?"

"And nothing."

"Don't give me that. You're blushing and you can't stop smiling. You look like a teenager who was asked to prom by the captain of the football team."

Rachel turned around and leaned against the counter. "And you're acting like we're in the eighth grade. We talked, nothing more. No big deal."

"You like him, don't you? Are you going to see him again?"

"I doubt it."

"Why not? He's really cute and he seems nice enough."

"Then you can date him," Rachel said. "I'm not in the mood for an inquisition."

Danielle scowled. "In all the time I've known you, you've not had a single date. I'm entitled to at least fifty million questions."

"Okay, but I'm going to keep count."

"Besides, if you weren't going to see him again, why'd you kiss him?"

Rachel's eyes widened and her mouth dropped. "You were spying on me!"

"I wasn't spying," Danielle said. "I was checking to make sure the windows were locked."

"I can't believe you spied on me."

Danielle pointed a finger at her. "Don't you dare turn this around on me. You're the one who kissed him and you're the one who went on a date with him."

"It wasn't a date. We had coffee and conversation. We didn't go out to a coffee shop, so it wasn't technically a date."

"No, it qualifies as a date."

Rachel clenched her jaw. "It was not a date."

"And I suppose it wasn't a kiss, either."

Rachel crossed her arms.

"You can deny it all you want, but it doesn't change the facts. You went on a date with him and you kissed him. You may not like it, but that's what happened."

"It was a mistake."

"That was one hell of a mistake. I think you enjoyed yourself and twenty bucks says you do it again." She reached for her purse and pulled out a twenty-dollar bill. She laid the money on the kitchen table.

Rachel stormed over to the counter and took a twenty out of her purse. She threw it on the table next to Danielle's money. "You never win our bets," she said. She whirled around and headed for her bedroom.

"Oh, I think I'll win this time," Danielle called from the hallway. "As much as you try, you can't control your life every single second. You'll buckle the next time you see him."

"Then I'll have to find another bookstore to go to," she yelled down the hall. She slammed the door shut before Danielle could respond.

Leaning against the door, Rachel closed her eyes and tasted Mark on her lips. The butterflies resumed their fluttering. Taking deep breaths, she counted backward from ten, opening her eyes when she reached one. It was time to forget him. Her life had no room for Mark Jacobson.

Chapter Five

The woods were always beautiful this time of year. Spring gave way to summer, and the plush trees welcomed the change of season. Green leaves in different stages of growth filled their limbs, and sunlight filtered through small openings in the branches above her. She stepped through the patches of light, enjoying the warmth on her skin.

The damp grass cooled her bare feet and the scent of rain moved along a mild breeze. A gust of wind rushed through her black dress and she looked down at the rippling silken material. Rustling leaves danced on the ground around her ankles in a celebration of nature.

The radiance of the sun dimmed as if setting, leaving the woods around her in hues of pinks, oranges, and blues. A soft glow in the distance drew her attention, and she moved in the direction of the light. After she took a few steps, an invisible pianist played a song for her. Tinkling notes clung to the air, each one caressing the next like lovers in the night. Even though she could hum every note of the hypnotic melody, she couldn't remember from where she knew the song.

A cardinal flew into view and circled her head, as if trying to catch her attention. It landed on her outstretched palm, and she giggled. The bird opened its beak. "Every fairy tale has a Prince Charming," it said, with a soft tone. "Go to him."

The bird flew away, and she glided toward the light. The sheer, black scarf around her neck floated behind her, as if trying to pull her in the opposite direction.

Halfway to her destination, she realized the light shined from behind a door. Without warning, the sun succumbed to the night. The warmth disappeared with the rest of the sun's rays. White clouds of breath formed in front of her mouth, and her nose tingled from the cold. She rubbed the goosebumps on her arms, but couldn't seem to get warm.

The light beckoned her forward, promising her safety and warmth. She ran over the now frozen ground, catching herself from falling several times. When she reached the door, light emerged from every side. She ran her fingers over letters carved deep into the wood. "Prince Charming," she read aloud. The piano's siren song became louder, despite no piano in sight. Why did the music sound so familiar?

She wrapped her fingers around the doorknob. The woods behind her disappeared, and she glanced back to see a windowless hallway with a black wall and cold, black marble tiles. The doorknob twisted beneath her fingers. She pushed open the creaking door, and the piano ceased playing. She lifted her hand to shield her eyes from the brilliant light.

As she stepped through the doorway, the light dimmed around her. In the middle of the otherwise empty room, a man sat in a chair with a snake coiled on his lap. The cardinal flew down and landed on the man's shoulder. "Don't worry, Rachel," it said. "It will be over soon."

The door slammed shut behind her.

Chapter Six

Rachel turned around at the sound of the screen door opening. Danielle emerged wearing pink pajama bottoms and a white cotton shirt, her hair twisted and clipped to the back of her head. "I tried not to wake you," Rachel said.

Danielle shrugged. "I'm used to it." She rubbed her arms through the long sleeves of her shirt and looked around the small backyard. "This can't be healthy. You wake up from a nightmare and you come out here, only to let paranoia sink in."

"It wasn't a nightmare," Rachel said. "It was one of those falling dreams."

Danielle sat down on the chilled concrete step next to Rachel. "Don't lie to me. You were in the woods again, weren't you?"

"Yeah," she said. Rachel rubbed at the tiredness in her eyes and wished the drowsiness away. She did not want to fall asleep again into the arms of the same dream.

"I hate to see you like this. You never sleep anymore." Danielle pointed at the handgun in Rachel's lap. "You sit out here all night with your gun, as if that's going to make the dream go away. When's the last time you slept the whole night through?" She didn't wait for an answer. "I know it's been at least two months, since you started seeing Mark. Isn't that when the dreams started?"

Rachel ignored Danielle's rhetorical question and stared at the gun. They both knew dating Mark was the cause of the dreams. The dream had never come before two months ago, the same night she invited Mark to her house for coffee. The dream started with menacing images, but nothing she could grasp onto after waking. There was only the memory of something sinister happening while she slept.

Over the last two months of seeing Mark, the dream had evolved into what it was now. As if Rachel did not have enough demons, the dream had become a monster in itself, bent on torment and destruction.

Despite knowing her relationship with Mark was the cause of the dream, Rachel could not bring herself to stop seeing him. He drew her to him in a way she could not explain or control. Even though she knew the time would come when she must leave him, she couldn't entertain the thought of her life without him.

"Well, whatever the cause," Danielle said, "you can't keep this up forever. Maybe you should take a sleeping pill or something to help."

"I would," Rachel said, "but I'm scared if I do, I won't be able to wake up."

"Maybe you should try anyway," Danielle said. "Sometimes when I have a nightmare, I realize it's only a dream and I'm able to control it. You can learn to do that, too."

"That'd be nice, but I don't know when I'm dreaming. Every part of it feels so real."

"You never realize you're dreaming?"

"Not until I wake up and come out here," Rachel said.

"But it's the same dream every time."

"It doesn't seem to matter. I still don't recognize it as a dream. Besides, I wouldn't even know what to do if I could control my dreams."

"For starters, you could shoot the bird."

Rachel arched her eyebrows. "Shooting a bird? That's pleasant."

"Sure," Danielle said. "Whip out a rocket launcher or something."

"A rocket launcher for a bird?"

A large grin crossed her face. "It's a dream so you can do whatever you want."

Rachel laughed. "I'd hate to be an innocent little bird in your dreams."

"But your bird isn't so innocent."

Rachel's laugh faded and her face sobered. She looked down at the gun. Comfort. Rachel expected the gun to bring it and Danielle tried to provide it, but she never truly found comfort. Danielle did what she felt she had to do, shouldering the responsibility of attempting to comfort Rachel, the same as Rachel had done for her from the moment they met.

Fourteen months earlier, when Danielle walked into her self-defense class at a women's shelter in Dallas, Rachel knew her life would never be the same. The timid girl that walked through the door was nothing like the Danielle she knew today. Eyes glued to her feet, Danielle shuffled across the room grasping her bandaged right hand close to her chest. Under the wrappings of the bandages, splints pressed against three of her fingers.

Danielle remained silent during the class and kept her head low, her hair covering up some of the healing bruises on her face. Rachel decided not to encourage Danielle to participate her first day at class. She never pushed any of the women if they weren't ready. The other women left after the class ended, but Danielle stayed behind and stared at the mat beneath her crossed legs.

Rachel sat beside her, but didn't speak. The silence continued for several minutes before Danielle said, "When I went to the emergency room, I told them I broke my fingers playing the piano. Damn Beethoven."

Hysterical, morbid laughter grabbed them both and refused to let go until tears rolled down their cheeks. "Maybe they would have believed you if you had told them it was Chopin," Rachel said. She wiped her moist eyes.

Fear soon replaced the laughter, and Danielle turned to Rachel. "I get scared moving from one room to the next. I keep thinking he's waiting for me in the hallway. Am I crazy?"

"Not at all," Rachel said. She took Danielle's good hand in hers.

"Can I sit here for a little bit?" Danielle asked.

"You can sit here forever if you want, as long as you don't mind me sitting here with you."

Danielle eventually relayed the true story of her bandaged fingers. Steve, her live-in boyfriend of a year, prone to the occasional knock-you-down-and-kick-you-in-the-ribs, had come home drunk from the bar. He accused Danielle of stealing fifty dollars from his wallet and giving it to a secret boyfriend who didn't exist.

Steve had decided to exact his own brand of warped justice. After he had beaten her, he broke three of her fingers, one at a time. She went to the emergency room, and he went to jail, where the police found the money in the front pocket of his jeans when they searched him.

Rachel shuddered as she thought of the abuse Steve had heaped on Danielle. One month later, however, justice had found its way to Steve. While out on bail waiting for his court date, his temper flared during a drunken moment at a bar, and he started a fight with someone who retaliated with a knife.

With her tormentor no longer alive, Danielle's recovery quickened. By then, her friendship with Rachel had grown to heights neither expected, but both welcomed. Piece by shattered piece, Danielle wrangled the truth out of Rachel about her own life.

When the time came for Rachel to move on, she made the mistake of going to see Danielle one last time, unable to leave her without a goodbye. But, Danielle refused to accept her goodbye and insisted on going with Rachel. Ever since, Rachel regretted telling Danielle the truth, always fearful of the possible consequences of Danielle's knowledge.

Danielle's hand landed on Rachel's shoulder. "Are you going to be okay?" Danielle asked. "I mean, really okay?"

"Of course I am. It'll go away in time, I'm sure." Rachel yawned. "Against my better judgment, I think I'm going to try to get some sleep." She stood up and opened the screen door.

"Rachel."

She turned around and looked at her friend.

"It's going to get better. I promise you that."

Rachel glanced at the gun, and her grip tightened on the handle. "Some people say it has to get worse before it can get better."

Chapter Seven

The dream haunted Rachel the rest of the night. After going back to bed, she laid awake and stared at the ceiling with tears spilling onto her pillow. For two months, night after night the dream visited her, and with it, pain that rubbed her soul raw.

Rachel spent the next morning contemplating the dream and rolling its images around in her mind. Danielle noticed her struggle to stop the nightmare from ruling her days, and offered sympathetic support. But, if Danielle saw her downward spiral, Mark would soon recognize it as well.

During her afternoon class at the shelter, she contemplated leaving Mark. An inevitable outcome of their relationship, they had maybe another week together. Until then, she would make sure he remained ignorant to keep their relationship intact while it lasted. The thought of leaving him still scared her almost as much as what would happen if she stayed. If she had a choice, she would stay with him forever.

Rachel walked from the back exit of the women's shelter to her car. She slid into the seat and turned on the ignition, ignoring the pain in her screaming muscles. She had pushed herself too hard at the gym before class, and she made a mental note not to do it again. The class had also been tough, and one of the women took her down while practicing self-defense techniques. Even though the progress of all the women made Rachel happy, the bruises forming beneath her skin told her she needed to take it easy.

The new girl and miracle at the shelter came to class, having recovered from her husband's final attack. Her husband had stabbed her eight times in her abdomen with a slender paring knife. The random impalements missed all major organs, but caused her to lose their unborn child.

As the others often did, she came up to Rachel after class and asked a timid question. Twirling the ends of her unruly red hair, she asked Rachel how she could defend herself against a knife attack.

Though the question never bothered her in the past, Rachel faltered with her words and a thin scar on the front of her neck burned with phantom pain.

I'd love the chance to use this knife on you.

She had thrown the voice out of her mind and told the girl they would discuss her question in the next class. Rachel's neck continued to throb all the way home.

As she turned down her street, Rachel told herself to forget about it. That particular question had been asked numerous times before and had yet to be problematic. The dream made the question sinister and made her remember things best forgotten. She needed to compose herself and reprise the role of Rachel Thomas, a woman with her life together. Letting those other thoughts and memories consume her would only destroy the new life she had built.

She longed to hop in the shower and wash off the residue of her afternoon class. A hot shower would go far in awakening her dull senses and erasing unwelcome memories. Besides, a shower was a necessity since she had a dinner date with Mark in a half hour.

She smiled and pulled her car into the driveway. She grabbed her duffel bag to go inside the house. It would be the perfect ending to her day to spend time with him. Mark had been a wonderful addition to her life, her light at the end of the tunnel in which she had been living, and it made the thought of leaving him so terrible.

He had a way about him, though Rachel couldn't quite put her finger on why he had such an effect on her. His uncanny ability made her forget herself and swept her into another world, where the concept of her and Mark had always existed. Everything he offered was hers for the taking, in exchange for the price of continuous nightmares.

When she reached the front door, she unlocked the deadbolts and pushed open the door. The security alarm squealed at her. She had it installed a month earlier, after the recurring nightmares drove her to her first panic attack. She thought the alarm would add to her sense of security and keep the nightmares and panic attacks at bay. So far, it had failed.

Rachel opened the white door on the alarm box and punched in her code. 7439. The display still read "armed" and the shrieking alarm crescendoed. She hit the buttons again. 7439. No response. She smothered the panic rising from her gut and tried again. 7439. The alarm continued its song.

"Dammit!" She threw her bag down by the hallway table and started out the front door. She thought about trying her code one more time, but decided against it since the code didn't work the first three times. She'd have to disarm the alarm.

A computer voice informed her that the police knew of her intrusion. Rachel froze on her front porch, consumed by the thought of disarming the alarm. The idea never should have popped into her mind. Sure, she could take out the alarm, but she wouldn't. If the police showed up while she worked on the alarm, she'd have a lot of explaining to do.

The phone rang, an uninvited accompanist to the shrill music of the alarm. Rachel ignored the sounds. She left the front door open and lowered herself down onto the front porch, incredulous she would ever consider manually stopping the alarm. But, the disturbing thought brought about a greater terror. She could take out the alarm faster than she could enter her code, and there were others who could do the same. People not so forgiving.

7943. Rachel closed her eyes. That was the right code. Police sirens added to the symphony behind her. Too late to enter the right code now.

A few moments later, a police car pulled against the curb. Rachel stood up and brushed off the back of her jeans. Two officers, one male and one female, climbed out of the patrol car and walked across the lawn toward her.

Rachel called to them while they approached. "I punched the wrong code into my alarm by mistake."

"What's your name?" the male officer asked when he reached her. He held a notepad, clipboard, and pen in his hands.

"Rachel Thomas."

"You didn't answer your phone when the security company called," he said. "Is everything okay?"

"When the alarm went off, I came outside and I didn't hear the phone ring. Look my code is 7943. Can you verify with the security company?"

The male officer didn't answer, but wrote in his notepad. Rachel glanced down at their names pinned to their uniforms. Scrawny and mousy, Officer Duncan's nameplate was askew on her disheveled uniform. Scuff marks stood out on her shoes and matched the food stain on her pants by her right knee.

Officer Shearn, her male partner, towered above her with his perfectly pressed uniform. He stared at Rachel from behind thick glasses. "Do you have some identification, Mrs. Thomas?" he asked.

"*Ms.* Thomas," Rachel said, "and yes. My driver's license is in the house." Rachel's heart sunk with the words. Her current driver's license was as fraudulent as it had been in every state she lived. She had not yet encountered police in her travels, and she prayed the license would stand up under scrutiny.

Rachel started for the front door, but the officers didn't move. "Did you want to come into the house with me?" she asked.

They followed her inside the house this time, but with vigilant and deliberate movements. Officer Duncan kept a wary eye on Rachel.

Rachel reached for her duffel bag, but Officer Duncan stopped her before she could pick it up. "I'll get it for you," she said.

She opened Rachel's bag and pulled out her purse. She sat the purse down on the hall table and rifled through its contents. The search seemed to take much longer than it should, and Rachel wondered if such a lengthy search was normal procedure. She started to ask, when Officer Duncan extracted a driver's license, studied it and handed the license to her partner.

"Can I use your phone?" Officer Shearn asked.

"Sure. It's in the kitchen, through there." Rachel pointed across the living room toward the kitchen. Rachel concentrated on controlling her breathing, and her heart rate increased. Why did he need to use her phone? He had a radio on the shoulder of his uniform, so he had no need for a phone.

Officer Duncan moved closer to Rachel and brushed away a strand of dirty brown hair that escaped from the tight bun on the back of her head. Stale cigarette smoke emanated from Officer Duncan's clothes, and Rachel had to stop herself from covering her nose.

The policewoman stared at her with skeptical, probing eyes, and Rachel's paranoia grew. Did she even know for a fact these were real police officers? What if they were legitimate cops and Officer Shearn ran a background check on her? What would come back?

Deep down, Rachel didn't care what the officers would find out about her. She didn't even mind if they learned her driver's license was fake. A background check would throw up a flare for the wrong eyes to see. Dark eyes searching for nothing other than her.

"Rachel!"

She rushed out of the hallway and onto the front porch. Mark ran full-speed across the lawn toward the house.

"Wait right there," Officer Duncan said to him. She placed her right hand on her gun holster.

Rachel hoped the motion was instinctual and not because she wanted to use her gun against Mark. Rachel's own gun was tucked in the drawer of her bedside table in her bedroom, too far away for her to get if the officers turned out to be anything other than sworn peacekeepers.

Mark halted at the edge of the driveway. "She's my girlfriend," he said, his words tinged with annoyance, as if the officer should have known.

"It's okay," Rachel said. "He's telling the truth."

Officer Duncan gave Mark the okay to move forward.

Mark went to Rachel, pulled her into his arms, and squeezed her tight. "What happened? Are you okay?" He released his hold on her and pulled back so he could look her over.

"I'm fine," Rachel said. "I entered the wrong code into my alarm. It went off and the police came."

Mark's shoulders dropped and worry departed from his face. "I'm glad it's nothing serious."

Eyes bore through Rachel, and her skin crawled with paranoia. She shifted her gaze toward Officer Duncan, who wore the same peculiar expression as she did earlier. Her eyes never left Rachel, inspecting her as if Officer Duncan knew her from somewhere. She shivered at Officer Duncan's stare and tried to squash her overactive imagination. Rachel looked back at Mark, who gave her a warm smile.

"Everything checked out," Officer Shearn said, and he walked down the front steps. "I called the security company back and gave them the all clear. They're resetting the alarm right now. Are you sure everything's okay?"

"Positive," Rachel insisted. At her words, the alarm stopped, though it continued echoing in her ears.

"Would you like us to check the rest of your house to be safe?" Officer Duncan asked her.

Rachel hesitated for a moment. There was no harm in the police looking through the house, but something in Officer Duncan's voice twisted Rachel's stomach with anxiety. "No, thank you," Rachel said. "I think we'll be fine since I set off the alarm by mistake and it wasn't an intruder."

"I noticed your license doesn't have this address listed on it," Officer Duncan said.

Rachel smiled and tried to quell Officer Duncan's suspicions. "I'm sorry, officer. I moved here almost three months ago and I haven't found time to make it to the DMV."

"You'll want to get it fixed right away," Officer Shearn said. He ripped a sheet of paper off his clipboard and handed it to Rachel with her driver's license. "It's a warning for your false alarm. There isn't a fine this time, but if you have another one, we'll have no choice but to fine you."

Rachel took the paper. "Thank you. I appreciate your quick response."

"No problem," Officer Shearn said. "Be more careful in the future with your code, and fix your driver's license." He walked toward his police car.

Officer Duncan kept her eyes on Rachel for a moment, and then followed Officer Shearn to the car.

After the officers drove away, Mark put his hands on Rachel's shoulders. "When I saw the police here..." He pulled her close and placed his hand on the back of her head. Worry filled his jagged breathing. "I thought something happened to you."

She rested her cheek on his shoulder and pressed her face into his neck. His tight hold comforted her, and she did everything she could not to cry. The past couple months had stretched her emotional stability to a breaking point. Her overwhelming feelings for Mark competed for control against her paranoia and anxiety.

Her obsession with security had reached an all-time high, having added the alarm last month and a hinge lock to the back door a few days ago. She fought the urge to put bars on the windows and lock herself up, away from the world. Everywhere she went, she looked over her shoulder and in her rearview mirror.

All the while, she made sure Mark remained oblivious to her self-destructive behavior and naïve to her torments, as well as the cause of them. No matter what it took, she intended to keep it that way.

Rachel pulled away from him. Hand-in-hand, they walked into her house. "I haven't had a chance to shower yet," she told him after closing the front door and securing the locks.

"I'm in no rush. Are you sure you're okay?"

"Yes, I'm fine. I promise." She slipped her driver's license and the written warning into her purse on the hallway table. "I'm going to take a quick shower, if you don't mind. Then we can go wherever you want for dinner."

"Unless you'd rather stay in tonight," Mark said. "We could order something for delivery. Maybe Chinese?"

Her taste buds jumped at the thought of fried rice and sesame chicken, and the world was back to right once more. "That sounds good." She leaned over and picked up her bag. "I'll be out soon." Her lips pecked his cheek, and she headed for the bathroom.

Chapter Eight

Rachel disappeared into the bathroom, and Mark's smile faded. As he held her, she erected another wall between them. The way she tensed against him, and then relaxed as if nothing was wrong. But, something *was* wrong. His conviction of that grew stronger every day.

Still standing in the hallway by the front door where Rachel left him, Mark caught sight of her purse sitting on the hall table. The officer's words came back to him about her driver's license having the wrong address. He peered down the hall and listened to the faint sound of the shower. Rachel would be occupied for at least another ten to fifteen minutes.

Mark stood over her purse, his hands ready to rifle through it to get out her driver's license. As far as he knew, she had always lived in this house since she came to Wichita. He couldn't fathom the reason why her driver's license would have a different address.

Mark left the foyer without sneaking a look at her license, and admonished his suspicious thoughts. He couldn't spy into Rachel's personal items, not without asking about the discrepancy. She might have lived at a different address before she moved to this house. He must have misunderstood that she always lived in this house, as the wrong address had no other explanation. Yet, it seemed his misunderstandings were piling up over time.

He stepped into the living room and glanced around for some kind of clue as to what mysteries controlled Rachel's life. He partly blamed his suspicions on the house. Aside from the feeling he had stepped back into the days of peace signs and orange Volkswagen vans, the house brought about no emotions, heightened no senses.

Cold and dead, the house lacked in the feeling of being a home. No pictures on the walls, no plants or flowers, none of the small touches to make him think Rachel and Danielle lived here. There was the candle on the coffee table, but he had been in the living room with Rachel when Danielle brought in the candle and set it there.

Mark's house at least had the sense of home. The pictures of Greg and Anna on his fireplace mantel. The mesmerizing Salvador Dali print hanging in his dining room. Two bookshelves full of broken spines in the living room. Rachel's house had none of those little things.

Mark couldn't be sure, but he had a hunch not one item in their house belonged to either girl, as if Rachel and Danielle had come to Wichita with nothing more than their clothes. Even the books on the short oak bookshelf in the back of the living room were ones Mark recognized as coming from his store, ones he had sold to Rachel. Their house felt more like a hotel, rather than a home in which they planned on staying.

He moved into the kitchen to get the menu and order dinner from their favorite Chinese restaurant. He stopped halfway across the linoleum floor, and his eyes fell on her backdoor. He counted the locks. One on the doorknob, two deadbolts, a chain, and a hinge lock. The hair stood up on his arms. First she added the security alarm last month, and now a new hinge lock. It seemed Rachel wanted to keep someone out.

A memory flooded his mind. Rachel had blamed their landlord for putting the excessive locks on the front door. Danielle later said they had the locks added because of a break-in at their old home. Now, a security alarm and a hinge lock had been added. Not for the first time in the past two months, Mark realized there were too many contradictions in the things Rachel told him.

Mark looked away from the door. He had suspected Rachel of dishonesty several times, but her motives eluded him. Locks seemed such a trivial thing to lie about, unless Rachel had something to hide, something she didn't want to share with him. Maybe Rachel wanted to keep more than burglars out of her life.

Mark swallowed hard. He didn't need to think those things. He wanted to keep her as part of his life, and doubting her would only drive her away. He went to the telephone and opened the drawer underneath it. He dug through a stack of menus until he found the one he wanted.

Rachel came up behind him right after he finished ordering their dinner. She slid her arms around his waist and laid her head down on his back, hair still moist from the shower.

Mark didn't mind the dampness penetrating the back of his shirt. The gesture kicked his heart into gear, and he took her hands, entwining his fingers with hers. Her smile warmed his back, and he closed his eyes, forgetting his earlier concerns. He had exaggerated the situation. Nothing was out of the ordinary with Rachel except his imagination.

"When's dinner coming?" she mumbled.

"Thirty minutes. Did you have a good shower?"

"Of course."

He turned around and she adjusted her hold on him. He kissed the tip of her nose. "Is Danielle getting off work soon?"

"Not until ten. Why?"

"I want to know how much time I have you to myself. It's bad enough I already had to share you with the police."

Rachel frowned. "I don't like the way the policewoman looked at me."

Mark chuckled. "Why? Did you knock over a liquor store on your way home?"

All humor from his statement was lost on Rachel, who didn't crack even a small smile. "I don't know why, but she was looking at me funny."

"Maybe she was jealous. It's not everyday people get to see someone as beautiful as you."

Rachel laughed and moved around him. She closed the menu for the restaurant and put it away in the drawer with the rest of the menus. "You are so full of it."

He put his hands on her shoulders and gave them a light squeeze. "I'm telling the truth, Rach. You're an angel."

A sharp intake of breath, tense muscles, and cords rising up from her neck. A second later, she was back to normal, and Mark questioned whether the momentary change had occurred, but he knew better. Another wall had gone up.

He turned her around and took her hands in his.

Rachel shied away from his gaze and bit down on her lip. "What did you order us for dinner?"

He smiled, knowing her real question. "Don't worry, I asked for extra fortune cookies for you. What was it about the way she looked at you?"

"I don't know. Creepy, I guess."

Mark recalled the woman to his mind, along with the expression on her face when she looked at Rachel. She seemed curious at first, but Mark remembered seeing something in the officer's eyes. More than just a normal glance, the officer studied Rachel, as if memorizing her features.

Definitely creepy.

Chapter Nine

Officer Shelly Duncan stopped pacing her kitchen tiles and ran her hands through her hair. She collapsed into a chair and rested her elbows on the small kitchen table, tired of wrestling with her conscience. Her good angel always lost anyway, having been weakened over time. It was all Frank's fault. If he hadn't taken up heroin as his drug of choice, she never would have been in this position.

Her mother warned her many years ago about her problem with men. They were Shelly's Achilles heel, her mother had said every chance she got. Her mother had been right. Frank was the perfect example. He couldn't be described as handsome by any means, but he was charming and great in bed. Shelly taught herself to look past the loud snoring, the tobacco he chewed, and the marijuana he smoked every so often, and married him. She wasn't the only cop on the force with a troubled homestead, and Frank's issues weren't too awful.

As time went on, her home life spiraled out of control. While she could ignore Frank smoking the occasional joint, the pills were a little harder to disregard. Then the pills morphed into cocaine, and later into heroin. It seemed no drug was off limits for Frank. Yet, she loved him, and she convinced herself love was enough reason to stay.

Maybe it wasn't entirely Frank's fault, Shelly thought. She accepted some of the blame for not saying anything to him, for not giving him an ultimatum to stop.

She fished a cigarette out of the crumpled pack on the kitchen table. She struck a match and held it to the end of the cigarette until the tobacco glowed orange, then shook the match to extinguish the flame. Tendrils of sulfur from the blown-out match drifted into her nostrils. She took a long pull off the cigarette and shut her eyes. The thick smoke curled into her lungs and comforted her.

Damn Frank. She always knew his heroin addiction would haunt her if he didn't stop using. It almost killed her five years ago when she woke in the middle of the night to a stranger pointing a gun at her head. She had buried Frank two days earlier. Her bastard of a husband died in a car accident, and not from the heroin she always assumed would be his demise.

The stranger standing over her bed with a gun explained Frank owed money to Graham Wilkes. Since Frank was dead, his debt of a little over twenty thousand dollars belonged to her.

Thinking about it now, Shelly muttered a curse. Of all the people Frank could have owed, it was Graham Wilkes. Frank's hospital and funeral bills had wiped out his measly life insurance policy before she received it. She didn't even have enough money left to buy a new car, since Frank had totaled their only vehicle on his way out of this world. How could she pay off Wilkes to the tune of twenty thousand dollars?

The stranger had the answer to wipe away her debt, and Shelly became an unwilling and unpaid addition to Wilkes's ranks. A mostly decent cop turned informant with no hope of ever getting out. At first, it had been easier than she thought. A small task here and there. Nothing too bad and nothing to destroy the last of her morals.

Until today.

Shelly stubbed out the half-smoked cigarette in an overflowing ashtray and dug her cellphone out of her pocket. She dialed the number written on the card in front of her. A second stranger had given the card to her a couple years ago when he confronted her in the parking lot behind her favorite bowling alley. As she listened to the fourth ring now, she wondered if the number was still good.

The phone clicked on the other end, as if someone answered, but no one spoke. "Hello?" Shelly asked.

"What do you want?" an angry male voice asked.

The cell phone shook against her ear, and she stammered out the words. "Are you still looking for someone?"

Silence.

She took a deep breath. She must have the wrong number. It was a long shot, anyway. So much time had passed since she saw the picture of the girl Wilkes wanted. This Rachel Thomas probably only resembled her. But, this afternoon, Shelly had been positive it was the same girl.

"Do you know where she is?" the voice asked.

Shelly's eyes widened. Maybe she had been right after all about Rachel Thomas being the missing girl. This could be the bartering tool she needed to get Wilkes off her back for good.

The thought made Shelly smile for the first time since leaving the girl's home earlier. "Yes," she said. "I know where you can find her."

Chapter Ten

Rachel reminded Mark of a child caught with her hand in the cookie jar. She stood in the doorway, her hair in a loose ponytail with rebel strands falling to the sides of her face. Hands clasped behind her back, she chewed her bottom lip. Her fidgeting bare feet stuck out below jeans rolled up to her calves.

Mark grinned at her expression, and she stepped aside to let him in. "I got here as soon as I could," he said. "What's so important?"

She motioned with her finger for him to follow her. He trailed behind her into the living room. The sight of the kitchen table and chairs positioned in front of the couch sparked his curiosity. He matched her steps around the furniture and stopped in front of the kitchen.

Rachel turned to him and said, "I think I broke the dishwasher."

Mark's eyes widened. He laughed and surveyed the damage. Soapsuds covered the floor like fog and vines of suds climbed the cabinets.

"I wanted to help Danielle in the kitchen for once," she said. Suds clung to her feet and gathered around her ankles as she walked toward the dishwasher. "I didn't think a dishwasher could be so complicated."

Mark stayed in the living room. "I'm sure she'd appreciate the effort, but I have a feeling you called me because you don't want her to know about this."

Rachel's sheepish grin answered his question.

"How much soap did you use in the dishwasher?"

"I filled up both wells and closed the door on the first well. It's the same thing Danielle always does. I turned on the dishwasher and went into my bedroom to read for a bit. When I came out to check on the dishes, I found this mess." She pursed her lips. "I don't get it. This never happens when she does the dishes."

"That's odd," Mark said. A thought occurred to him. "What kind of soap did you use?"

"I used dishwasher soap." She waded through the suds and opened the cabinet door under the sink. "We ran out of the other stuff, so I used this one," she said. She held up a bottle of Dawn.

Mark's eyes widened. "Rach, that's not dishwasher soap."

Her brow creased and her eyes traveled across the label. "It's not? But it says right here it's for dishes."

Mark dropped down on the living room carpet and pulled off his tennis shoes and socks. "It's used for washing dishes by hand. Put it in the dishwasher and you get this." He gestured at the suds on the floor.

Her shoulders dropped in defeat. "Great."

"I understand why Danielle doesn't let you near the kitchen," Mark said. He rolled up the bottom of his jeans and stood up. "What did you do before you met her?"

"I ate out or used paper plates," she said, a despondent expression crossing her face. "I'm such an idiot when it comes to the kitchen."

"Don't say that. The kitchen may not be your forte, but you're the smartest person I've ever met." He paused and noticed her downcast eyes. "It's okay, Rach. We'll get it cleaned up before Danielle gets home. She'll be none the wiser."

Rachel pointed at the dishwasher. "What about that thing? It didn't finish running yet."

He squished his way through the soap bubbles and flipped the latch on the dishwasher. Suds spewed out like froth from a rabid dog's mouth. Mark laughed, and he pushed the latch in the opposite direction, quieting the machine. "I guess we should clean out the soap before letting the dishwasher run its course. Otherwise, we might be here for days cleaning the floor."

Thirty minutes later, his soaked jeans adhered to his skin. The floor now showing in some areas, Mark dipped suds off the floor with a large pitcher while Rachel worked on the dishwasher itself, using a sponge to wipe out soap and suds.

Mark filled the pitcher again and rose on his knees so he could rinse it out in the sink. His eyes fell on Rachel, and he stopped to watch her work. Rachel's beauty ran deeper than the bronzed, smooth skin that required no makeup to hide flaws or imperfections. Her beauty flowed through her veins, rushing through her body and escaping through her fingertips when she touched him. It radiated from eyes an unusual shade of green and seized Mark's heart.

She turned her head and caught Mark staring at her. A playful smile teased her lips. "What?"

A small cluster of suds clung to her cheek. He smiled and walked toward her on his knees. "You have some suds on your face," he said when he reached her. He lifted a hand and wiped them away.

She looked down and bit her bottom lip, as if embarrassed by his touch. He continued caressing her cheek, hypnotized by the feel of her skin. She moistened her lips and stared into his eyes. Her actions struck Mark in the chest with a sharp thrill and stimulated his heart. Every time he touched her, she captured his heart a little more.

He dropped the pitcher to the floor beside him. He lifted her chin and touched his lips to hers. One of his hands settled on her lower back while the other found the back of her head and tangled itself in her hair. Slow and sensual, his mouth moved in tandem with hers. Mark never wanted the kiss to end.

Though their physical relationship always stopped with a kiss, Mark never pushed the boundaries. Rachel had an innocence about her that he wanted to preserve, even if his body disagreed.

Her fingers curled into his sides and clenched his shirt. She made a soft sound and pressed her lips tighter against his. Her hands ran down to his hips and halted. She hinged her thumbs on the waistband of his jeans and slowed the kiss. Mark wondered if she faced the same conflicts as he.

His wet jeans reminded him of the task at hand. He broke the kiss, but lingered close to her, his nose touching hers, her soft breaths warming his skin. "You really are an angel, Rachel," he whispered.

She recoiled, and her eyes flew up to meet his. An almost painful shadow flashed across her face, followed by a gratuitous, content look. It wasn't the first time he had seen this happen in the past two months, and it bothered him almost more than the walls she kept putting up between them.

Five days had passed since Rachel's alarm summoned the police. Since then, Mark watched her and searched for signs of things she did to make him wary.

What he found only added to his unease. Distant eyes, as if she were in another place and time. Quick recoveries when he asked if she was okay. Impeccable, scripted answers to questions, as if she was placating him, telling him what she thought he wanted to hear instead of the whole truth.

He had been good at dismissing it in the past. Today, however, apprehension clawed at him. "I didn't mean to upset you," he said.

Her expression remained the same. "You didn't upset me," she said and leaned in for another kiss.

Mark reciprocated, and the corroding doubts vanished from his mind, as they usually did when she kissed him. It wasn't fair to Rachel to continue to distrust her when he had no solid reason for his suspicions.

Shelving his concerns once again, he pulled away from her and said,

"We better finish this up before Danielle comes home and finds out what happened."

"You're right. Thanks for helping me," Rachel said. After a quick kiss, she rested her forehead against his shoulder.

Mark circled his arms around her, ignoring the wet denim plastered to his knees. A little water and suds couldn't keep him from this moment with her.

Chapter Eleven

The conference room door shut, followed by two sets of footsteps, one heading toward the front door, the other coming toward Paul Pettis. The deliberate slamming of the front door confirmed Paul's suspicions, and he moved into position near the top of the stairwell.

He listened to the footfalls and held his breath until he caught a glimpse of Sean rounding the corner. Paul grabbed a fistful of Sean's shirt, whirled him around, and threw him against the wall with all the force he could muster.

Sean's breath came out with a grunt. "What the hell?"

"You found her, didn't you?" Paul asked. He pulled Sean away from the wall and slammed him into it again. Sean's small stature made him easy to toss around when Paul deemed necessary. "Where is she?"

"Take it easy!" Sean said. "She's in Wichita, Kansas."

Paul frowned. Kansas? What the hell was she doing in Kansas? He thought she should have left the country a long time ago, but she did not have the same idea. "Give me the envelope," Paul said.

Sean held up a manila envelope and waved it in Paul's face like a white flag. "All you had to do was ask."

Paul released Sean and took the envelope. He reached inside and pulled out a thin handful of photographs. "You didn't take many pictures this time," he said.

Sean smoothed down his shirt to eliminate the wrinkles left behind by Paul's grip. "I took as many as I always do. He kept most of them."

Of course he did, Paul thought. He tucked the envelope under his arm and flipped through the photos. His disgust with Sean grew with each picture. When he got to the fourth picture, he almost dropped the whole stack. "Who's the guy with her?"

Sean ran his hands over an oil slick of gel on the top of his head. Paul never understood the dark wave of plastered hair. "His name is Mark Jacobson," Sean said. "He's twenty-nine and he owns a bookstore with his brother, Greg. The bookstore is right by where she's staying. She's been spending a lot of time with him outside of the bookstore."

The details didn't interest Paul. "You gave all of these pictures to him? Even the ones with her and this guy?"

"I had to show him—"

"Why the hell did you show these pictures to him? You could have left the ones with the guy out."

"Get off my back. It's my job to take the pictures and show him all of them. He'd kill me if he found out I didn't give him all the photos. I'm not going to put myself in jeopardy over this girl to make you happy."

Paul lowered the pictures and glared at Sean. "It's your job to find her, not get her or this guy killed."

"It's my job to find her, but what happens to her or the guy in the pictures after I do my job is none of my business."

Paul narrowed his eyes and backed Sean up against the wall, resisting the urge to choke him to death right there in the hallway. Pushing a finger into Sean's shoulder, he said, "You're nothing but a slimy, sick, worthless bastard. You know what happened to the last guy like you who lived here? I put a bullet through his head. Slime oozed out with all that blood. Now, get the hell out of my sight before I do the same thing to you."

Sean eased his way along the wall and scrambled out of Paul's reach.

"And I want a copy of the written report," Paul said before Sean could start down the stairs. "Go downstairs and bring it back to me right now."

"I can't do it this time. I'd have to get the report back from him to make a copy, and you know I'm not supposed to show anyone the reports. Nobody's even supposed to know where she is, especially not you."

Paul restrained his temper. Sean's hands were as tied as Paul's, and it did no good to take everything out on him. "I don't care if you have to rewrite the damn thing from memory, just get it to me." He softened his voice and locked eyes with Sean. "Please. I need to see it."

"I'll see what I can do," Sean said, "but like I said, she's not worth me losing my life." He hesitated by the stairwell. "Give me back the envelope."

"I'll give it to you when I'm done with it," Paul said, his tone dismissive. He waited for Sean to head down the steps before taking a closer look at the pictures.

The first one was standard, like so many he had seen in the past. Rachel was opening her car door, oblivious to Sean's camera capturing her face. Paul wondered why she made no attempt to change her appearance this time. She always changed the color or style of her hair, always wore colored contacts, yet there she stood with her natural hair and eye color for the whole world to see.

The next two pictures also caught her engaged in daily activities. Getting mail, walking from her house to her car. The fourth picture strayed from the norm. She stood beside her car again, but not alone. A man, Mark Jacobson, was turned toward her, his face dangerously close to hers. She held her head down and a smile played on her lips. Further down the picture, Mark's hand touched her hip.

The fifth picture also showed Mark in front of her, but this time they were frozen in a kiss, his fingers raised to her cheek in a loving gesture. They looked like any other normal couple enjoying each other's company on a date.

Paul smiled at the sixth picture. It showed more of Mark than it did of her, and Paul recognized the expression on his face. His eyes radiated an innocent yearning and appreciation for Rachel. It reminded Paul of how he felt looking at his wife when he first saw her, back when the world still rotated to the east. Mark loved her, and from Mark's expression, Rachel returned that love. With Mark looking at her like that, Paul understood why Rachel had stayed long enough in Kansas for Sean to catch up to her again.

Paul continued studying Mark's face, glad for the first time in three years she found someone to make her happy. Then something else occurred to Paul. Mark didn't know the truth about her. She hadn't told him yet, if she ever planned on telling him. His eyes lacked the torment often reflected in Paul's eyes, in Rachel's eyes.

If she stayed in Kansas much longer, Mark would find out about Rachel soon enough. Once he did find out, he would wish he'd never met her.

Paul turned to the last picture. Rachel stood next to Mark, holding his hand, her head tilted toward his, her face paused in mid-laugh. Paul touched her through the photograph and whispered a warning she would never hear. "Run, Rachel."

Chapter Twelve

Rachel plopped down on her bed. She hiked one leg up on the mattress, tugged at her shoelaces, and pulled the shoe off. The shoe flew across the room and hit the wall with a bang.

As she battled a knot in the shoelace of her other tennis shoe, Danielle appeared in the doorway holding a half empty roll of cookie dough, her waitress apron tied around her waist. She glanced at the shoe on the floor and frowned. "Bad day?"

Rachel gave up on the shoelace and yanked the shoe off with a grunt. "You don't know the half of it. All I want to do is soak in a hot bath and forget I ever woke up this morning."

Danielle walked over to the bed and offered her the cookie dough. "What happened?"

Rachel scooped some dough onto her finger. "We got a new one today. Sixteen years old," she said. She placed the dough in her mouth.

"Oh, no."

Rachel chewed the chocolate chips, and the dough melted on her tongue. "This is good. Exactly what I needed," she said.

"I don't understand how you handle being there day after day, seeing the things you do. I have a hard enough time working there part-time. I couldn't stand being around the shelter as much as you. It would tear me up."

"I wish I could say I'm used to it," Rachel said, "but I don't ever want to get used to that. At least by the time I've heard their stories, they're already out of the situation. That's about the only thing that gets me through."

"Yeah, but overall, you should feel good about what you do."

"What do you mean?"

"Think about it. At least you know if they go back or end up in another abusive relationship, they're able to defend themselves against an attack."

"But I never want any of the women to have to use what I teach them."

Danielle sat down on the bed and faced Rachel. "It's not only the self-defense, Rach. You teach them so much more than how to protect themselves. You teach courage, strength, confidence. That's everything you taught me, and it helped me get past what that bastard did to me. You showed me how to look forward and not be a victim of my past."

"I didn't teach you those things. I showed you where to find them in yourself. There's a difference." She stood up and grabbed an elastic band off her bedside table. Pulling her hair up in a ponytail, she said, "I'm sorry. I didn't mean to unload my day on you. I'm going to do the bubble bath thing and then go over to the bookstore. Mark and I are going to see a movie tonight and—"

Danielle gasped. "I almost forgot!"

"What is it?"

"Come here."

"Why?" Rachel asked.

"Do you have to question everything? Just come here."

Rachel followed her into the kitchen. On the table, red roses surrounded by baby's breath flowed from a glass vase. "What are these?"

"They're roses."

"I know what they are, but where did you get them?"

"They were delivered today. They're for you."

Rachel stared at the flowers and rested her hands on the edge of the table. "Who delivered them?"

"Mark. He said he wanted you to come home to something beautiful."

Rachel flinched. "Why would he bring me roses?"

"Well," Danielle said, her tone as if she was speaking to a child, "sometimes when a boy likes a girl, he'll send flowers. It's what some people call 'courting' and it's a well-recognized and accepted practice." Danielle sighed. "I'm so jealous."

Rachel glanced at her, stunned by the statement. Danielle jealous? Rachel thought she was the only one who battled with envy in their friendship. Laughing, she asked, "Why are you jealous?"

"Mark's one of the good ones."

The simple statement summed up Danielle's entire view of relationships. Good ones, bad ones. "Yes, he is," Rachel said. She looked back at the roses, taking in their exquisite beauty and wondering what she had done to deserve them and him.

Scrutinizing Rachel's expression, Danielle asked, "Haven't you gotten flowers before?"

"No," Rachel said. She reached out and stroked a petal on one of the roses, then withdrew her hand as if the rose bit her. Her cheeks flushed and she fought a smile.

"You're blushing!"

Rachel tried to hide her face behind her hands. "I am not."

"Your face is red and you tell me you're not blushing. We need to work on this chronic lying problem you have. Repeat after me. You're right, Danielle. I am blushing."

Rachel lifted her eyes toward the ceiling. "You're right, Danielle. I am blushing. Are you satisfied?"

"A little. Now, I have to go to work and you have a date. I'm going out after work, so don't get worried like you do. I want you to write, 'I will not lie to Danielle ever again' one hundred times on the chalkboard before I get home and I'll forgive you."

"We don't own a chalkboard," Rachel said.

Danielle took one last look at the roses before heading toward the front door. "Definitely one of the good ones," she murmured.

Chapter Thirteen

"Name one real girl that can take on a guy," James said. "And those fake professional wrestlers don't count."

Rachel bit her bottom lip in frustration. She sat on the back of Mark's truck bed behind the bookstore, waiting for Mark to finish closing up for the night. She had arrived early, hoping to get a few peaceful moments to herself.

Instead, James found her sitting outside and lured her into a one-sided conversation. Rachel had welcomed the opportunity to get to know James better, as he was Mark's closest friend. James, however, seemed to enjoy the chance to grill her on her ability to defend herself. From his excited questions, she got the impression he had been waiting a long time to bring up the topic.

James stood in front of her, his eyes challenging her. "You can't name any, can you?" he said, continuing the debate he started when she arrived ten minutes earlier. "See, those self-defense classes don't work in real life. In the movies, maybe, but not in real life."

Mark came through the backdoor of the bookstore, saving her from having to choose a patient response. "You guys should have come in," he said.

"That's okay," Rachel said, hopping off the truck bed. "We kept ourselves entertained."

James grunted in agreement.

"Weren't you going home?" Mark asked James.

"I was, but then Rachel walked up as I was leaving. We were having a discussion."

Rachel glared at him. "More like a disagreement."

Mark laughed. "I'm not sure I want to know, but tell me anyway."

"I don't get how a little girl like Rachel is supposed to defend herself against an attacker," James said.

"Little girl?" Rachel said. "I thought you said you didn't want to offend me."

"Well, you're what? Five feet tall and 90 pounds?"

"You're way off in your guessing skills," Rachel said.

James ignored her remarks. "So what if a guy was three times as big as you?" he asked, turning to face her. "How could you defend yourself?"

"If a man was triple my size, I'm inclined to think he couldn't run faster than me."

"I don't think those self-defense classes are any good. They teach a girl to fight back when there's no way she can win. She'll get herself hurt even more."

"Oh, really?" Rachel smirked and pointed to the grass between the parking lot and the street. "Why don't we go over there and I'll show you how it works."

"Oh no. There's no way I'm going to fight you."

"Why not?"

"I'm like a hundred and eighty pounds heavier and twelve inches taller than you. I don't want to hurt you."

"Again, a massive exaggeration. But, don't worry, you won't hurt me. If you accidentally do, I won't hold it against you."

"I'll hold it against him," Mark said.

"Mark won't hold it against you, either," Rachel said.

"It doesn't seem right," James said. "I'd feel bad if I hurt you."

"Then let's make it interesting," Rachel said, grinning. "Say, a hundred dollars."

His eyes widened. "A bet?"

"Sure."

"A hundred dollars is a lot of money."

"That's what you get if you win."

"And what do you get?"

"An apology." She smiled before adding, "And the knowledge of your utter humiliation because you were taken down by a 'little girl.'"

James extended his hand and they shook on it. "I sure could use a hundred dollars," he said. He strolled on the grass.

"Rachel," Mark said, "this is crazy."

"No, he's crazy, and he needs to learn," she said. She moved onto the grass until she stood about five feet in front of James. She spread her feet into a comfortable stance and bent her knees to center herself in preparation for his attack.

"Okay," James said. "What should I do?"

"Attack me."

"Man, I wish more women would say that to me."

"James," Mark warned.

James looked at Mark. "Sorry, but she's the one who said it." He turned back to Rachel. "How do I attack you?"

"Do you think if a man is going to attack a woman in an alley at night, he's going to ask her how to do it first?"

He laughed. "I guess it does sound a little stupid."

"Hurry up," Mark said. "I don't want a cop to drive by. The last thing we need is to get arrested because of a bet."

James stared at Rachel for a moment. "I don't know. There's a lot of pressure with you and Mark staring at me. I don't think I can do it."

Rachel shrugged. "Your call," she said. She turned around and started walking toward Mark, knowing James was bluffing.

His footsteps closed in behind her, as she expected. As soon as he grabbed her shoulder, she reached around and locked his arm up with hers. She tightened her grip and turned sideways toward him. Her knee jerked up and landed in his stomach, but she restrained the impact so as not to hurt him too much.

Rachel loosened her grip on his arm, and he doubled over. She twisted his arm up and behind his back, forcing him to stand up straight. She swept her foot in front of his legs and pushed him facedown to the ground. James landed hard and groaned.

She crouched beside him and put her knee into the small of his back, using her weight to hold him down. "And just like that, you're on the ground and I'm not even out of breath."

James gasped for air between his words. "Let me up."

Rachel ignored him. "The element of surprise was pretty good," she said, "but do you want to know what your biggest mistake was?"

"What?"

She smiled. "You called me a little girl. Now apologize."

"I'm sorry, I'm sorry! Can I get up now?"

She got to her feet and joined a wide-eyed Mark at his truck. James stood up, dusted himself off, and walked toward them. When he passed by, he pointed at Mark. "Don't you even think about telling anyone about this," he said.

Mark laughed as soon as James left. "That was great."

"He had to learn somehow he shouldn't underestimate all of us little girls."

Mark looked at her in amazement. "I guess I always knew you could do that, but it's still strange seeing it." He paused and his stare became inquisitive. "You could beat me up, couldn't you?"

She laughed. "I wouldn't even try."

"What if we got in an argument? You could do some damage."

"Don't worry. I only use my powers for good."

"What a relief."

"Besides, it's not like I'm stronger than you or even James, for that matter. I just know how to use what strength I have to defeat my opponent."

"That salvages some of my ego. When did you learn to do what you did to James?"

"I started going to a gym after my parents died. It was good for me to take my frustrations out on a punching bag or by lifting weights and sparring with others." She grabbed Mark's hand. "The strangest thing happened to me today. Some misguided flower delivery man delivered roses to our house by mistake. We have some girl's flowers in our kitchen."

Mark smiled. "That poor girl. I bet she would have liked getting them."

"Probably. They're beautiful."

"I suppose you'll have to take good care of them for her."

"I will. No one has ever given me flowers before." Rachel didn't know why she spoke the words, but couldn't stop them from leaving her mouth.

"Ever?" Mark asked.

"Never."

"If I had known that, I would have made sure you had them every night since the day we met. It's shameful you had to wait so long to get flowers."

Rachel shrugged. "But it makes getting them for the first time that much better." She let go of his hand, took a few steps forward, and gazed up at the sky. "It's an incredible night. I think I can see every star."

Mark stepped up behind her and wrapped his arms around her waist. "Why don't we skip the movie tonight?"

She twisted her head and frowned. "I was looking forward to seeing this one."

"We can see it another time."

"Every time we make plans, we never end up doing what we say we're going to do," Rachel said with a laugh. "What do you propose we do instead of seeing a movie?"

"Come here." He led her back onto the lush grass behind the small parking lot and pulled her down with him. She sat in between his legs and relaxed against him. He waved his hand at the sky. "I say we sit here and watch this movie," he said.

"What kind of movie is that?"

"I'm pretty sure it's a chick flick."

"Then this must be the part of the movie where you identify all the constellations," she said.

He paused. "I think that happens in the sequel."

She laughed. "What if I don't like the movie?"

"Oh, but ma'am, satisfaction is guaranteed in this theater."

"And what if I'm not satisfied?" she asked.

"Well, then I'd have to find a way to make it up to you. Like maybe a candlelight dinner or a midnight stroll through the park." He brushed her hair back and kissed her face, lingering at the top of her neck. "Or maybe I'll pick you up some Saturday morning and we can take a little road trip, find a hideaway for the weekend."

She bit her bottom lip and tried to ignore the sensations he created with both his mouth and his words. "Hmm, those all sound great, but there's one problem. I like this movie."

"That's okay. We can still do all those other things."

"Promise?" Rachel asked.

"I promise," Mark whispered.

Rachel smiled. Everything he said sounded so perfect that tonight, just for tonight, she would pretend all of it could happen for them. Later, when she sat alone with her paranoia and her gun on her back porch, she could return to the reality that they would not be together for much longer. Rachel closed her eyes and tuned out her thoughts, imagining a world where she could stay with him forever.

Chapter Fourteen

Spending an hour sitting in Mark's arms behind the bookstore had been therapeutic, despite the weather cutting their time short. Interrupted by the cracking of thunder, Rachel bowed out of going somewhere else and Mark drove her home. The calming smell of rain followed them on the short drive to her house. Sparks of lightning outlined dark clouds, confirming the radio's warnings of thunderstorms arriving soon in their county.

In her driveway, Mark brought up the subject of dinner Sunday night at Greg's house. Rachel said she would go, but only because she couldn't think of a good excuse to get out of the commitment.

She wanted to have a normal life, to do the meet-the-family things that came with a relationship, however, with dinner would come the dreaded questions. Even though asked with routine curiosity, the questions would seem threatening, suspicious, angry. Most questions would elicit a reluctant lie, something Rachel did only when necessary.

Rachel thought Mark sensed her hesitation regarding the invitation to dinner. To avoid raising too many suspicions, she widened her smile and did her best to convince him that dinner with his family would be enjoyable. Sunday was still several days away. By then, she would find an excuse not to go.

After kissing him goodnight, she entered her house and tossed her keys on the couch on her way to the kitchen. Rain tapped out a beat on the roof that only nature could compose, and the sound comforted Rachel. She poured a tall glass of skim milk and put the carton back in the refrigerator. She turned around and faced the table, letting the cool liquid refresh her throat. The sight of the roses drew her to the table. She reached out to touch one of the silky red petals.

Creak.

Rachel's head snapped around and she froze, her ears alert, unsure if she had heard the noise. Her deliberate breathing echoed in her ears, and she crept toward the living room, toward the sound. When she reached the doorway of the kitchen, thunder rattled the windows, and she jumped back. She stood still and waited for another sound, but the house remained quiet.

Relief forced her lips into a sheepish grin. Either she had heard things or it was a case of an old house settling. She put a hand on her chest and closed her eyes, coaching her breathing to try and control the impending panic attack. Inhale. Exhale. Inhale. Exhale. In—

Creak.

Her eyes flew open and her breathing sharpened. She squeezed the glass and the cold milk inside chilled her hand. She stared into the living room with large eyes.

They're here.

The thought reverberated through her mind like a pinball unable to flee through the escape hatch. Her breathing quickened, becoming a pant. Her eyes shifted to the left. The hallway leading to her bedroom beckoned her, and her mind zeroed in on the gun in her bedside table. She had to move. *Now.*

Rachel released the glass and bolted for the door, ignoring the shatter behind her. Rounding the corner, she dashed into her bedroom and slammed the door shut. She opened her bedside table drawer, pulled her gun out, and slid over her bed. She crouched against the wall in a position where she could see the door.

She drew her knees up and held the gun close to her chest. She stared at the doorknob and waited for it to turn. The light from her floor lamp reflected off the cheap gold-colored knob and mesmerized her. At any second, the doorknob would rotate and they would enter the room.

"Go away." She meant to yell, but the words barely left her throat between her frantic gulps for air. Her head bobbed with each gasp and she tried to slow her breathing, to no avail. Her fingertips numbed, and her grip on the gun loosened.

Leave me alone.

She wished someone would lift the boulder off her chest, but no one came to help. Her tongue thickened and the sound of her breathing melted with the background drumming of rain. Throat tight, she let the darkness take over.

Chapter Fifteen

Rachel opened her eyes and acquainted herself with her surroundings. Slumped down on the floor of her bedroom, the gun had tumbled out of her hand and now rested below her fingers.

She sat up and tried to clear her mind. According to her watch, she had been out for over an hour. Danielle had not returned home yet. If she had, she would have woke Rachel and launched into a stern lecture on passing out with a loaded weapon, one that Rachel admitted she needed.

She flipped on the safety and laid the gun down on her bed. She used the edge of the bed to pull herself to her feet. Her mind drifted from the anxiety attack and focused on the dream that found her while the attack rendered her unconscious.

Another dream, the same as all the others. Vivid, realistic details. The leaves various shades of green, the fresh smell of tree bark and rain. Walking through the woods in the black evening gown. The bird fluttering down to her hand, telling her what to do. The piano playing a song she used to know. Moving across the forest floor toward the door. The door opening.

Rachel went into the bathroom, where she washed her face and brushed her teeth. She had overreacted at a small sound. She couldn't afford to have a panic attack every time the house settled, which was what the sound had been. If she had heard someone else in the house, if she had heard *them*, they would have already made their presence known.

She put her toothbrush away and caught her reflection in the mirror. Pictures from the past flashed in front of her eyes, blurring with the weary face of the girl in front of her, a girl she did not recognize. Dark circles outlined eyes that were absent of strength, while lines of surrender encompassed her downturned mouth.

A shadow stood behind her. Ghostly hands landed on her shoulders and crawled down her arms with determination. A seductive voice whispered in her mind, reminding her of who she was, promising her the world, and enticing her to return to where she belonged.

Rachel turned away from the mirror and moved into her bedroom. The dream drained her of all strength, and she tried to convince herself she could still handle the stress it caused. She longed for one night of uninterrupted sleep with no nightmares. No bird, no door, no damn piano.

Unable to hear the rain outside, she decided she needed fresh air. She picked up the gun from her bed, ready to begin her nightly ritual.

Her face hardened at the sight of the gun. She detested everything it reminded her of, everything it represented. She didn't want to sit outside in the backyard anymore and ponder the night away with the gun acting as her sole source of sanity.

She returned the gun to her bedside table and left her room. In the kitchen, she cleaned up the forgotten broken glass and used a sponge to mop up the milk. All evidence of her panic attack erased, she opened the refrigerator door in hopes of something to eat. A half empty carton of skim milk, a tub of butter, a bottle of ketchup, and three cheese slices stared back at her.

She shut the door. Sleep was out of the question and there was nothing to eat. She desired Danielle's company and conversation to take her into the early morning hours, but it could be several hours before she waltzed through the front door.

Rachel sat at the kitchen table and stared at the roses. If only she were strong like Danielle, who survived the unthinkable, yet still had the courage to go out into the world and let go of the past. Rachel was unable to forget the things haunting her.

In some respects, she was getting better because she had let someone into her life for the first time in three years. Any change in her, no matter how small, was only because of Mark. With Mark, she had no past. There were no panic attacks, no fading nightmares. With Mark, life was bearable, livable, wonderful. With Mark…

A voice in the back of Rachel's head nagged, telling her what to do.

Unwilling to put up a fight with her smarter side, she withdrew a pad of paper and pen from the kitchen drawer. She scribbled a quick note to Danielle and threw it on the table. She grabbed her keys from the couch, set the alarm, and secured each of the deadlocks.

Chapter Sixteen

Concern flashed across Mark's face when he opened the front door and saw Rachel standing on his front porch. "Is everything okay?"

Rachel hesitated and took in his image. He was barefoot and dressed in a pair of navy pajama bottoms. She let out a nervous laugh. "I just realized how stupid this is. I'm sorry I woke you." She turned to leave.

"Wait," he said, and he grabbed her hand.

She bit her bottom lip and faced him.

"You didn't wake me. Come on in."

Rachel followed him down the hall into the living room and inhaled the familiar scent of citrus multi-purpose cleaners. As usual, his house was spotless. Two bookshelves held books lined up and categorized by author. The glass coffee table was free of fingerprints, and there was not a hint of dust on any surface. Chaos had no place in his world, and his perfect, organized life had no room for her.

"What's wrong?" he asked, sitting on the couch.

She sank into the couch cushions and crossed her arms. "Nothing's wrong. I couldn't sleep." She laughed at herself. "I'm not quite sure why I'm here."

"It's okay. I was still awake, paying bills. That's enough to keep anyone up at night, sweating profusely, unable to stop shaking in terror."

She laughed again and tucked some stray strands of hair behind her ear.

"I'm glad you're here," he said.

Her smile lingered despite the changing tone of her voice. "You know

I never meant for this to happen with us. All I wanted was a cup of coffee." It was a rare moment of truth for her.

He drew her head down on his shoulder and kissed the top of her head. "That makes two of us."

She closed her eyes, and he stroked the back of her head. Tension flowed from her body and the last remnants of the dream disappeared. For the first time in years, she felt protected.

Safe.

Rachel sensed him move, and she opened her eyes.

"You fell asleep," he said.

"I did?" She sat up and rubbed the back of her neck. "What time is it?"

"A little after two."

"I suppose I'd better go," she said, with a yawn.

"Oh, no you don't. You're exhausted. There's no way I'm letting you drive anywhere. You can sleep in my room and I'll sleep out here on the couch."

"I don't want to impose."

"You're not imposing." Mark stood in front of her and scooped her up.

She threw her arms around his neck. "What are you doing?"

"Trying to break my back." He groaned and pretended to buckle under her weight.

She smacked his arm. "Now you're being mean," she said. She squirmed in his arms and giggled.

"Are you ticklish?"

"I guess," she said. A soft, embarrassed laugh escaped her lips. "What's wrong with that?"

"There's nothing wrong with it, I just never thought of you as ticklish." He maneuvered her through his bedroom door and laid her down on his bed. Sitting down on the edge of the bed, he took off her shoes.

"This is what I call royal treatment," she said. "Does a massage come with this package, too?"

He winked and rose from the bed. "It could." He covered her with the blanket. Bending over, he kissed her forehead. "Goodnight, my lady." At the doorway, he flipped off the light switch.

As soon as the darkness fell on her, the dread of being alone overcame her. Her stomach tightened, and she feared another panic attack. "Mark?" she whispered.

"Yes?"

"Please stay."

Chapter Seventeen

"Wait a minute." Greg stopped his work on the computer and looked at Mark in disbelief. "She slept in your bed right next to you, and you never once thought about sex?"

Mark wiped his hand across his desk, brushing away dust only he could see. "Strange, huh?"

"I'd say. Aliens have invaded and taken over my brother's body."

"Remind me which one of us is older."

"You have to admit that everything about you has changed. You used to have a new fling every week."

Mark frowned. "Not every week."

"Close enough. You've been seeing Rachel for over two months, which is some kind of record, and now you're telling me that you don't want to sleep with her?"

Mark glanced at his watch, impatient to open the store and end this conversation. "I didn't say I don't want to, but I haven't really thought about it. I'm content spending time with her. Sex isn't always a necessity."

"I think my heart stopped."

Mark ignored him. "Last night, it felt so natural to have her there. It was like she's always been there. Then this morning, I woke up and the first thing I saw was her face."

"And?" Greg asked.

"What makes you think there's anything else?"

"There is."

"And all I could think was how much I want to wake up every morning and see her there."

Greg grinned. "You know what this means, don't you?"

"Are you going to start talking about aliens again?"

"It means you love her."

The realization of his emotions washed over him, and he could no longer ignore what he felt every time he thought about her. "I know I do."

"Have you told her?"

"Are you crazy? My stomach is in knots having this conversation with you. If I told her how I feel, she might say she doesn't feel the same, or she may outright reject me. I don't want to take the risk of losing her."

"I've seen you two together a lot, and I can tell you she's definitely in love with you, the same as you are with her. What makes you think she doesn't love you?"

Mark's smile faded and all his insecurities rushed in at once. "I don't know. Sometimes I think she does. Other times, I feel like she's not all there. It's like she's holding part of herself back from me."

"What do you mean?"

Mark paused. He never considered telling anyone about his fears, but Greg might be able to shed some light on the subject. "It's hard to explain because it's nothing specific. It's like she's not always being honest or not telling the whole truth. Something about her doesn't make sense. It sounds strange, but I feel like there's something else to who she is."

Greg creased his forehead and leaned back in the office chair. "Like she's hiding something?"

"Yeah, but I don't know what it could be or why she would think she has to hide something from me. If she has the same feelings for me that I do for her, then I don't understand why she would do that to me."

"What do you know about her?"

Mark shrugged. "She's from California. Her parents died in a car accident when she was ten and she went to live with a foster family. She teaches self-defense at the shelter and lives off a trust fund her parents left her. She lives with Danielle, her best friend, and they came here from Indianapolis."

"That's it?"

Mark's inability to think of any additional facts about Rachel unsettled him. "I thought I knew her better than that."

"There's more to knowing someone than factual data. You know her, but you don't seem to know a lot of things about her life before she moved here."

"It's almost like she has no past."

"Don't get all mysterious on me. It sounds like you're operating on suspicion, and nothing concrete. Have you ever asked her about her life? Like specific questions?"

"I guess not."

Greg waved his hand. "There you go. You can't expect to know everything about her if you've never asked."

Mark couldn't deny Greg's logic. Rachel had answered every question Mark ever asked. If he didn't know many facts about her life before she came to Wichita, it was his fault for not asking. He couldn't expect her to offer up information about herself every time they saw each other. He needed to ask her some questions to fill in the gaps. Tonight.

Chapter Eighteen

Did you sleep with him?" Danielle asked.

Rachel sat cross-legged on Danielle's bed, while Danielle tore through the clothes hanging in her closet in search of something to wear. Danielle had bombarded her with questions in the ten minutes she had been home from work, and Rachel wasn't sure how to respond to them anymore.

"I take it that's a no," Danielle said when Rachel didn't answer. "Do you want to sleep with him?"

"Am I supposed to answer that?"

"Come on. You stayed at his house last night. What am I supposed to think?" She tossed a red tank top on the floor behind her and resumed her search.

Rachel leaned over the edge of the bed and picked up the shirt. She folded it and laid it next to her on the bed. "You're not supposed to think. It's my life."

"Why are you so upset about this? Isn't it what you've always wanted? To live a normal life and to be a real girl?"

Danielle managed to strike the one nerve in Rachel that always made her jump. There was nothing Rachel wanted more than normalcy, but she didn't know how she could have it in the midst of all the chaos. "You know it is," Rachel said.

"Then go for it."

"And what? Forget the past? Ignore who I am?"

Danielle turned around, holding a pair of black pants in her hands. "What do you mean? You're Rachel Thomas. You know, the girl who gets anxious every time her boyfriend Mark comes around."

Rachel frowned. "Will you stop with all the boyfriend stuff? You know what I'm talking about. Why do you care about it so much anyway?"

"Because you're my best friend, and I want you to live a little."

"I am living."

"No, I'm living," Danielle said. She slipped off her denim shorts and stepped into the pants. "I'm not sitting around in a little glove compartment shutting everyone out like you are. I'm enjoying life and making the most of it, like you told me I should. Maybe you ought to take your own advice. You're not living. You're surviving."

"And survival is all I'm concerned about. I don't like complications."

"Is that what Mark is? A complication?"

"Yes, and I'm going to take care of it," Rachel said. She had been thinking about the idea ever since she woke up in his bed that morning. There were no other options but to push Mark out of her life right away. Being careless and naïve any longer could prove disastrous.

"Take care of it?" Danielle asked. She grabbed the red shirt off the bed and pulled it over her head. "You mean you're going to tell him it's over."

"That's what I mean. After tonight, Mark will no longer be a part of my life."

"Like that will ever happen," Danielle said. "Can we bet on this, too? I sure could use another twenty dollars."

"It has to happen, Danielle. I can't afford to live in this fantasy world. I'm losing track of what's important."

Danielle stopped primping her hair in the full-length mirror and studied Rachel. "You've already made up your mind, haven't you?"

"It scares me, Danielle. I have no control over this. When I'm with him, I forget about everything else. It's like my life didn't begin until I met him."

"Oh." A smile formed on Danielle's lips. "You're in love with him."

Rachel's frown deepened. She followed Danielle out of the bedroom and toward the front door. "I'm not in love with him. There's no such thing as love."

"There's the cynical girl I know."

"A greeting card company invented love to make money."

Danielle paused, her hand on the doorknob. "It looks like they've succeeded in creating meaningless, false feelings in yet another sucker."

"I'm not in love with him and I'm going to prove it to you," she said.

"Who are you trying to convince?"

Rachel pursed her lips and crossed her arms.

"Would you like me to drop you off at his house or are you taking your car?"

"Mark is working at the bookstore, so I thought I'd walk over there."

Danielle touched Rachel's arm. "You need to stop trying to control your life. It's okay to allow yourself to live and love again." She went out the front door, leaving Rachel alone with her thoughts.

Chapter Nineteen

Rachel pulled open the front door to the bookstore and a loud bell rang out, announcing her entrance. From behind the cash register, Sarah informed her Mark was in the office with James. Rachel thanked her and headed toward the back of the store. On her way through the store, she waved to Greg, who was helping a customer.

In the office, Mark and James leaned against the desk, fixated on a television that rested on top of the file cabinet. "Anything good on TV?" Rachel asked.

Mark turned to her and smiled. "James wanted me to watch the news with him." He gave her a quick kiss. "I could have picked you up."

"It's okay, the walk always does me good. Since when do you watch the news, James?" she asked.

"I watch it every night. I brought in this old TV so Mark could watch it with me while he was waiting for you."

Rachel made it a habit to not watch the grim tales on the news. She'd had so much of that in her own life that watching the sorrows of others was too much for her. "What's so special about tonight's newscast?" she asked.

"Senator Cal Robbins gave a speech in Kansas City today and they're going to show some coverage of it," Mark said.

"He's a senator from California, running for President," James said. "He's been in office for quite some time now. You've probably heard of him, Rach, since you're from there."

"I have heard of him," Rachel said. "He's the only politician I know about."

"Here it is," James said. He used the remote control to raise the volume.

A picture of Senator Robbins popped up in the top corner of the screen next to a polished anchorwoman. "This morning, Senator Cal Robbins visited Kansas City on his Midwest tour," she said. "We take you there now, live, with Neil Crawford of our affiliate station."

A young man in a pressed suit appeared on the screen. He clutched a microphone as if his life depended on it. With perfect posture and his best anchorman smile, he stood in front of a makeshift stage covered with red, white, and blue campaign banners.

"Thanks, Susie," he said into the microphone. "Behind me is the stage where Senator Cal Robbins stood this morning and gave one of the most memorable and passionate speeches of his tour to date. Kansas City is one of the many stops he is making on his tour through the Midwest, and his supporters turned out in droves. This outdoor venue was so overrun with those who came to watch the Senator, many people had to be turned away due to lack of space.

"Senator Robbins is already a forerunner in the race for the White House, and the turnout this morning lends credence to the overwhelming support Senator Robbins has received since announcing his candidacy."

Rachel wondered how much longer the newscaster would speak. She wanted to rush to the television, turn it off, and drag Mark far away from any media outlet, but she knew her actions would be called into question.

"Though many topics are hot in this election," the newscaster continued, "Senator Robbins focused on crime prevention and the need for stricter sentences for convicted criminals, as many expected. Today marks the third anniversary of one of the highest profile murders in the last several decades. Emotions ran high and tears were shed as Senator Robbins recalled the unsolved murder of his close associate and dear friend."

Rachel leaned back on the desk and her fingers brushed against the desk organizer. She glanced at Mark and James, who were intent on the television. Her hand swept across the desk behind her and connected with her intended target.

"Three years ago today, Jona—"

Crash.

Mark jumped off the desk and James turned around. Rachel looked down at the desk organizer on the floor. Pens and pencils rolled away from the impact site while paperclips jumped across the tiles.

"I am so sorry," Rachel said. She crouched on the ground and collected paperclips. "I can't believe I did that, considering how OCD you are about everything being clean."

"Don't worry about it for a second." Mark knelt beside her to help clean up. "Are you okay?"

"I think so. I just moved my arm and the caddy went flying. It must have been right on the edge of the desk." Rachel hoped Mark bought her excuses and didn't think she was over-explaining. She glanced up at the television. The anchorwoman had moved onto a new story. "I'm such a klutz today," she said.

"Quit worrying. It was an accident," Mark said.

James picked up a pen by the sole of his shoe and wiped the end of it on his jeans. "Maybe they'll repeat the report later. I want to hear more about the guy that got killed." He shoved the end of the pen in his mouth and chewed.

"I'm sure they will since it's such big news," Mark said. "I remember when that happened. It was all over the news back then. Very tragic. What was his name?"

James shrugged. "I know his name, but I can't seem to remember it right now. He was some bigwig in home security. That was messed up because he was killed while he was at home. Imagine that, a security guru being murdered in his own house." James sucked in his breath and his eyes grew wide. "Unless the person that killed him was someone he knew. That makes it even worse."

"His name was Tom something, wasn't it?" Mark asked.

Rachel returned the organizer to the desk, replacing the last of the pens.

"No," James said, "It began with a 'J,' like Jerry or Joseph."

Rachel couldn't let the conversation continue in the direction it was heading. "I didn't realize you were so into politics, James," she said.

"James has always been into politics," Mark said. "He knows every President and Vice President we've ever had. He knows all about everyone in Congress. He even knows who's who on the local school boards."

James shrugged. "For some reason it fascinated me in elementary school when we learned about the Presidents and it stuck."

"What are your thoughts on Senator Robbins?" Mark asked.

"He'd make a fantastic President," James said. "He makes friends with everyone, no matter their political persuasion, and he figures out a way to make everyone happy on issues. Since his friend died, he's done so much with crime control and…" James scrunched up his face and scratched his head. "What was that guy's name?"

The bell announced the entrance of a customer. "This is real exciting," Rachel told James, "but I need to steal Mark away from you now. I'm starving and he owes me dinner."

They said goodbye to James and Mark took her hand. Halfway to the back exit, he stopped walking. "I forgot my keys."

"We'll be here all night," she said.

"Come here," he said. He grabbed her arm and pulled her toward him.

He brushed the hair away from her face. "I promise I won't let James sucker me into a daylong conversation and if he does, I'll—"

"You'll what?" she asked.

"I don't know, but it'll be good."

Rachel laughed, and he kissed her. He turned and headed back into the office. Her smile fell from her lips. If he were more than a minute or two, she'd have to go in and get him. Anything to keep him away from the topic of the news story.

She glanced around the bookstore, studying each patron she could see as she walked up the center aisle. To her left, a young woman with several books tucked under her arm read the synopsis on the back cover of a romance novel. Sarah headed toward two teenagers flipping through magazines on the back wall.

Somewhere in front of her, Greg conferred with an older couple about travel books. Jason, a young college student who worked in the bookstore part-time, collected money from a middle-aged man at the register.

The bell on the front door rang out through the store, and Rachel's nerves jumped. Lead lined her stomach and blood pumped through her veins with unusual vigor. Her claustrophobia closed in the walls around her, and the store seemed to get smaller with each passing second.

"Look, Mommy!" a girl's voice exclaimed.

Rachel walked toward the voice coming from the children's book section, as if drawn by an invisible force.

"This is the book where Cinderella goes to the ball," the girl continued.

Rachel stopped walking. Her throat constricted against the quick breaths she drew of thick, hot air.

"Her dress is pretty and she dances with the prince, but has to leave before she turns into a pumpkin."

The piano's keys tinkled in Rachel's mind, beginning its haunting melody, unaware that it was only supposed to play in her dreams.

"Please, can I have that book, Mommy?"

Rachel fought the darkness that enveloped her vision.

"Excuse me, miss?"

The panic attack ended with the man's words. Rachel turned to him and forced a smile.

A return smile peered at her beneath his trimmed mustache. "I'm sorry to bother you," he said, "but do you work here? I'm having trouble finding a book."

"No, I don't. He should be able to help you," she said and pointed in Jason's direction. Jason waved to let her know he was on his way. The stranger insisted on small talk about the hot weather and high humidity until Jason reached them. Jason greeted the customer and steered him in another direction.

Mark appeared next to her, dangling his car keys by his side. "There you are," he said. "I'm sorry I took so long. You were right about James starting another unending conversation." He studied Rachel. "Is everything okay? You're a bit pale."

Rachel shrugged and gave him a quirky smile. "It's probably my blood sugar dropping since you're letting me starve to death," she said. "I could pass out at any moment."

Mark smiled again. "We can't have that happening here in the store. We'd lose some customers for sure. Let's go eat."

Rachel accepted his hand and let him lead her out of the store. He always made things better when he was by her side, and it made leaving him that much harder. Lying to him was soul wrenching, but the greater her paranoia, the more abhorrent her dishonesty became. Her actions in his office, albeit necessary, were inexcusable and deceitful.

If she stayed with him, Mark would discover her motives, and he would never forgive her once he did. It solidified her thoughts that she needed to end what they had now, before her heart refused to let her go.

Chapter Twenty

Mark reached his hand through the soap bubbles and pulled a plate out of the sink. Armed with a sponge, he scrubbed the soap over the plate and handed it to Rachel. She rinsed it off in warm water and laid it on a towel spread across the counter.

"I can't believe you talked me into letting you help with dishes," he said, "especially after your dishwasher incident."

"Quit complaining and get busy. I'm way ahead of you in the rinsing department." With a mischievous grin, Rachel flicked some water from her fingers onto the side of his face.

"Don't start a water fight if you can't finish it," Mark said with a laugh.

Rachel raised her hands up in the air. "Then I surrender before you decide to retaliate," she said. "By the way, you were right. That was the most incredible lasagna I've ever had. How did you learn to cook like that?"

"I started cooking out of necessity. Greg and I were stuck having to fend for ourselves half the time, with Dad being on the road and Mom being knee deep in vodka and prescription narcotics."

Rachel rinsed a glass and contemplated his words. Mark endured serious neglect and trauma as a child, and survived much more than most people do in a lifetime. Yet, he adapted to his misfortune and never let it overcome him. Rachel craved that ability, and she wondered if it was too late for her to be more like him.

"Greg's culinary skills were zero," Mark continued. "He burnt anything and everything. I guess I got sick of eating peanut butter and jelly, and I taught myself how to cook."

"I wish I knew how to cook," Rachel said. "I burn things, too. I think I get that from my dad because I remember my mom's cooking wasn't that bad."

She laughed at a memory and took a soapy dish from Mark's hands. "One time my mom had to work late and Dad was stuck cooking dinner. He got this brilliant idea he could make meatloaf. He even put on one of Mom's aprons. I laughed at him and he kicked me out of the kitchen."

The words rolled off Rachel's tongue without thought as to how much information about her life came out. At that moment, she did not care about the secrets she held under lock and key.

"About an hour later," she said, "I went to check on him. I opened up the door between the kitchen and living room and all this smoke rolled out. He had burned the meatloaf. All the windows in the kitchen were open, and he had snuck out the other door so I wouldn't know what happened. I found Dad in his bedroom and he looked crushed. As soon as he saw me, his expression changed. He ushered me back in the living room, telling me not to worry, he would fix it.

"Another hour passed and I was ready to eat the black meatloaf. Then the doorbell rang and it was the pizza delivery guy. I don't remember ever having pizza that tasted so good. As we were eating, Dad said, 'Now you can tell your mother what a wonderful cook I am.' We laughed until we cried." Rachel paused, and sorrow flooded her heart. "A few months later, he was dead."

"You still miss them, don't you?"

Missing her parents was a weak phrase for what she felt, but it was the best way to describe her emotions with words. "Yes, all the time," she said. Confused by the surprise in his voice when he spoke the question, Rachel asked, "Don't you miss your parents?"

Mark shrugged. "Your parents really loved you when they were alive. I can tell by how much you still love them. I never experienced that. They were my parents, flesh and blood. I should miss them, but I don't think about them much. Sometimes I feel guilty, but it's hard to miss parents who were never there in the first place."

He yanked the plug out of the sink's drain, and water whooshed down the drain. He rinsed the soap off his hands under the running water Rachel used to rinse silverware. As he dried his hands on a dishtowel, he asked, "Why is it always like pulling teeth to get you to talk to me?"

It was a question Rachel expected at some point, but she still feigned ignorance. "What do you mean?"

"I think the story about your dad is the most you've ever talked about yourself at once, and I didn't have to ask."

She took the dishtowel from him and rubbed her damp hands against the material. She shrugged and answered the best she could without saying too much. "I don't like talking about myself. There's nothing interesting to say."

"Everything about you is interesting to me."

He wasn't going to let the topic go, Rachel realized. "I guess I don't ever have to talk about my life, so I'm not used to it. Danielle's the only person I've been close to for so long and she already knows everything there is to know. I've never had anyone else besides her to talk to." Rachel reached over and took Mark's hand in hers. "At least, not until I met you."

"So what's the difference between talking to her and talking to me?"

"I imagine there's some sort of comfort level I reached with her after knowing her for a long time. As I came to know her and trust her, it became easier to talk to her."

"So what will it take for you to reach that comfort level with me?"

Unsure of how to reply, Rachel took a deep breath and let go of his hand. The turn in the conversation once again upset her plan for the night. Yet, that was how it always went with Mark. Every time she thought about leaving him, he reminded her of how much more she needed him.

"Rachel, how can I convince you it's okay to talk to me about anything?"

"Those are some loaded questions," she said.

"Ones that I'd like the answers to."

She picked up the last plate in the sink and focused on the circular motion of the towel over its damp surface. "You're making this sound long-term."

He stepped closer to her. "I'd like to think it is."

She put the towel down and raised her eyes to his face. Inches away from her, warmth radiated from his body onto hers. She opened her mouth to say something, and then changed her mind. She creased her forehead and bit her bottom lip hard to stop from saying anything at all.

Mark lifted his hand and brushed her hair out of her face. "Rachel, what is it?"

Rachel could no longer hold her thoughts to herself. "I am so in love with you." Before he could say a word, she raised herself on her tiptoes and touched her lips to his in a tentative kiss.

Mark placed a gentle hand high up on her arm and kept the kiss sweet and pure. Rachel wanted more. She pressed into him and intensified the movement of her lips over his. Mark's hands wrapped around her back and he pulled her closer to him.

Without looking, she set the plate on the counter and ignored the shatter when it fell back into the sink. She put her hands on his face and rested her thumb on the corner of his mouth. His hands journeyed around to the front of her shirt. The buttons came undone with ease, his mouth never straying from hers. Her shirt dropped off her arms to the floor, and the heat of her body counteracted the chill that caressed her skin.

Mark broke away from her and moistened his lips. Desperate to get back to where they left off, she couldn't seem to catch her breath. She needed to be with him more than she needed anything else. She didn't want to stop now and risk never allowing herself to get back to this point with him.

Mark brushed her cheek with the backs of his fingers, and Rachel trembled under his touch. She watched his eyes through a haze of desire. A large smile crossed his face. "I love you, too, Rachel," he whispered, "more than you could ever know."

Chapter Twenty-one

Rachel floated through the strange fog as if walking on clouds. She smoothed down the silky material of the black dress she wore and stopped walking to admire its simple beauty. She lifted her eyes and saw a shadowy figure at the other end of the room. Her eyes adjusted, and the person moved toward her.

Mark came into view and held out his hand. "Come with me, Rachel. I have something to show you."

She smiled and took his hand. He led her down a shadowed hallway that seemed to have no end. The dark curtains covering the windows allowed minimal light to pass through. The thick fog clinging to her ankles covered the cold tiles beneath her bare feet.

The piano started playing the same song she remembered from long ago. The tune brought vague images to the front of her mind, but she couldn't grasp onto any of them to see what they were.

"Why does that song sound so familiar?" she asked Mark.

"All songs are the same in fairy tales."

"Who's playing the piano?"

"Prince Charming. Every fairy tale has a Prince Charming."

"Where are we going, Mark?" she asked. She frowned when he didn't respond. "Mark?"

A slight breeze chilled her skin. She looked down the hallway, and when she squinted she could distinguish the outline of a door. "Mark, where are we going?"

Mark turned toward her. A sadistic grin crawled across his mouth and into his eyes. "I'm taking you home."

"No!" She willed her legs to stop, but an unseen power forced her to continue down the hall. "Stop it! Don't take me there!"

"Rachel, are you ready to go home?" Mark tugged her arm and pulled her through the fog, closer to the door. "It's time to go home. Time to go home."

"I don't want to go!"

He chanted faster. "Going home Rachel is going home you're going home going home—"

"No! Please, Mark, make it stop!"

"Going home going home going home home home home."

The door materialized in front of them and they stopped walking. The sound of her labored breathing filled her ears. Her head swam and when she turned to look at Mark, her movements were in slow motion.

He smiled. "Don't worry, Rachel. It will be over soon."

The hallway disappeared and she was transported to another room, the one behind the door. A dim light glowed in the background, outlining the silhouette of a man in a chair. Her eyes fell on his hands and the red rag he held. Fear gripped her as the man spoke. "Welcome home, Rachel."

She screamed.

Chapter Twenty-two

Fear spilled over from the dream and paralyzed Rachel when she woke. She remained frozen until reality washed away the last of the images from her mind. She repeated to herself that it was only a dream, though she wasn't entirely convinced.

Disoriented, she forced her head to move so she could glance around the dark room. The silhouette of Mark's shoulder disturbed the shadows and she remembered she was at his house. In his bed. The events of last night reentered her mind. What was she doing? When she told Danielle she would get Mark out of her life, she meant it. Instead, she allowed their relationship to escalate.

She didn't sit back helpless while they took their relationship to a new level. She instigated it. She couldn't explain her actions, couldn't figure out why she let it happen. All she knew was she needed him more than she needed the air in her lungs. She needed to touch him, taste him, feel him. The passion, the fire, it all seemed so right.

But it was so *wrong*.

The oversized, red numbers of the alarm clock on his bedside table displayed 6:14 am. She turned her attention back to Mark. He faced toward her, his patterned breathing controlled by a deep sleep. Her hand reached for him. Her trembling fingers hovered above his bare shoulder for a moment before she retracted her hand to her mouth.

A range of emotions surged through her, the most prominent of which was sadness. She didn't belong here. She didn't deserve him or the innocent love he brought into her life. Though he had never seen the hidden side of her, the tainted and broken side, the moment he realized she was not the girl he loved, he would run away and never look back.

She needed to sneak out before he woke up. Once she was alone at her house, she could figure out the best way to end the relationship. As much as she wanted a life with him, as much as she loved him, she had no choice but to leave him. If it came down to it, she would leave him without a goodbye.

Rachel leaned over and touched her lips to his. She inched herself sideways across the bed, but stopped when she saw the movement was waking Mark. He opened his eyes and smiled at her. "Have you been awake long?"

"A few minutes."

He looked at the clock and yawned, then turned his eyes back to her. "Are you always up this early?" he asked, still grinning.

His innocent, almost playful question reminded Rachel of his naivety. She bit down on her lower lip in an attempt to hold back tears.

Mark studied her face, and his expression changed to one of concern. "Did you have a bad dream?"

"Yes," she said.

"What was it about?"

"I can't remember now." She cringed inside with the lie. She remembered every image as if it were a real memory and not a dream. The uneasiness trailing in the wake of the nightmare still disturbed her.

At his coaxing, Rachel moved closer to him and laid her head down on his chest. He wrapped his arms around her and his lips brushed her forehead. His warm skin reassured her of his presence, and the sound of his slow and steady heartbeat comforted her.

She closed her eyes and drifted toward a dreamless sleep, wishing she could stay like this forever.

Chapter Twenty-three

Mark woke two hours later. Sunlight streamed through the bedroom windows and across the blanket on the bed. Rachel rested on her side with her arm thrown over his stomach. He ran his fingertips over her skin and traced the muscular contours high up on her arm.

He cocked his head to better see her sleeping face. In sleep, peace surrounded her, and her face appeared far more serene than during waking hours. A hint of a smile teased her mouth. Out of the corner of his eye, her chest rose and fell, allowing for the soft breaths she emitted from her parted lips.

For Mark, sex had always been for the sole purpose of pleasure, the temporary satisfaction of a superficial desire, leaving him empty and alone. With Rachel, it had been an unparalleled experience, fulfilling a very real emotional need. In the end, both lost the intense battle for control. She awakened a part of him he never knew existed. No matter how close he held her, how deeply he kissed her, or how much he touched her, it hadn't been enough.

Even now, the desire to touch her overwhelmed him and he stroked his fingers through her hair. The small gesture caused her eyes to flutter open. She rolled onto her back and glanced around the room to orient herself to her surroundings. Her eyes landed on his and she smiled.

"I'm sorry," he said. "I didn't mean to wake you."

"It's okay, it was probably time I did. Besides, I woke you up first."

He leaned over and kissed her. He propped himself up on his elbow. Looking down at her, he asked, "How about some breakfast?"

"Sounds good. I'm famished. Do you mind if I shower first?"

"Go ahead. I'll find some clothes for you and set them outside the bathroom door. I can get yours washed while we eat." He chuckled. "There's a broken plate in my kitchen sink, isn't there?"

She bit her bottom lip and guilt washed over her face. "I think so. I'm sorry. I'm sure I made quite the mess."

"For the first time in my life, I don't care about a mess." He twirled the ends of her hair between his fingers. "Rachel, about what I said last night. I've never said that to anyone else before you. I've never even come close to feeling it until I met you."

Rachel lifted her head off the pillow high enough to touch her lips to his.

Mark put his hand behind her head and lowered her head back down to the pillow, as his mouth moved over hers. Their bodies were separated by a blanket, and Mark thought it was for the best or they might not make it to the kitchen for breakfast anytime soon.

Their lips parted and Rachel smiled. "I love you, Mark. I'm not saying it just to say it, or because it's expected of me. I couldn't stop myself from feeling this way even if I tried. I want you to believe me when I say that."

Her words seemed a little odd, and he wondered why she thought he wouldn't believe her. "Of course I believe you," he said. "I'm glad to hear you say all that because I feel the same way." He moved away from her. "Go ahead and shower, and I'll get your clothes in the wash."

Rachel gave him another quick kiss and sat up. She swung her feet over the edge of the bed, and gathered a blanket around herself to use as a cover.

Mark's smile disappeared at the sight of her back. Unsure if the light played tricks on him, he leaned over and squinted. Dozens of thin scars ran diagonal and horizontal across her back, too many for him to count. He reached out his hand and his fingertips connected with her back. She jumped off the bed as if lightning hit her, and brought the blanket around her body.

"Are you okay?" he asked.

Rachel put her hand on her chest and exhaled. "I'm fine. You startled me."

He sat up at her statement. Her trembling voice told him that she was a long way from being fine. The image of the scars lingered in both his mind and the pit of his stomach. His voice quieted. "What happened to your back? How did you get those scars?"

Her eyes darted around the room and the blanket twisted between her fingers. "It… it was an accident. I was hiking and I fell down a small hill and I skidded across some rocks and branches."

His voice reflected his skepticism. "Hiking."

"It was a long time ago. I'm going to shower now." She retreated to the bathroom before Mark had a chance to respond.

Chapter Twenty-four

The palpable tension crushed the air between them while they ate their omelets in silence. Rachel finished her cup of coffee and stood up. "Would you like some more coffee?" she asked.

Mark didn't answer. She walked to the coffee pot, and the drawstrings of his pajama bottoms bounced around her knees. A day ago, he would have enjoyed watching her walk around in his clothes after spending an incredible night together, but the scars on her back completely obliterated all feelings of joy.

The steady sound of her clothes tumbling in the dryer reminded him she would leave soon. If he wanted his questions answered, if he was going to push her, now was the time. He took a deep breath. "You said you love me."

"I do love you, Mark," she said without turning around.

"Then when are you going to learn to trust me?"

Rachel tilted the carafe until her cup was full. Returning it to the burner, she turned around and leaned against the counter. "It takes a long time to trust someone. Trust is a tricky thing."

"No, it's not. You trust Danielle, right?"

"Of course, but I've known her for a long time. I know she won't—"

"Won't what? Betray you? Hurt you? Leave you?"

"Sure. All of those things."

"Why won't you trust me? Do you think I'm capable of doing any of that to you?"

Rachel averted her eyes to the floor. "I don't know."

Mark pushed his chair back from the table and stood up. "I feel like I'm walking around with a sign on my forehead that says 'Bad Guy' in neon letters, but what have I done to deserve that? I've done nothing to warrant your mistrust, nothing to warrant being lied to."

"Lied to? When have I lied to you?"

Her words rang hollow, and he could tell she knew what he was talking about. "For starters, your explanation of the scars on your back seems strange."

"I told you. I was hiking."

"I'm sorry, Rachel, but we both know you're not telling the truth, and I don't understand why."

Rachel's silence confirmed his suspicions that she lied to him about what happened.

"Then let's start with something smaller," Mark said. "How did you get the scar on the front of your neck? It's hard to see, but there is one there." He pointed to his own neck, mirroring the location of hers. The thin scar was in an odd place for an accident requiring stitches, but until he saw the scars on her back, he hadn't given the one on her neck much thought.

Her lips tightened and she remained silent.

"You have nothing for that one? Not even, say, a childhood roller-skating accident? Or maybe a cat scratch?"

Rachel took a sip of her coffee and ignored him.

Mark let out his breath in a huff. He wasn't sure how he would ever get her to open up to him, and he regretted starting down this road. For the first time since they started dating, he worried he would drive her away, despite the recent revelation of their mutual feelings.

He had gone way too far and had too many unanswered questions to stop now. "Rachel, when I ask you questions, your answers are vague, and the things you say don't always make sense. It's obvious you're hiding something."

Rachel avoided his eyes. "What am I hiding from you?"

"I don't know, but there are all these inconsistencies with you. Like last night, when you told me the story about your dad. I was excited to hear a memory that means so much to you. Then I thought about it. You told me you had a cook when you were growing up, so why would your dad make meatloaf? I believed every word you said last night. That was a genuine memory, but you were also telling me the truth when you said you had a cook. So did you have the cook when you lived with your foster family? Because if they were the ones who had money, then your trust fund didn't come from your parents. Did it come from your foster family? And why is it you never talk about them, Rachel?"

Her knuckles whitened with her tight grasp on the mug handle. She continued staring at the floor, as if frightened to look in his direction.

Mark took a step forward. "I know you aren't telling me everything. You're shutting me out of your life when I very much want to be a part of it."

She met his eyes and spoke in a hushed tone. "I'm not shutting you out, Mark."

"Okay, then let's try something more simple than your scars. Where is your home? Where did you grow up?"

She set the coffee mug down on the counter behind her and crossed her arms. "California."

"You've told me that before, but California's a pretty big place. Can you narrow it down?"

"I don't want to talk about it. I have a lot of sad memories with my parents' death."

"My parents died when I was young, too. Hell, my mom committed suicide and I found her body, yet I still talk about my life. Please, answer this one question. Where did you grow up in California?"

"What does it matter if I answer you or not? You won't believe me," Rachel said.

"I'd believe you if I knew you could be honest with me."

"I am honest with you."

"Only when it suits you."

"Only when it won't hurt you."

Mark stepped back and anxiety sliced through his chest. Her wide eyes and open mouth revealed she had no intention of blurting out a confession. Until now, he wasn't convinced she was hiding anything from him, since he only had a suspicion and nothing concrete. For the first time, he realized her eyes were stripped of innocence and held a deep-seated torment that distressed and even frightened him.

He laid his hand on her arm, his eyes stinging with tears. "What happened to you, Rachel?" he whispered.

Her lips parted as if she was going to answer. She appeared to battle with herself to speak, and a tear escaped from her moist eyes. She brushed past him and walked toward the living room without a word.

Mark cursed under his breath and ran to catch up with her. He grabbed her arm and whirled her around. "I know you wouldn't hide things from me unless you had a damn good reason for it. You have to realize that I love you, and I am not going away. Ever. Do you understand me?"

Rachel kept her eyes lowered to the floor.

"Rachel, please."

"If you knew me, you would never say anything like that. If you knew, you wouldn't love me, you wouldn't want me."

Mark wrapped his arms around her and she buried her face in his shoulder. "I don't care what's happened in the past," he said. "Nothing can change how I feel about you. You may think there are things you can't tell me, but you can. Whenever you're ready, tell me and I will listen."

He held her away from him and looked at her. "I'm on your side, Rachel. I'm not one of the bad guys. I'm never going to leave you and I am never going to hurt you. I need you to trust me on at least that much."

Rachel moved into the living room. She settled into the couch cushions and said, "San Diego."

He sat beside her and took her hand.

"I was born in San Diego and lived there until I was ten. Then my parents died and I moved to Northern California."

"With your foster family?"

"Yes. When my parents died, the world I knew came to an end. If I don't talk about the other family, it's because I would rather remember what life was like when my parents were alive. The worst thing is I don't remember what my parents look like." She looked up and met his eyes. "Isn't that horrible? To love someone so much and not be able to see them after they're gone? I have a few memories of them, but their faces are always blurred. The harder I try to see their faces, the fuzzier they become."

"You don't have any pictures of them?"

"The only thing I have is a baseball cap my dad had bought me a week before he died." She smiled to herself. "My mom made the mistake of sending us out to buy a dress for some school concert. I didn't want to wear a dress, so I told my dad if he bought me a baseball cap, I'd get a dress. At the time, I didn't realize he could take me home and let Mom deal with me. After all, dresses were her department, but he bought me the hat."

Rachel took a deep breath before continuing. "Sometimes I wonder if he had a feeling something was going to happen to him. He shouldn't have let me get away with that kind of manipulation, but he did. It may seem like a small gesture, but that hat helped me through their deaths. I slept in it the first few nights at the es… with the foster family. It made me feel closer to my dad, like he was still alive somewhere."

She almost slipped, Mark thought. Her first few nights at the what? She started saying something else, but she corrected herself. Her face was calm and joyful with the memories of her father, her voice steady and strong. But, when she corrected herself, Mark saw a flicker behind her eyes. While her expression did not change, he sensed a tremendous pain inside of her. Despite his desperation to know, he didn't ask, worried she might stop talking again if he questioned her story.

He wanted to comfort and soothe her, but without knowing what caused her pain, he didn't know how to help. He needed to get her to talk about her parents again. Every time she spoke about her father, she seemed happy. "You've never really talked about your mother before," he said.

Rachel creased her brow. "I don't remember much about her, not like

I do with my dad. I don't know where she worked or other details like that." Her face softened with a smiled. "I do know she sparked my interest in books."

"So I have her to thank for you coming into my bookstore," Mark said.

"It's all her fault we met. As far back as I can remember, she not only read to me, but she made up stories of her own. I would sit beside her in a rocking chair on the back porch and she would tell me fairy tales. The first time she had me make up my own story, I got to the end of it and realized I forgot to include a Prince Charming. I was stuck at the end, with no one to save the princess from the evil witch."

"What happened to the princess?"

"Nothing. I couldn't finish the story because the princess couldn't be saved. I think my mother was distraught, but she didn't show it. Instead, she coaxed me to start over and reminded me not to forget Prince Charming. I asked her why and she told me that every fairy tale has a Prince Charming." A deep hurt strangled her voice and her brow creased. "I've never forgotten that."

Mark squeezed her hand, and his gut twisted with anxiety. He wanted to drive straight to the cause of her anguish, but he stopped himself from asking more questions. Whereas before he searched out the truth, he was now afraid he had opened a door leading straight to that truth. Hearing the pain in her voice, seeing the agony in her eyes, he was no longer certain he wanted her to stop lying.

Chapter Twenty-five

Twirling a black permanent marker between her fingers, Rachel pretended to study the map of the United States when Danielle entered the living room. Spread out on the coffee table before her, Rachel looked at the black dots that peppered the map and wondered where they would go next.

Danielle walked over to the table, leaned over Rachel, and found Kansas on the map with her finger. A black dot covered the city of Wichita. "You're kidding, right?" Danielle asked.

Rachel kept her eyes glued to the map. Each black dot marked a city where she lived at some point during the past three years. "We've been here far too long," she said.

"I know you've been bouncing around this crazy idea of leaving Mark, but I thought we were staying here for another few weeks no matter what happened between you two."

Rachel shrugged and said, "I've changed my mind." She set the marker down on the map.

Alarm flooded Danielle's voice. "What happened with Mark? You stayed with him again last night, so did you break it off this morning?" Danielle sat down beside her on the couch after Rachel didn't answer. "Honey, what's wrong?"

"I have scars." Her voice trembled and her eyes welled with tears. "On my back. I'm not supposed to have any scars."

"Come here." Danielle drew Rachel's head onto her shoulder. Her hand stroked through Rachel's hair.

"Did you know I have them?" Rachel asked.

"Yes, but they are fading."

"Why didn't you tell me?"

"You thought you didn't have any scars. I didn't think you needed to know otherwise. I knew how much it would upset you."

"He saw them." Rachel took in a jagged breath. "He saw them and asked me what happened."

"Mark?"

"I told him a lie. Another lie. It wasn't even a good one. He said he didn't believe me."

"It's never bothered you this much to lie in the past."

"My whole life is nothing but a lie. I know I'm doing it to protect him, but I'm tired of lying to him all the time."

"It only bothers you because you love him."

"I am not in love with him," Rachel said.

"Then what's the problem?"

"It's never going to end. The rest of my life will be like it is now and it won't ever be normal. I want it to end once and for all. I need some sort of peace in my life. I might not deserve peace, but that doesn't stop me from wanting it."

Danielle's melodic voice soothed her. "Remember when you used to do this for me? Whenever the pain became too much to bear, you were always there to comfort me. You would tell me it would pass, that one day all of my bruises and scars would disappear. You were right. One day your scars will be gone, too. Maybe not on the outside, not all the way, but they will go away on the inside. I think you're somewhat in control of how fast they disappear."

"What are you trying to say?"

"You need to tell Mark. If you tell him everything, you'll have no more reason to lie or to hide. It can give you some of that peace you're searching for."

Rachel lifted her head from Danielle's shoulder and wiped the tears from her cheeks. "There's no way I can tell him anything more than I already have." Rachel rose from the couch and moved behind it, toward the hallway. "I need to start packing."

"Rachel, wait a sec." Danielle twisted in the seat to look at her. "What did you tell him?"

"This morning I told him I was born in San Diego and that I moved to northern California after my parents died."

"That's nothing. It's not even a scratch on the surface of who you are, let alone being good enough. You have to tell him everything."

"Why? So he can follow me to all ends of the earth? I already have one groupie."

Danielle stood up. "Hey!"

Rachel held up her hand. "I'm sorry. That wasn't fair. The truth is I don't want you going with me this time. Every minute you spend with me your life is in danger."

"I am fully aware of the consequences and I accept them," Danielle said. "Do you understand how you have changed my life? I wouldn't even have much of a life right now if it hadn't been for you. Everything you have done for me has always meant so much."

"I don't expect or want you to repay me for what you think I've done to help you."

"I'm not repaying you. I know I could never do for you what you did for me. Could we live without each other? Probably. We could go our separate ways and in the end we would somehow be fine. But, life is far more interesting and enjoyable for me with you in it. Any risk that comes with having you around is worth it. You know if you were in my shoes, you'd do the same thing for me."

"I appreciate that, I really do," Rachel said. "And yes, I would do the same thing for you without hesitation."

"Rach, despite the fact that I'm willing to go with you, no matter where that takes us, I'm not going to lie to you. It's time for you to stop running. You have to face this."

"It's too late for that. It's out of the question."

"What's the absolute worst thing that could happen if you did stop running?"

"You could die. Mark could die." Rachel's face reflected the anguish inside. "And I could live."

Danielle took a deep breath. "Do you think they're still searching for you after so long? I'm sure they gave up a long time ago."

Rachel's mind numbed at the thought. They. The ominous They. Though speaking in private, Rachel and Danielle always referred to the people looking for her as They, not daring to use any names. Those names were bitter on the tongue, fingernails on chalkboard to the ears, and terror to the mind.

Even now, Rachel could not bring herself to think one of those names. She was scared the moment she did, They would hear her through some science fiction telepathy and come charging through her front door to take away her freedom and the remainder of her sanity.

"I know they're still searching for me," Rachel said. "It doesn't matter how long it takes, they won't give up until they find me."

"Then let's go to the authorities."

"There's no way we can do that."

"Why not?"

"You know damn well why."

"You're right, no authorities," Danielle said. "But you have to tell Mark. Maybe between the three of us, we can figure out a solution to this whole problem."

"There is no solution."

"I know of at least one solution," Danielle said. "You do own a gun."

Rachel looked down, unwilling to accept Danielle's suggestion.

"If it came to that, you wouldn't use it, would you?" Danielle didn't wait for her to answer. "I didn't think you would. Why not give it to me then? I'd be more than happy to use it for you."

"That's murder, Danielle, not a solution." Under her breath, she added, "Maybe I shouldn't have ever started running."

Danielle clenched her jaw. "Tell me those words didn't come out of your mouth. Rach, you cannot believe that."

"Well, look at where it's gotten me! I'm stuck in this life where my only option is to keep moving and keep hiding, and now I've put both you and Mark in danger."

"And you would have been so much better off staying there?"

"I don't know." Rachel's face flushed and she whispered, "I gave up so much. I could always go back and all of this would be over. It would get you and Mark out of harm's way."

Danielle moved behind the couch and grabbed Rachel's arm. "Why don't we go into the bathroom so you can take a good look at your back in the mirror? Then you can tell me if your life there was so great." She let go of Rachel's arm. Her voice lowered and her eyes narrowed. "Do you remember the pain? Was it so worth everything you gave up that you would want to go back?"

Rachel slid down the back of the couch until she rested on the ground. "I don't know anymore." She covered her eyes with her hands to catch the fresh river of tears. She wished she could disappear and escape Danielle's rousing of the past. Mark had dug deep enough that morning for her to be forced to endure more questions.

Danielle crouched beside her. "I think you feel guilty about being with Mark, and there's no reason for that. You need to realize it's okay for you to be with him. Has it ever occurred to you that, after trying for over two months, maybe there's a reason you can't kick him out of your life?"

Rachel hesitated and bowed her head. "I lied earlier."

"About what?"

"I do love him."

"I know you do, and I know that he loves you, too. It's okay for you to love him, but it proves my point that you have to tell him. If you love him, you won't keep lying to him. Let him decide for himself what to do. You owe him that much."

"He doesn't deserve something as horrible as hearing the truth. He's one of the good ones. You said so yourself."

"If you think telling him the truth will hurt him, how is he going to feel when you run and don't tell him you're leaving? That's going to hurt him far worse than any words coming out of your mouth. Rach, you can't leave him like this. If only because he's one of the good ones."

"He won't understand and it's wrong for me to expect him to try. I can't do that to him."

"You have a lot of great excuses lined up and I'm sure you'll find even more if we keep going back and forth like this." Danielle stood up and thrust her hands onto her hips. "I'm not going to argue with you anymore. If you don't tell him, I will."

Rachel's jaw dropped. "You can't do that to me. It's not fair to me or to him."

"I don't care. I'm not about to watch you screw up the best thing that's ever happened to you. At least give Mark an opportunity to decide how to react to your past, instead of assuming how he's going to feel."

Rachel opened her mouth to object, but Danielle's stubborn expression warned her of the futility of further argument. Somewhere deep inside, she knew Danielle was right. She loved Mark too much not to tell him the truth, and she really did not want to leave him. "Okay, you win. He's working the rest of the day, so I'll talk to him tonight when he gets off."

"You're making the right decision. Now, when are we leaving Wichita?"

"As soon as I can get us hooked up with some new identities," Rachel said, rubbing her temples. "I made contact with a guy who owns a pawnshop across town. He does a little forgery work on the side. I'm meeting with him for lunch to place our order, so let me know what name you want to use and then I'll pick them up tonight. Tomorrow morning we'll head out to our next exotic destination," Rachel said with a tinge of sarcasm.

"Where are we going?"

"I don't know yet." Rachel eliminated any desire to stay in Wichita, even if it meant leaving Mark. Soon enough, he would know who she was, and he would want her gone from his life. Wherever she and Danielle ended up, Rachel would never make the mistake of getting involved with a man ever again. She looked up at Danielle. "You can pick a place this time if you want. I don't care anymore."

"Okay. Let's start packing."

Chapter Twenty-six

Kansas was flat, much more so than Paul Pettis expected. He was skeptical when he first heard he had to come here, but now that he was here, he thought he could learn to like it.

He tossed the nine millimeter gun to the ground and looked at the endless field ahead of him. He couldn't see even a hill to obstruct his view under the darkening pink and blue hues of the sunset clouds. He thought if he looked hard enough, he might see the Rocky Mountains.

"I hate this place," Sean said, interrupting Paul's serenity. "Too hot and humid."

As soon as they stepped off the jet a few hours earlier, Paul's suffering under the summer humidity began. An invisible force field holding back much-needed rain from providing the ground with moisture, the humidity seemed to raise the temperature by at least twenty degrees. Sweat penetrated Paul's jeans and black t-shirt, both of which stuck to him like a second skin.

Even though Paul agreed with Sean about the heat, he wanted nothing in common with the man, not even a small point like their disdain for Kansas humidity. He took a deep breath to cleanse as much hatred from his tone as he could. "Do you think I care if you like Kansas? I'm sure the natives will be cheering when you leave. They might even have a parade."

Sean scowled. "Don't be a jerk because you're in a bad mood about the girl."

Paul clenched his fists and released them as he blew out the breath he was holding.

"I have to get out of here," Sean said. He scratched the skin around his dark mustache. "He's waiting for me."

Paul closed his eyes. "You do that," he said under his breath.

"You're supposed to stay here and clean up. Someone will be here soon to help you finish up and take you back to the jet."

As if Paul didn't already know that. Sean's authoritative tone was a slap in the face, but Paul wasn't in charge anymore. All of his tenure disappeared the moment they stepped foot on the Kansas plains. He would be nothing more than a grunt until things calmed down. No one wanted him to interfere with the job at this stage.

"Sean, please don't hurt her," Paul said. "I know that's asking a lot, but please don't."

Sean pursed his lips and shrugged. "That's not really up to me, is it? At least she'll be alive still. The guy is a different story. We both know he probably won't make it through the night."

Paul looked down. Sean's words were true, but he didn't want to consider them. Rachel had finally found herself, her real self, and it would soon be taken away.

Sean's footsteps moved away from him and toward the car. Paul reached into his shoulder holster and pulled out another gun. He lifted the barrel of the gun and aimed, his finger on the trigger, his left eye shut. He had a clear shot of Sean's overinflated head. All he had to do was squeeze.

His shoulders dropped, and he holstered the gun. He wouldn't kill Sean today, he thought. Soon, but not today. There were too many other things to deal with rather than getting rid of Sean's body and trying to explain how Sean ended up dead.

Paul turned around and looked down at the task at hand. Flies swarmed around Officer Shelly Duncan's open eyes and slack jaw, but it did not bother Paul. He just wished she'd had the courtesy to shut her eyes right before he shot her.

At least she had died quickly. No begging, no whimpering. A single shot in the back of her head and she fell. Sean would fall as well, but in the end, he would plead for death. Maybe Paul would shoot him in the stomach and let him bleed out. Or shoot him in the kneecaps and let him live. The only time he saw someone shot in the kneecaps, it had been a pleasure to watch him suffer. Sean needed that kind of agony in his life to knock him back a few notches.

A throaty chuckle escaped Paul's lips and he picked up the shovel by his feet. It was time to stop dreaming about ending Sean's pathetic life. He had work to do if he was going to get back to the jet on time. All the loose ends had been tied up with Duncan's death, and he was left to dispose of the body.

Chapter Twenty-seven

Unable to focus on the paperwork he promised Greg he would get done, Mark paced the floor of his office. Sarah had come back to the office a few minutes earlier, and concern crossed her face when she noticed his restless movements. He stopped pacing when he saw her, not wanting his mood to reflect in his actions.

He answered her quick question and, as soon as she left his view, he resumed shuffling back and forth along the tiles. He knew he should send her home given the slow business so near closing time, but he desired solitude instead of dealing with the occasional customer.

Mark glanced at his watch. He had forty-five minutes until he was supposed to meet Rachel at her house. Her phone call an hour earlier stirred up endless questions. With a controlled voice, she had asked Mark if he minded staying at her house in lieu of going out.

It wouldn't have been an alarming request, except the events of that morning kept coming to mind. Though he wasn't much in the mood for being in public, he sensed the real reason for the change in plans. Rachel wanted to talk, and the prospect of hearing what she had to say filled him with dread.

One question floated through his mind since driving her home that morning, and his imagination took liberties with the answer. What kind of woman spent her days volunteering at a battered women's shelter? The answer came too easily: the kind of woman who was abused.

When the realization struck him that she might have been a victim of abuse at one time, his first thoughts were of a superficial relationship. A boyfriend or even husband who did the occasional Jekyll-to-Hyde transformation and took a bad day at work out on her. But, the simple explanation lacked something, though Mark couldn't fathom what. It also didn't account for the scars on her back or help him understand the cause of them.

He knew what happened to her, but he didn't want to admit it. The thought was too horrific. No matter how he tried to spin it, no matter what other ideas he came up with, he always came back to the same cause. Only one thing could be responsible for the angry scars that marred her back. Multiple, random wounds cast on her skin in different directions. Straight, yet overlapping. Thin, but varying in length. Oh, yes. He knew.

He pushed the image of her scars out of his mind as hard as he could and slammed the door against it. He didn't know anything for sure, and he wouldn't allow himself to play agonizing guessing games. If she wanted him to know, she would tell him tonight.

Instead, he focused on her nonexistent foster family. She had no contact with them, and she purposely avoided talking about them. He didn't know their names or if they had other children living with them besides Rachel.

Abuse as a child would explain her reluctance to talk about them. It also explained why she went to a gym as a child, finding solace in sparring with others and learning how to defend herself. But, like with so many other explanations, something didn't feel right about that one, either.

The bell rang through the store to announce a customer, disturbing Mark's train of thought. He stepped out of the office and frowned at James jogging up the center aisle.

Mark raised an eyebrow. "There had better be something wrong for you to run in here like that," he said.

James walked past him. "You're going to need to sit down for this one," he said.

Mark frowned and followed him into the office. Sitting behind his desk, he asked, "What is it?"

James pulled up a chair to the other side of the desk and sat down across from Mark. "Remember that guy that got killed?"

"Lots of guys get killed."

"The one that they were talking about on the news last night, the friend of Senator Cal Robbins. We couldn't figure out his name, remember?"

"Oh, yeah," Mark said. "What about him?" He had put the news report out of his mind in the wake of the amazing night he spent with Rachel, and then seeing her scars that morning.

"I found out his name and raced over here to tell you," James said, excitement resounding through his voice.

Mark waited for a moment, but James didn't speak. "Are you going to tell me or are we playing twenty questions?"

"Jonathan Thomas."

Mark caught his breath at the unexpected name. Chills rushed through him as he recalled the desk organizer falling off the desk before the newscaster finished speaking the deceased man's name. It was quite a distraction to clean up the mess on the floor instead of listening to the rest of the news story about his murder. Would Rachel knock it off the desk on purpose? She would if she had a secret she wanted to hide, and considering everything else, it seemed she had a lot to hide.

Jonathan Thomas.

Rachel Thomas.

"He has the same last name as Rachel," James said.

"I realize that," Mark said. "It doesn't mean anything."

"It does if Rachel pushed the organizer off your desk before the newscaster said his name," James said, as if he had read Mark's thoughts about Rachel's suspicious actions. "That thing was nowhere near the edge of your desk like she said. I know because I stole a pen from you when I came in the office."

"Why would she do that?" Mark asked, his voice almost a whisper. He tried to wrap his mind around the revelation. "That doesn't make sense."

James scooted to the edge of the chair and put his elbows on the desk. "What if she didn't want us to hear his name?"

"But that doesn't make sense," Mark repeated. "What's the big deal about her having the same last name as some guy that was murdered? Thomas is a common last name."

"What if she's related to him? What if she knows something about his murder?"

"There's no way she's related to him. She's an orphan, remember? And I doubt she knows anything about his death just because they have the same last name. That's a stretch under any circumstance."

"They're both from California," James said, unwilling to give up.

"A lot of people in California have the same last name."

"But when did she leave California?"

Mark searched his memory. "I think she said she moved away three years ago."

"And Jonathan Thomas was murdered three years ago yesterday," James said. "That's a little coincidental given that they share the same last name."

"People move away from California every day. Nothing you've said means that she knew him or knows anything about his murder."

"But there's also too much coincidence *not* to mean something. You have to admit something about her isn't right. I know you've noticed it. Greg said you were talking to him about it yesterday morning."

Mark frowned at hearing his brother had broken his confidence. "Sure, she's a little secretive, but I think maybe something happened with her foster family and she doesn't want to talk about it. There's nothing wrong with that, and we can't go around accusing her of anything. I don't even like that we're having this conversation without her present to defend herself."

James bounced in the chair like a child, his eyes jumping with excitement. "Wouldn't that be crazy if your girlfriend knew something about a billionaire's unsolved murder?" he asked, as if he heard none of Mark's words.

"It's a coincidence, James, nothing more."

"Maybe." He leaned forward and grinned. "But wouldn't it be cool?"

"I don't see anything 'cool' about the idea."

"What if she witnessed his murder and now she's running for her life because the killer is after her?"

"This isn't James Bond or some spy flick."

"You know what I think?" James asked, pointing a finger at him. "I think you need to wise up. Don't call her anymore, and don't go see her. Disappear from her life. Guys do that all the time."

The thought had never crossed Mark's mind. "Why would you say that? I would never do that to her."

"Yeah, but if she's messed up in the murder of Jonathan Thomas, you don't want to get wasted by some mafia-type guy because of her."

"That's not going to happen."

"I mean Rachel's cute, but she ain't *that* cute."

Mark stood up and set his palms down on the desk. "James, I'm in love with her. I'm not going to disappear because you come in here with some wild theory that Rachel may know who killed Jonathan Thomas."

James also rose from his chair. "Hey, that's great, man. I'm happy for you and all, even though I think you're crazy for sticking around when you don't know what she might be mixed up in or who may be after her."

"Thank you. Now will you leave the matter—"

"But I think I'm going to figure this out for myself." He shrugged. "Morbid curiosity." He walked out of the office.

Mark groaned and chased James down an aisle. "Where are you going?"

"To learn about Jonathan Thomas." He turned around and spread his arms. "You do own a bookstore."

Mark caught up with him. "Fine," he said. "But at least let me do the research with you, okay? She is *my* girlfriend." He led the way to the true crime section of the store. He ran a finger over the spines of the books until he found one that caught his eye, a biography authorized by the Thomas family on the life and murder of Jonathan Thomas. Holding up the book, he asked, "How's this one?"

James grabbed a second copy off the shelf. "Works for me."

Mark detoured to the cash register and asked Sarah not to disturb him unless it was an emergency. He went back to the office and settled into his chair. James had his book open on the desk, already lost in the world of Jonathan Thomas. Mark opened his book and skimmed through the details as fast as he could.

Jonathan Thomas had lived an impoverished childhood in the outskirts of San Francisco. His mother died from complications after giving birth to her youngest son, who also passed away. Jonathan, the second oldest, was left to help raise the younger three siblings with his older sister, while his father moved from job to job in search of good pay and steady work.

After graduating from high school, Jonathan skipped out on college to find a job and help support his siblings. He found employment with a local security company that hired out security guards to area banks. He worked his way from a clerical assistant to vice president in seven years.

At twenty-five, unable to convince the president of the security company to explore other areas of the security industry, Jonathan ventured out on his own and opened Thomas Security. He specialized in hiring out security guards and bodyguards and built a clientele that surpassed his previous employer's. Jonathan then branched out his company to commercial and residential security, including the installation, servicing, and monitoring of alarms systems.

Jonathan succeeded beyond his wildest expectations. At the time of his death, his security company was one of the largest in the nation, second only to another company owned by a man named Donovan King. The author spent a chapter detailing the well-known and explosive rivalry between the two men, who were complete opposites.

Whereas Jonathan built his company from the ground up, Donovan inherited his father's already successful security company. Jonathan loved the media and had no aversion to interviews or photographs. Donovan, on the other hand, remained private and elusive, and the press soon found him uninteresting, though the occasional desperate journalist would find a reason to write an article about him.

Mark's own interest waned and he closed the book. Looking up at James, he said, "This is stupid. I mean, he seems like an upstanding guy and I'm sorry he was murdered, but there's nothing here screaming out that Rachel knew him."

"You might want to turn to page three fifty-six."

"How did you get to page three fifty-six already?"

"I started reading from the back. If you're going to solve a mystery, always start at the end of the story, closest to the time they died. Everyone knows that."

Mark rolled his eyes at the sudden spurt of wisdom. He flipped through the book. Halfway down the page, he found what James was talking about. Jonathan was considered one of the nation's most eligible bachelors and family members reported he was a target for many single women looking for quick wealth in the form of a man. His younger brother, Cory, disclosed in an interview with the author that Jonathan avoided serious relationships.

A week prior to his murder, however, Jonathan made reference to a younger woman who captured his attention, commenting it was the one woman who was untouchable even for him. Jonathan never revealed the name of the woman, and all attempts to learn her identity after his murder were fruitless.

Mark paused in his reading. At his death three years ago, Jonathan was forty-three years old. Rachel would have been twenty-three at the time, which passed for a younger woman.

"I guess you read it," James said.

"It's nothing but another coincidence."

"They have the same last name, she moved away from California at the same time he was murdered, and he was messing around with a younger woman. That's a lot of coincidences."

"If Rachel were this mysterious woman, she wouldn't share his last name unless they had been married. The book says Jonathan was never married. And, how in the world would she meet this guy? It says right there he avoided serious relationships because of gold diggers. If I were him and had that much money, I'd also be wary of women."

James set the book down on the desk. "Okay. That must mean she's related to him and she lied about having no family."

Mark opened the book up to the beginning and found the information on Jonathan's family. "His older sister's name is Melissa. There are the twins that are younger than him, Cory and Courtney. His youngest brother is named Stephen." Mark looked up. "The name Rachel isn't in the book."

"What if she was his daughter?"

"But he wasn't married and there isn't anything about illegitimate children. And, Rachel isn't his niece because both of Rachel's parents are dead and all of Jonathan's siblings are still alive, except the one that died during childbirth. Even if her dad were related to the Thomas family, but not mentioned in the book, why would she have to live with a foster family after her parents died if she had other family members alive?"

"What if—"

Mark glared at James. "No more what ifs. There's no proof, there's no link to Rachel, there's nothing. We're wrong, so let's leave it alone."

"Okay, okay." James rose from the chair. He laid the book down on the desk. "I need to head home anyway, but I wanted to let you know about the dead guy. I'm sorry I jumped to conclusions about Rachel, and I am happy that you guys are in love or something."

Mark smiled. "Thanks. You know, I'm glad we didn't find anything. I was starting to think..." The corners of Mark's mouth dropped into a frown and his mind wandered back to the book. No matter how he tried, he couldn't make the pieces fit, couldn't find proof of a solid connection between Rachel and Jonathan Thomas. The only explanation that seemed right was Rachel had knocked over the desk caddy on accident, and it was nothing more than coincidence that she shared the man's last name.

But then again, there was the nagging feeling that something didn't seem right.

"You okay, man?" James asked. "I know this is a lot to swallow without having any answers."

"Yeah, I'm fine. Thanks again, James. I know you meant well." James left the office and Mark stared down at the book. In just a few minutes, he would learn what Rachel had to say, and finally have his answers. He hoped he could handle it.

Chapter Twenty-eight

Rachel slipped a contact lens into her eye. Blinking it into place, she looked in the mirror over the bathroom sink. She had one blue eye and one brown eye. "Hey, Danielle!"

Danielle strode into the bathroom. "How's the makeover going?" she asked.

"Okay, I guess. Which eye color do you like better?"

Danielle scrutinized each eye. "Are you still going to dye your hair blonde?" she asked. She walked over to the counter and looked through several wigs that were laid out, all different shades of blonde.

"I think so."

Danielle picked up a longer blonde wig. She arranged the wig on Rachel's head and tucked her natural hair underneath. "Go with the brown contacts. You'll stand out too much with the blue."

"I hate this. For the first time in three years, I've had my natural hair and eye color and now I have to change it." Rachel examined the boxes of hair dye kits lined across the counter. She picked one up and held it next to the wig. "Does this one match?"

"It's pretty close, but please hurry up and decide what you're doing. Those eyes are starting to spook me."

"Sorry." Rachel set the hair dye box down and removed the blue contact from her left eye. She inserted the match for the brown contact into her eye. "What are you changing this time?"

Danielle sat on the edge of the bathtub. "I'm going to cut off all my hair."

Rachel gasped. "No, don't do that. I love your hair with all those curls."

"I do, too, but I think it's time it went into the trashcan. It might be fun having short hair."

"How short?"

"Shorter than yours." Danielle held her hand up an inch above her shoulder. "I think right about here should do it."

Rachel scowled. "Maybe you should think about it more."

"Too late. It's getting cut tomorrow morning before we go." She walked back over to the wigs. "Do we have a short black one?"

"No, but there's a long one in the box along with black hair dye," Rachel said, pointing to a cardboard box by the bathtub. "I knew you were going to get around to black hair one day, as much as I didn't want you to."

Danielle took out the black wig and put it on in front of the full-length mirror on the back of the bathroom door. Her deep blue eyes stood out against the black strands of synthetic hair, and Rachel smiled. She thought she would hate the look on Danielle, but no matter what color of hair or contacts Danielle tried on, she always looked beautiful and natural.

Rachel picked up her digital camera from the bathroom counter. "Ready for your picture?" She waited for Danielle to stand in front of the light blue backdrop they had tacked to the wall. The forger would adjust the color of the backdrop as needed to match the standard backdrop for any state's driver's license. Danielle gave a large smile, and Rachel frowned at her. "Nobody looks good in their driver's license photo."

Danielle rolled her eyes, but traded her smile for a blank, expressionless stare.

"Much better," Rachel said. She snapped three quick pictures to make sure not to catch Danielle with her eyes closed or in a blurry photo. She reviewed the pictures on the camera's LCD screen. "These are perfect. You look like you were waiting at the DMV for about six hours."

"I don't know if that's a compliment because I took the picture right, or if you're saying I look terrible," Danielle said. She took the camera from Rachel's hands. They traded spots and Danielle took several pictures of Rachel. "We're all done," she said and handed the camera back to Rachel.

"All done," Rachel echoed. As she scanned the photographs Danielle took of her, the blonde wig reminded of another time she wore a similar wig. Rachel turned and examined herself in the full-length mirror. It was as if everything she did was a reminder of things best forgotten. She tugged on the blonde ends of the wig and twirled the hair between her fingers.

You are far more beautiful without it.

Rachel pulled the wig off her head, as the unwelcome voice rolled through her mind. Maybe blonde wasn't such a good idea, not with all the panic attacks and memories that insisted on surfacing.

Danielle walked up beside her. "Are you okay?"

"I'm fine," Rachel said, glad that Danielle could not read her thoughts.

"I know you're torn on talking to Mark, but I still believe it's the right thing for you to do."

Rachel wished she could avoid the topic, but Danielle hadn't forgotten her ultimatum. "Even though I agree with you, it doesn't make me any less sick and terrified to tell him. There are so many ways he could react."

"And I'm sure you've already analyzed every possible end scenario," Danielle said with a smile. "Mark will be more understanding than you ever imagined. Does he know you're going to tell him about your past?"

As she removed the contacts from her eyes and placed them back in the case, Rachel thought about her earlier conversation with Mark over the phone. Mark's tone had changed when she said she wanted them to stay in that night, revealing that not only did he know she was going to tell him about her life, but that the truth frightened them both. "I think he suspects," she said.

"When is he coming over?"

"The store closes at ten, so it won't be too long after that. I should be back from the pawnshop by then. Our guy will slide in the new photos and then we'll be set. Do you still want to go to South Carolina?"

"I've always heard it's beautiful there in the fall," Danielle said. "If we stay there for two or three months, we should be able to see the seasons change."

"I'm all for that, but when we get there, we need to get our IDs fixed right away with the address of where we'll be living. When the security alarm went off, the cops asked for my license, and, of course, the address was wrong since we got it in Indianapolis. I don't want to make the same mistake again."

"I couldn't agree more. I'm glad they didn't realize the whole thing was a fake."

"Me, too, but I guess that's why we pay so much for them to be done right."

"Maybe after you talk to Mark tonight we won't have to pay for them ever again," Danielle said. She started toward the bathroom door.

"Do you mind letting me know when it's about 9:00?" Rachel asked before she could leave. "I want to get to the pawnshop on time so I can be here when Mark arrives."

Danielle glanced at her watch. "Rach, it's almost ten now."

Rachel rotated her wrist and looked at her own watch. "No, it's only a quarter till nine." She noticed the second hand was not moving. "Damn it, my watch stopped. I should have been at the pawnshop a half hour ago." She walked out of the bathroom and down the hall.

Danielle followed her. "I'll go for you."

"No, it's okay." Rachel slung the camera over her shoulder. "I need to get some fresh air and clear my head before Mark comes over. Besides, even though this guy has seen a photo of you, he won't be expecting you there. He might get spooked. I don't want to delay because we have to find a new person for our IDs. I shouldn't be gone more than forty-five minutes and maybe Mark will be late. You can keep him entertained until I get back, right?"

"Of course. The good ones are always easy to entertain."

Rachel paused at the front door. "Danielle, even though I wish you wouldn't go with me this time, I'm glad you are. I don't know how I'd ever survive without you."

"You'd make it," Danielle said. "After tonight, I'm betting you'll have Mark to keep you company as well."

Rachel smiled and dug her car keys out of her purse. "I hope you're right. I don't think I could live without him either."

"You're realizing this now?" Danielle scoffed. "Get out of here and hurry back. I don't want to have to keep him entertained for too long."

Rachel held up her car keys as an acknowledgment and ran out the front door.

Chapter Twenty-nine

After James left his office, Mark chastised himself for his suspicions. Guilt over his subversive actions gnawed at him. He never should have read parts of the book about Jonathan Thomas without talking to Rachel first. He needed to trust that she would tell him everything he needed to know on her own time, whether she had known a murdered billionaire or she had been abused by her foster family or both.

As he sat in his quiet office with his thoughts, Mark realized he felt something new in his life. His love for Rachel made his heart a bit lighter, yet because of his concerns for what she may have gone through, the burden of responsibility pressed down on his neck and shoulders. Outside of the bookstore and his mortgage, he had never been accountable to anyone or anything.

With loving Rachel came the vow that he would help her through whatever plagued her. If something affected her, he would be right there to lift her up and carry her through. He refused to let her travel the road alone, no matter the cost.

Mark rose from his chair and stretched out his legs. He moved into the bookstore and replaced the books about Jonathan Thomas on the shelf. His watch showed a few minutes to ten. Time to lock up the store and go see Rachel. He sent Sarah home before making a quick check of the aisles of books.

As he worked on closing out the register, the bell on the front door rang. Mark walked out from behind the register and came face-to-face with two men. The first man looked no older than seventeen and was much shorter than the second man, who clenched his square jaw and stared at Mark with cold eyes.

"I'm sorry, but we're closed," Mark said. "We open back up at nine tomorrow morning."

His words failed to stop Square Jaw, who moved around Mark. His bald head bobbed through the aisles of the store and toward Mark's office. "Hey!" Mark said. "You can't go back there!" He turned and walked toward his office.

"Are you Mark Jacobson?" Short Man asked.

Mark spun back around and faced Short Man. His professional tone made Mark wonder if he was a cop, but his instincts negated that thought. Their odd behavior had him on full alert. He suddenly wished he wasn't alone at the store and that he hadn't left his cellphone in his office. "That's me," he said. "What can I do for you?"

Square Jaw came back up to them without saying a word.

"What's going on here?" Mark asked.

Short Man pulled back his black overcoat and revealed a shoulder holster. He took out his gun and aimed it at Mark's chest with a cocky smile. "You can take us to go see Rachel."

Mark took two quick steps back, his wide eyes focused on the gun. Though throughout his life he had friends that went hunting on a regular basis, Mark had never been around a gun and he didn't know much about them outside of what he saw in the movies. This gun appeared to be a standard, black handgun, and just as deadly as any other.

Submerged in fear, his flesh turned cold and a tremble rattled his insides. But, gun or no gun, his impulse was to protect Rachel. "No," he said.

Before Mark could register what was happening, Square Jaw moved next to him, also holding a gun on him. Short Man took out a long, cylindrical part from a second compartment of his shoulder holster. As he screwed it on the front of his gun, Mark realized it was a suppressor.

Short Man smirked, his gestures almost comical despite the seriousness of the words he spoke. "You don't seem like a stupid man, Mark, so let me put it this way. I'm not opposed to the idea of killing Rachel. If you take us, I imagine she'll live." He arched his eyebrows and stepped forward, cornering Mark against the register counter. "Or I can go do things my way, which won't end so well for either of you. Now, would you like to revise your answer?"

Mark remained silent and weighed his limited options. He swallowed hard and nodded.

"See? That was easy." He waved his gun toward the back of the store. "Let's go. Lock it up like you normally would."

After Mark secured the bookstore and exited through the back, Short Man climbed into the passenger seat of Mark's truck. Square Jaw followed them in a black SUV. Holding his gun on Mark at all times, Short Man instructed him to approach Rachel's house from the opposite direction with his lights dimmed so his truck could not be seen from the front windows.

Mark turned off the ignition and reached for the door handle, but Short Man's voice stopped him. "Not yet. We're going to sit here for a minute."

Mark took a deep breath and tried to sort out his thoughts. Small rays of relief broke through his terror-clouded mind when he noticed Rachel's car was not in the driveway where she always parked, nor was it on the street. A voice inside told him it didn't matter that she wasn't home. These men would stay until she returned.

He felt Short Man's eyes on him, as if he were sizing Mark up. Despite the gun held on him, Mark became irritated at the man's inspection of him. "What?" he asked, not sure where the bold question came from.

Short Man laughed. "You don't look like Rach's type."

Mark's brow creased with confusion. Short Man spoke as if he knew her well, like a close friend, yet he had threatened to kill her.

"It's also funny because you're a dead man walking," Short Man said. "Do you know that phrase, Mark?" He did not wait for an answer. "I'm sure you do. It's a phrase they use in prison to describe a man walking down death row to his execution. Except for you…" Short Man paused and studied Mark for a moment. "You became a dead man walking the minute you got involved with Rachel."

Mark looked down as more chills coursed through his body. Short Man wanted to scare him, and it was working. Despite his fear, Mark needed answers and he forced himself to speak once more. "What's your name?" he asked.

Laughter bubbled out of Short Man. "This isn't 'The Dating Game,' Mark. You don't get to ask questions, let alone know my name."

Mark ignored his statement and spoke again. "Are you going to hurt Rachel?"

Revenge danced in his eyes and the corner of his mouth turned upward. "I would love to hurt Rachel after what she did the last time I saw her. I would hurt her so bad she wouldn't remember her own name after I was done. But, lucky for her, that's not for me to do. He's the only one who is allowed to hurt her, and boy, is he pissed about you." Short Man laughed out the last half of his statement. "I suppose that will have to suffice for me."

Defeat curled around Mark like a poisonous viper. Though he wanted to know what Rachel did to this man to warrant his response, something else in the man's words caught his attention. There was someone out there who intended on hurting Rachel. Someone powerful enough to stop others from hurting her, so that he alone held the right to do with her as he wished.

"Who is he and why would he want to hurt her?" Mark asked.

"That's enough questions. He's coming."

Mark had no time to look out the window when two other men walked up to the truck. One of them opened the driver's side door. "Time to go," he said. He grabbed Mark's arm and dragged him out of the truck.

Mark caught his balance before falling onto the asphalt of the street. A man with a gel-filled mass of hair tightened his grip on Mark's arm, but it was the man's thick, dark mustache that sparked recognition. "You were in my store yesterday," Mark said. "You talked to Rachel." His stomach churned, and he understood that not only was the man casing the store, but he was also checking on Rachel.

"Shut up and get moving," Moustache Man said. He nudged Mark with the barrel of his gun.

Mark barely caught a glimpse of the fourth man before Moustache Man forced him across the lawn and up the steps. The four men stood off to the side of the porch, away from the front windows and away from the sightline of the peephole. Conscious of the guns three of the men held, Mark lifted his heavy arm and pressed the doorbell.

He closed his eyes and listened to footsteps approach the door from inside of the house. The sounds of each lock disengaging pounded in his chest. Danielle's smile disappeared behind two of the men, who pushed her into the house. The other two forced Mark inside.

Square Jaw and Short Man moved through the rest of the house. Moustache Man grabbed Danielle by the arm and shoved her into the living room. Danielle stumbled forward, and Mark caught her before she hit the ground.

"Both of you sit down," Moustache Man said in a gruff tone.

Mark held onto Danielle's arm, and they sat close together on the couch. Moustache Man followed their every movement with his gun. Taking hold of her hand, Mark turned his head to look at her. "I'm sorry. They said they'd kill Rachel. I didn't know what else to do."

Danielle managed a faint smile through her stressed and fearful expression. "Don't be sorry, Mark. I would have done the same thing."

Mark examined the fourth man, who walked around the living room, scrutinizing every item. He was the only one out of the four who did not carry a gun, and Mark first thought him unimportant. Now, Mark realized the man's demeanor was his weapon, and he determined that this man was in charge.

Dressed in an immaculate black suit, his stern face held an air of authority and confidence. The man ran a hand through his closely cropped dark hair, and even that mundane gesture had meaning and purpose. This was a man who believed the whole world jumped at his every whim. A man who did not need to use weapons and threats of imminent death to force people to comply with his will. This was a man Rachel would fear.

The thought startled Mark. Fear was the last emotion he would associate with Rachel. Of course, until now, fear was not an emotion he would associate with himself. He couldn't remember a single moment in his life when he felt fear. But, the man who stood in the center of the room, his clear, amber eyes exploring every corner of the living room, yet never once settling on Mark, this man demanded fear.

The two men from the bookstore came into the room. Square Jaw trained his gun on Danielle and Mark, while Short Man walked over to his boss. He held a blonde wig at his side. "No one else, but she was here." He jiggled the wig in his hands for his boss to see. "From the looks of things, I'd say we almost missed her again this time."

The man in charge took the wig from Short Man's hands. He stared at it for a long moment and ran his fingers through the synthetic strands. He tossed the wig on the coffee table and walked over to Mark and Danielle. Standing before them, he looked at Danielle and asked, "Where is she? Where is Rachel?"

"She's not here," Danielle said. "She already left and she's not coming back."

"Is that so?" His eyes narrowed. "I don't believe you."

"I'm telling you the truth. She left me behind this time, and she's gone."

He paused and inspected Danielle's face. Mark looked at Danielle as well, wondering what her words meant. He recognized in her composed expression that Danielle was not surprised by the events around her, not like he was. He wanted to ask what was going on, but something told him to stay quiet.

"Again, with the lies," the man in charge said. "Do you know who I am?"

Despite her monotone voice, Danielle's sharp breathing gave away her apprehension. "You're Donovan King," she said.

Mark's heart skipped a beat, his mind recalling the man's name in reference to Jonathan Thomas.

Donovan continued speaking to Danielle. "Then you know what I'm capable of." The words held no hint of pride.

"Yes," she said. "I know."

"Then let's try this again, and I expect you'll be honest with me this time. Where is Rachel, and when will she return?"

"I told you," Danielle said. "Rachel is gone and she's not coming back. It doesn't matter how many times you ask, it won't change the fact that she's gone for good."

Donovan pressed his lips together and stared at Danielle, as if deciding what to ask her next. He regarded her for a moment, then rotated his head to look at the wig on the coffee table. His head bounced up and down, and he looked at Short Man. "Joe," he said. He nodded the side of his head toward

Danielle.

Joe lowered his gun and fired three muffled shots into Danielle's chest. Mark jumped sideways. His eyes popped open and jagged breaths burned his lungs. Danielle's hand became lifeless in his as her body slacked.

Mark hopped up from the couch and rested his knee on the couch next to her. Leaning over her body, he pushed his hands down on her chest where he saw blood and tried to stop the bleeding. He looked at her face, into her cloudy, blue eyes. "Danielle?" he asked.

She did not respond.

Though Mark knew she was dead and he could not bring her back, he called her name again. "Danielle! Danielle!" He pressed harder against her chest.

Joe nudged Mark's shoulder with his gun. "She's dead, Mark," he said. "Nothing you can do for her now, so it's time for you to sit back down. Donovan's not done with you yet."

Terror pounded through Mark and he stared at her unmoving body, his mind unable to digest the reality of the image. He raised his hands off her chest and twisted around so he could sit back down on the couch. He hung his head and lifted his wet hands. Danielle's blood had painted his skin red.

Mark became aware of Donovan watching him. He shifted his gaze upward, toward Donovan. As Mark stared into his emotionless eyes, trepidation grasped his spine and prickled his flesh.

Donovan turned to Square Jaw. "Tony, why don't you go ahead and get Mr. Jacobson out of here. The rest of us will clean up this mess and wait for Rachel."

Tony obeyed by walking up beside Mark and raising his gun. Mark barely registered the thud of the blow to the side of his head before the darkness came.

Chapter Thirty

Since leaving the pawnshop with their new IDs, the same black sedan trailed behind Rachel, or at least she thought it was the same one. There were enough cars on the darkened roads that she couldn't be sure. On her way to the pawnshop, she had been wary of a white van that had the nerve to stay behind her car for more than three blocks.

Paranoia had taken over.

She turned down a side street and followed it to a T in the road, where she opted to turn left. She continued through the large neighborhood for a bit, making a series of quick right and left turns.

After several minutes, she exhaled with relief at the absence of the sedan in her rearview mirror, but then cursed herself for being foolish. She was lost, having paid more attention to her would-be pursuer than to her location. Worse, she rarely traveled to this part of town and the streets were unfamiliar. Had it not been so dark, she would have found her way back to the main road without a problem. Instead, she ended up on a different thoroughfare she didn't recognize.

Two sets of directions from gas station clerks and forty minutes later, she found her house. Mark's truck was parked on the street. She stayed in her car. Her heart raced and the thick air in the close confines of her vehicle constricted her throat. She grasped the steering wheel and squeezed it until her knuckles turned white.

Rachel let go of the steering wheel and her expression cleared, becoming confident. She gestured with her words. "Mark, there's something I need to talk to you about." She wrinkled her nose and tried again. "Mark, I haven't been honest with you." She laughed and looked at the front window. "And you're probably in there right now looking out the window at me talking to myself, thinking I'm half crazy."

It didn't matter how much she practiced what she would say. Once she got inside and saw him, it would all change. She would forget any rehearsed monologue and the words would come out jumbled.

She didn't want to go inside, didn't want to face Mark, didn't want to acknowledge her past, but she forced herself out of the car and up the walkway.

Rachel shut the front door and secured the locks. In the short hallway by the living room, her mind prickled and realization came over her. The chains on the front door were unlocked. Danielle always remembered to lock them. With robotic movements as if controlled by someone else, she turned into the living room, took a few steps, and stopped.

Across the room, Donovan King sat in a chair.

Her weak legs refused to turn around and run back outside. No forest surrounded her, no black dress adorned her body, no piano played in the background. The nightmare seemed so real this time, much more so than all the others, but her inability to control the dream remained the same.

Donovan smiled, and her heart dropped to her stomach.

An unseen assailant grabbed her arm from behind, and instinct took over. Her arm flew up and the back of her hand connected with his mouth. She whipped around and her fist lashed out, smashing against the man's mouth.

The hit knocked him against the living room wall with a loud thud. Before she could attack him again, she recognized the man's face and her breathing quickened. She had spoken to the man in Mark's bookstore yesterday.

She heard a noise behind her and whirled back around. She froze at the sight of Joe's gun leveled at her head.

"Remember me?" he asked. He palmed the gun and the backside of his hand smashed against her cheek. The weight of the gun threw her to the ground.

The other man wiped his mouth and blood smeared across his cheek and the back of his hand. He grunted and cursed under his breath. He lifted Rachel off the ground and jerked her arms behind her back.

"I tried to warn you about her," Joe said, holding his gun flush against the side of her head. "You should have listened to me. She's a feisty one."

Rachel attempted one last struggle to get out of the man's arms, but he only tightened his grip.

"Not anymore, she isn't," the man said. "I'd say she's pretty docile now." He put his mouth near her ear. "Aren't you, sweetheart?" he asked. He gave another strong tug on her arms.

Rachel gnashed her teeth together and groaned against the strain on her shoulders. The man continued pulling her arms tighter until her shoulders were on the verge of dislocating. She cried out with the pain and begged for him to stop.

Donovan raised his hand in a silent command to the man behind her. The man loosened his grip on her arms in response. Though the pain let up somewhat, he kept her arms pulled tight enough so she couldn't squirm her way out of his grasp.

Donovan rose from the chair and walked toward her, his hypnotic, amber eyes never departing from hers. Rachel realized with dismay that even after three years, his power over her had not diminished in the slightest.

His knuckles moved over her cheek. "Rachel *Thomas*, is it?"

Her chin trembled at his tender, loving touch, and lines of tears marched down her face. "I'm sorry," she whispered.

Donovan didn't respond. Joe stepped up next to Donovan and held out a syringe and alcohol swab. Donovan took the swab and hinged the short sleeve of her shirt on her shoulder. He rubbed the cold alcohol swab against her upper left arm. He turned to Joe and exchanged the alcohol swab for the syringe.

Rachel bit down on her bottom lip and her neck muscles tightened when the needle entered her skin. "I'm so sorry, Donovan," she repeated.

"So am I," he said. He pulled the needle out of her arm. "Joe, Sean, you can leave us now. We'll be right out."

Sean released her arms. Rachel's arms and legs went limp, and she tried to take a step forward. She lost her footing and fell into Donovan's familiar arms. Her vision blurred and her thoughts scrambled in her head.

Donovan brushed her hair out of her eyes and kissed her forehead. "It's all going to be okay, Rachel. When you wake up, you'll be back home with me."

Chapter Thirty-one

Rachel woke with a start. She pushed herself into a sitting position and took in her surroundings. She was in her old room, the room she'd hoped to never see again.

Her head ached from where Joe hit her with the gun. Placing her hand on her upper arm, she rubbed at the soreness where the needle entered her skin. She realized Donovan gave her a sedative, and she remembered nothing after falling unconscious.

Pulling the covers off her body, she climbed out of the plush, king-size bed. The bare walls, the white carpet, the lack of decoration. Everything remained the same. Even though she could have decorated the room in any manner she wished, with any amount of lavish she desired, she never cared for anything more than what was in the room now. She always enjoyed the simplicity.

She stood in the middle of the room and turned around in a circle. It was as if she had been transported back in time by three years. The same king size bed protruded from the far wall and was covered with a simple down comforter. The same short, oak dresser stood across the room. She knew if she opened the drawers, they would be filled with her clothes that she left behind. The same overstuffed, comfortable armchair rested in the corner of the room. Towering over the armchair was the same brass floor lamp she used for late night reading.

She walked to the dresser. A hardback compilation of stories by Edgar Allen Poe sat in the same location where she left it. She flipped the book open to the bookmark and saw it marked the same page where she stopped reading three years earlier.

She set the book down. Her eyes landed on the large, black jewelry box next to the book. She opened the lid of the box and placed her hand on the delicate diamond necklace inside the box without directly looking at it. A memory flickered in the back of her mind of a dance she shared long ago while wearing the necklace. Not wanting to dwell on the memories, she snatched her hand back from the ornate piece of jewelry and replaced the lid on the box.

Rachel rubbed her sore arm again and moved into the walk-in closet, where the dark colors of her old wardrobe greeted her. They were a stark contrast to the white of the rest of her room. Her eyes fell on a leather garment cover in the front of the closet. She rotated the garment bag on the hanger until it faced her. Though she already knew what she would find, she unzipped the bag.

She peeled back the flaps to reveal a black dress, the same one from her dreams. She stepped back and her insides curdled. This was not a nightmare from which she would wake. She zipped up the garment bag to hide the dress, and rushed back to her bed, as if it would provide her sanctuary.

Her bedroom door opened a few minutes later. Donovan stepped out of her nightmares and into her bedroom. She knew someone would be close by, standing guard. He wouldn't allow her to escape a second time. She rose from the bed to meet him, and watched each step he took toward her.

His chilling smile reached inside her body and took hold of her heart. "Rachel," he said. "It's so good to have you back. Seeing you here again…" His fingers traced her cheekbone. "I have missed you so much," he whispered.

His familiar touch burned through her skin, but she restrained herself from jerking away from him. "Donovan, I don't—"

Before she finished speaking, he struck her cheek. The sudden force of the blow threw her back onto the bed.

His voice hardened. "I gave you everything you could ever want or need. I gave you every part of me. You were the only thing I lived for, Rachel. Then you stole from me and left me here alone." He hit her again.

She raised her hands to protect herself, but somehow his fist found her face twice more, each hit harder than the last. Her brain bounced against her skull, and she sank deeper into the bed, hoping to disappear and stop him from hurting her more. He didn't stop, but punched her several more times before walking away from the bed.

Rachel's tears dried up in her eyes, and the pain replaced all the air in her lungs. She tried to call out his name, tried to beg him to stop, but no words came out with her raspy breaths. Everywhere she looked, she saw red.

"Three years," Donovan said, oblivious to her struggle for air. "I've been searching for you for three years and when I find you, someone else has taken my place." His fist connected with her face again.

"No," she managed to say when he pulled back his hand. Hard as she tried to talk, to give him some sort of explanation for her actions, nothing else came out.

Donovan's eyes smoldered with anger. "Did you have sex with him?"

"No, of course not," she said. She hoped he didn't detect the lie.

"I believe you, which is good for his sake."

Rachel tried not to show her relief to know Mark was alive, and she wondered about Danielle. "Please, Donovan," she begged.

"But you let him kiss you, and hold you, and touch you," Donovan said. He picked her up off the bed and slammed her against the wall. The back of his hand smacked against the side of her mouth. "Did you think I wouldn't know?"

Warm, salty liquid seeped into her mouth and onto her tongue. Red polka dots of her blood stood out on the white carpet, but it did not compare to the amount of blood soaking into the comforter on her bed.

"Don't you remember what happened the last time you let someone do that?"

Her eyes once again produced tears. "Not again," she said. "I'll do anything, just please, Donovan, not again."

"You are mine, Rachel. You belong to me. That's never going to change." He leaned over and his lips covered hers. Even though three years had passed since the last time she experienced his kiss, she remembered every detail as if she had never left his arms.

She wanted to collapse on the floor and sleep until the pain was gone, but she let him lift her shirt over her head and unbutton her jeans. Done with punishing her physically, he now wanted her to sleep with him. Her jeans slipped down to the floor and she stepped out of them, as his eyes drank in her exposed skin.

His fingers tightened on her arm. "Show me," he said.

He didn't need to say anything else for her to know what he wanted to see. Rachel turned around and lowered her head. She closed her eyes, and her cheeks and neck burned crimson.

His fingertips traced her scars and electrified her back. Every movement of his fingers sent phantom pain throughout her body. He moved closer to her and lowered his mouth near her ear. "I knew they would still be there," he said. "I'm sure you thought of me every time you saw them. Your little reminder that you'll always be mine."

He turned her back around kissed her again. His mouth strayed down and trailed the base of her neck. The loving and tender kisses were a stark contrast to the outburst of violence he demonstrated only moments ago.

Even though he wouldn't hurt her anymore tonight, Rachel would sleep with him without fighting him. She didn't want to take a chance of what might happen if she resisted. She had to show him that she wanted to be with him.

This same sequence of events had occurred so much in the past that it was like the proverbial bike ride for Rachel. A beating, followed by sex, and then apologies or explanations for his actions. Over and over, the cycle never changed with Donovan.

She would somehow make it through the intimacy without so much as a whimper, no matter how bad the pain. It was the only way to regain his trust, something she needed to do if she wanted to survive. In the short time she had been back, she resigned herself to the idea that her days of running were over.

Rachel was home.

Chapter Thirty-two

Paul wanted to kill someone. The desire was growing by the minute and was already stronger than he had ever felt before. If he couldn't take his anger out on Sean like he wanted, then anyone would do. But, he was as defenseless as Rachel, now that she was back at the estate.

At this moment, as Paul wore out the grass beneath his feet, Donovan was in her room. Paul could not bring himself to think about what atrocities Donovan committed against her, and Paul could do nothing to help. It had been made clear to him that he was not allowed anywhere near Rachel, at least not for the first several weeks she was back.

Still paying for her fleeing the estate, he gladly faced unending punishment on her behalf while she was gone. He would have continued forever if it kept her safe. But, he always knew that at any moment, the time would come when Donovan would catch up with her. Paul had managed to sabotage the search for her a couple of times before, but his efforts only bought her a short amount of time. Donovan was nothing if not determined, and with endless resources, there was no place Rachel could hide.

If she had not met Mark, she wouldn't have stayed so long in Wichita, and she would not be here now. All the excitement Paul should have felt at her finding someone to love, and someone who loved her, was washed away in the reality that Donovan found her and brought her home. What would be a wonderful and romance-filled time for anyone else in the world, backfired on both her and Mark.

Now that she was back, Paul needed to save her more than ever, but there was no hope for either of them. Mark would not be alive for much longer, maybe another twelve hours if he were lucky. Rachel would revert back to the state she was in before she left the estate three years ago.

Rachel was a smart girl, Paul thought, smarter than most. She had always used her intelligence to her advantage in every situation. More than that, she was a survivor. Paul knew that even if she stayed, she would find a way to survive again. She would make it through, no matter how many new scars she acquired. She would recommit herself to both Donovan and to her role at the estate. Paul took small comfort in that. If he could not help her, she would somehow be okay in the end.

An idea formed in his mind, and Paul halted his pacing. Maybe there was a way to help her, but hope would come only through one person: Mark. He could reach Rachel in a way Paul never could. Mark had to convince her to leave the estate again, convince her to run far away this time and never stop running.

It was risky, as Paul's plan relied on a man he had never met, but there wasn't much choice. Getting her out was the only way either of them would make it through this alive.

Chapter Thirty-three

Rachel rolled over in bed and watched Donovan dress. She held out her hand. "Why can't you stay?" she asked.

He slipped his arms into his shirt and buttoned it up. "I have to go into town to take care of some things and meet with Graham," he said.

Though he had gone into her bathroom and washed her blood off his face and hands, smears of her blood stood out against his white dress shirt. Rachel knew he would change his clothing before he left the estate, but her blood would never come out of his shirt.

A pang of guilt racked her, and she took responsibility for ruining his clothing. The clothes she wore when she arrived at the estate were also tainted with her blood. She would throw those away not only because of the blood, but because they were a reminder of her time away from Donovan. He would not want her to keep them, since anything that was not from the estate did not belong here.

She withdrew her arm and pulled the covers over her bare chest as she sat up. Under the surface of her eyes, a well of tears threatened to spill over from the pain in her face. The swelling on her face grew with every passing moment and intensified her pain.

A dull ache spread across her cheeks and mouth, adding to the pain from Joe hitting her. The only unaffected area was her nose. Donovan always made it a point not to hit her there, so it wouldn't break and alter her appearance. The rest of her face and body were open targets, but he always preferred hitting her face.

She resisted the urge to assess the damage with her fingers. She did not want Donovan to know she was concerned with what he did to her, and call attention to his abuse. She risked sending him back into a rage if he noticed her dwelling on her injuries.

He rarely lost control like he had with the agonizing beating she had suffered, but the difference between now and then was he had stored up three years of good reasons to punish her the way he did. One more hit, even the slightest slap, seemed all that her face could tolerate before it shattered into pieces.

Donovan pulled on his suit jacket. "I'll be back in a few minutes. Get dressed," Donovan said, and he left the room.

Rachel looked down at the blanket she wrung and her forehead creased. Donovan's absence from the estate would be the perfect opportunity to somehow get to Paul and find out what happened to Danielle and Mark.

Guilt flooded her as Mark entered her mind. It was wrong to think about Mark, to wonder about him. This was exactly what got her into trouble the last time. Donovan should be her only concern. Falling back into the role she had played, into the life she had lived was much too easy.

Rachel forced herself out of bed and over to her dresser. She found a low-cut black camisole lined with lace, and black pajama shorts, a nighttime outfit that was one of Donovan's favorites on her. All of her clothes smelled fresh, as if Donovan had kept her room and clothes cleaned in anticipation of her return. Both of them knew she wouldn't be gone forever.

She slipped on the clothes, wincing from the pain in her face as the shirt came down over her head. Even bending down to pick up her dirty clothes pushed the limits of her broken body. From what she could tell, it would take about three days for the bruises to begin healing and a full ten days or more for them to disappear. At least, that's what she remembered from the last time she sustained similar injuries.

Donovan returned, and she welcomed him with a warm smile. He held a silver tray in his hand, the contents of which were covered with white linen. He sat down on the bed next to her and placed the tray beside him. He ran a finger under one of the straps of the camisole and lowered it down over her shoulder. "You look so beautiful in this," he said. He leaned over and kissed the crook of her neck.

Rachel prickled with goose bumps at each brush of his lips against her cool skin, and she hated her body for reacting to him.

"Are you trying to get me to stay with you longer?" he asked.

She wanted nothing more than for him to leave and had only dressed in clothing she knew would please him, but she couldn't tell him that. "I wish you could stay, but I know you have things to do," she said.

"I'll be back later tonight and I'll stay with you then. We'll spend a lot of time together over the next several weeks. We have three years of lost time to make up."

Rachel forced a smile. "I can't wait."

Donovan lifted the linen off the tray on the bed. On top of the tray, another syringe filled with a menacing liquid sat next to an alcohol swab and a bandage.

Rachel could not contain her tears. "Please don't do this, Donovan," she said. Even as she spoke, she knew he had no other choice but to drug her. He would do it today, tomorrow, and for many days, even weeks, to come until she convinced him she would not leave again.

"I'm sorry, Rachel," he said. "I don't want to do this." He raised his hand to her face and wiped away her tears. "You know I only have the best intentions. It's going to take some time for us to get back to where we were."

Rachel took a deep breath. "I know that I destroyed your trust in me and I ruined everything we had together. I am so sorry that I left you, and I wish I could take it back. Things will change things between us, Donovan, and all of my actions will be made up to you. I know what I did was wrong." She laid her hand on top of his and pressed his hand against her aching face. "But you don't have to do this. I'm never leaving you again."

Donovan cradled her face in his hands and kissed her. The kiss was filled with sensuality, yet laced with innocence. Donovan had never before kissed her in that manner. His kiss was always hungry and full of desire, but his lips now contained all the love he still felt for her, even after so much time apart. It reminded her too much of the way Mark kissed her.

Again, Mark invaded her thoughts at the absolute worst time. There was no more room for Mark, not while she was with Donovan. Their relationship would forever be in the past so that she could rebuild her tattered life with Donovan. She never wanted it to end like this with Mark, but here she was at the estate, in Donovan's arms, tasting her future with him. The situation in itself eliminated Mark.

Donovan broke the kiss, but kept his face close to hers. "I have spent the last three years trying to figure out why you left me. I came to understand I never gave you what you needed."

"Donovan—" Rachel started.

"I know you're sorry for what you did," he said. "You don't have to try and convince me of that. But, I also bear some responsibility." He took the alcohol swab off the tray and carefully opened the package. The cold wipe rubbed against her skin, high up on her right arm.

"I know you wanted more than what I gave you," he continued. "You wanted more freedom than I thought I could spare. Once we patch things up between us, our lives together will be different. You will have everything you need from me and more. When I know you're here to stay, you will have more freedom than you ever wanted. You won't have to do another job, not unless you want to. I want you by my side at all times." He stopped rubbing the alcohol on her skin and held her eyes with his. "I'll give you everything else you want, too."

"All I need is you, Donovan. You don't need to give me anything else."

"That's exactly what I am going to give you. Me. I want us to get married, Rachel, and I don't want to wait. Then you can move upstairs so we can spend our lives together. We can start a family. I never thought I wanted children, but I do want them with you. I admit, I wasn't ready for any of this before, but I am now. I need to share my life with you."

Rachel jerked her head back at his revelation. He had never hinted that marriage or children were ever a possibility in their world. Her chin quivered and the tears started again. She was glad he never offered her such things when she lived here. If he had, she might have never left. Without hesitation, she would have married him and had children with him.

Now that he offered her these things, she wasn't sure she wanted them with him. If she had been a normal girl, she would be back in Wichita with Mark, building their relationship until it climaxed into marriage, kids, and an eternity filled with nothing but love. Even now, she knew that is where they were heading before being ripped apart.

But none of what she felt for Mark mattered now. She had to erase him from her life and from her heart. Even though she did not know where Danielle was, Mark was still alive and she was his only chance of staying that way.

To keep him alive, though, she needed to prove to Donovan that he, not Mark, was her future and her only choice in life. Then, after she successfully convinced him to let Mark go, she would continue on the path that she jumped off of three years ago when she left so abruptly. Donovan would hold true to his word and marry her. They would have children that they could raise together.

It wouldn't take much for her to fall in love with Donovan again. She would truly want to be with him and have a family with him. She wasn't sure how his settled down lifestyle would impact the affairs on the estate, but she would find out soon enough.

"You want that with me, don't you?" Donovan asked.

She believed more and more that she did want it. Left with no other option for her future, she needed to embrace their life together fully and unconditionally.

Rachel allowed a small smile of approval at Donovan's words. "Very much so," she whispered in response, taking the first step to getting back in his good graces. "I'm yours, Donovan. I always will be."

He kissed her again. His love for her again filled the kiss, and she did her best to reciprocate the emotion. When he broke away, he said, "I am so glad to hear that. For now, however, I have to do this." He held up the syringe. "I am sorry, but I know you understand the reasons behind my actions. I don't want you to be upset with me."

"I'm not angry in the least," Rachel said. "I broke your confidence in the worst possible way. I know you're only doing what you have to for now." She clutched the blanket in her fist and braced herself for the stick of the needle.

"This is the same thing I gave you before we left Kansas. As you know, the effects are immediate," he said. "Tony will be down in a few hours with another one. Once I return to the estate tonight, I'll come back to see you."

The needle stung as it pierced her skin and tore through her muscle. She couldn't help but look back at her arm and watch him push the liquid into her system. He took the needle out and covered the injection site with the bandage. As with the alcohol swab, the small act of care and concern contradicted the way he had beaten her without mercy.

Once he was done, Rachel glanced back up at Donovan, her vision already blurry. Her body gave in to the sedative, and Donovan put his arm around her to help her lay back down in bed. He covered her body with her sheet and comforter and pressed his lips to hers once more. She closed her eyes, with no recollection of ending the kiss.

Chapter Thirty-four

There was no way to escape.

The entirely white room had no windows or furniture. No matter how many times Mark turned the doorknob, each time hoping for a different outcome, the door was consistently locked from the outside. The absence of anything in the room to cut through the white made the tiles and walls seem exceptionally bright, magnifying the growing headache that radiated from the spot Tony hit him with the gun.

Between the lingering exhaustion that had no explanation, and a tiny mark on his arm which felt like he had received a shot, he deduced he had been drugged. After Rachel's house, he remembered nothing else except waking up. Hitting him with a gun wouldn't have kept him unconscious for long, so they must have drugged him, too.

Unable to construct a weapon and with no hope of exiting the room, Mark sat on the cold tiles and leaned against the wall with his legs stretched out in front of him. He had replayed the events at Rachel's house in his mind a hundred times since waking up. The sound of the gunshots that killed Danielle echoed in his ears. He tried to close his eyes to shut out the sound from his mind, but then he saw the image of bullets jerking through her body. He could not stop seeing and hearing Danielle die over and over. Thankfully, someone had cleaned her blood off his hands while he was unconscious.

Mark didn't want to think about death, but here he was, most likely knocking at death's door. Sitting in a cold, empty room, not sure of the time or what day of the week it was. He didn't know what state or even what country he was in. The dirt on his jeans and invisible bruises on his arms made him think he had been dragged into the room. That and being drugged was about all he could figure out.

His fate was still unknown to him. No one had visited him since he woke up in the room. He had not been given any indication of what Donovan King wanted with him or why he had been put in this room. All Mark knew was Danielle was murdered without hesitation or remorse while he held her hand.

The rest of us will clean up this mess and wait for Rachel.

Donovan's words reminded Mark that they must have Rachel somewhere. He prayed she was alive and unharmed, but the memory of Donovan wouldn't allow him to believe she was safe. Question after question formed in his mind. Who was Donovan King and how was he connected to Rachel? As each minute passed, he grew more convinced he didn't want to know the answers.

The door opened, but he did not recognize the man who came in as one of the men that had been at Rachel's house. With gray hair threatening to erase the remainder of the brown, yet minimal wrinkles around his eyes or mouth, Mark guessed the man was in his late forties, early fifties at the most. A long range, two-way radio was clipped onto his belt and a shoulder holster wrapped around his large, muscular build.

Mark pushed himself up off the floor, his eyes glued to the gun resting in the man's shoulder holster. "Where's Rachel?"

The man squinted behind wire-rimmed glasses. "You must be Mark," the man said, looking him over with the same interest that the men at Rachel's house had shown. "Why don't you sit back down? We'll be here for a while."

Mark lowered himself back down to the floor, his gaze not wandering away from the man for even a moment. He was too afraid to look away, for fear the man would reach for his gun and shoot. "Who are you?" Mark asked.

"My name is Paul and right now, I'm the closest thing to a friend you have."

Mark flinched. He had no friends in this circumstance, let alone a man with a gun. Confused by Paul's words and reason for being there, he asked, "Where's Rachel?"

"Rachel's in her room down the hall."

Mark's heart picked up speed. She was so close, much closer than he had thought. Mark resisted the urge to run out the door to try to find her, reminding himself of Paul's gun.

If Paul was his only ally, then Mark thought he was safe for at least a short time. He also believed Paul may be willing to give him some much-needed information about what was happening.

"Please," Mark said. "I need to know if Rachel's okay."

"She's about as good as she can be in this situation."

His words caused Mark to fear the worst. "Is she hurt?"

"I… probably." Paul's eyes moved off Mark as he faltered. "I honestly don't know."

Mark's confusion and frustration grew. "What do you mean you don't know?"

"I've been unable to see her since Donovan went in her room. He left the estate, but I can't go in there yet. Her room is being guarded, and I am not allowed to see her."

"Why can't you see her?" Mark asked. "Who are you?"

Paul held out his hand and gestured as he spoke. "Look, I know you're confused. I'm going to do the best I can to explain everything. I've been waiting to do this for some time now. When I found out about you, I figured that Donovan would bring you here when he brought Rachel back. He wouldn't want to kill you, at least not right away. That would be too simple." Paul's radio crackled to life and he held up a finger. "If you value your life at all, do not make even the slightest sound."

Paul's lips moved in the direction of the radio, but the words he spoke did not reach Mark's ears. Too simple. What did that mean? Too easy? Too quick? Too painless? The only thing Mark knew was that at any moment a bullet could rip through his heart. Through his skull.

Death was a certainty, and he had already seen it once. The gun lowering. The flash in Danielle's eyes. The flicker across her mouth. The knowledge she was going to die. He had felt death, too, as Danielle's hand slipped in his and became heavy while she let go of life. The way her face fell emotionless as the last of her lifeblood flowed between his fingers.

Paul secured his radio and studied Mark. "Are you scared?"

There was no room for any emotion except fear. It controlled his heartbeat, his thoughts, his every movement, and every breath. But, as much fear as he felt in the masked face of death, a greater terror prevailed. He met Paul's eyes. "I'm afraid for Rachel."

Paul's gaze wavered. "So am I."

There was no air for Mark to breathe. Paul's words sucked it all out of the room. "What the hell is going on?" he managed to ask.

"Have you ever heard of Donovan King?"

Mark's thoughts turned to the book about Jonathan Thomas. "Yes, but I don't know much about him."

"That doesn't surprise me. He's a very private person."

His curiosity took control and he interrupted Paul. "Who is Jonathan Thomas? Did Rachel know him? Is she related to him?"

Paul hesitated. "Why would you think she's related to… oh, her name, Rachel Thomas. I couldn't believe it when I heard she was using that alias."

"Alias?" Mark echoed. "Her name isn't Rachel?"

"Oh, it's Rachel all right, but not Thomas. Her real last name is Pettis, Rachel Pettis. How did you hear about Jonathan Thomas? Did Rachel mention him to you?"

More confused than ever, Mark ignored Paul's questions and said, "I don't understand any of this. Rachel, Jonathan Thomas, Donovan King. None of it makes sense."

"I assume you know Jonathan Thomas was murdered three years ago," Paul said.

What if she knows something about his murder?

James's question hit him hard. Mark's mouth went dry, but he managed to ask the question. "What does his murder have to do with Rachel?"

"That's what I'm here to explain to you, but I don't have a whole lot of time. I'm risking both our lives by even being in here."

"Then why are you doing this?"

"I owe Rachel. I should have helped her a long time ago." He took a deep breath. "Rachel's my niece."

"No," Mark said. "No, her parents died when she was ten and they had no siblings. She was orphaned and went to live with a foster family." He spewed out the facts Rachel had told him, as if saying them aloud would make them true.

"No siblings." Paul snorted. "I suppose that's better than telling people I'm dead."

Mark opened his mouth to protest further, but stopped himself when he recognized the same green eyes he knew so well staring at him from behind Paul's glasses. "So if you're her uncle, does that mean there's no foster family?"

"She told you the truth about her parents. They died when she was only ten years old, but when they died, she came here to live with me. That was sixteen years ago."

Part Two

Chapter Thirty-five

Sixteen years earlier

In the ten years of her life, Rachel Pettis had never been so scared or so alone.

Rigidly seated on an ivory couch, the material stained with age and the occasional spill, Rachel held her head down and concentrated on her fingers twisting in her lap. Her nose started running again, but she didn't ask for a Kleenex. Her throat was too tight to speak.

She shifted under the weight of the uncomfortable stares and whispers of her fourth-grade teacher, the school counselor, and the social worker. The group of adults sat at a small table in the teacher's lounge at school. One came over every so often and checked on her.

Since nine o'clock that morning, when she learned her parents had died in a car accident, she sat in the same room while waiting for Uncle Paul to pick her up. Her teacher said it would be quite some time since he had to fly down to get her. The quiet of the school's hallways reminded her that her classmates had already gone home to their families. Rachel would never again go back home to her parents.

She raised her arm, wiped her nose on her sleeve, and replaced her hand in her lap before she was caught. She didn't want to get in trouble for forgetting her manners. Her fingers resumed twisting and turning. As hard as she tried, she found it impossible to think of anything besides her parents.

Tears streaked down her face and she realized there would be no more evenings where her daddy picked her up and swung her around when he came home from work. Her daddy's laugh would echo through the foyer and he would hug her tight. Long after he let her go, Rachel could smell his aftershave, a warm, musky scent that lingered in her nostrils.

No longer would Rachel squeeze beside her mother into the rocking chair on the back porch. They would rock for hours, taking turns making up elaborate fairy tales about princes and princesses who lived in castles far away. That morning, all of their make-believe castles came crashing down as her fairy tale life with her parents ended.

The sound of the door opening snapped Rachel back into the present, where her daddy's aftershave had long since faded and there was no such thing as happily ever after. She had not seen her Uncle Paul for a few years, ever since he'd had what her daddy called a nervous breakdown. Rachel wasn't sure what a nervous breakdown was, but it had something to do with her Aunt Maria's death and Paul's decision to leave behind a career in medicine to become a security guard for some rich jerk. She wasn't allowed to say the word her daddy normally used to describe Paul's new boss.

She had heard her daddy rant and rave about it enough to understand why Paul didn't visit them anymore. She loved her daddy, but she thought he was too hard on his brother. Her daddy always told her she could be whatever she wanted when she grew up, and Rachel reasoned the same thing should apply to Paul.

Rachel stood up and Paul knelt down to her level. She gave him a fierce hug and didn't want to let go. He held her tight, the dark stubble on his face rough against her cheek, his voice melodic in her ears. "I'm so sorry, honey."

She pressed her face deeper into the cool leather of his thin jacket. "I'm scared, Uncle Paul."

"There's no need to be scared anymore." He let go of her and lifted her chin. "I'm going to take care of you now. Is that okay?"

"Yes, Uncle Paul."

"Good. Sit here for a few minutes while I talk to the social worker, then we'll leave."

Rachel sat back down, her hands folded and resting quietly in her lap. Paul stood in a corner of the room with the social worker. She heard the social worker thank her uncle for coming, but then their voices became hushed and Rachel couldn't discern what they were saying. Paul's impatient gestures reminded Rachel of how her daddy sometimes looked when he talked on the telephone, pacing back and forth.

Paul came back to her and took her hand. She picked up her backpack, spoke a strained goodbye to her teacher, and walked through the halls of her school for the last time. Paul opened the orange, metal door to the outside. They walked down the steps from the school, and Rachel squinted against the rays of the late afternoon sun reflecting off the blacktop. She pointed to a lone green car in the visitor's parking lot. "Is that your car?"

"No, it's a rental," Paul said. He slipped on a pair of sunglasses. "We'll leave it at the airport when we leave."

"Where are we going and when are we leaving?"

"We're going up north, but we'll still be in California. You're going to live with me now. We'll leave right after the funeral, which will be in a couple days. Until then, we'll stay at a hotel."

"What about all my stuff at the house? How can we take that on an airplane?"

"I've already gotten you some clothes from your house to get you by for the next few days, along with your toothbrush and some other personal effects. Before we leave San Diego, we'll go back to your house so you can pick out what you want to take with you. The rest of your belongings can be shipped, or we can get you new clothes and other things. It's up to you, but you don't have to make the decision now. You can always change your mind up until the point that the house is sold. That could take a long time, depending on probate."

Rachel shrugged with indifference. She was relieved they didn't have to go back to her now empty home, at least not today. "I've never been on an airplane before," she said once they were inside the car.

"I hate flying, but it's quicker than driving. I'm just glad we have a private jet all to ourselves and don't have to fly with other people."

Rachel's eyes grew with Paul's words. "A jet for us? That must cost a lot of money."

Paul laughed. "I'm sure it does. Wait until you see our hotel suite. It has two bedrooms and a kitchen in it. Good thing we don't have to pay for that, either."

"Why don't we have to pay for it? Where's your house?"

"I live at the estate. I work as a security guard there."

Rachel rolled her eyes. "So we have to live at the same place as the rich jer—I mean, guy?"

Paul laughed. "You've been listening to your father too much. Besides, that rich jerk is responsible for getting me here so fast. It's his jet we're using, and he's paying for the hotel, too."

Rachel pursed her lips. "I guess that's nice of him, but Daddy called him a lot worse names than jerk." She cocked her head to the side. "Does daddy know him?"

"No, but he was upset with me for going to work for Donovan. He was also mad because I'm not a doctor at the hospital anymore."

"Why did you stop being a doctor? Daddy said you were a great doctor."

"I'm still a doctor, but I don't work at the hospital."

"Do you miss Daddy?"

"Of course I do, honey. He's my brother and I loved him. I still love him, no matter what happened between us, but I wish we could have made amends before now."

She reached into her backpack on the floorboard and brought out a black baseball cap with no sports team name or logo stitched across it. She pulled her ponytail through the hole in the back and secured the cap on her head. A warm melancholy clenched her heart and she felt a little closer to her father for wearing the hat she begged him to buy.

She tugged on the curved bill and tried her best not to cry. It wasn't fair they were gone. She turned to her uncle, the only person she knew who could explain it to her. "I don't understand why God took them away from me."

Paul exhaled heavily. "Rachel, sometimes God is the only one who knows why things happen. It's not for us to question, but to accept it and move on."

Rachel narrowed her eyes, her jaw set in defiance of Paul's words. "Well, I might not question it, but that doesn't mean I have to agree with God."

"Don't be angry at God. Be angry at the jerk who was driving drunk at seven-thirty in the morning."

Rachel sniffed. She turned her head away from her uncle's view so he would not see the tears she rubbed out of her eyes. She placed her clenched hands back in her lap, pushed aside her anger, and stared out the window as San Diego passed her by.

Chapter Thirty-six

The first day at the estate was a blur for Rachel. She stayed in her room, crying and sleeping. All she could think about was her parents. The funeral had been nice, but it went by so fast Rachel had no real time to mourn. A lot of people she didn't know had come up to her at the funeral and told her they were sorry for her loss. Rachel took little solace in the rushed sympathies tossed her way.

Paul visited her several times that first day to bring her food and try to talk to her. She barely acknowledged him, but soon she regretted her indifference toward him, remembering her mother's frequent admonitions to always be polite.

On her second day there, she ventured out of her room with Paul as her guide. Her large eyes took in the wonders around her while he led her around the estate, starting the tour from her room in the basement. The basement acted as a separate house, with everything they needed to live on their own if necessary. He first showed her his room down the hall and she was relieved to know he was close.

They wandered into the gym, and she smiled at the equipment that surrounded the large, black mat on the floor. Paul let her try each machine and warned her never to go in the gym without someone else so she wouldn't hurt herself.

Not too far down the hall from the gym was the game room, with a pool table, four dart boards, a poker table, and a foosball table. Next to the game room was a small kitchen that included a microwave, stove, and a dishwasher. Paul let her know that the refrigerator and cupboards were always fully stocked, but to be sure not to ruin her dinner by snacking.

He took her upstairs and into the main kitchen where he introduced her to the three cooks that worked at the estate. Rachel had never before seen a kitchen so large. She walked over to one of the counters. Palms down, she lifted herself up until her feet dangled above the floor. She rolled her head down, and her reflection in the stainless steel made faces back at her. She dropped down to her feet after Paul reprimanded her for acting silly.

Rachel jogged across the room and poked her head in the pantry that was as big as her bedroom at her old house. She was excited to learn that their meals would be cooked for them every day, but only after she confirmed she wouldn't have to eat broccoli and no longer had to do the dishes.

Their next stop, the library, had bookshelves built into the walls throughout the hexagonal-shaped room. In the center of the library, several leather reading chairs were scattered with tables and lamps next to each one. Wooden ladders were set on rails around the room so books on the higher shelves could be reached.

A slim spiral staircase reached for the second floor of the library, and Rachel thought it would be fun to run up and down the stairs until she became dizzy. Instead of racing to the stairs, she twirled around the center of the room. Te colorful spines of varying thickness blended in front of her eyes, until Paul put his hand on her shoulder and stopped her movement. Rachel vowed to read every last book.

Paul led her across the hall into the conference room. Black leather chairs were pushed up to a cherry wood table. Paul explained that while Donovan had an office an hour away in the main corporate building for his company, he did most of his work out of his home. He said Donovan held important meetings in the conference room, and she wasn't allowed to go in there unless she was told otherwise.

Rachel found the room boring and didn't mind it was off limits. She followed him to the set of heavy, wood doors at the far end of the conference room. Before he opened the doors, he told her the waiting room was on the other side of the doors.

"What's a waiting room?" Rachel asked.

"It's where people sit and wait."

"What do they wait for?"

"They wait to have a meeting with Donovan in the conference room."

She wrinkled her nose. "That doesn't sound like much fun."

He laughed. "It probably isn't," he replied, and he pulled the doors open.

She gasped as she walked in. "Wow! This is so cool!" Four leather chairs with majestic, high backs were positioned in the center of the room. Rachel moved past them to examine the cases on the walls, each housing different weapons. Guns, knives, whips, swords, and crossbows, along with some other weapons she had never heard of or seen before, were all contained behind glass on the walls. "What is this?"

"This is Donovan's collection."

"Why would you want to keep your collection in a waiting room?" Rachel asked. "Why not have books and magazines to make people more comfortable, like in the doctor's office?"

"He doesn't want them comfortable. He wants to make them nervous. It gives him an edge during meetings."

She shrugged. "Makes sense to me." She moved over to one of the cases, which contained three crossbows. Her fingers grazed the glass. "Can I shoot one of these?"

"Don't you play with dolls or something?"

She wrinkled her nose and stuck out her tongue. "Yuck," she said. She walked out of the room and gazed out the French windows at the other end of the foyer. The small glimpse of the woods made her long for playing outside with her friends. "Can I go outside?" she asked Paul.

Paul shut the waiting room doors behind them. "In a little bit. First, I want to take you upstairs."

"What's up there?"

"That's Donovan's private floor. His bedroom, office, study, and some other rooms are all up there. We aren't supposed to go upstairs, but I know he's anxious to meet you. He asked me to bring you to his office when we were done taking a tour of the estate."

"If he wanted to meet me why didn't he come see me sooner?" Rachel asked, as they climbed the flared staircase. She kept her hand sealed to the rail and fought the temptation to run her fingers over the wrought iron balusters. "Doesn't he care that I'm here?"

"Yes, he does care, but he wanted to give you space and meet you when you were ready. He lost both of his parents, so he understands how hard it is."

Rachel realized she had not thought of her own parents since Paul started the tour. The pain of her loss once again crept into her chest and threatened to smother her. She pushed back at the sadness and tried to focus on the carpeted steps she climbed. At the top of the stairs, she peered down the dark hallway and hesitated.

"Do you have any questions for me before I leave you here?" Paul asked.

"Can we go outside later?"

He laughed. "Yes, I'll take you outside in a bit." He took her to a door halfway down the shadowed hallway. "Come back down when you're done. I'll wait at the bottom of the stairs for you. There are other people here that can't wait to meet you."

She smiled. "Thanks, Paul."

Donovan rose from his seat behind an antique desk as they entered the room. Rachel stepped onto the first of two extravagant rugs and trailed behind Paul across the long, intimidating room. In front of her, Donovan shut the monitor of his laptop. As she neared the desk, Rachel wanted to touch the handcrafted moldings, but she kept her hands clasped behind her back so she wouldn't misbehave.

"Rachel, this is Donovan King," Paul said.

She accepted Donovan's outstretched hand across the desk. Her hand bobbed up and down in his, and she hoped he didn't feel her hand trembling.

"I'll be downstairs when you're ready," Paul said to her with a wink.

"It's nice to meet you, Rachel," Donovan said after Paul shut the door. "I understand you'll be staying with us."

She swallowed hard and straightened her posture. Donovan towered over her. Much taller than Paul, he seemed larger than life to her. "Yes, sir. If that's okay with you."

"Of course it's okay, but only if you promise to call me Donovan." A warm smile softened his face and Rachel smiled back, relieved to know he was friendly. He sat down and indicated the chair on the other side of his desk. "I'm glad to see you came out of your room. I was starting to get worried about you. Did Paul show you around?"

"Yes." She slid into the leather chair across from him. She placed her hands in her lap and crossed her legs at the ankles. "It's a really big house."

"Do you like it?"

Rachel looked past the desk at the inset bookshelves. Some had books on them while others had vases and other décor. She was sure if she accidentally broke a vase it would cost more money to replace than she even knew existed. "Yes," she said. "I like the house a lot." She leaned her head in closer and whispered in a conspiratorial tone. "The waiting room is the best. I would like to learn how to shoot the crossbows."

"I bet you would. The cases are only opened for cleaning, so you won't be able to shoot one of those crossbows, but maybe one day you can try a different one out. My father started that collection when I was about your age, and I kept it going over the years," he said. "How are you doing? About your parents, I mean."

Her smile faded and tears forced their way into her eyes. Paul was always trying to get her to talk about her parents. Even though she didn't want to discuss them anymore, she also didn't want Donovan to think her rude. "I miss them a lot. I wish they would come back, but I know they can't."

"I understand that. It's hard when you lose someone you love so much. I was seven when my mother died of cancer. Her death made me sad for a long time, but after a while it got better for me. It will for you as well, even though it may not seem like it now. Do you believe that?"

"Yes," she said.

"Now, let's talk about your future. The room you're in now is temporary, so don't unpack too much. I'm having some rooms in the basement remodeled so you will have a large room with your own bathroom. I've also spoken with Paul and we both expect you to continue with school," he said.

Rachel's mood brightened. "Oh, don't worry, I love going to school. I get all A's and I never get sick and miss days. When can I go? I hope there are lots of nice kids there."

"You won't go back to an actual school building. Do you know what homeschool is?"

"Kind of."

"It's where children can learn at home instead of going to school with other kids in a formal classroom setting. That's what you're going to do, if you agree, of course."

Rachel frowned, disappointed she wouldn't get to go to school and make new friends. "I think that's okay, but don't I need a teacher or something?"

"Of course you do. Paul is going to teach you everything you need to know. We ordered your schoolbooks yesterday, so you can start on Monday. You'll also go on rounds with Paul whenever he's scheduled. You will learn a lot by doing that."

"What are rounds?"

"That's what we call patrolling the grounds to make sure no one trespasses."

Her eyes lit up. "Do I get a gun, too, like Paul?"

Donovan laughed. "I'm afraid not for quite a few years. You have to learn how to shoot one and care for one first. Even then, you'd have to show that you're responsible enough to own your own gun."

"I've always wanted to learn how to shoot a gun, but my daddy would never let me. He didn't like guns much."

"Maybe after you get settled in, I can teach you all about guns. Is that acceptable?"

"Yes, thank you."

"Now, do you have any questions for me?"

She pursed her lips as she thought. "I didn't see any televisions."

"That's because we don't watch television here."

"Why not?"

"We don't have time. Everyone always has work to do, and television can be quite distracting."

"Oh. Are you married?"

He let out a nervous chuckle. "No. I'm afraid I don't have time for that, either."

"What do you do for work?"

"I own a security company. It takes a lot of hard work to run the business."

Feeling comfortable for the first time since arriving at the estate, Rachel narrowed her eyes, ready to challenge Donovan. "How old are you?"

"Twenty-eight."

"Are you Paul's boss?"

"Yes."

"But you're younger than he is. How can you be his boss?"

"He's only five years older than me and sometimes it works out like that. Are you always so full of questions?"

Rachel tilted her head. "I like to know things."

A smile tugged at the corner of his mouth. "That's not always a bad thing."

"I know," she said. "Can I go outside now?"

He stood up. "Sure. I'll take you downstairs and we'll find Paul. He'll introduce you to the rest of his team, and then you can go outside."

"How many other people are there?"

"Four more. Tony, Joe, Eric, and Aaron. They help with security and also live here. Paul is in charge of all four of them, as well as some others that you'll see from time to time."

"You mean they live in the other rooms in the basement? Do the maids and the cooks live here, too?"

"No. They go to their own homes at the end of each day. There are a lot of people that come and go here, and you'll get to know all of them in time."

"I've never known anyone with cooks and maids before."

"You'll be spoiled by it. In fact, one of the maids is yours alone. Claudia now works only for you and she will help you out with everything you need. If you need clothes or shoes or anything at all, let Claudia know. It's like having your own personal assistant."

Rachel couldn't help but smile. "Am I that important?"

"You are," Donovan said.

Rachel followed Donovan out of the office and back down the steps. She restrained herself from running down the staircase like she would do at her house. She always seemed to be in trouble with her mom and dad for running up and down the steps, and did not want to get into trouble with Paul or Donovan for doing it here.

Halfway down the stairs, she saw Paul talking with four other men and one woman. When they noticed her, all of them turned to watch her finish descending the stairs. Rachel lost her smile and her nerves took control again. She was reminded of the first day of school, worried that the other kids wouldn't like her. At the last step, she forced herself to smile as big as she could, showing most of her teeth like her mom told her to do whenever she had her picture taken.

She was greeted by six return smiles, including Paul's. Paul walked over to her and guided her to the others, introducing them one by one. Rachel shook hands with each of them.

Tony, the tallest of the group, came first. Rachel thought he was the funniest looking out of all of them, with a square face and a bald head. When he smiled, she noticed he was missing a couple of teeth in the back of his mouth.

She met Aaron second. Pulled back in a ponytail, his long hair was such a light blonde that at first she thought it was white. She had never seen a man with a ponytail before, but her mom had teased her dad about wearing a ponytail before Rachel was born. Aaron's pale face matched his hair, and Rachel wondered if he had to wear a lot of sunscreen when he went outside. His thick glasses magnified his blue eyes, which made them look cartoonish. Rachel had to stop herself from giggling at the sight.

Eric was the third in line. His hair was shaved close to his head, so she could only see little bits of brown. His face matched his head, with dark stubble from ear to ear. He shook her hand, squeezing it so tight she thought it might crush her.

Joe was the last of the group, and Rachel liked him at first glance. She could tell he liked her, too, as he called her "Kiddo" and tousled her hair. He told her a knock-knock joke that Rachel had heard many times from other kids at school. She knew he was trying to make friends with her, so she laughed along with him, even though she never found the joke funny.

After meeting the four men, Donovan told them they could leave. Rachel turned around to look at Donovan and he flashed another smile. "Rachel, this is Claudia," he said as he gestured to the stout, Hispanic woman standing beside Paul.

Rachel waved a shy hello to her. "Nice to meet you, Claudia," she said. She wanted Claudia to like her the most out of everyone since she would have to ask Claudia to buy things for her.

Claudia walked over to Rachel and knelt down in front of her so they were on the same level. "Nice to meet you, Rachel. I think we'll be real good friends. If you need anything, let me know and I'll go into the city to get it for you."

"Can I go with you?" Rachel asked with excitement.

Claudia looked above Rachel's head at Donovan. She looked back at Rachel, her face now somber. "I'm sorry, Rachel, but I have to go alone. The city is so far away that it takes a long time to get there. I also have other errands to run when I go to the city, and I'm gone most of the day. I don't want to take you away from your studies."

Rachel scrunched up her face. "It's okay," she said, even though she was disappointed. "I know school is important, too."

Claudia rose to an upright position. "I have to go now, but if you need anything, come find me. I am usually on this floor cleaning."

Rachel didn't want Claudia to go yet. She lunged forward and hugged her waist as tight as she could. Claudia's warm arms surrounded her for a moment before she let go.

After Claudia left the room, Donovan looked down at Rachel. "I still have quite a bit of work to get done today so I need to go as well, but I will see you soon."

"Thank you, sir… I mean, Donovan."

"You're welcome." He turned and climbed back up the steps.

Paul put his hand on her shoulder. "So what do you think?"

"I think I'm going to like it here, but I still want to see the backyard."

Paul laughed. "Okay, okay. Let's go outside."

Chapter Thirty-seven

Careful with her footing, Rachel stepped across the slate roof until she stood a few inches from the edge. The warm rays of the mid-morning sun streamed over the forest that started at the estate's fence.

Though she had lived on the estate for eight years now, the view still invigorated her. Endless miles of trees came together in the finest of nature's many symphonies, composed for only those who listened. She filled her lungs with fresh, clean air and smiled, grateful to have the opportunity to grow up on such beautiful land.

The only thing that had changed on the estate in the last eight years was her. As a ten-year-old child, Rachel was an unexpected addition to the estate, which brought about challenges of its own.

The scenic views were just one of the things that differed from her life before her parents died. Rachel's upbringing had been unlike any other. Every morning, she worked with the schoolbooks her uncle brought her. She studied English, history, math, and science like any other child attending school. Paul assigned her homework each night and gave her exams on the material to ensure she learned on the same level as other kids her age.

Most afternoons, she patrolled the grounds with Paul until darkness claimed the land. She loved being able to enjoy the sunset through the tops of the trees each night, almost as much as she enjoyed her long discussions with Paul about all sorts of things. After rounds each day, she went with Paul to the gym, where he taught her how to fight and how to defend herself against an attack.

When she turned thirteen, Paul succumbed to her requests to teach her how to play poker and she became a regular at the poker games with the others on the estate. At a time when girls her age were discovering boys and makeup, Rachel discovered another lifestyle, a criminal one. Paul's schoolbooks were accompanied by Joe's lessons on bypassing security systems. Eric taught her how to open a safe without the combination and how to pick even the most complex lock.

Tony and Aaron were the only ones who didn't play a role in her education. Aaron was a walking encyclopedia of drug information, and he often worked offsite. He could identify any illegal substance and knew all the sciences behind manufacturing drugs, including taking an existing drug and breaking down the chemical compounds. Rachel had no need for that knowledge.

She fought Paul to learn about explosives from Tony, but he remained steadfastly against the idea. She gave up when Donovan told her it was out of the question; explosives were too dangerous.

To placate her, Paul allowed her to start going on rounds alone and she received her first gun, a present from Donovan. Every morning before the rest of the world stirred from bed, Donovan took her shooting in the back of the estate's grounds, and she soon hit the middle of the target with every shot.

When she turned sixteen, Paul declared her education complete and she no longer studied schoolbooks. Instead of getting a driver's license and being giddy with friends about first loves and homecoming dances, Rachel committed her first burglary. It was a rite of passage, a final exam of sorts, and one she easily passed.

She hid the guilt she felt from the others and silenced her nagging conscience by telling herself it was like the cops and robbers games she played as a child. Some people chose the law, and others chose to rob. She happened to be a robber. Standing on the roof now, she was fully immersed in that role.

Rachel spun around at a noise behind her. She smiled at Donovan standing against the mountainous background. His casual dress of jeans, a black t-shirt, and hiking boots surprised her. He rarely walked around the estate in less than suit and tie, and only dressed down for a job.

"Are you trying to kill yourself?" he asked, as he crossed over to her.

She laughed. "No, I'm not trying to kill myself. What are you doing up here?"

"I was in the middle of a telephone conference and Tony barged in to tell me you're on the roof. Naturally, I changed clothes and climbed up here to see for myself." An amused expression softened his face. "But maybe I should ask what you're doing up here."

"I was checking something out for the Halsey job."

"Halsey is already taken care of," he said.

"Your plan is way too complicated."

"We don't have many choices, Rach. Those damn dogs are causing a lot of problems."

"You don't have to worry about the dogs. If you take them out of the equation, then it's real simple."

Donovan paused, as if mulling over her words. "Tell me."

"You guys are so concerned about entering from the ground level. If you enter from the third floor, the dogs aren't a problem."

"That would be great, but we can't get to the third floor unless we go in the backyard and use a ladder to get up to the balcony. Besides it being too much equipment to bring, the dogs are in the back."

"But there's no need to ever touch the ground in the backyard. On the west side of the house, there are two large oaks next to each other and they straddle the fence. From the pictures, the branches where the trees intersect are more than strong enough to hold one man at a time. It's you, Aaron, and Eric going in, right?"

"Yes," he said.

"Can you eliminate Aaron?"

"Possibly."

"If it's you and Eric, you'll have enough time to climb the first tree, get over the fence, and then cross the branches to the second tree. Next to the second tree is a small flare on the edge of the roof."

"So we use that to get onto the roof."

She smiled. "Exactly. The roof has slopes similar to this one," she said, pointing to the roof under her feet. "I've been able to get from one side to the other several times on this roof without any trouble. Once you get on the roof, scale the slopes to the other side of the house. On the east side, there's a third story balcony you can jump down to. The doors on that balcony have flimsy locks. Since the security system hasn't been set up yet, you won't have any problems getting in."

"And we've avoided the dogs. It's brilliant, except I feel a little old for tree climbing."

Rachel regarded him skeptically. Age did not control Donovan King. Strong and agile, a tree wouldn't have the slightest advantage over him. Her eyes raked over his body. A light breeze blew against his t-shirt and she could discern the definition of almost every muscle.

Not for the first time, she wondered what it would be like to have the warmth of his body against hers, how his touch would feel on her bare skin, and how his kiss would taste. She cut the thoughts from her mind before he could read them. "You're not too old to climb a tree. How long did it take you to get up here?"

"A few minutes once I figured out how you managed to do it. Although you could have done me a favor and used a ladder." He chuckled. "Okay, I see your point. Looks like I've got some tree climbing to do. Not that I don't appreciate your help with Halsey, but I thought you would have been more concerned with your own job."

Rachel took a deep breath. She was trying to focus on everything but her job. Working to solve the problems with the Halsey job helped distract her overactive mind. She did not want Donovan to see her appear weak regarding her own job. Instead of responding to his statement, Rachel asked, "Why are we always doing favors for Wilkes?"

"I think you know the answer to that, Rachel."

Yes, she knew the answer. Graham Wilkes was a powerful force whose criminal influence far surpassed Donovan's. Beneath his legitimate chain of Bella Hotels and Resorts laid a complex network of drug running. The largest drug outfit in the nation, it was so well buried it was hard for anyone to keep up with his movements. Because of Aaron's vast knowledge about drugs, Donovan lent him out to Wilkes on a regular basis.

Donovan often commented that despite their lifelong friendship, he and Wilkes had traveled different roads in life. Wilkes played in the drug arena. Donovan preferred art and jewelry; more specifically, the extraction and illegal sale of it. Rachel had a feeling that even if Donovan had not grown up with Wilkes, they would still be trading favors with him if not outright working for him.

"Besides," Donovan continued. "Graham has always been there whenever I've needed him. He's never hesitated, and we don't either."

"You're right. I know he's done a lot for you in the past, and if you were in his shoes, he would help you out with this."

Donovan tilted his head. "Are you having second thoughts about the job?"

She hesitated for a moment too long. He moved closer to her and laid his hand on her shoulder. She almost jumped at his touch and wanted him to walk away before she did something stupid.

His presence overwhelmed her and stole every thought from her mind. The slight afternoon breeze shifted direction and forced the combination of cologne, soap, and skin into her nostrils. The familiar scent squeezed her heart until she thought it would rupture. The sun adhered her clothes to her skin, along with the heat that crept over her flesh.

Donovan seemed unaware of the trembling in her body. "I have confidence you can do this, Rachel. This is important, not only to Graham, but also to me."

She agreed. Wilkes's oldest daughter, Jill, had been drugged and raped. A jewelry box was missing from her condo. Of course, the job was important.

"You don't know how much I wish I could keep you out of this one," Donovan said.

"But you know that with a guy like Jeff Cox, the best way to lure him to the hotel room is with a woman," Rachel finished for him. "I also think he'd be more willing to give up the location of the jewelry to a woman."

"After what he's done, I need you to be careful. I couldn't stand it if anything happened to you."

"Nothing is going to happen," Rachel said, not for the first time.

"Have you seen Graham's daughter?"

Rachel had only seen Jill Wilkes once, two years earlier when she came to the estate with her father. Aaron, Joe, and Eric still talked about her on occasion. Blonde hair that cascaded down her back like a waterfall. Perfect almond-shaped blue eyes that hypnotized any man who dared to gaze into them. Creamy skin which blemishes shied away from.

Then there were the things they latched onto and candidly spoke about, even in front of Rachel. Though Aaron and Joe both shared their lustful thoughts about Jill, Eric was far worse than the rest, commenting on things he would like to do to her, things Rachel wished she had not heard.

Rachel was sure Donovan had those same thoughts about Jill, since no one else at the estate could seem to forget her. She wondered for a moment if Donovan had ever dated Jill, or if he wanted to. Standing side by side the day Jill came to the estate, Donovan and Jill looked like they were made for each other. Suffering from a lingering case of jealousy, Rachel wished she had never met her.

"Compared to Jill," Donovan continued, "I think you'd be a little more enticing to Cox."

Startled by his statement, Rachel looked up at him and waited for the punch line. But, Donovan rarely joked and his expression confirmed his seriousness. She stopped herself from laughing at his misguided perceptions of her. "I don't think you have anything to worry about."

"I hope you're right," Donovan said. "Paul is still incensed I'm sending you."

"Paul will get over it."

"Probably. I heard the dresses came yesterday. I'm sorry I wasn't here to help you with that. Did you get one picked out?"

"It took some time, but we found one." The dress was considered the most important part of the job, as it would help Rachel grab Cox's attention amongst an influx of women all vying for him to return to their hotel rooms with them.

Since Donovan was absent from the estate when the dresses arrived, Paul decided Joe would provide the male opinion for selecting the right one. Paul was too biased, Aaron too meek, Tony too unwilling, and Eric too eager.

For over an hour, Rachel tried on dress after dress and modeled them for Joe until they found one they both liked.

"Are you sure the dress will work?" he asked.

"The dress is perfect," she said. "The plan is perfect. The job will get done perfectly."

"I'm sorry," Donovan said. "I should know better than to doubt you. I still have my concerns, but I'll keep it to myself for now. I'm flying down to Los Angeles this afternoon for a meeting, but I'll be back late tomorrow afternoon, before you leave for the job." He moved to the edge of the roof and peered over the side. "By the way, did you have a plan for getting down?"

She walked up beside him. "Of course I have a plan," she said. "What in the world would you do without me?"

He looked at her and grinned. "I probably wouldn't be standing on my roof right now."

Chapter Thirty-eight

Donovan's smile fixed itself in her mind and followed her throughout the day. She dazed her way through her rounds and into the poker game that night.

Each of those who lived at the estate headed up their own security teams, made up of men from Donovan's security company, while Paul was in charge of the entire operation. The rotations allowed for them to have one day off every two weeks.

To help relieve the team from the strenuous work schedules, Paul brought in an off-site team once a month so they could have a night off together. On that night, the residents gathered in the game room for intense, alcohol-infused competition. Though the chips they played for were only assigned low dollar amounts, every hand was layered with pride, as if thousands of dollars were at stake.

"How many, Rach?" Tony asked.

Rachel studied the five cards in her hand, and her mind calculated the possibilities. It could go either way. Two aces, two sevens and a lonely queen begged to become a full house, a great hand in a game of five card draw with no wilds. If she forfeited the queen, though, she risked getting stuck with nothing more than a two-pair, most likely a losing hand given the high bidding. Then again, the queen, one ace and one three were all clubs, and a flush could also take the pot, now standing at fifty-three dollars in chips.

"Come on, Rach," Joe said. "The fate of the world doesn't rest on this hand."

"Yeah, but the fate of that pot does," she said, She placed the queen face down on the table. "Give me one, Tony." She took a large swallow of her beer. She lifted the new card off the table, and did her best to not let her disappointment show. She had traded the queen for a five. With only a two-pair, she would have to fold.

Tony dealt himself three cards before the second round of betting began. Aaron, Paul, Joe, and Eric all said, "Check," when their turn came to bet, and Rachel's strategy changed. Four out of five opponents declined to bet, which told her no one's hand was as spectacular as they originally thought.

Rachel looked at the neat stacks of chips in front of her. She had already won over four hundred dollars in chips that night so her ego wouldn't be too bruised if she lost this one hand. She picked up a blue chip, designated as the five-dollar chip for the game, and tossed it into the pot.

Tony groaned and dropped his cards down in front of him. One down, she thought. When Aaron folded next, she stopped herself from smiling at her luck. Paul met her bet of five dollars, while Joe folded. Eric raised her five more dollars.

Rachel didn't hesitate, seeing Eric's five and adding five more. Paul folded. Eric threw in another blue chip and called. Knowing Eric's competitive nature wouldn't allow him to fold anytime soon, Rachel also called. Eric fanned out his hand on the table displaying a two-pair, kings over fives. Rachel showed her aces over sevens with a large smile.

"Damn," Aaron said. "I folded with a three of a kind and all you guys had were two-pairs."

Joe pushed his chair back and headed to the makeshift bar in the corner of the room. He filled a shot glass with tequila. "Anyone else want one?" he asked.

"Over here," Eric said. "Make it a double."

Rachel glanced at her small collection of empty beer bottles and declined.

Tony shuffled the cards. "I'm ready to get out of here." After their monthly poker game, it was custom for the others to leave for town, where they drank and played pool and darts until early morning. Tony had a girl named Gina that he visited while in town, and the others almost always found someone to keep them company.

Paul usually stayed at the estate with her, but left on occasion, if for no other reason than to get out. From the stories of the others, she knew Paul kept to himself while out, remaining true to his deceased wife in a way that caused the dormant romantic side of Rachel to ooh and ah.

"Can I go this time?" Rachel asked. She had always wanted to go with them to town and rediscover the world she left when her parents died.

Joe patted her shoulder. "Rach, you're eighteen. You can't get into a bar until you're twenty-one."

"I could get a fake ID," she said.

Paul pushed his chair back and stood up. "No way, Rachel. That's illegal."

"So when did obeying the law become part of our code of ethics? Come on, guys. How is it possible that given all the expertise in this room, we can't come up with one fake ID?"

"Truth?" Tony asked. "We don't want to get into a fight because some jerk won't leave you alone."

Rachel scowled. "You act like I can't take care of myself."

Joe laughed. "Oh, so we let you get in a fight instead and then have to explain to Donovan why his sweet little Rachel is in jail."

"I promise I'll be good. Nobody will go to jail."

"Sorry, Rachel," Paul said. "It's not going to happen." His fatherly tone told her it was the end of the discussion.

Rachel threw up her hands in defeat and stood up. "Fine. I guess I'll roam the grounds aimlessly again." She started out the door.

"Make sure you call ahead and let George know you're out there," Paul said. George was the security guard that headed up their relief team.

"As always. Have fun, guys." Rachel climbed the stairs two at a time. Near the employee entrance in the back, she grabbed a radio out of the closet that housed their security gear. Holding it close to her mouth, she said, "Hey, George. You out there?"

"Go ahead, Rachel," George said.

She stepped onto the back patio and continued with their routine, monthly dialogue. "I'm headed outside."

"We'll keep an eye out for you. Tell me when you're off the grounds, okay?"

"Sure thing, George." She secured the radio onto her belt and started down the slight incline that led to her favorite place on the grounds. Next to the chain link fence and barbed wire was a patch of land under a large oak tree where Rachel wasted countless hours as a child. From this spot, she had an incredible view of the forest rising and falling with the mountainous curves. Not quite as good as the roof, she thought, but still a beautiful view.

The King estate was built as a gift to Donovan's mother from his father. Tucked away in a corner of the world where the Sierra and Cascade mountains collided, the estate provided his mother with a home that, for her last year on earth, could help her forget the cancerous cells that knew nothing of mercy. Rachel had heard the story numerous times over the years from Paul. It was an example of a real-life fairy tale, one that Rachel held as dear to her heart as the ones her mother told her when she was young.

Rachel turned at the sound of footsteps and rolled her eyes at Eric's approaching silhouette. It wasn't that she didn't like him, although Eric didn't top her list of favorite people. She had been looking forward to a quiet evening alone with her thoughts and nature.

"I thought you went with the others," she said when he reached her.

He shrugged. "Changed my mind. Paul scheduled me for rounds in the morning, so it's probably not a good idea to go out." He glanced around, his brow creased. "So this is what you do when we're gone, huh?"

"Pretty much."

"Seems kind of boring."

"I enjoy it," she said.

"So, you've got your big job tomorrow. Are you nervous?"

"Not really. It's just another job."

"It's one of the biggest jobs in recent memory. Are you sure you can pull it off? You can still back out if you don't think you can hack it."

"I have to pull it off and backing out isn't an option. Wilkes is counting on us to get this job done, and I'm going to do it right. But, I don't want to talk about it right now. I had hoped to come out here to help get my mind off it. That's why I wanted to go with the others tonight."

He took a few steps toward her, standing much closer to her than Rachel liked. "Well, since King's in Los Angeles until tomorrow and the others are gone for the night, I guess I'll have to volunteer to take your mind off the job."

The strong stench of tequila wafted from his breath and toward Rachel. She stepped back from him. "I'll probably go inside soon and rest up."

"What, don't want to spend time with me?"

"It's not you, Eric. Like you said, I have a big day tomorrow."

"Back to the job, are we? That's all we ever talk about."

"That's what our lives consist of, rounds and jobs."

"It must have been hard for you, growing up here."

Confused at the strange turn in the conversation, she asked, "What do you mean?"

"You never got to go do high school things, like others girls your age. Instead, you did rounds and jobs."

"Somehow I don't think I would have done well in high school," she said, laughing. "I'm not exactly pep squad material."

"You're right. That's definitely not you." Eric paused. "But there are other things you missed out on. You never got to do the dating thing."

As the words left his lips, stale air wrapped around her. Though she was accustomed to Eric's inappropriate comments, tonight his eyes seemed different, as if they were seeing every part of her. She regretted not taking the shot of tequila, positive it would have made the exchange and his presence easier to digest.

"I never wanted to do the dating thing," she said.

"Surely you don't want to go through life not knowing what it's like to be touched by a man." He moved closer to her. "Don't you want to know how good it can be?"

Rachel shifted her weight and backed up again. Dangerously close to the oak tree, she became concerned with being cornered against the bark. "Eric, I don't think we should have this discussion," she said.

"Oh, I see how it is," he said, with a condescending tinge in his tone. "You're waiting for him, aren't you? You keep hoping that one day King's going to tell you he wants you."

Rachel swallowed and hoped Eric couldn't see the scarlet streak spreading across her cheeks and creased forehead. "I… I'm not quite sure I know what you're talking about."

Eric guffawed. "You think I don't know? That I don't see how you look at him? Even an idiot could figure out what scenarios start running through your head every time he walks into the room."

"Eric—"

"Are you that stupid to think he would want anything to do with you? You're the hired help, Rach. The only thing he'd want is to use you." He rested his hand beside her on the tree trunk, his whisper harsh and the toxic fumes of alcohol harsher. "You can do so much better than him. One night with me, and I'll make you forget that King ever existed."

Rachel threw her hands up. "That's it. This conversation is over." She jerked sideways and moved around him so she could go back to the house.

"You better forget it, Rach," he called from behind her. "It's never going to happen with him."

She grabbed the radio off her belt and let George know she was leaving the grounds for the night.

Chapter Thirty-ninc

Rachel hit the mat with a thud. She laid still and tried to catch her breath. Paul's face appeared over her. "We're finished. I'm not sparring with you anymore. That's the third time you've gone down today."

"I know, I know."

"Are you worried about tonight?"

Rachel sat up. Her frustration peaked at the same question being asked of her over and over by everyone she ran across that day. Of course, she was worried. She had promised Donovan perfection. She couldn't be sure of the consequences if one thing went wrong.

"Hey, Rach," Paul said. "Still alive down there?"

"Yes, I'm worried about tonight. Every last detail is planned, every possibility is accounted for, but what if something happens? I don't want to be responsible for that."

He sat down beside her. "This job comes with a lot of pressure, maybe too much. You're not just doing it for Donovan, you're doing it for Graham Wilkes. Nobody would blame you if you dropped out now. Someone else can do it, maybe someone from Graham's camp."

"No, they can't, which is why it's my assignment. Wilkes doesn't have any women on his payroll, remember? That's why he farmed it out to Donovan."

"True, but we could find someone else with time."

"But Donovan volunteered me. I can't let him down. Backing out now would reflect poorly on not only me, but him as well."

"Are you sure you want to do it?"

Rachel wasn't sure about anything at the moment, but she would do the job without complaint. "I'll be fine."

"Good. Maybe you ought to go rest."

"Paul, I think I'm old enough to decide when I need to rest."

"I know, I'm sorry. I keep forgetting you're an adult now."

"It's okay." She was silent for a moment. "I think I'll go rest for a while," she said, and she got to her feet.

He laughed. "As stubborn as ever."

In her bedroom, Rachel sat on her bed with the intention of lying down for a bit. After a moment of sitting, though, she became restless again. She decided it was best to take a shower, knowing her anxiety level would never let her rest. She needed calm, and a hot shower would go a long way in bringing it, even if it were temporary.

When she moved into the estate eight years earlier, Donovan brought in contractors to enlarge her room by knocking down walls between three adjoining rooms. He had the contractors work in teams of five around the clock so Rachel would have her room ready quickly.

Rachel couldn't contain her excitement during construction, the commotion of the improvements being the only thing that took her mind off the death of her parents. Donovan had the contractors turn one of the rooms into a large bathroom, commenting that every girl needed not only their privacy, but an extraordinary bathroom.

Within a week, he delivered on his promise. Rachel had never seen such beautiful tiles and fixtures. The bathroom not only had an extra-large shower with two shower heads at competing angles, but a separate tub with whirlpool jets and a pillow to rest her head. Around the tub were small recesses in the walls, sized to hold candles. Rachel could not remember seeing a more extravagant bathroom.

Rachel never once took the bathroom for granted, but it was the only bit of luxury she allowed herself. Her bedroom was the stark opposite of the bathroom, white walls with only a bed, a dresser, and an armchair. Donovan had instructed the contractors to make the bedroom twice as nice as the bathroom, but Rachel had stopped him. She did not want to take advantage of his generosity since she was a stranger in his home. Not only had he already done too much for her, she also concerned herself with how long she would be at the estate, having learned quite early that everyone dies.She could be left alone at any small twist of fate.

Standing under the steady stream of the shower heads now, Rachel was glad she allowed Donovan to have the bathroom built to his specifications. He was right that every girl needed an extraordinary bathroom, a sanctuary to relax her cares away. She closed her eyes and let the hot water roll off her back. She coaxed her tense muscles to relax and took in deep breaths of the therapeutic hot steam.

Back in her bedroom, she dressed in a pair of jeans and a black, ribbed tank top. Sitting on the edge of her bed, she ran through every step of the job several times. The more she thought about it, the more nervous she became, erasing the benefits of her shower. Time became her enemy as her watch ticked off the minutes faster than ever before. A freight train running at her at top speed, she couldn't freeze the hands of time to jump out of the path of collision. Before she knew it, the job would be done, and she was sure she would never be the same.

No matter how strong her fears, backing out of the job was the last thing on her mind. She needed to prove to everyone she could do it. After several years, she gained acceptance among the other residents of the estate. If the job did not go right, it could destroy everything she achieved. Of course, so could the issues she now had with Eric. She couldn't avoid him forever, but after his behavior last night, she wanted to stay far away from him until their conversation was a distant memory.

A polite knock on the door interrupted Rachel's thoughts. "Come in," she said.

Donovan entered the room. Rachel rose from the bed and greeted him, her eyes fixated on his smile. The sight of him was of great comfort to her, and it helped relieve some of her apprehension over the job. She wished he was going with her tonight to do the job, as it would make it much easier for her.

"You're back," she said. "Did your meeting go well?"

"Always does. Are you ready for tonight?" he asked.

Rachel knew better than to let her fears come through in her tone. "Yes," she said.

"Paul mentioned you might be a little nervous," he said.

She wanted to strangle Paul for saying anything of the sort, especially to Donovan. "I'm not nervous."

"Eric also said you were acting strange last night."

Rachel bit back all the remarks she wanted to make about Eric. That he would bring up such a thing to Donovan seemed too much like sabotage, although she couldn't fathom what his motive might be. "I'm fine. Please don't worry about me."

"I can't help it. This is a big job and you've never done anything like it before. Are you sure you can go through with it? That you won't falter at the last second?"

"Yes, I'm sure. Everything will go smoothly with no hitches."

He moved toward her. "You would tell me if you didn't want to do it, right?" he asked, not letting the subject go.

No, she wouldn't tell him because whether she wanted to do it or not no longer mattered. She had accepted the job and now she had to do it. No one ever denied Donovan when asked to do a job, let alone back out of one once they were committed. "Trust me, I'm okay," she said.

She did not notice her fingers twisting in front of her waist until he put his hands over hers. "You don't seem okay. I mean, you sound okay and that's what you keep telling me, but I know you're not. You only do that thing with your hands when you're nervous."

Rachel flushed, unaware anyone knew of her habit. "Maybe I'm a little anxious."

Donovan brushed her hair out of her eyes and rested his hands on her shoulders. He frowned. "You're tense. So much for being fine."

His hands gave her shoulders a quick squeeze, and crimson traveled around her neck. She hated being this close to him and felt guilty for enjoying his touch and wanting more. Her attraction to him burned through her. She tried to look at him with normal eyes, but she knew they exposed the feelings she tried to hide from him. There were moments when she thought he wanted her, too, but they were fleeting. A glance here, a gentle touch there.

Donovan appeared uneasy, as if he could read her innermost thoughts and did not feel the same. He cleared his throat, and dropped his hands from her shoulders. Stepping back, he asked again, "Are you sure about this?"

Rachel looked away from him, unable to conceal her disappointment that he had retreated from her. "I'm sure, Donovan. There's no need to worry."

"Good. When you're dressed, please meet us in the waiting room."

As soon as he shut the door she flopped backwards on her bed, wishing she could sink into the mattress and disappear. She squeezed her eyes shut and forced Donovan out of her mind. More important things deserved her full attention.

After she dressed, she walked to the bathroom and pinned up her hair. She arranged the wig on her head and examined her appearance in the oval, full-length mirror in the corner. The blonde curls of the wig helped her appear at least five years older and rendered her unrecognizable.

Donovan came up with the idea to use a blonde wig to match the hair color of Jill Wilkes. Donovan assumed since Cox chose Jill as his rape victim, sticking with a similar look would trigger him into action again. Rachel was not afraid of Cox trying anything since she could easily defend herself. She was more concerned with whether Donovan preferred blonde hair over her own lackluster, brunette locks.

A few days earlier, Claudia showed her how to apply makeup. Claudia had only been told that Paul was taking Rachel to a musical. During her training session, Claudia gushed about all the musicals she had seen and how much she wanted to go to Broadway someday to see even more. Rachel soaked in all the tales, knowing that even though Paul was taking her to a building where a musical was being performed, she would not be in one of the seats watching the scenes unfold onstage.

Rachel was unfamiliar with makeup in general, but learned the differences between blush and eye shadow, lipstick and eye liner. Using her newfound knowledge and a large array of makeup to choose from, Rachel selected more natural colors so she wouldn't look like a doll that a child used as a coloring book. Her lipstick, however, was a striking bright red that matched her dress in shade. Her intention was to draw Cox's eyes to her mouth in order to better lure him.

The red dress fell to Rachel's ankles and had a slit in front of one leg that stopped close to the top of her thigh without giving away any secrets. Thin spaghetti straps held up the top of the dress, and the neckline plunged drastically into a V-shape, revealing cleavage she never knew she had.

The body of the dress clung to every curve and though she felt like she was on display, a sensual excitement overrode her doubts. With a gleam of mischief, she reached into the front of the dress and positioned her breasts for maximum exposure. She reassessed her appearance with satisfaction.

She bunched up the skirt of the dress into her hands and jogged back into her room, where she slipped into a pair of open-toed red heels that revealed her manicured red toenails. Donovan had a manicurist and pedicurist come in earlier in the day to perform their magic on her, and she detested every moment of the pampering, even though she knew it was necessary.

The shoes were not as quick a trick to learn as the makeup. She spent three weeks practicing in them before she could go from one end of a room to the other without falling. Her first painful steps in the shoes resulted in a couple sprained ankles during her crash course in walking. Now, she glided upstairs to the waiting room, where Donovan and Paul sat engaged in conversation.

Both men stood as she entered the waiting room, each with a different expression when they saw her for the first time. Paul's face wrinkled up. "I don't know about this."

"I think she looks fine," Donovan said. His eyes moved over her body, and Rachel hoped he had good thoughts. "The dress is much better than we thought and it's sure to work."

"She might attract too much attention. We can't risk someone remembering her later."

"Most men will take notice, but there will be a lot of other women dressed in a similar fashion. Women won't notice her since they will be too busy trying to get Cox's attention. As long as she's the one Cox goes for, then nothing else matters. This dress is the best way."

"It's really… tight," Paul said.

"It could be much worse. I think they did a great job picking this one out. It's perfect."

"Excuse me," Rachel said, "but you don't have to talk like I'm not here."

"Okay then, how do you feel about the dress? Be honest, Rachel." Paul crossed his arms. His tone expected her to side with him.

She shrugged to play it down so as not to upset Paul, but also not to disagree with Donovan. "As long as the dress does its job, it's fine. Besides, it's too late to try to find another dress, so I don't see why we're having this discussion."

"Alright, I'll let it go, but I still disagree." Paul's forehead creased. "Where's your bag? We can't forget that."

"I put it in the car earlier," she said.

"Are you both clear on what you are to do?" Donovan asked. They nodded in response. "Good. Paul, go ahead and pull the car around. I need to speak with Rachel alone for a moment."

After he left, Donovan moved closer to her. "Are you sure?" he asked her once more.

"Yes," she said. For a moment, she forgot all about the job, unable to focus with his body so close to hers. She wanted to grab his shirt, pull him closer, and kiss him. She restrained herself, knowing that nothing would be accomplished through such a scene.

The ups and downs of not knowing how he felt about her, if he felt anything at all, frustrated her to no end. If only she could ask him why he violated her personal space every time they were alone together, why he intruded on her thoughts all day long, and why he wouldn't let her rest at night as he invaded her dreams.

His voice pulled her back into reality and reminded her of the task before her. "You realize how important this is." It was not a question.

"Of course."

"You'll be entirely on your own. You won't have contact with Paul at all. If anything goes wrong, he won't be in a position to bail you out. With that in mind, don't let Cox get control of the situation. You are to remain in charge at all times. Is that understood?"

Rachel had heard the same warning several times before, but with the job looming over her, it sounded more severe this time. If she wasn't careful every second, she could place herself in a dangerous situation. "Yes, I understand," she said.

"Stay confident and focused. No distractions. When the time comes, don't think, just act." He laid his hands on her shoulders and his mouth brushed against her cheek, his lips sweeping closer to her mouth than she expected. "Good luck, Rachel," he said.

"Last minute advice?" Paul asked, as she settled into the passenger side of the car.

She touched her cheek where he had kissed her. "Something like that."

"I still don't like the dress," Paul mumbled, and drove the car away from the house.

Chapter Forty

Two hours later, Paul parked the car on a side street. Up a small hill to their right, a circular, stucco building interrupted the night sky. The stars illuminated the building and the concrete walkway surrounding it.

Rachel had seen the building many times in photographs, but seeing it in real life put a lump in her throat and a weight on her chest. She wanted Paul to turn the car around and drive back to the safety of the estate, but she knew there was no use asking. Every opportunity she had to turn away from the job was now gone. She had no choice left but to go through with it.

Oblivious to her internal struggle, Paul pointed to a door on the side of the building. "Right there is where you enter," he said.

The light above the door appeared burned out as a coincidence, but coincidence didn't exist in her world. Everything about the job was planned down to the second, including the burned out light. Donovan had worked closely with Wilkes to ensure his men were as active in the job as she and Paul. His men arrived at the building earlier that morning, long before the rest of the city was awake, to cut the wires to the light and take care of other details of the job.

"The door is unlocked," Paul continued. "Remember the way you go in because you'll come out that way, too. Try not to let anyone see you going in or leaving because they'll be sure to remember you later since you're not using the main entrance. Once you're inside, find the restroom near the lobby. Stay in one of the stalls until the musical is over, then go into the lobby and get into the receiving line."

Rachel absorbed the details one last time.

He handed Rachel a ticket stub to the musical and a hotel room keycard. "The ticket stub is in case someone asks. Slip the hotel keycard to Cox and meet me back here. You should be gone no longer than twenty-five minutes."

Rachel placed both the keycard and ticket stub in a clutch purse that also held a tube of lipstick and a compact mirror. She tucked the clutch under her arm, steadied her breath, and climbed out of the car.

She entered through the door Paul indicated, and peered both ways down the halls. The building appeared empty. The attendees of that night's play were enjoying the last scenes of the performance, but soon the hallways would fill with people and conversation.

Rachel moved to the restroom and hid in the middle stall. The smell of antiseptic and the shine on the walls of the immaculate bathroom stall sparked a memory of a vacation to Disneyland with her parents the summer before they died. When they stopped off at a gas station during their road trip, Rachel raced to the bathroom.

Inside the first stall, she found graffitied walls with language she had never heard before. Wide-eyed, she used the restroom and ran back to her mother, wishing she could undo what she saw, even though she wasn't sure what most of the words meant.

As Rachel waited in the stall for the musical to end, she wished she had some graffiti to help her pass the time in the stall. Instead, she only had her nerves to keep her company, and she second-guessed her role in the job. Doubts had not corroded one of her jobs before tonight, and she couldn't let them get the best of her now.

More than ever, she wanted to impress Donovan by making this job the smoothest they had ever done. She wanted to solidify herself as much more than a valuable asset to him. She only wished that he saw her as something more than an employee, as Eric pointed out last night. But, a man like Donovan had a world of attractive and sophisticated women to choose from, women like Jill Wilkes. Eric was right. There was no need for Donovan to go near the hired help for companionship.

Women filtered through the bathroom door to use the restroom and freshen their makeup. They conversed in rushed, gossiping tones about the musical's handsome star, Jeff Cox. Rachel drew a shaky breath and removed the hotel keycard from her purse. She sealed her left hand around the keycard, gripping it like a tiny security blanket.

She exited the stall unnoticed and found her way to the receiving line. All of the performers had changed into dresses and suits after the musical ended, and Rachel wondered what fantastic costumes they wore during their time on stage. She shook the hands of men and women she had never seen, and told them what a wonderful performance they gave in a musical she knew nothing about.

As she neared the front of the line, she craned her neck to get a better view of Cox. He still had makeup from the play on his face, but it didn't interrupt his ability to attract members of the opposite sex. A handsome man, Cox had blonde hair, blue eyes, and smooth features, but he exuded arrogance, even more so than Eric. Women almost fell over each other trying to shake his hand and grab his attention, while he appeared to regard them as objects created for his pleasure.

Rachel bit her tongue to stop herself from laughing out loud at the lustful scene. Many hotel room keycards enter his hands, which he dropped into a trashcan beside him after the adoring fan left his sight. Now she understood why Donovan insisted she wear such an alluring dress.

Rachel transferred the keycard to her right hand when she reached the front of the line. Cox took her hand and she leaned into him. She whispered the name of the hotel in his ear in a husky tone. He took the keycard from her hand, and she walked toward the entrance, swishing her hips without overdoing it. She glanced back in time to see him slip the keycard in his suit pocket.

"Well?" Paul asked when she returned to the car.

"He took it."

"That doesn't mean I changed my mind about the dress."

Rachel rolled her eyes, but didn't let Paul bait her into a debate.

At the hotel, she retrieved her bag from the trunk of the car. Holding the straps of her shoes between her fingers, she used a designated stairwell to climb to the fifth floor. At the top of the stairs, she slipped on her heels and took a special key out of her bag to gain access to a freight elevator.

She rode the elevator to the closed restaurant on the twentieth floor. From there, she walked through the restaurant to a private elevator that waiters used to take room service up to the penthouse. Using a keycard similar to the one she gave Cox, she unlocked the penthouse door. She made her way down the lengthy entryway, her heels clicking against the flawless wood flooring.

She had some time before Cox would come strutting through the door, so she familiarized herself with the penthouse. Though she had memorized the floor plan, Rachel's meticulous side did not want any surprises once Cox showed up.

From the entryway, Rachel entered a cozy sitting area. Two white sofas with delicate, stitched patterns were arranged in an L-shape around a glass table standing on iron, claw legs. The sitting area opened up to a much larger living room, with another couch, two light blue armchairs, and a luxurious chaise lounge. The dining area next to the living room boasted a dark wood table large enough to seat eight beneath a crystal chandelier.

In both the living room and dining area, sheer blue curtains covered glass doors leading to the balcony, and abstract oil paintings graced the walls.

A partially open door on her left revealed a white marble floor and Rachel imagined if she opened the door she would find the first of two bathrooms she remembered from the floor plans. The bedroom on her right, however, interested her more.

Her eyes took in every detail of the bedroom. The finest of linens dressed the California king size bed, and she noted with approval the rails on the headboard of the bed. She placed her bag next to a telephone and reading lamp on an oak table in the front of the room. She pressed on the headboard, but could not make it touch the wall. Once Cox was there and on the bed, she didn't want any unnecessary noise, despite her nearest neighbors being two floors down.

With the stage set, she exited the bedroom and turned her attention to the balcony off the living room. She yanked back the curtains and the lights of the city greeted her. The balcony included another chaise lounge and several oversized chairs for relaxing under the stars.

The door tempted her to go outside for a moment. She thought of the people the lights represented and wondered what they were doing. The world she stared out on greatly differed from the one she knew. There were times when late at night she would lie awake, dreaming about that world and what it would be like to go back.

No distractions, Donovan's voice reminded her. She needed to focus on the job and nothing else. She returned to the bedroom, removed her high heels, and sat down on the bed. There, she waited for Cox, and allowed Donovan's voice to float through her mind without censor.

An hour later, the door to the penthouse opened. She walked to the doorway and leaned against the frame. Jeff Cox slipped out of his coat and threw it over the side of the chaise lounge. His eyes journeyed over Rachel's body and he grinned. "You're even more beautiful than I originally thought," he said. He started toward her, hunger gleaming in his eyes.

Repulsed by his quick action, she shuffled backward into the bedroom and stayed a couple steps beyond his reach. He held his arms out to her, and Rachel tasted bile in the back of her throat. "I have a better idea," she said. "Get on the bed."

He stepped out of his shoes and climbed onto the center of the bed. "Aren't you coming over here?"

Rachel went to her bag and took out two pairs of handcuffs. She tossed one pair onto the bed. "Put this on first."

He attached one of the cuffs to his wrist and snapped the other cuff onto the headboard without hesitation. She expected some resistance, but it seemed he had done this before.

She walked around the bed and did the same with his other hand. She returned to her bag and pulled out a pair of gloves. She tugged them over her hands and reached back into her bag.

"What are you getting now?" he asked.

"I'm afraid you won't like it too much." She turned around and pointed a gun equipped with a suppressor at his head.

"What the hell is this?" he asked.

"Eight weeks ago you were in Los Angeles, preparing for your musical. You met a woman named Jill at a bar near the performance hall. Sound familiar?"

"Never heard of her."

"You went back to her condo with her, where you slipped drugs into her drink when she changed her mind about having sex with you. After you raped her, you stole a large jewelry box out of her room. The box contained hundreds of thousands of dollars of antique jewelry, which her mother had given her before she died two years ago."

"Is this a joke?"

"Jill identified you to her father, Graham Wilkes. He's someone you don't want to cross."

The terror in his eyes unmistakable, he asked, "Are you mafia?"

The corner of her mouth turned upward. "No, I'm freelance."

"I didn't do anything to this girl. I don't even know who she is. I would never do anything to upset Graham Wilkes."

"I'm not here to listen to your pathetic denials. We both know what you did. Wilkes wanted me to cut off your little friend and bring it back to him on a silver platter. I convinced him we should let you stay intact, but only if you tell me where the jewelry is. These are his wife's family heirlooms. I'm sure you understand his motivations behind wanting them back."

His lips tightened.

"Fine, have it your way." She reached into the bag and took out the hunting knife she borrowed from Paul.

"Okay! It's at my home. Look, I took the jewelry box, but I didn't rape her. It was consensual." Cox raised his eyebrows and smirked. "Why don't you put down the knife?" Even though his eyes remained fearful, his tone changed to one of seduction. "I can show you why she loved every minute of being with me. I have a feeling you're a bit more feisty than she is."

His words disgusted Rachel, but she pretended to consider his offer and walked to the foot of the bed. She ran her tongue over her lips and crossed her arms. "Why don't you tell me where the jewelry is, and we then can see about the rest? You are already tied up, after all. No one ever has to find out. You can keep a secret, right?"

Cox relaxed a bit and flashed a cocky smile. "I knew you'd come around to my way of thinking."

Rachel softened her voice to make him think he would get what he wanted. "Is the jewelry in your condo in Los Angeles or your house in San Francisco?"

"San Francisco."

"Where is it in your house?"

"It's in my bedroom on the second floor, in a wall safe. The safe is in the back of my closet on the right-hand side."

"I need the combination."

He hesitated.

She waved the knife.

He told her the combination.

"You don't mind if my guys check it out while we wait, do you?" She picked up the phone on the desk and dialed. Into the phone she said, "It's me. San Francisco." She paused and ran her fingers over the blade of the knife. "It's in his room on the second floor. There's a safe in the wall of the closet."

"Wait!"

"Hold on." Rachel lowered the receiver to her shoulder. "Yes?"

"I lied."

She lifted the receiver to her mouth. "I'll call you back," she said. A recorded voice finished giving her the three-day forecast, and she replaced the receiver. "I'm standing here with a gun and a knife, ready to use either. Why would you lie?"

"I hoped you were bluffing."

"Do I look like I'm bluffing?"

"No, and I'm sorry for trying to trick you. The jewelry is in Los Angeles, under my bed."

"Is there a safe?" Rachel asked.

"No."

"Thank you."

"Why don't you get yourself out of that dress and come over here with me?"

His ego oozed out with his words, and Rachel shuddered. She put the knife back in her bag and gave herself a rapid, silent pep talk. It was time. She pointed the gun at his head.

Terror returned to his face. "What are you doing?"

"I have the information I came for."

"Wait! I lied again! It's not in Los Angeles!" As Rachel anticipated, the headboard moved according to his frantic struggle against the handcuffs, but it did not touch the wall.

"Yes," Rachel said, "it is in Los Angeles."

"But you can't kill me. Someone will find my body here in your hotel room and they'll trace this back to you."

"Don't you know who owns this hotel? Graham Wilkes."

His eyes widened.

Don't think, just act.

Her index finger squeezed the trigger, releasing a bullet that entered his forehead. She lowered the barrel of the gun and fired two more shots into his chest, as Donovan instructed her to do. The gun had more kick than she remembered and the exiting bullets jarred her arm. His body slacked when the bullets hit his body. Rachel forced out the breath she was holding in a rough wheeze that scraped against her lungs.

There was no need to check his pulse to confirm Jeff Cox was dead. Blood was spattered behind him across the headboard rails and the wall, and more blood ran down his body onto the bed. A small amount of blood trickled from the wound in his forehead, forming a thin river and flowing past open, foggy eyes that stared back at her, accusing her, damning her.

She tore her eyes away from the sight. Even though Cox deserved death, her stomach churned at what she had done. In the past two years, she had broken into seven homes. Now, she was a killer. She wondered what her father would say if he were alive.

The job not yet complete, Rachel forced herself to move. She picked up the phone again and dialed a predetermined extension. "I need fresh bedclothes, please," she said when a male voice answered the phone.

Opening her bag, she removed a pair of jeans, a t-shirt, and tennis shoes. She left the wig on her head and changed her clothes. Without looking at Cox, she threw the dress, heels, and gun on top of his body. She set the hotel keys and ticket stub to the musical down on the edge of the bed. All of it would be disposed of in a manner that wouldn't be traced to her or anyone else involved, but that was left for others to do.

At the sound of the door opening, she picked up her bag and moved into the front room. Two men under Wilkes's employ stood waiting, both dressed in all black. One of the men pulled on latex gloves and the other walked toward her.

Pointing to the bedroom, she said, "He's in there." She handed a small key to the man closest to her. "Here's the key for the cuffs. The jewelry is at his condo in Los Angeles, under his bed. Tell Wilkes to contact King." Fighting another wave of nausea, she left to meet Paul.

Chapter Forty-one

Silence filled the two hour drive back to the estate. Images of lifeless eyes and bullet holes ran through Rachel's mind. The longer she sat in the car with Paul, the more she thought about what she did. She couldn't deny Cox was a distasteful person, but disposing of even a bad person who did horrible things still made her a much worse person.

With every passing mile, Rachel wished she could turn around and run. She knew she would have Donovan's approval of her work, and as much as she coveted that from him, she wanted to receive it under different circumstances.

Now that she had jumped from cracking safes to removing a target, she wondered how many more times Donovan would ask her to take someone's life, and how many times she would be unable to refuse him. If Donovan came to her with the request to do a similar job, she would have no choice but to follow through.

Donovan stood in the foyer when they returned to the estate. "How did it go?" he asked.

Rachel glanced at him. "It's done." She brushed past Donovan and moved with determination down the back hallway toward the stairs. As she walked away, she heard Paul and Donovan conversing. She thought Donovan said her name, but she didn't care. She wanted to get downstairs, shower, and climb into bed. Sleep would not come easy and once she did fall asleep, her dreams would resurrect Cox.

As she untied her tennis shoes, Donovan came through her bedroom door. Shutting the door behind him, he asked, "Are you okay?"

She remained seated on the bed and didn't look up. "I'm fine." She tugged off her shoes and placed them on the floor.

Donovan sat down on the bed beside her. "Rachel, you're not okay. Your face is pale and your hands are shaking."

"I said I'm fine," she said through her clenched teeth.

He touched the ends of the wig. "As good as the dress was, I didn't like this thing on you," he said. "You are far more beautiful without it."

Any other time, Rachel would love to hear the words that came from his mouth, but tonight they rang hollow. She didn't want him to placate her to take her mind off the job, instead of being sincere with his compliment.

Somehow she thought when she returned to the estate she would feel elated at her success and be met with affection from the man she pined for. Her expectations were childish at best, and her heart broke over what he made her do and that he was still unattainable.

Donovan removed the wig from her head and laid it on the floor by her shoes. Strands of her hair tumbled down to her shoulders with each bobby pin he extracted. "I spoke with Wilkes. His men raided the condo and found the missing jewelry. He's very pleased with the work you did. So am I."

Rachel closed her eyes and tried to control her jagged breathing. She wished he would go away, but she also wanted him to stay. Frustration contorted her face and no words came out as she tried to speak, leaving her chin trembling.

"Hey," he said, touching her shoulder with concern.

"I killed a man tonight."

"Yes, you did."

"You don't understand. He was alive and he was breathing and he was talking and moving and now he's dead." Rachel could not control the words that flowed from her panicked lips. "He's dead because of me."

"I understand a lot more than you realize," he said. "Jeff Cox wasn't a good man and he deserved to die. After what he did to Jill, it was the right thing to do. What you did was okay."

She shook his hand away from her shoulder. "It's not okay! I killed him!"

"Come here," he said with a soothing tone. She let him pull her head down to his shoulder. "It's okay, Rachel. I'm proud of you for going through with it. Most people would not have been able to do that. It's fine if you feel some guilt, that makes you human, but you can't let it overcome you. You did nothing wrong."

Her defenses broke down with each stroke of his hand through her hair. Thoughts of Cox evaporated, replaced by a cloud of comfort that settled around her. Her immediate feelings frightened her and she spoke through her muffled sobs without thinking. "Please don't touch me. Not now."

Donovan stiffened and moved away from her. Standing up, he said, "You should try to get some sleep."

"I don't know if I can sleep," she said. Rachel kept her eyes averted from his face.

"Stay here," he said. "I'll be back shortly."

As soon as the door shut, she cupped her face in her hands and broke down. She wiped away the tears as fast as they flowed. It was bad enough she already fell apart in front of Donovan. She did not want him to know how much the job affected her by seeing her reduced to tears.

As the last of her tears dried on her cheeks, Donovan returned to her room carrying a glass of water in one hand, his other hand balled into a fist. He handed her the glass and opened his fist.

Rachel pointed to the small white pill in his hand. "What is that?" she asked.

"It's a sedative. It will help you sleep tonight."

"I don't want to take anything. You know how much I hate pills."

"In this case, it's okay to make an exception," he said. "This will relax you into sleep, which you desperately need right now. In the morning you will see things more clearly and feel better about what you did."

Rachel knew he was trying to help her cope, but she was unsure if she would ever agree with his last statement, no matter who she killed. She did not want to discuss the job any further. The best way to get him off the topic was to divert his attention. "Where did you get the sedative?"

"Paul keeps all kinds of things around. One of the many benefits of having a doctor on staff." Donovan turned her hand over and placed the sedative in the center of her palm. He closed her fingers and covered her fist with his hand. "I wouldn't let you take anything that wasn't safe," he said.

His eyes always convinced her of things that words never could. She trusted the light in those caring, amber eyes, her beacon of hope to pull her through anything. Those eyes now told her he was not lying. He wouldn't endanger her by exposing her to pharmaceuticals that may harm her.

He also wouldn't make her do something that wasn't right, Rachel reasoned. Killing Cox only made her feel bad because she extinguished a life. Cox, however, was not a person that deserved to continue living, especially after what he did to Jill Wilkes.

If Cox did something so horrible to Jill, he may have done it to others in the past, as well as planned to do it in the future. By killing him, Rachel saved countless potential victims from enduring the same horror as Jill. That was enough for her to accept her role in his fate. Lingering guilt was normal under the circumstances, and she would find a way to live with it.

Rachel set the pill on her tongue toward the back of her throat. She tipped the glass and drank just enough to wash the pill down. She only hoped it worked fast.

He took the glass from her and placed it on her dresser. He sat back down on the bed, his body much closer to her than she liked. "Do you want to talk about it?" he asked.

"No."

"Would you like me to leave you alone?"

Rachel contemplated before answering. "I don't really want to be alone right now." The tension under the silence unnerved her and her thoughts started revolving around Cox again. "Do you ever regret—"

"Regret what?"

Rachel cut off her thought. Donovan was so purposeful in everything he did that he had no reason to regret his criminal lifestyle. Instead of answering his question, she changed the subject. "Why do you do it? You have everything you could ever need. The company, the estate. So why do all the other stuff?"

He shrugged. "The company was what my father did. The other stuff is what I do."

"So your father was a businessman and you're a spoiled rich criminal?"

Donovan stifled a laugh. "I suppose you could say it like that. But, that's enough analyzing me. Why do you do it?"

She did the jobs because he asked her to, but she couldn't tell him that. "There's a rush, I guess."

"Ah, the proverbial rush knowing stolen art or jewelry worth millions of dollars is in your hands."

Rachel looked up at him. When she returned from a burglary, the goods were transferred to the hands of expert fences, but she had no concept of the value of what she stole. She always assumed it was not for her to know.

Value did not matter to her. Donovan took good care of her, providing shelter, food, and enough of what she needed to satisfy her basic needs with a shot of luxury. Everything they had was costly, even their meals. Nothing on the estate was cheaply done. Everyone who lived there would be taken care of until the day they died, including her. It was part of the deal they made when they gave up their lives in the real world.

Donovan also gave her protection against the world, which could be very cruel. She fast learned this idea with the death of her parents and with the atrocities Cox committed against Jill Wilkes. Because of Donovan, she would never know how horrible life could be.

Although Donovan would never suspect her of getting greedy, she still believed value of goods was the part of the business belonging to him alone. After he brought it up, though, she became curious at his hints of value. "Have I ever stolen something worth that much?" she asked.

"You'd be surprised. Or maybe you wouldn't. You are my rising star, after all."

Rachel frowned. He always referred to her as the best safecracker around, or an excellent employee. "Rising star" was another way of putting a barrier around their relationship, one she wished she could destroy. She wanted to be so much more to him than another employee, no matter how valuable he considered her. If she could get his mind off her skills and onto her, maybe he would see her in the same way she saw him.

"Are you still thinking about Cox?" Donovan asked.

She ignored his question and turned to look at him. "You said you understand what I'm going through. Does that mean you've killed someone, too?"

Donovan's eyes fell to the floor. "Yes, here and there. They all needed killing. I never would have asked you to do this if I wasn't willing to do it myself."

The revelation surprised Rachel, as she never thought of Donovan as someone who had killed before. Knowing she was not alone made her feel better about her job, and reignited her attraction to him. Though still riddled with guilt over Cox, she enjoyed sharing something as intimate as her guilt with him, and learning from his wisdom.

"Did you feel guilty after the first one?" she asked.

"The first time I did a little. It was a job for Graham, something he didn't trust any of his people to do. I was only a few years older than you when it happened, and it bothered me for a little bit. After that first one, I didn't feel much of anything. There were reasons for each of them, so the kills were always justified. That doesn't leave much room for guilt."

"Have you killed anyone since I came to the estate?"

"Some, and I'm sure there will be more to come," he said. "Don't worry, Rach. After a few days, you won't think about it much. Then, next time you do it, you won't think about it at all. It only gets easier each time. Maybe when the next one comes along, I can go with you and we can do it together."

Next time. Rachel didn't want to think he would ask her to take another life, but he clearly trusted her more than anyone else on the estate, much like Graham trusted him. He was training her to be like him, and she took comfort in knowing he was willing to help her through the next job. With him by her side, it would make killing someone much easier.

A strange calm rushed over her mind, the sedative making its presence known far quicker than she imagined. Her voice sounded distant as she spoke. "I have a question about the job. What was Paul's problem with the dress?"

"The dress." Donovan paused. "The dress was… revealing, and Paul didn't like that."

"But you said the dress was okay."

"It was the perfect dress for the job. We had to ensure Cox met you in the hotel room and the dress…" He swallowed hard and looked away from her. "Well, never mind. Paul didn't want you to have to wear it, that's all. He has a hard time realizing that you've grown up. Sometimes he still sees you as a child."

Her eyes studied his face. He was so close she thought she felt the warmth of his skin radiating onto hers. Her heart pounded in her chest and a fever set her face on fire. The desires she associated with his presence crept through her unchecked. "Do you still see me as a child?" she asked.

"How could I?" Donovan brushed his knuckles across her jaw line. "You're an incredible, beautiful woman." He kissed her hesitantly, and then pulled away from her. "This is wrong, Rachel." He rose from the bed.

She looked down and bit her lower lip. Her chest tightened, part from frustration, part from heartache. After tasting him for the first time, she wanted so much more than a small kiss. He seemed to want less.

In the corner of her eye, his hands gestured aimlessly, as if he was unsure of what to say. She glanced at his face and saw the conflict in it. She had never seen this side of him, insecure and less than strong.

"This is so wrong," he repeated. He briefly met her eyes and put forth the best excuse he could find. "You're half my age. I'm sorry, Rachel," he said, and started for the door.

Rachel shot up from the bed, emboldened by the sedative's grip on her. "Donovan, wait." Her fingers twisted in front of her waist.

Donovan turned around. He stared at her for a moment, but she couldn't interpret his expression. His eyes fell to her restless fingers and he inched toward her. He reached out and stilled her hands.

"I don't care if it's wrong," she said. She searched his eyes for some hint of his thoughts, and she thought he would leave.

This time his firm kiss bubbled over with passion. Her body reacted to him and her need for him consumed her. His mouth moved off hers and he lifted her shirt over her head. He tossed it to the floor and reached for the button on her jeans while she worked on unbuttoning his shirt.

She could see him touching her, tasting her, but when he lowered her down on the mattress, the sedative unleashed its power over her. She fought to stay awake, and forced her eyes open every time they closed. Even though she felt his warm skin against her, his hands pinning hers down, his fingers intertwined with hers, it was as if it was happening to someone else. She closed her eyes and fought off sleep, praying she would remember every moment of experiencing him when she woke in the morning.

When she opened her eyes again, Donovan stood beside the bed, buttoning his shirt. He knelt down next to the bed and kissed her softly. "You are mine, Rachel," he whispered, as her heavy eyelids closed. "You belong to me."

Chapter Forty-two

Few things remained secret on the estate, so Rachel was surprised that for five months after the night in her bedroom no one knew of her involvement with Donovan. His sneaking in and out of her room most nights went unnoticed. The looks they shared, even in front of the others, remained just between them.

Five full months, and not one person at the estate suspected the blossoming romance between employer and employee. When they did find out, Rachel wished she could take back the kiss she stole from Donovan in the library when Joe came through the door. Within an hour, Rachel discovered Joe's gossiping skills rivaled his ability to disarm security systems.

In the wake of everyone learning about their relationship, Donovan insisted they remain discreet. He did not want to deal with any of the other residents questioning his decisions, nor did he want their relationship to appear as if it tainted his capacity to run their operations. He gave Rachel no preferential treatment. If anything, he was harsher with her and placed her under greater scrutiny. He expected nothing but perfection from her, and she gave him everything she had, both in her assigned jobs and in their relationship.

A year after Joe told her secret to the others, still no one had dared to approach her directly about the matter, but they didn't have to. From the looks she received, she ascertained each resident's reaction to the news. Joe and Tony seemed indifferent, though she suspected Joe wanted to give her a high-five. Aaron could only manage his trademark blank stare, the one he disappeared behind when a conversation went down a road his mind couldn't travel.

She suspected Paul had his reservations, but after knowing about her relationship with Donovan for the past twelve months, he never spoke of it. His mannerisms remained the same toward both her and Donovan. Every now and then, though, standing in the same room with Paul and Donovan, she detected a slight twitch in his jaw that told her he was thinking about it and he wasn't happy.

But now, as she stood in the game room watching Paul throw darts in the general direction of the dartboard, Eric's reaction came to mind. Like the others, he had not spoken his opinion, at least not to her. His actions, however, reflected his feelings.

"Eric hates me," Rachel said.

Paul threw the last dart.

She walked to the dartboard and tugged on each dart until she retrieved all of them. "Are you sure you don't need new glasses?" she teased. "Donovan will be real upset if you put a hole in the wall."

Paul grunted. "We can patch it. Besides, it's not like you're doing any better than I am."

"Oh yeah? Watch this." She ran her tongue over her lower lip and concentrated on the target. The dart whistled through the air. Bull's-eye. She turned around and smirked. "You were saying?"

"Keep up the smart comments and I'm not playing anymore."

"Yes, you will. You can't stand for me to beat you and that will be your downfall." She threw the rest of the darts, each one landing far away from the bull's-eye so as not to show off too much.

"I hate it when you win, but with throws like that I have nothing to worry about." Paul retrieved the darts and walked back to the line. "What makes you think Eric hates you?"

"Eric has never been overly friendly to me or anyone, but lately he's been more brusque than usual."

Sarcasm filled Paul's voice and he avoided her eyes. "Eric brusque? I don't believe it."

She glared at him. "Come on, what do you know?"

Paul hesitated, as if trying to decide what to tell her. "Eric's upset that Donovan put you in charge of the Stein job. He doesn't think you can do it."

Rachel shook her head. She should have known Eric's behavior was tantamount to a childish temper-tantrum over the Stein job. She recovered from the mild blow to her ego. "Eric can have the responsibility for all I care, but Donovan put me in charge, not him. He has to get used to me being in charge every so often, but I don't see what his problem is. He's not even assigned to this job."

"He made it clear to Donovan that he wanted to be in charge of this one, but Donovan gave it to you. That's quite an insult to an already somewhat unstable guy." Paul threw a dart. "I also might have overheard Eric telling Aaron that he thinks Donovan shows you preferential treatment because of your relationship with him."

"Nothing could be further from the truth," Rachel said. She did not want anyone thinking like that and was incredulous Eric would voice his opinion to others without approaching her first. "Everyone knows Donovan is harder on me than anyone else out there. Eric is grasping at straws because he can't stand for me to be in charge. I'm sure he'll say anything to get me taken off the job so he can take control."

"Rach, I don't know if this is such a good idea."

"I think I can handle being in charge of this job."

"I'm not talking about the job."

His words quieted Rachel for a moment. They had never spoken about her relationship with Donovan, let alone admit that there was one to discuss. Rachel dropped into a chair at the poker table and crossed her arms. "Okay," she said, resigned to a stern lecture. "Let's have it."

Paul clasped his hands together as if praying and paced in front of her. "I've known Donovan a lot longer than you. Most of the time you've known him, you've been a child, incapable of judging character. You've spent over nine years of your life cut off from society, but biologically, you're the same as any other nineteen-year-old. You have the same physical needs and—"

"Will you stop getting all doctory on me and say what you have to say?"

He took a deep breath and stopped pacing. "Donovan has sheltered you for nine years. I wonder if you aren't confusing dependence with something else."

"That's not the case."

"And I didn't expect you to say anything less. At least let me tell you this much. Donovan is a possessive man in every aspect of his life. I know how he gets. I don't want you on the receiving end of it. Do you understand?"

Donovan's voice entered her mind, repeating the phrase he had spoken so often. *You are mine.* After being involved with him for almost seventeen months, he had never said he loved her, though she knew he did. Despite wanting to hear those three words from him, she accepted everything else he said as confirmation of his love.

He always told her that she belonged to him, that she was his life and he was hers. That he couldn't breathe without her, let alone survive a single moment. She had never defined his words as a form of possession, but Paul's description was accurate.

Rachel pushed herself up from the chair and held her hand out to Paul. He handed her the darts and sat down behind her. She put her toe up to the piece of tape on the ground and aimlessly threw the darts at the board. She was no longer concerned with her score or with beating Paul. She only wanted the conversation to end.

"Rachel," Paul said, letting her know the conversation was far from over, "I know it's your life and I can't tell you what to do. I'm also not belittling your feelings for him, or whatever it is you have with him, but I wanted you to know my thoughts about it. I know what it's like to be young and to think you're in love."

For the first time since Donovan kissed her after the Cox job, Rachel experienced guilt over their relationship. She had never considered Paul's feelings on the matter or what affect her relationship with Donovan would have on him.

As a young girl, Paul acted as her father figure, though she had been raised by everyone at the estate in one way or another. Despite being her uncle, Paul rarely interfered with her decisions. That he was unsupportive of her relationship with Donovan bothered her and she questioned her actions. Paul wouldn't warn her away from Donovan without reason.

"I appreciate your honesty," she said. She yanked the darts out of the board.

"But you won't stop seeing him," Paul deduced from her words. "I can't force you to end it with him, but please think about everything carefully. As for Eric, he tends to run his mouth so his feelings about you are no secret. I've never trusted him and I'm starting to think he's up to something. He would do anything to put you out of favor with Donovan."

Rachel held the darts out for Paul to take, but he motioned for her to take another turn. She stepped back up to the line. "Why doesn't Eric like me?" she asked.

"When you first came here, it was hard for everyone to adjust. A ten-year-old girl on the estate?"

She smiled. "I guess it would be pretty strange."

"Especially strange when it's a child as feisty and stubborn as you. Joe always liked that about you and never minded that you were here. I think you won over Tony when you sat in on a poker game for the first time and cleaned Eric out. He saw that you weren't afraid to try anything and that's what it takes to live here. Aaron wasn't so sure about you and still has his moments. Of course, he is somewhat influenced by Eric—"

"Somewhat influenced?" Rachel said. "Aaron can't tie his shoes unless Eric is right there, showing him how to make bunny ears."

Paul laughed. "That's Aaron all right. But, when Eric isn't around, Aaron admits to liking you. I think he admires your courageous nature, which is something he lacks. Eric, on the other hand, is simply intimidated by you. He's also jealous that Donovan has always adored you. Over the past several years, his relationship with Donovan has been rocky, at best. I think he's scared that one day Donovan will eliminate his position."

Rachel's heart skipped a beat, and she pondered Paul's statement. "Would Donovan really get rid of Eric?"

"If Eric becomes too much of a problem, yes. Donovan chose each of us for the roles we fill. We all have our place on the estate with our own area of expertise. You were the only unexpected addition to the team, but you learned quickly and you fit in well. The problem with that is that you and Eric are both masters at lock bypass and safecracking."

Even though she had been taught several different skills and could perform most of them with ease, Rachel took a shine to opening safes. She enjoyed the challenge and treated each safe as a puzzle for her to solve.

As the resident safecracker, Eric spent a lot of time with her, training her in the craft. She never imagined having two people with the same skills would be problematic, but considered it to be an advantage for Donovan. "What's wrong with us both being able to open safes?" she asked.

"Why does Donovan need two experts in the same field? Besides that, you have an edge over Eric. You're more valuable to Donovan because you're intimately involved with him. Eric knows that if he screws up too bad, Donovan won't hesitate to take him out."

Rachel whirled around to face Paul. She knew that's what Paul had been saying all along, but the words still struck her. "Take him out?"

"It's always a possibility."

Rachel stared speechlessly at Paul. Over the years, Rachel had done a lot of bad things for Donovan. She had broken into homes and stolen art or jewelry that he could sell on the black market. She helped plan out intensive jobs that resulted in the deaths of others. She had killed Jeff Cox, as well as two others Donovan convinced her needed killing. Rachel was the only one at the estate who had ventured into contract killing, and it was only because she wanted to please Donovan.

The thought that Donovan would so callously eliminate someone at the estate frightened her. If he asked her to kill another resident, she knew she could not do it, not even if it were Eric. But, if he considered getting rid of Eric, there was a chance that he may one day decide he no longer needed her.

Rachel wouldn't bring herself to believe that Donovan could kill anyone at the estate, no matter what they did. Paul's fears had to be unfounded. Otherwise, they would all be at risk. "I doubt Donovan would ever get rid of Eric," she said. "But Eric being jealous of me is ridiculous. If Eric is screwing up, it's his own fault."

"That's not how he sees it. He blames you."

Rachel pursed her lips. "Maybe I should talk to him and get things out into the open."

"That's the last thing you should do. Let's get through this job. Maybe he'll get over it and things can calm down."

Chapter Forty-three

Jobs were not a frequent occurrence at the estate, and the ones they had were spread out in both time and location. The team also never worked two similar jobs in a row. Donovan made sure everyone was cautious every step of the way, eliminating every possible chance of getting caught.

Three people were chosen for the job based on their individual skills. Some jobs were worked in conjunction with Graham Wilkes and his men, but most of the time those who lived at the estate were the only ones involved. If the job required an additional person from the estate, Donovan would go. He didn't stand on the sidelines barking orders, but spent plenty of time on the playing field.

Rachel mentally divided every job into two phases: preparation and execution. The painstaking preparation lasted anywhere from two weeks to a year, until all foreseeable problems were resolved before they occurred. Issues ranged from driving time to merchandise delivery to body disposal.

During the preparation phase of the Stein job, Rachel dedicated every waking moment to the job. She altered her routine to include an hour nap each day to help keep her mind clear and body refreshed. She spent more time in the gym and daily ran a path through the back of the estate.

She reviewed every twist and turn of the job, memorizing each detail, no matter how insignificant. She could perform the job in her sleep if asked. Nothing less than perfection was expected from the team, but Rachel pushed herself beyond the limit, knowing Donovan demanded more from her than the others. As her first job in charge, she was convinced of her ability to finish it successfully.

"I wish you would stop thinking about Stein," Donovan said. "I'd be happy to have five minutes alone with you without the job in your head."

His words stopped Rachel's thoughts in the middle of running the small details of the job through her mind. Donovan reached out his hand and lightly traced an unseen picture on Rachel's back. His touch tickled her bare skin and a small giggle left her lips.

She turned on her side to face him and lowered her left cheek onto the cool pillowcase. His eyes focused on his fingers as they danced over her arm, but Rachel kept her eyes on his face. "I'm not thinking about Stein. I'm thinking about you."

Donovan raised his eyes to meet hers, his fingers not stopping their movements. The corner of his mouth turned upward. "Don't lie to me," he said.

Rachel grinned. "I'm only lying a little bit."

He lifted the sheet away from her skin and lowered it down to her hip. His eyes and fingers followed the exposed curves of her body.

Her skin prickled with his touch. "Let's not talk about Stein now," she said.

"It's a big job," he said.

"They are all big jobs."

"We have serious bidders on this one. Lots of serious bidders." His hand stopped moving and he caught her eyes with his. "Twenty million dollars, Rachel. This will be the biggest job we've ever done with a single piece. I've wanted this one for years. And, now, it's just sitting in a safe, waiting for you."

Rachel recognized the childlike light in his eyes. Not too many things sparked that in him, and Rachel was always glad to see him come to life. The stern, businessman side of him was present all too often in his day-to-day activities. If he didn't need his company to mask the occupation he loved, she knew he wouldn't hesitate to sell the company and do these types of jobs full time.

The double life was wearing on him, Rachel noted as she studied his face. Lines radiated from the corners of his eyes and a few gray hairs trespassed on his five o'clock shadow. She stroked the side of his face, the scruffy texture both rough and seductive against her fingers. She loved the feel of his face when he hadn't shaved in a couple of days.

"If this job doesn't go right, I could lose a lot of contacts, not to mention future work," he added.

"I thought you didn't want me to worry about the job."

"Okay, so maybe I'm worried, too." He tucked her hair behind her ear, and his thumb created intimate sensations along her cheek. "Even though I have my best girl on it and I know she's going to come through for me, it's still a lot of pressure."

"Tell you what," she said. "I'll stop worrying if you do." She moved toward him until her body pressed against his skin. She moistened her lips and pulled the sheet back up to cover them both.

"You have a deal," he said, tangling his hands in her hair. He pressed his mouth to hers and took both of their minds off the job.

Chapter Forty-four

Rachel fought off another yawn, as she had all day. It was a seemingly losing battle, just like trying to hide the dark circles under her eyes with a bit of concealer. Donovan had stayed in her room too late, giving her only a few hours of sleep. She wouldn't have minded so much if she didn't have the Stein job to finish.

Paul never scheduled her for rounds the same day of a job, and the time off provided her with a much-needed break to align her thoughts. She spent the last few hours of her day alone in her room with Donovan. The time with him helped calm her nerves, even though they shot right back up when she left the estate for the job.

Getting into the house was easy enough. The Steins left for a three-month trip to Canada two weeks earlier. Dennis Stein was an up-and-coming director who started filming a highly anticipated movie, one that was predicted to launch his career into Oscar territory. Rachel did not care much about the film or Dennis Stein's directorial abilities. She only cared that the movie would take the Steins away from their home for an extended period of time.

Normally, Sylvia Stein would not go with her husband. The past several months, however, the tabloids took extreme interest in an exposed affair with a young actor that starred in her husband's last film. The fallout was Dennis Stein now kept his wife close at bay, monitoring her every move rather than go through a messy Hollywood-style divorce.

Sylvia's toy dogs went with them on the trip, so there were no animals with which to contend. Access into the home resulted from hard labor. Javier, one of Graham Wilkes's best men, snagged a position with the gardening crew that worked at the home. He was in the position three months before the job, so as not to have fingers pointed at him when the painting disappeared from the safe.

Since the gardeners tended to the large mansion while the Steins were on the movie set in Canada, Javier set it up so Rachel and her crew could get onto the grounds. From there, Rachel disarmed the security alarm.

Rachel and Paul entered the home undetected, while Tony waited in the car to keep an eye on the outside. The only part of the job she couldn't control was the security guard. With only thirty minutes in between each security check, they had to get in and out with no delays.

The hardest and most time-consuming part of the job involved the safe. While it should have been quick and easy to open, Donovan's constant reminders of all the bidders he had lined up for the painting echoed in her mind while she worked. Gloves clinging to her moist palms, Rachel pushed Donovan out of her mind and turned the dial on the safe.

Paul stood in the doorway of the study, scanning the hallway as a safety precaution. Rachel had another member of Wilkes's crew loop the security tape that monitored the interior and exterior of the home, so none of their movements were caught on camera. Still, she concerned herself with time and wanted to get into the safe so they could make a hasty exit and go back to the estate.

Rachel did her best to block out Paul's presence. Through her stethoscope, she listened for the distinctive clicks that gave away the safe's secrets. She counted each click as naturally as she could recite the alphabet.

The safe proved a bit more difficult than most, but Rachel assumed her nerves to be the reason. After a few amateur mistakes brought on by the immense pressure of the job, Rachel heard the last click in her stethoscope. She pulled on the safe's handle and took the stethoscope out of her ears.

"Took you long enough," Paul said from behind her. "I thought we'd be here all night."

"I'd like to see you do it next time," she said, opening the door. Expecting to see a twenty million dollar painting the Steins recently acquired, only darkness peered back at her. She blinked a few times, but the painting did not appear. She drew a sharp breath. "No."

"What is it?"

"The safe." She turned around, and panic set in. "The safe is empty."

Paul laughed, and he walked into the study. "Very funny." He moved behind Rachel and looked into the safe. His face sobered. "Where's the painting?"

Rachel's breathing sharpened. "It's supposed to be here," she said. "Where is it?"

"Is there another safe?" Paul asked.

"There's only one safe, and the security tape showed they put the painting in there before they left for Canada." She closed her eyes. "What are we going to do? We can't go back empty-handed."

Paul didn't respond.

Her radio gave off a series of beeps, letting her know it was time to leave. "We stopped taping two days ago to run the loop," Rachel said. "Someone who knew we ran that loop must have come in during the last two days. We've been set up."

"Rachel, we have to get out of here. If you're right about a setup, cops could be here any minute."

She continued staring into the safe. "No, there's got to be something we're missing here. We can't leave without that painting."

"Come on, Rachel." He grabbed her arm and pulled her up. She shut the safe and spun the dial. They moved through the house, erasing all evidence of their intrusion on the way to their predetermined exit.

They reached the car less than three minutes later and right on schedule. Tony waited for them in the car with the engine running. "What happened?" he asked, as he jerked the car away from the curb. "Where is it?"

"Don't worry about it," Paul said, and fastened his seatbelt.

Rachel remained silent in the back seat. Her hands wrung the straps of the black duffel bag that carried her equipment. She ran the job through her mind to figure out who knew enough of their plan to get in the house after the tape was looped. All she could think was it didn't matter who did it. Donovan would not be happy with her when they returned.

"What's going on?" Tony asked. "Where the hell is the painting?"

"It wasn't there," Paul said. "Just shut up and get us the hell out of here."

Tony dug his cell phone out of his jacket pocket. "We've got to call Donovan," he said.

Paul grabbed Tony's cell phone out of his hands. "Damn it, Tony, just drive! He'll find out when we get back." Paul twisted around in his seat to face her. "Don't worry, kid. Everything's okay. We'll simply tell Donovan what happened and he'll understand. This was out of our control."

"No," she said. "I'll talk to Donovan by myself."

"I can't let you do that."

"I have to. It was my job and it's my responsibility. I'll talk to him."

Chapter Forty-five

Rachel's stomach dropped to the floor when Tony pulled the car through the estate's front gates and down the long road leading to the circular driveway. The three-hour drive back to the estate had flown by, and she still had no answers about what went wrong.

She remained planted in the backseat of the car after Tony turned off the engine. Paul opened her door and held his hand out to help her. Rachel waved off his gesture and climbed out of the car.

"Rach, it's not your fault," Paul said. "Any one of us could have headed up the job. You did everything right and you had it all planned down to the last detail."

"Donovan won't care about that," she said. She handed him her duffel bag. "We don't have the painting. That's all that will matter to him."

"Let me go with you to talk to him," Paul said again, as he had several times on their drive home.

Rachel ignored him and walked up the stone steps to the front doors of the estate, with Paul and Tony on her heels.

Eric greeted her when she entered the house. His thin lips twisted into a smirk, he arched his eyebrows. "How did your first big job go?" he asked.

His sarcastic tone and haughty expression told her exactly what went wrong with her job. Eric was behind the missing painting. Every muscle in her body tensed and rage took over. Her fist smashed into his jaw.

Paul wrapped his arms around a red-faced Eric before he could retaliate. Tony grabbed Rachel's arm and shouted at her to calm down.

"You sabotaged my job!"

"Oh really?" Eric asked, as he continued leering at her. "How did I do that if I wasn't there?"

"I don't know how, but you did," Rachel said. "We both know it was you."

"Where's your proof?" Eric laughed. "Of course you don't have any. Maybe you're not old enough to handle a job by yourself. You never would have taken the lead on this one if you weren't King's personal call girl."

She lunged at him again, but Tony pulled her back. "That has nothing to do with it! I got this job on my own!"

"What is going on?"

Rachel turned toward the hard, angry voice. Donovan stood at the edge of the foyer, his hands shoved in his pockets, eyes narrowed toward Eric.

"Looks like your prodigy isn't all she claims to be," Eric said. "She returned sans painting."

Rachel bit her lip to stop herself from saying something she would regret. She didn't want to lose control in front of Donovan.

"Rachel?" Donovan's cold stare went right through her. "Is this true?"

"The painting was missing when I opened the safe." She couldn't stop the words from leaving her tongue. "But Eric knew about it before we said the painting was gone. He must have had something to do with it."

"Rachel, come to the library," Donovan said.

Rachel kept her eyes on Eric, waiting for him to say something to give away his role in the botched job. But, Eric only arched an eyebrow at her and pursed his lips in victory, incensing her all the more.

"Now, Rachel," Donovan said.

Tony let go of her arm and she stormed into the library. Donovan shut the doors behind them. "What happened tonight?"

"The safe was empty."

"And what does this have to do with Eric?"

"He sabotaged the job."

"Do you have proof of that?"

His firm tone stopped her cold and removed all confidence behind her suspicion of Eric. "No, but he—"

"Let me get this straight. You brought back nothing and you attacked him because you think he sabotaged the job, but you have no proof?"

"I don't need proof, damn it," she said. "I know he sabotaged me."

Rachel barely registered Donovan's hand flying out. One moment she was standing, the next she was sprawled out on the ground. The involuntary tears that jumped out of her eyes at the second of impact streaked down her face. She lifted a jittery hand to her burning cheek.

"You were in charge," Donovan said from somewhere above her. "You are the one who is responsible for this twenty million dollar mess."

Her voice was reduced to a whisper. “I swear I didn’t screw it up. The painting should have been there.”

“It should have been, but it wasn’t. An empty safe is your fault, not Eric’s. He wasn’t there, nor was he involved in the planning of the job so he couldn’t have done anything to sabotage you.”

The pounding in her head raced against her heart and she covered her mouth with her hands. He had never been angry with her before, had never even raised his voice to her. Why would he hit her? Didn’t he love her?

“Stand up,” Donovan said.

Rachel forced herself to her feet and stood before him, her spine curved, shoulders slumped, head bowed. She rolled her eyes toward his face and the ice from his stare found its way into her veins.

“Not one of you has ever come back empty-handed,” he said. “Not one of you has ever screwed up a job. If it were anyone else, I would think they were stealing from me. This will never happen again. And, you will never attack another person on this estate. Is that understood?”

Rachel’s chin quivered and she forced out the words. “Yes, Donovan. I understand.”

“I have to make some phone calls and explain why I don’t have that painting.” He stopped beside her on his way out. “I am very disappointed in you, Rachel.”

As soon as he shut the library door, Rachel collapsed to the floor and hid her face in her hands.

Chapter Forty-six

Rachel sat under her favorite oak tree, her arms linked around her knees. Her sun-streaked hair fell loose around her shoulders, one side tucked behind her ear. She stuck out her lower lip and blew upward to get the hair out of her eyes once more.

She usually pulled her hair back to keep the wind from blowing it in her eyes while on rounds, but the past few days, she wore it down. The hair falling over her ear and cheek concealed the discoloration toward the back of her jaw. The bruise covered the same area of skin the first bruise did, the one that appeared after he struck her in the library four years earlier.

That night in the library still seemed like a bad dream. After a restless night of wondering what went wrong so fast, Donovan visited her while the rest of the estate dreamed about more pleasant things. His apologies had been sincere enough, his explanation more than plausible.

With the painting missing from the safe, Donovan spent the entire night doing damage control with his bidders. Promises had to be made to each of them, who had come to expect so much more from him. There was more than she realized riding on that painting, and the pressure overwhelmed him. When she snapped at him, he momentarily lost control, and he was sorry that he took it out on her.

Rachel forgave him, understanding she had caught him off-guard during a stressful moment in time, for which she took responsibility. As he apologized, she knew better than to bring up her running conspiracy theory about Eric sabotaging the job. Donovan hadn't believed her the night before, and there was no reason to raise his blood pressure again.

For the next several months, they were back to being in love and eternally happy. And then, it happened again. Another stressful moment where she said the wrong thing at the wrong time. A couple months later, another punch, another plausible explanation, another sincere apology.

Instead of the violence being predictable, it turned sporadic, and she never knew what might send him into a fury. Sometimes months would go by without an incident, other times it was hours. Without warning, rage flashed in his eyes and turned him into the monster that was taking over the man she loved. For the next few years, Rachel's feet glided over eggshells, but it didn't matter how carefully she stepped. She always managed to rouse the monster.

Footsteps caused her to look up, and she managed a smile as Paul approached her. She never spoke to Paul about the anger inside Donovan, and he never asked her about it. The bruises were as secretive as her initial relationship with Donovan.

After the first time Donovan hit her four years ago, she learned the importance of leaving her hair down, of placing a hand or a clump of hair over part of her face when someone passed by. Other times, when someone caught a glimpse of a bruise, she made up stories to explain it away. Learning to lie and hide was easier than facing the truth.

She would do anything to keep Paul in the dark, even if it meant dealing with her hair flying in her face during her rounds. As fearful as she was becoming of Donovan, Rachel was more afraid Paul would someday talk to her about the bruises.

Rachel pushed another cluster of renegade strands away from her eyes and greeted Paul. She lifted her fingers to make sure her hair was still in camouflage mode. As an additional safety measure, she propped her elbow up on her knee and hovered her hand over her bruised cheek like a shield.

Paul gestured at her black short sleeve shirt and black pants. Her radio was clipped on her belt, and her gun secured in a shoulder holster, the standard outfit she wore to patrol the grounds. "You don't have rounds for another hour," he said. "Are you enjoying this wonderful summer day, or are you out here for a reason?"

"Daydreaming, I guess."

He lowered himself into the soft grass next to her and leaned against the tree. "I hope it's at least a good one."

"Maybe." She squinted her eyes and studied his hair. "What is this?" she asked. She put her hands in his hair and looked for the culprit.

"What?"

"Hold still." She pinched a short hair between her fingertips and yanked it out of the side of his head.

"Ouch!"

"It didn't hurt that bad." She examined the thin strand of hair. "You have a gray hair."

"I do not. Let me see." He took the hair from her and threw it down after examining it. "Thank you. You've ruined my day."

"Oh, it's one little gray hair, old man," Rachel said.

"Are there any other aging imperfections you'd like to point out?"

Rachel pressed her lips together to stop the smile as she took in his receding hairline. "Nope, just the gray hair."

He looked off in the distance. "I guess we can't stay young forever."

"Tell me about it," Rachel said, echoing Paul's melancholy.

"What are you complaining about? You're only twenty-three to my forty-six."

"Yeah, but twenty-three feels pretty old to someone who's never been that age before."

Paul paused as he thought about it. "I guess I can understand that. So what are you doing out here, old maid?"

"I'm trying to figure out what it's like out there." She waved her hand in front of her.

"Well, there are lots of trees and the ground is still a little soft from that rain we got yesterday."

She scowled. "That's not what I'm talking about. I've been here for thirteen years. I don't remember what life is like beyond the estate's fences. Tell me something about that world."

He smiled, caught in a memory. "It was a good one when Maria was alive."

Surprised by his statement, Rachel turned her body to face him. Paul rarely mentioned his deceased wife. "You loved her a lot, didn't you?"

"It's too bad you were so young when she died. I wish you could have known her better. She was the most wonderful woman in the world." He swatted her arm with the back of his hand. "Next to you, of course."

Rachel allowed a smile at his compliment. "Did you ever want to find someone else?"

"I often wondered what my life would have been like if she had lived, but from the moment I saw her, I never wanted anyone else besides her."

Another fairy tale, Rachel thought. Paul lived for one woman and one woman only, even if she was no longer alive. He would never stray from Maria as long as he breathed. Rachel wondered if Donovan felt the same way about her. Aloud she said, "People my age are out there falling in love, getting married, starting families."

"Do you want that?"

When Rachel was eighteen and starting her relationship with Donovan, she would have answered yes to that question without doubt or hesitation. Even after the first several times he hit her, maybe even up until a few months ago, she still would have answered yes.

She wanted to tell Paul she welcomed all of that with Donovan, but something held her back. She had spent many nights wondering if this was the way all relationships were. Thinking back on her parents, she never knew her dad to touch her mom except out of love. She wondered if her mom hid the bad parts of their marriage from Rachel, the way Rachel hid her bruises from Paul.

Still, she thought Donovan loved her as much as she loved him, even though he hurt her sometimes. After each outburst, he always showed her how much he loved her, and he was always so sorry. He would tell her it wasn't her fault, and he would never hurt her again.

At first, she believed him. Now, she was simply confused. She lived her life bracing herself for his next attack, knowing it could come at any time. It didn't matter whether he was angry with her or if they had just spent hours in each other's arms. Inevitably, he would hit her again.

"I don't know what I want," she said. "I wonder if my life was supposed to turn out like this. If it were preordained that I would live here on the estate forever and never have a normal life."

"Having what people out there call a normal life is impossible here, isn't it?"

"Can you imagine? 'Sorry I can't make it to dinner, honey, but I have to drive all the way to Sacramento and take out this target. Don't wait up.' I don't think it would go over too well."

Paul laughed with her. "No, it wouldn't." After a moment of silence, he asked, "Do you want to tell me what this is really about?"

Her smile faded. What could she tell him? There were so many things she could say. She could tell him how the guilt from the jobs was destroying her. With every safe she opened, with every person she killed, she felt as if the devil himself had broken away another piece of her soul for his gnawing pleasure.

She could tell him about Eric and how much she disliked him. How she avoided him as much as possible, and ignored the snide comments tossed her way if caught alone with him. At times his words were beyond crude, when he told her exactly why she would love spending time alone with him in his room. The looks he gave her, as if he stripped away her clothing every time he saw her, made her shudder with disgust and a bit of fear.

After her accusations that he sabotaged her job, she couldn't tell Donovan anything he said. Eric would deny it, and Donovan would assume she was trying to undermine Eric. Her aggravation with Eric had built to the point that she thought at any moment she could snap and either take her frustrations out on him or just plain kill him.

She could tell Paul her relationship with Donovan didn't resemble a single fairy tale her mother had told her. She wanted to get back to the way things used to be before the night he hit her in the library. She longed for the times when he would hold her in the early morning hours, or sneak kisses around the estate when they thought no one was watching. Back then, she didn't jump at his slightest move.

"Rachel?" Paul asked.

She looked at Paul's tired face. She wouldn't tell him anything. She never did. Paul had enough on his mind without having to worry about her problems. They were so minor anyway: not being able to stomach her work, Eric's jealous outbursts, Donovan's tendencies toward violence. She could handle it.

She opened her mouth to once again tell Paul that life was perfect. "I don't think Donovan loves me," she said.

Paul wrapped his arm around her and she rested her head on his shoulder. He brushed back her hair and kissed the top of her head. "Honey, he loves you in his own way, but he's not good at showing it. In fact, he sucks pretty badly in that department. The question is, do you love him?"

"I'm not even sure what that means anymore. I thought I did, but now I feel more like his mistress than anything else." The uninvited words flowed without thought, spilling out from the dark place inside where she hid her fears from the rest of the world.

Rachel lifted her head, her mouth twisted into a frown. "And sometimes I feel like a prisoner to this place. The only time I'm allowed to leave is for a job. I'm twenty-three years old and I don't even know how to drive a car. I couldn't leave on my own if I wanted to." Rachel hesitated, and she drew a deep breath. "No one's ever told me I can't leave, but it's unspoken, isn't it? 'Rachel doesn't leave by herself.' Why is that?"

Paul appeared unfazed by her rant, as if he expected it. "You're the only one who didn't know the stakes when you came here. Every one of us came to the estate knowing what we were giving up and what was expected of us. We all had our own reasons for leaving that life behind." He gestured toward the boundaries of the estate. He lowered his voice and looked at her. "You know how it is here, Rachel."

She closed her eyes and rubbed her forehead, the reality that she had always tried to avoid washing over her. She *was* predestined to spend her life here. She would never know the world outside of the estate.

It was time for her to forget the fairy tales her mother told her. In real life, Cinderella never went to the ball; her hands were always too dirty from her work. And, in real life, Prince Charming fell off his white horse and snapped his neck before he could rescue the princess.

"You were a child when I brought you here," Paul said. "You had no idea what it was like or what you were giving up. If you had known, would you have come here willingly?"

Rachel thought about his question, but was afraid to respond. She didn't want to admit she doubted everything she ever knew. Instead of answering him, she said, "You never told me why you came here. I remember you were a doctor and Aunt Maria died, but how did you meet Donovan?"

"I met him because Maria died." He paused for a long moment and stared off in front of him. "Do you remember when Maria and I used to take you to church?"

Rachel searched the depths of her mind. She saw a vague image of a petite, dark-haired woman standing next to a much younger Paul, but no distinct memories came with the picture. "No, I don't remember that," she said.

"I didn't think so. You were only five when she died, and six when I left to come here. Maria and I attended church every Sunday. Even though we lived in Los Angeles at the time, we went to San Diego every few weeks for a visit and we took you to church with us. We were both active in our church. Maria was in the choir."

"You never told me she could sing," Rachel said.

A wistful smile crossed Paul's face. "She had an angel's voice, like God Himself sang through her. We taught Bible studies to the younger kids after church every Sunday. We even read the Bible and prayed together every night. I don't suppose your dad ever took you to church after I left, did he?"

"I went with a friend of mine a couple of times, but that was it. Mom and Dad never cared much about going to church."

"Our parents were religious, but your dad didn't carry it with him into adulthood. Your dad was named after the apostle Luke and I was named after Paul. Do you know the Bible story about Paul?"

"I think I've heard it before, but I can't remember what it's about."

"Then here's a quick Sunday school lesson. There was this real mean guy named Saul who spent his time persecuting Christians in the early church. He'd round them up and jail them or take them off to be killed.

"One day, when traveling on a road that led to Damascus, he saw this light from Heaven. Then Jesus spoke to him. He told Saul to stop persecuting Christians. The experience blinded Saul. After three days, he could see again, both physically and spiritually. He became one of the most famous Christians of all time and his name was changed to Paul. That's the gist of the story, anyway.

"Before Maria died, I worked at the hospital and Maria was getting her Master's degree in psychology. We held off on having kids mainly because she wanted to finish college first, but we made up for it by spoiling you."

Rachel smiled at the thought. "You're probably making that up since I don't remember so well," she said.

"Trust me, your dad was always upset with all the presents we brought you on our visits, especially the ones that made lots of noise." Paul's smile faded. "One night, Maria walked out to her car from the campus library and this guy jumped her. He forced her out to a wooded area right by the library.

Raped her and left her there. At some point during the struggle, he smashed her head against a rock. Her…"

Paul abruptly stopped speaking and swallowed hard. Rachel placed a reassuring hand on his arm, and he continued the story. "Her brain swelled until there was no more room left. They did emergency surgery, but she had a seizure and went into a coma. Three months later, I had her removed from life support and she died. Being a doctor, I knew she wouldn't survive, but I couldn't let her go. So I kept her like that, and prayed for a miracle. She never regained consciousness."

All these years, Rachel never knew how Maria died, and now she understood why her parents had not told her.

"Her rapist was caught two days after the attack," Paul said. "He was seen on the security cameras that were in the library and around campus, so the police had an easy time tracking him down. He claimed he was so strung out on a cocaine-heroin speedball mixed with Jack Daniels that he didn't know what he was doing.

"The prosecutor charged him while Maria was still on life support, and he pled guilty to attempted murder. They dropped the rape charges in exchange for a plea bargain. He wasn't charged with her murder because, out of purely selfish reasons, I left her on life support so long. Since it was his first offense, the judge gave him one year of rehab for his drug addiction followed by another couple of years in prison." Fury doused Paul's voice. "He raped my wife and left her to die, and they patted him on the back and told him it was okay because he was stoned."

Rachel brushed the tears off her cheeks. She could tell by the tone of his voice that he still blamed himself for the events that followed Maria's death. He had no way of predicting that by holding out hope for her recovery, he also paved the way for her killer to get off easy. Rachel wanted to console him, but no words could take away the pain etched deep in his soul.

"After the sentencing," Paul said, "I went out to her grave. As I was leaving, this man approached me. I recognized him from being in the courtroom during the sentencing hearing, but I had no idea who he was. He introduced himself as Donovan King, and told me he wanted to talk about the criminal justice system. Of course I was full of opinions about justice, plus I was curious why he was so interested in the case, so I had a few drinks with him. Mind you, I didn't drink back then, but after Maria's death I did a lot of things I normally wouldn't have.

"After a few shots and lots of whisky, Donovan had my attention. He was only twenty-three at the time, but he was much like he is now: smart, knows what he's doing, and confident as anything. He could charm a starving lion out of a meal if he wanted."

Rachel early on learned that side of Donovan. He had charmed her on her first day at the estate and hadn't stopped since. The same charm drew her back into his arms no matter how many times she was on the receiving end of his temper.

"Donovan told me about Graham Wilkes," Paul said. "It turned out the guy who killed Maria was into Wilkes big time. He owed him more money than he could ever repay since he was going to be put away for a bit, so Wilkes wanted him dead to send a message. Donovan asked me if I'd like to do it, and if I'd like to come work for him as the head of his onsite security team, as well as provide onsite medical care when needed. In exchange, everything I could ever need or want would be taken care of for the rest of my life. I didn't hesitate."

Paul shrugged. "I guess sometimes justice can only come at the end of a loaded gun. At least that was my rationale back then. Your dad and I argued about my career change, so I left on bad terms. I remember though that I brought you this big book of fairy tales as kind of a going away present."

"I loved that book," Rachel said. "Every time I read it, I thought of you and hoped you were coming back to visit soon."

"I think the hardest thing about the whole deal was leaving you, but what an offer." He locked eyes with her. "You see, Rachel, Saul turned into Paul when Jesus appeared to him. I started out as Paul and turned into Saul when the devil appeared to me in the form of Donovan King."

A chill coursed through her body as she considered his analogy. "If you could go back in time, would you still do it?" she asked.

"Every time. But, if I could go back, I never would have brought you here."

Rachel contemplated his words. When she spoke, her voice was almost a whisper. "I know I love Donovan, and I know he loves me. I just always thought there was more."

Chapter Forty-seven

Paul had witnessed Rachel's deterioration over the past four years, since the night of the failed job. It was like watching the slow decay of a live corpse, and he had done nothing to help her.

Not anymore.

He moved with purpose up the winding staircase, and made his way down the long, darkened hallway. Halfway down the hall, he opened the door to Donovan's office without knocking.

Donovan looked up, more with curiosity than surprise, his cellphone pressed to his ear. "Let me call you back," he said into the receiver. After he set his phone down on the desk, he asked, "What's wrong?"

"We need to talk," Paul said.

"This couldn't wait?"

"It's already waited long enough."

Donovan motioned to the chair on the other side of his desk, but Paul waved his hand. "I'll make it quick. Rachel's questioning things."

Donovan leaned back in his chair. "What things?"

"Like why she's living in a prison. Why she doesn't ever leave the estate unless she has a job."

"Paul, we talked about this before she came here."

"I know, and I understand why it was necessary back then, but she's an adult now. I don't think it's a risk for her to leave as long as it's controlled and kept to a minimum."

"You brought a child, a ten-year old girl to the estate. Business had to remain intact, without her disturbing it, so we trained her as an employee. If you recall, that was your solution to the problem, not mine."

"Yes, that was my idea," Paul said. "So far it's worked out just fine."

"I agree that it has worked, but she came here on the condition that she would not leave. It was way too risky and would raise questions. I couldn't put our operation in jeopardy. I did the best I could given the circumstances, and I wouldn't have done it for anyone else but you."

"And I appreciate that," Paul said. "It was a difficult time for all of us, but I had the responsibility as her only living relative to care for her. I didn't see any other way of handling it. I couldn't leave her to the system, jumping around from foster home to foster home with no promise of stability. People don't adopt 10-year olds, they just don't."

"Which is why I agreed to your suggestion to bring her here, but only with those conditions," Donovan said.

"But now she's grown. Prior to her arrival, we never discussed what would happen when she became an adult."

"That's true and I understand your concern, but I don't know how good of an idea it is to let her start leaving after so long. At least not yet."

Paul knew he was getting through. He placed his hands on the desk and leaned forward. "Rachel loves you. She's dependent on you and looks to you for everything she needs. She trusts you, and she's given her entire life to you." Paul lowered his voice. "She's human, Donovan. Flesh and bone."

"I know."

"She has emotions and dreams that can be crushed."

Donovan remained silent, his eyes fixed on the desk.

Paul's vision blurred with tears and his body trembled with his words. "She bleeds, too."

"I know that!"

After a tense moment, Donovan rose. Paul took a step back, once again struck by Donovan's powerful presence. If the man walked into a room full of marines, they would all stand up a little straighter in the shadow of his authoritative stature.

Yet Paul knew there were many facets to Donovan King outside of his public one. Over the years, he had witnessed the different personalities of Donovan, all coming from the same shell, all as varied as the shapes of snowflakes.

Donovan braced his hands on the edge of his desk, his face rigid. Without looking up, he asked, "What is it that you want me to do?"

Paul flinched. This was the first time he had seen Donovan humbled to the point of asking another for direction. A surge of hope rushed into Paul's heart. "Senator Cal Robbins is hosting a dinner at his home next week. I think you should take Rachel."

"I'm leaving for Seattle that afternoon."

"Reschedule your meetings," Paul said.

A twitch in Donovan's jaw revealed his otherwise imperceptible debate, but he did not respond.

Paul decided to press the issue. "For Rachel."

Donovan lifted his eyes. The edge of his voice was unusually soft, regretful, and apologetic. "I never meant to fall in love with her." He sat back down and reached for his phone, his actions dismissing Paul.

Chapter Forty-eight

Rachel looked up when Donovan came through her bedroom door. She placed a bookmark in her book and closed it. "I thought you had to go to Seattle," she said, as she hopped off the bed. She laid the compilation of Edgar Allen Poe stories down on her dresser and walked over to him.

"The meetings were rescheduled." He tucked a strand of hair behind her ear and twirled the ends of it between his fingers. "I know it's short notice, but do you think you can be dressed and ready to go in an hour?"

Rachel tilted her head. "I suppose that's a possibility. Is there a last minute job?"

"Senator Cal Robbins is hosting a dinner at his estate tonight." Donovan paused before adding, "I would like to take you as my date."

"I'll be ready," she said, her eyes brightening.

"Then I'll see you upstairs in one hour." He gave her a quick kiss before leaving her room.

Paralyzed by Donovan's visit, Rachel remained still until it fully registered in her mind what he said. She was going to leave the estate for something other than a job for the first time in thirteen years. More than that, Donovan was taking her out on an actual date, in public, surrounded by his peers.

Rachel's feet had trouble keeping up with her legs as she sprinted out her door and down the hall. The sides of her fists banged on Paul's door. "Paul!" she called. "Paul!"

"I'm coming," he said.

"Hurry up!"

He opened the door. His rumpled hair and wrinkled clothes told her she interrupted a late afternoon nap. "Rachel, honey, you know I love you, but this had better be important. I was having the best dream."

"No time for that. I'm going with Donovan to a dinner for Senator Robbins."

Paul smiled knowingly.

Rachel's eyes widened. "You talked to Donovan, didn't you?"

"Don't question it, Rach. Accept it and enjoy it."

"I only have one hour to get ready! You have to help me. I have nothing to wear!"

"Okay, okay. Calm down. Everything is already taken care of for you. Let's go make you beautiful."

Forty-five minutes later, she was dressed and ready to go. Paul stood at a distance and watched Claudia squirt hairspray over Rachel's head. Rachel squirmed and wrinkled her nose at the mist that showered her neck and shoulders.

"All done," Claudia said. Paul and Rachel thanked her, and she left the room with a basket full of makeup and hair supplies.

Rachel walked into the bathroom and took in her reflection. The slit of the long, black evening gown tastefully stopped just above her knee, and the neckline of the sleeveless top fell several inches below her collarbone without being too revealing. A sheer, black scarf wrapped loosely around her neck and traveled down her spine to her lower back.

Rachel patted the French twist on the back of her head, and turned her head to the side to see the profile of her hair. Satisfied with what she saw, Rachel couldn't resist bobbing the tendrils of hair bordering her face.

"Much better than the last dress you wore," Paul said when she waltzed back into the bedroom.

"I don't even recognize myself."

"You look exactly like your mother."

Tears formed in her eyes at the thought. "How did you manage to pull this off?"

"A magician never reveals his secrets. But, I've had the damn dress on hand for nearly a week waiting for Donovan to decide he was taking you."

She hugged him. "You're amazing."

"No, you're amazing." He held her away from him. "Like Cinderella going to the ball."

"Then you must be my fairy godmother."

He frowned at her. "Enough analogies." He walked her to the foot of the stairs.

"Thank you, Paul."

"I'm going back to bed. I'm beat and I have a great dream waiting for me. Have a great time." He gave her a wink before walking away.

Rachel moved up the stairs and into the foyer, where Donovan stood wearing a black tuxedo. She had never seen him so dressed up, and her heart skipped a few beats before racing out of control. She was like Cinderella going to the ball. She only hoped that there would be many more to come.

Donovan let out a low whistle and looked her over. "You are absolutely breathtaking," he said. "Everyone will have their eyes on you tonight."

"But I'll only have my eyes on you," Rachel said. She moved closer to him, and he encircled her with his arms. His lips found hers and, for a moment, Rachel thought they might not make it to the dinner after all. When the kiss broke, a large smile overcame her.

"As beautiful as you are, something is missing," Donovan said. He walked over to the table in the foyer and opened the drawer. When he turned around, he had a large black jewelry box in his hands.

Rachel gasped with surprise when she raised the lid of the box. Inside was a silver colored necklace with three large diamonds seated in a delicate, lace-like design.

"The necklace is platinum," Donovan said, "so it won't damage easily. The diamonds are each a full carat. I know it's not a lot, but I didn't think you'd want something too fancy."

Rachel raised her eyes to meet his and smiled innocently, unable to speak.

Donovan chuckled. "You don't have any idea what that means, do you?"

"None at all," she said.

"It's a one-of-a-kind necklace. I had it designed for you. I thought you would like something simple, yet elegant at the same time. It needed to at least match your beauty."

Rachel couldn't take her eyes off him. At that moment, he had shown her more love than he had in the entire five years of their affair. She wanted so much to tell him that she loved him, but she was afraid he wouldn't say it in return. He had not said it before, and there was no reason for her to believe he would say it now. Not wanting to ruin the night, she instead said, "Thank you so much. It's gorgeous."

"I'm glad you like it," he said. He took the box from her hands. "Let me help you with this." He walked behind Rachel and untied her black scarf. He handed her the scarf and box to hold while he secured the necklace around her neck. Rachel gave him back the scarf, and one hand instinctively reached for the necklace. It fit on her neck like it was part of her.

After he finished retying her scarf, she turned around to face him. "It's perfect," he said. He reached up and touched her right earlobe. "If you had your ears pierced, I would have gotten you matching earrings. We may have to fix that."

"No one has ever given me something so amazing or thoughtful."

"You deserve nothing but the best," he said. "Speaking of which, the limousine is waiting outside for us. We better not keep the driver waiting too long."

Rachel smiled, and her fingers continued their inspection of the necklace. She took his hand and they made their way to the front door, the sheer, black scarf trailing after her.

Chapter Forty-nine

Rachel's lips remained glued into a smile for the entire drive. When they reached their destination, her eyes widened at the sight. The limousine followed a lighted circular drive and stopped near the front of a white French Colonial mansion behind several other limousines.

Donovan took her hand and squeezed it. As they waited their turn to get out of the limousine, she took in the luxury around them. She turned to Donovan. "This is amazing."

Donovan laughed. "You haven't seen anything yet."

"Is his house bigger than yours?"

"Ours," he said. "You live there, too. Yes, his house is much bigger than ours. I imagine if the estate wasn't my parents' home, I would have had one as large as his, but that would be showing off, I suppose. I'm content in our house. I grew up there, so it's special to me."

"It's a great house," Rachel said. "Our house, that is."

"It's only great because you're there."

She smiled. "What's this dinner for?"

"Cal will most likely run for President in the next election. He's vetting his supporters, making sure we're aware he's still around, so when he comes asking for donations, he'll know who to come to first."

"Sounds like there will be a lot of important people there. Makes me a little nervous."

"Don't be nervous," he said. He turned his knees toward her and put his hands over hers. "Before we get up to the front, there are some minor points I want to go over with you. You've always handled yourself so well in strange situations, and I'm sure you'll do the same tonight. It is a little different, though. If you're unsure of which fork to use or how to eat something, watch me without drawing attention to yourself."

"There's more than one fork?" Rachel asked. "What about the spoon?"

Donovan chuckled. "Yes, there's more than one fork and more than one spoon. In fact, quite a few things on the place settings will have duplicates and even triplicates, each used for different things. If we'd had more time, I would have gone over this with you back at the estate."

"I think an etiquette lesson would have definitely come in handy," Rachel said.

"If you mimic what you see me do, then you'll survive the night without breaking too many fancy dinner party laws. One more thing. As we meet people at the party, you'll see some people whispering while they are looking at us. I know you can be self-conscious so I don't want you to think that they are talking negatively about you. They won't be. They'll be talking about me."

Rachel creased her forehead. "Why would they talk about you?"

"I have never brought a date to one of these gatherings. You will be a source of great interest to the busybodies there."

"I understand," Rachel said, somewhat untruthfully. She understood why they would talk about him, but could not comprehend that Donovan had never brought a date to a social event before tonight.

Before they became involved, she had spent many nights jealous while he was off at a soiree, always wondering if he had a beautiful woman on his arm. The revelation that he had not done that on even one occasion warmed Rachel's heart and made her realize how much she meant to him, even if it didn't seem like it at times.

"Rachel, I'm not so good at expressing my feelings," he said, as if he had read her mind. "I know that's a major flaw I have, among many other flaws."

Rachel tilted her head, unsure of where his words were heading.

"We have been together for so long now, and we will be for the rest of our lives. I know I've never expressed how I feel about you, and maybe it seems at times like I take you and our relationship for granted."

Butterflies flew around in Rachel's stomach so fast that it felt like they were trying to break out. "Donovan, I know how you feel about me."

"I also know how you feel about me. I don't think either of us have any questions about our feelings for each other, but I've never told you. I know that is something I need to do more often, so you always know how much you mean to me."

The limousine inched forward, and Rachel turned her head to see how close they were to the front of the line. There was only one other limo ahead of them, and she worried that their intimate conversation would be interrupted at any second.

She turned back to Donovan. "I don't need to hear you tell me how you feel about me," she said. "I don't want you to feel guilty about not saying it."

Donovan leaned in and gave her a quick kiss. He laid a hand on her cheek, his face close to hers. "Rachel, I love you. I have loved you for a very long time, and nothing will ever change that for me. I may not say it, but I don't ever want you to doubt that, no matter what. You're my life, you're everything I live for. I could never make it in this world without you."

Rachel fought off tears of joy, knowing they would only ruin Claudia's makeup. She had waited so long to hear those words, but she didn't want to seem too excited at the sound of them. She gave him another kiss, and said, "I love you, too, Donovan. I can't remember a time when I didn't love you. Nothing will ever change that for me, either, I promise. I'm yours forever." She pressed her mouth against his for one more kiss.

The limousine moved again and stopped in front of the walkway leading up to the house. "We're here," Donovan said. He squeezed her hand before letting go.

Rachel's door opened and she accepted the driver's extended hand. As she exited the limo, she looked past the driver at the house in amazement. Four white columns flanked a double set of French doors, and the glow from inside poured out onto the front steps. Donovan walked up beside Rachel, and she slid her arm through his.

A man in a white tuxedo and white gloves welcomed them at the top of the steps and opened the door. Rachel stepped onto the marble floor of the foyer, her eyes following the gentle curve of the staircase that opened up in front of them. Another tuxedo-clad man greeted them. They followed him down a long, winding hallway to an arched beveled glass door.

The door swung open, and Rachel held her breath with her first glimpse inside. A short flight of stairs led down to the dining area. Round tables covered with lace cloths filled the room, the lighting provided by crystal chandeliers suspended from the ceiling.

Donovan took Rachel's hand, and they walked to the railing above the large dining room. Guests mingled among the tables, gossiping and laughing. Some turned to look at the latest arrivals, and Rachel recognized the whispering Donovan warned her about. Soft orchestra music piped in from the other side of the room. Tables were absent in the center of the room, and Rachel imagined the area was reserved for dancing after dinner.

It was a fairy tale.

She felt Donovan's eyes on her, and she could not contain her large smile. "This is incredible."

"So are you, Rachel," he said. "So are you."

"Well, Donovan King!"

Rachel turned toward the voice. The man approaching them stood only a few inches taller than her. His bulbous nose and grandfather-like smile made her think of a younger version of Santa Claus.

He shook hands with Donovan. "We were taking bets earlier on whether you'd make it. I guess I lost." His hearty laugh filled the immediate area, and he rested his hands on his protruding stomach. He turned his attention to Rachel. "And who is this beautiful young lady you've brought to help light up the room tonight?"

"This is Rachel Pettis," Donovan said. "Rachel, I would like you to meet Senator Cal Robbins."

Senator Robbins took her hand and, to Rachel's surprise, brushed his lips against her knuckles. "It's wonderful to meet you, Rachel. I have a feeling you're the one to help this lifelong bachelor settle down."

"What's this rumor I hear about you running for President?" Donovan asked, in a quick attempt to change the subject.

"The election is over three years away and the rumor mill is already grinding." He shrugged. "Then again, maybe it never stopped grinding after last year's election."

"A lot of your constituents were very disappointed you didn't go for it then," Donovan said. "You know you'll win by a landslide, no matter who you're up against."

"Let's not get ahead of ourselves," Senator Robbins said. "I know there were some upset people, but they don't understand there is a time for everything and the last election was not my time. This next election, however, is a strong possibility. Becoming President has always been an ambition of mine."

"Well, you have my support, mostly financially, of course." The men shared a laughed.

"Thank you, sir. If I do this, I'll need all the support I can get, financial and otherwise." He cleared his throat. "Since we're on the subject of support, I'm glad to see you have someone here to keep you happy tonight."

"Why is that, Cal?"

"I hate to tell you this, but the idiot my assistant used to plan this little get together screwed up bad. You're seated at the same table as Jonathan Thomas, and it's much too late to change anything."

Donovan scowled. "And you wonder why I don't come to these things. If you'd given me the heads-up before we made the drive, I might have turned right back around."

"I'm truly sorry. If it makes you feel any better, he's not exactly thrilled about it, either. Who knows? Maybe you two will kiss and make up." He laughed again. "Rachel, my dear, I hope you have a wonderful evening, and that we get to meet again very soon. Try to keep this man out of trouble." He walked off to greet another guest.

Rachel looked at Donovan with only one thought in her mind. "Jonathan Thomas? As in Thomas Security?"

Donovan's smile disappeared, and he scanned the room. "That would be him. Are you ready to meet my biggest competitor and the one man I sincerely hate in this world?"

She took a deep breath and Donovan led her through the sea of people to a table near the front of the room. Four people sat around the table that contained their place cards. The two men stood as they approached, and the younger man smirked. "You actually showed. Cal thought you might not make it, which would have made tonight a bit easier given the unfortunate seating arrangements."

"Looks like I picked the wrong dinner to come to," Donovan said. "Of course you could always leave now and save us both the trouble."

"I wouldn't dream of giving you the pleasure of watching me cower away."

"Now, now," the older man said. "There will be no arguing tonight, not in front of such lovely women."

"Speaking of which, King, aren't you going to introduce your friend?" the younger man asked.

Donovan introduced Rachel to the other guests. The older man, Stanley Meade, had features more stereotypical of an aging schoolteacher, not a wealthy banker. His graying hair, hooked nose, and wiry stature reminded Rachel of her third-grade teacher. Stanley's wife, Vera, sat next to him wearing a bright violet dress with a scooped collar lined with faux fur. Several strands of oversized pearls adorned her plump neck.

Beside Vera sat their nineteen-year-old daughter, Kimberly, a rather pretty girl whose blonde locks, heart-shaped face, and blue eyes resembled neither her father nor mother. Her impatient expression and crossed arms informed the room that she resented being dragged to the dinner with her parents.

The younger of the two men was Jonathan Thomas. As much as Donovan disliked him, she expected a devilish looking man, but no horns jutted from his sandy brown hair. His light and playful expression contrasted Donovan's intense features, and his youthful face lacked the same lines that graced Donovan's eyes. Rachel chided herself for comparing the two men and for finding Jonathan attractive.

"So, Rachel," Jonathan began after they were seated.

Donovan interrupted before Jonathan could finish his thought. "I see you couldn't scrounge up a date tonight, Thomas. You might be losing your touch."

"Obviously you haven't. Where did someone like you manage to find someone like her?" Jonathan leaned in, a conspiratorial edge to his voice. "You didn't have to hire her, did you?"

Vera gasped and clutched her pearls, and Kimberly choked on her drink. Stanley took interest in the conversation and moved his chair closer to the table. Rachel was relieved Donovan didn't bring a gun with him, though, from his expression, she could tell he might just kill Jonathan with an instrument of opportunity.

Rachel didn't flinch at Jonathan's statement, having heard much worse from Eric over the years. "Actually, he did hire me," she said to Jonathan. Donovan grabbed her hand under the table as a warning, but she ignored him. "But you know, he's such a gentleman that I might throw in the sex for free."

Stanley failed to stifle a laugh, while Vera fanned herself and Kimberly pretended to ignore the exchange. Donovan squeezed Rachel's hand and a satisfied grin took control of his mouth.

Jonathan raised an eyebrow and a smile tugged at his lips. "The angel speaks and she's a feisty one."

"Well," Vera said, her tone expressing disapproval. "I think it's good Jonathan was unable to bring a date this evening. My sweet Kimberly will make the perfect dinner companion for him." Her superficial smile evolved into a natural one. She chirped in Jonathan's direction, "And she's single, too."

"Mother!" Kimberly said, her cheeks flushed.

Vera ignored her daughter and began her sales pitch. She leaned across the table so Jonathan could hear her better. "Kimberly has won every beauty contest she entered since five years of age. She's also exceptionally talented. She can play five instruments and speaks fluent Japanese. She's at the top of her class at—"

The sound of champagne corks popping interrupted Vera's speech. Rachel jumped in her seat and turned to see several waiters moving throughout the tables, filling champagne glasses. Donovan placed his hand on her thigh and whispered, "Cal likes to put on a show."

Rachel chuckled and whispered back, "It's a good thing. Otherwise, we'd be hearing how Miss Kimberly won her first grade spelling bee with the word ubiquitous."

Donovan suppressed his laugh. "Be nice, Rach."

Mischief glinted in her eyes and she smiled. "I could say the same thing to you."

He bowed his head in compliance, and a soft laugh escaped Rachel's lips.

She was glad to see Donovan keep his promise, and they made it through dinner without another altercation between the two men. Rachel imitated every move Donovan made as they dined. Rachel savored every bite of the multi-course meal, which consisted of seared scallops, arugula salad, a medium-rare filet of Kobe beef, and a beautiful flan in a decadent caramel sauce.

Content to listen to the others around her, Rachel contributed to the conversation only when necessary. Vera's attempts to pawn her daughter off on Jonathan amused Rachel. Kimberly's face remained flushed during dinner, revealing a slight crush on Jonathan along with discomfort at her mother's domineering manner.

Donovan and Stanley kept busy discussing business and politics, and their conversation focused on their gracious host's bid for the Oval Office. Having been shielded from the world for so many years, Rachel did not understand most of their discussion. She decided that even if she had lived a normal life in the outside world, she would still have little interest in political matters.

Though amazed at the conversation around her, she was even more in awe of Donovan. Though she always knew Donovan was an important man, the conversation between Stanley and Donovan demonstrated just how important. Rachel realized she was lucky that he chose her to be by his side, and her love for him grew in the short time they had been at the dinner.

Waiters came to clear the tables, and the music that accompanied dinner peaked in volume. Couples rose and moved to the center of the room to dance. Rachel watched them glide across the floor, and her mouth turned upward. Violins and champagne worked together to form a blissful haze in Rachel's mind, and she understood the true meaning of the word romance. It danced in her eyes, keeping time with the graceful figures sweeping across the room. Rachel didn't want the evening to end.

"You know, Jonathan," Vera said, "my Kimberly is an excellent dancer."

Kimberly rolled her eyes.

"I'm sure she is," Jonathan said, and he pushed his chair back. He walked around the table and stood beside Rachel. He took her hand and pulled her to her feet. "You don't mind, do you, King?" Not waiting for a reply, he led her toward the other dancing couples.

Horrified, Rachel asked, "What are you doing?"

"I'm going to dance with an angel."

"And I don't get a say in this?"

He wrapped his arm around her waist and planted his hand in the middle of her back. "Maybe later."

Rachel stood still. "I… I'm not sure I know how to dance."

"It's easy." He took her hand and placed it on his shoulder. "Follow me, and you'll be fine," he said. He grasped her other hand in his and drew her near his body.

Claustrophobia overcame Rachel. "You're much too close," she said.

"I'm sorry you feel that way," Jonathan said. He pulled her closer. "Is that better?"

His body pressed against hers and her breath caught in her throat. Her feet surprised her by keeping up with his every move, and she tried to preserve her composure. "You are the most arrogant bastard I've ever met," she said under her breath.

"I would have thought that privilege belonged to King." He glanced over her shoulder, in the direction of their table. "He doesn't look too happy at the moment."

"I don't blame him. I'm not, either."

"That's too bad. You should learn to relax and enjoy yourself more." He continued before she could speak. "What do you do for a living?"

She answered his question with reluctance. "I work for Donovan."

"I was under the impression that you weren't a prostitute."

Rachel glared at him. "I'm security at his estate."

"Are you here for business or pleasure?"

"Until a few moments ago, pleasure."

"You really don't like dancing with me?"

She hesitated, not wanting to admit that a part of her did enjoy dancing with him.

"Nothing smart to say? I take it you find me irresistible." He slid his hand down to the small of her back.

"If your hand goes any lower, you'll learn just how resistible I find you."

Jonathan slowed his movements. "I'm not a bastard like you think. If you want, I'll be happy to escort you back to King right now. I'll even apologize to him for my rude behavior. I'm sure he will gloat about that for years, but I'm willing to make that sacrifice for you."

His green eyes fixed on hers and she thought they were probably the most incredible eyes she had ever seen, more hypnotizing than even Donovan's eyes. Something about him was much different than Donovan, and that intrigued her. The way he held her was in stark contrast to Donovan. She had never experienced such gentle arms. "Maybe in a little bit," she said.

He smiled and they danced in silence. She followed his graceful steps over the floor and she floated on air, comfortable in his arms, his body natural against hers. It really was a fairy tale.

Every fairy tale has a Prince Charming.

The thought brought her back to reality. She grew uneasy at her unexpected attraction to him and became aware of Donovan's watchful eye. "I think I should go back now," she said, though she wished he would refuse and keep her longer.

Despite her mental urging, he stopped. "Thank you for dancing with me, Angel. Maybe we can do it again very soon." His lips found her cheek and lingered for a moment on her skin.

When they reached the table, Donovan stood up and took her hand from Jonathan. "Thank you for letting me borrow her," Jonathan said. "I apologize if I've insulted you in any way." He walked over to Kimberly and held out his arm. "I would be honored if you would dance with me."

Kimberly blushed and took his arm.

"You'll have to excuse us," Donovan said to Stanley. "It's getting late and we have quite a drive ahead of us."

"Of course," Stanley said.

"It was very nice to meet you both," Rachel said.

"Likewise, my dear," Stanley said. Vera flashed a spurious smile.

Rachel risked a glimpse in Jonathan's direction. He held Kimberly at a distance, and over her shoulder, his eyes reached out to Rachel. She drew a sharp breath and then clamped her mouth shut. Donovan led her out of the room with a tight grasp on her hand.

Chapter Fifty

Rachel Pettis trailed behind Donovan King until they disappeared up the steps and out the door. Jonathan's eyes roamed to his left, where Cal Robbins twirled his wife. Cal met his eyes and gave him a slight nod as if to say, "I saw what you did."

Jonathan nodded back. *All right, you caught me.* He chuckled softly at their silent exchange. He and Cal had been friends for so long that Jonathan couldn't hide any of his motives from him. Of course, Cal was also friends with King, and that put Cal in the precarious position of having to play diplomat between the two men at social events.

It was widely known that Cal's friendship with King was more political than amicable, but they were friends nonetheless. King had been one of the driving forces behind Cal's campaign for his Senate seat. With the help of Graham Wilkes, King practically got Cal elected and kept him in that position.

Jonathan shuddered at the thought of Graham Wilkes. Though he appeared to surround himself with respectable businessmen as associates, Wilkes was nothing more than a glorified drug dealer. If it hadn't been for keen business sense and sharp criminal instinct, Wilkes would have been dealing from a street corner by a school in between jail stints. And, Wilkes and King were as close as brothers.

There were rumors about King, about his nose being not so clean. About his business dealings not always being legitimate. The rumors, however, were unfounded. Nothing more than supermarket tabloid headlines coming from the mouths of prominent and allegedly upstanding men and women. Over the years, King proved predictable and almost boring, making

Jonathan think that maybe he remained impervious under Wilkes's influence.

But tonight, King threw Jonathan for a loop. A woman. How interesting. Even more interesting was Jonathan's reaction to her. He had seen her from across the room the moment she stepped foot through the door. Her smile had captured his heart before he noticed she was on the arm of Donovan King.

As King had introduced her, Jonathan took his first glimpse into those angel eyes and he never wanted to look away. Then, she had responded to his gibe at King and surprised Jonathan with her sharp tongue. Throughout dinner, her gestures and her conversation had proved her to be graceful, elegant, and natural. Much different from other women thrown at him by overbearing mothers like Vera Meade.

Jonathan grimaced, having almost forgotten the woman he danced with now. He smiled at Kimberly and reinforced through his rigid arms that he had no intention of letting her body get close to touching his. He wanted to keep the residual feeling of Rachel pressed into him for the rest of the evening. The warm scent of her skin clung to his lips, and he wondered who could blame him for wanting to share a dance with such an intriguing and beautiful woman.

King did, Jonathan thought. Damn King. He had stolen Rachel out of Jonathan's arms. Well, after Jonathan stole her first, that is, but it didn't matter. He would find a way to make it clear to King that he had unexpected competition. After all, Jonathan always got what he wanted.

It was the only trait he shared with Donovan King.

Chapter Fifty-one

The entire ride back to the estate, Rachel kept her eyes lowered to the floor. Her fingers twisted and turned, turned and twisted. When they first climbed into the limousine, she attempted conversation, but Donovan did not respond so she gave up. She had nothing left to do but wring her fingers, and the silence consumed her thoughts.

The limousine hit a slight bump in the road before driving through the front gate of the estate. Donovan's cell phone rang once. He didn't move to answer it. Twice. He did not shift his penetrating stare away from her face. Three times. Why wouldn't he answer his phone? Four rings. She willed him to speak, cough, anything to break the silence between the ringing of his phone. Rachel's fingers twisted and turned faster.

He was upset, there was no avoiding that fact. Nothing she could say now would change his mood. The silence between them during the long drive only fueled her fear. She had never been more afraid of him than she was now, even though she had done nothing wrong to upset him.

That wasn't entirely true, she told herself. At the beginning of the fateful dance, she may have been at the mercy of Jonathan Thomas, but after he had offered to take her back to the table, she chose to continue dancing with him. Something about him fascinated Rachel. Even during dinner she stole a number of glances his way. While they had eaten, she convinced herself she looked at him to take part in the conversation, but she knew that wasn't the only reason.

Then came the dance and the way his body had felt against hers. He had held her in a gentle, comforting manner that was difficult to ignore. At the moment when his lips touched her cheek, something had happened inside of her. She loved Donovan, she had told him so before the dinner, but that emotion was threatened by this unexpected outside force named Jonathan Thomas.

Rachel cringed inside. She had done so much wrong, to the point that it felt as if she had betrayed Donovan, the man she told she would always love. She still loved him now, but after being in the warm, kind presence of Jonathan, she wondered if there was something wrong with the way Donovan loved her.

The driver helped her out of the limo again, but unlike at the home of Senator Cal Robbins, she did not wait for Donovan to get out before she moved up the stairs and through the front door. Once inside, she rushed down the back stairwell and into her room. She hoped he would retire to his own room and not say anything about Jonathan.

But Donovan continued to follow her. The closer he got, the more his palpable anger smothered her. Rachel walked to the other side of her bedroom, and Donovan shut and locked the door behind them. She removed the scarf from her neck and dropped it to the ground when he came up behind her, latching his hands onto her shoulders.

Donovan shoved her, and the side of her face crashed into the wall. His body pressed into her back, not allowing her any room to breathe. He took her hands and slid them along the wall until they were above her head. He forcefully ran his hands down her arms. "Is this what you want?"

Her fingers curled into the wall, and her hands fell next to her head. She twisted her head to the side, but couldn't see his face. A high pitched zip jerked tears from her eyes. The flaps of her dress rolled open and cool air breathed on her exposed back. He tugged her dress down and it bunched around her ankles. He ordered her to step out of the dress, and he kicked it aside with his shoe.

His uncontrolled emotions seeped through rough hands that groped her body, touching her in ways that excluded love. He pushed her harder against the wall until she thought her ribs might snap.

The clasp on the back of her bra unhooked, and Rachel's stomach dropped. "No, Donovan," she said. "Please don't."

He moved back to give her a bit of room between her body and the wall. "Is this the way you want it? So you can pretend he's the one you're with?"

"Don't do this, Donovan. Please don't do this. I don't want him."

He grasped her arm and whirled her around, his fingers so tight it was as if they pierced her skin and cut off the circulation. Her hand reached up and held her bra in place, so she wouldn't be even more exposed. His nostrils flared and anger radiated from his narrowed eyes.

Her trembling hand touched his face. "I don't want him," she repeated.

She inched closer to him. "I only want to be with you. You know that I love you."

At her words, Donovan released her. His rage-filled expression relented to despair, as if someone else had taken over his body and forced him to hurt her. For a moment, she thought he would cry.

Donovan bowed his head. "I don't know what's wrong with me. I never want to do those things to you. It just happens. I'm trying, Rachel, I really am. I can't lose you."

"You won't lose me," Rachel said. She wrapped her arms around him. "I'm yours, Donovan. That won't ever change." For the first time, as the words left her mouth, her cheek stinging with every syllable, she wasn't sure she meant what she said.

"You are mine," Donovan whispered. "You'll always be mine, Rachel." His desperate kiss told her what he wanted from her, and Rachel always gave into his desires, no matter how bad the pain. She never dreamed of denying him, and tonight was no different, despite what he had done.

In the early morning hours, after his lengthy apologies, his seeming disgust with his actions, and his promises of change, Donovan left her bedroom to retire to his own room for a few hours of sleep. Rachel rolled over on her side and drew her knees up. With the comforter snug around her tattered body, she touched her cheekbone where it hit the wall. The tenderness assured her a bruise would appear later.

All she wanted was to love him. He made it so difficult.

Chapter Fifty-two

Jonathan rapped the end of a pen against the mahogany desk in his office. He had been in the same position for over an hour, only moving to ask his executive assistant to cancel his appointments for the day. Ever vigilant about his schedule to ensure he remained on track, Rita grilled him about his reasons for clearing his calendar. Jonathan placated her by stating he wasn't feeling well.

The excuse wasn't necessarily a lie, as Jonathan didn't know how he felt. Since meeting Rachel Pettis last night, his emotions were all over the place and impossible to pinpoint. There was something about Rachel he had never seen in another woman. Her beauty called to him when she entered the room, and her quiet strength grabbed him as the evening wore on. He had an overwhelming desire to watch her all night, but he kept her in his peripheral vision so as not to incite King.

King did not scare Jonathan. He had dealt with King enough to know he was an obstacle. A stubborn one, but an obstacle all the same. Jonathan made a living and lived his life working around much bigger obstacles than King.

Jonathan's feelings toward this woman he barely knew frightened him far more than King ever could. After leaving Cal's estate, Rachel remained planted in his mind. He only closed his eyes for a few brief hours of restless sleep, where she appeared in his dreams.

This morning, he thought of nothing else but finding a way to see her again. Seeing her would help him straighten out his emotions. He needed to know if he was attracted to her because she was on the arm of his competition, or if it was a pesky case of love at first sight. He hoped it was the former, as the latter presented more complications than he desired. The only problem was he didn't know how to find her.

He ran his conversation with Rachel through his mind in hopes of remembering something to assist him in his search. He didn't have a lot to go on, but he knew someone who could help.

Jonathan leaned forward and pressed the intercom button on his phone to page Rita. When she answered, he asked, "Can you get Walt on the phone for me, please?"

"Last name?" Rita asked.

"Walter Sykes. The only Walt we know."

"Do you want me to schedule an appointment with him?"

"No, Rita, thank you. I'll wait on the phone until you can connect us."

"Yes, sir," she said. "Is there anything else?"

Jonathan paused. Depending on what Walt found, he might need a couple days to figure things out. As long as the end result was getting his mind off Rachel, taking time off would be worth it so his life could return to normal.

"Please cancel all of my appointments for the next two days," he said into the phone.

A long silence came from the other end of the phone. Jonathan started to ask if she was still there when Rita said, "*All* of your appointments? Are you sure?"

"If there's anything urgent, let Cory handle it. He's more than capable." Jonathan trusted his brother Cory more than anyone else in the company. Cory could take care of any pressing matters while Jonathan straightened himself out.

"Okay, sir. I'll get Mr. Sykes on the phone for you now." There was a long beep followed by silence.

Jonathan resumed tapping the pen against his desk. If anyone could find out more about Rachel Pettis, it was Walt. He had done contract private investigating work for Jonathan a number of times in the past and was discreet about everything. Looking into King's girlfriend required the utmost discretion.

Rita came back on the line. "Mr. Sykes for you, sir."

Jonathan waited to speak until a beep signaled that Rita disconnected herself from the call. "How are you, Walt?"

"Jonathan Thomas!" Walt said. "I wondered when I would hear from you again. You always have the most interesting cases."

Jonathan chuckled. "This one is no different, I'm afraid. I need you to look into someone for me."

"Sure thing," Walt said. "What's the name?"

"Rachel Pettis. She's in her early twenties."

"Where does she live?"

Jonathan thought for a moment. "Actually, I'm not quite sure. It is somewhere up north, though. That's pretty much all I know about her." He wasn't sure he wanted to reveal her relationship with King quite yet.

"You don't give a man a lot to go on, do you?"

"I'm sorry, I wish I had more." Jonathan remembered another fact from his conversation with Rachel, but he hesitated before telling Walt. Maybe he'd have to share the information about her relationship with King, after all. "Walt, I need your discretion on this one."

"Of course. I'm always quiet about what I do for you."

"But this one really calls for it, more than any other case you've handled for me. I don't want you to hand this one off to anyone else. I want you to take care of it yourself."

"You've got it," Walt said. "Although, I have to admit that you're making me a bit nervous."

"I'm sure it's nothing to be nervous about," Jonathan said. "Rachel works for Donovan King. She's a security guard at his estate. I'm pretty sure they're… together."

Walt whistled into the phone. "Donovan King. Not someone I normally go poking around and you want me to look into his girlfriend? That can't possibly end well."

Jonathan sat up straight in his chair. Walt's words instilled a bit of fear into him. If Walt stayed away from King, maybe Jonathan should as well. He already knew the answer to his next question, but asked anyway. "What have you heard about King?"

"It's rumors."

"What are the rumors?"

"Nothing good," Walt said. "He's mixed up with Graham Wilkes, and they've known each other since childhood. We both know Wilkes is not a good man, so I highly doubt King is one, either. I don't know what you want with this girl, but I'd stay far away from anyone associated with King, especially if you know she works for him during the day and spends her nights in his bed."

Jonathan shook the image out of his mind. He didn't want to think that King had ever touched her in that manner, but he knew Walt's words were true. Rachel had been cozy with King during dinner, and the entire night King watched her with a careful eye. Not only was their relationship apparent, but they had been together in that capacity for quite some time.

"You're probably right," Jonathan said, "but I still want whatever you can find on her. Can you run a basic check for me and at least find out where she lives? Along with any other information you can get, of course. I need it right away. I'll be glad to pay a rush charge."

"I can run by your office tomorrow afternoon with whatever I find.

Have a check ready for me."

"The usual fee?"

"Yes, plus whatever the rush is worth to you. I know you're always more than fair."

Jonathan smiled. "Thanks, Walt." He replaced the receiver and leaned back in his chair. He hadn't considered that Rachel Pettis might be wrapped up in King's dealings with Wilkes. If she was both working for and intimately involved with King, anything was possible.

He closed his eyes and envisioned Rachel standing before him. Her emerald eyes tore through him and convinced him it was love at first sight. She felt it, too. He could tell as she argued with him that she hadn't expected the undeniable chemistry between them. He knew he somehow had to see her again, no matter what her story was with King.

Chapter Fifty-three

The fog settling around the trees mirrored the one in Rachel's mind. Unable to focus on her rounds, she wandered across the grounds in the general direction of her patrol route. Two days had passed since she met Jonathan Thomas, and both the dance they shared and Donovan's outburst still affected her.

Her fingers retreated to her cheek, which ached with the bruise from hitting the wall. Rachel could deal with the smudge on her cheek the color of a bruised rainbow, as long as no bruises emerged where he grabbed her arm. She hated seeing marks the shape of his fingertips on her. Those were the fingers that knew how to touch her, that loved her and memorized every part of her body a thousand times over. But, they were also the fingers that could reduce her to tears, crushing her spirit and imprisoning her in a world of pain.

In the limo before the dinner, Donovan said everything she ever wanted to hear. She assumed it to be a turning point in their relationship, but nothing had changed, except now she had experienced something greater than his anger. The jealousy that fueled his outburst was far worse than anything she ever felt at his hands before that night.

The invisible wounds were much more painful than the bruise on her cheek. Donovan had drilled into her head that she belonged to him, but that night was the first time she ever felt like his property to do with as he pleased, no matter how much it hurt her. She had never felt so inhuman as when he pushed her up against the wall and stripped her dress off her body. She would much rather take a hundred beatings than suffer through that humiliation again.

Then yesterday, the morning after the dinner, the apologies and excuses came, as she learned to expect. He was sorry. He loved her and didn't mean to hurt her. He had overreacted and if he could go back, he would handle the situation better. Seeing her dance with another man, seeing another man touch her in a way only he should touch her drove him over the edge. Overcome by jealousy, the identity of that man compounded his anger. If it had been anyone besides Jonathan Thomas, he wouldn't have reacted in that manner.

Rachel couldn't help but think his reaction would have been the same if she danced with the Pope. She despised the onslaught of excuses almost more than the actual act. His words ensured she would forgive him and forget his temper until the next time. With each apology, however, she grew more jaded and now she wondered if he was capable of change.

Paul's voice cut through the tranquil morning air. "How are things on your side of the world?"

Rachel removed her radio from her belt, glad for the distraction from her thoughts. Pressing the button on the side of the radio, she said, "We're all clear over here. Minus the fog, that is."

He laughed. "I'm sending Eric out to relieve you. He should be there in about ten minutes."

"Thanks."

"Rachel."

The radio fell from her hands at the sound of the vaguely familiar voice. She freed her gun from her shoulder holster and whipped around with her gun trained on the intruder.

Jonathan Thomas stood behind her, his clothes more suitable for a day in the office than a stroll through the woods. He recoiled at the sight of her gun and his hands flew up in surrender. "Hey, hey, hey!"

"Do you realize I could have shot you?"

"I'm sorry," he said. He dropped his hands to his sides. "I guess I underestimated you."

"Don't let it happen again." She put her gun away and tried to slow her heart before it escaped from her body. She couldn't be sure if the rapid knocks against her chest were caused by the adrenaline rush of being startled or by Jonathan's unexpected presence. "What the hell are you doing here?" she asked.

"I had to see you."

What kind of answer was that? He couldn't waltz into her world as if it was nothing out of the ordinary and throw her life into chaos. The longer he stood in front of her, the more her head spun and stomach knotted. He was a detriment to every aspect of her life and he had to leave.

"This is insane," she said. "You can't be here. Not only are you trespassing on private property, but someone could come along at any time."

"Your relief will be here in eight minutes."

Though he was right, Rachel had to convince him to leave. No good could come out of him staying longer. If he stayed, she might…

She destroyed the thought before it could reveal her emotions to her stubborn mind, and tried another tack to get Jonathan off the grounds and out of her life. "If Donovan knew you were here—"

"What exactly would he do?"

"Well, it wouldn't be pleasant."

"Okay, sorry, you're right. It's entirely inappropriate to show up like this, but I didn't know how else to get in touch with you. Where do you live? Maybe I can meet you there when you get off work and take you to dinner."

"Jonathan, I'm full-time, onsite security."

His forehead creased and he contemplated her words. "You mean you live here?"

"Yes."

He tightened his lips and looked off to the side. "I wasn't expecting that."

"You have to leave now."

"Can't you meet me somewhere later?"

"That's not possible," she said.

"Why not? Are you and King—"

"What?"

"You know."

Surely the truth would force him leave. "Yes, we are." She glanced around the woods to make sure they were still alone. "You have to go now. Eric will be here any second, and Donovan cannot find out you were here."

Rachel expected him to walk away, but he remained still. She opened her mouth to demand that he leave when he grabbed her arms, pulled her to him, and kissed her. Her mind battled him and she wanted to shove him away.

Instead of resisting, she relaxed against him and she returned the kiss. His kiss was pure, without a hint of the hunger that led to sex. But, desire was there, and it was as if she could feel his soul as he enveloped her in his arms. She was no longer on the estate, but raptured into a new world created by the perfection in his kiss.

Without warning, sanity restored itself and she pulled away from him. "This can't happen," she whispered.

"It's already happened," he said. "I can't explain it, but you know it's right."

"It can't be right," she said. "I don't want you in my life. You have to forget that I ever existed."

"It's too late for that," Jonathan said.

"I was fine, my life was fine, without you."

"I'm sure it was perfect. Everything you've ever dreamed of." He touched the bruise high on her cheek. "You don't belong here, Angel. He doesn't deserve you." He turned around and vanished into the fog, leaving her staring after him.

"Slacking on the job?"

Rachel whirled around and faced Eric. Had he seen Jonathan? If he had, he probably saw their kiss and heard their exchange as well. If Donovan was that incensed over the dance they shared, she did not want to find out how he would react to a kiss.

"Don't ever sneak up on me like that again," she said through clenched teeth. "You know procedure is to warn others before you approach. What you just did could get you killed." She started walking away when his voice stopped her.

"Don't forget your radio," he said in a mocking tone.

She stiffened and turned around. Not looking at Eric, she picked up her radio and hurried back to the house and toward the safety of her bedroom before he could say anything else.

Anger and frustration coursed through her veins like torrents. Jonathan had thrown her world into turmoil. How dare he talk to her like that! He knew nothing about her. He had no right to judge or criticize her life, which is exactly what he did with two simple sentences.

But seeing him again stirred up emotions inside her, the same ones that plagued her while they were dancing. She had done her best to block him out of her mind for the two days since she'd met him, but things were different now. That night she was in another world, one she hadn't been in since she was ten and one she would probably never be in again. Today, Jonathan had broken into her world.

Then he had the nerve to kiss her. Her anger flared as she thought of the way he pulled her to him and kissed her with no regard for her feelings or for her relationship with Donovan. He acted like she would enjoy his kiss and the feeling of being that close to him.

But she did enjoy it. His kiss excited her, which upset her even more. She knew better, but her body betrayed her and succumbed to him. Her mind screamed at her that it was wrong, but it was unable to provide her with any means of controlling the feelings levitating her toward Jonathan.

Rachel wandered into her bedroom and slammed the door shut behind her. In her bathroom, she propped her hands on the counter and she stared at her reflection in the mirror. She had to forget that Jonathan Thomas ever existed so she could return to her life with Donovan. She was already terrified of what would happen if he found out about the kiss. Somehow, she had to get things back to the way they were when he simply loved her, before the night she provoked his dark side in the library.

She jumped at a rap on her bedroom door. "What?" she asked.

"It's me," Paul said through the door.

She left her bathroom and opened the bedroom door. "I'm sorry, Paul. I didn't mean to yell."

"It's okay." In his hands, he held her black jacket that was used for formal security situations. "Listen, Donovan needs you upstairs for a meeting he's having in a few minutes."

"I just got off rounds and I'm exhausted. The last thing I want to do is stand in at a meeting."

"I know, but he specifically requested you."

"Who is it with this time?"

"He didn't say, but whoever it is, they're in the waiting room right now. He wants you to escort them to the conference room and stay for the meeting."

Rachel threw up her hands. "Fine." She snatched the jacket from his hands and pushed past him.

"What's wrong with you? You seemed okay a half hour ago."

Without turning around, she said, "PMS."

In front of the waiting room, she slid her arms into the jacket and buttoned it, hiding her gun and shoulder holster. She exhaled and tried to soften her demeanor. She wasn't about to bite the head off some poor soul.

She opened the door to the waiting room, wearing her best false smile. The smile left her face when the man in the room turned around. "No," she said.

"What is this room?" Jonathan asked.

She closed her eyes, hoping she could wish him away, but it didn't work. He was still there, wide-eyed and smiling when she reopened them. She should have known Donovan was meeting with him, but she hadn't been able to stop thinking about his kiss long enough to question why he had been on the grounds in the first place.

"This collection is incredible," he said. "I've never seen anything like it. I guess he wants to unsettle me by having me wait in here. Is that how it works?"

Of course, she thought. By having her in the room during the meeting, Donovan figured he could distract Jonathan. Under her breath, she said, "Son of a—"

"I hope you aren't directing that comment toward me," Jonathan said. "I thought you liked me more than that."

"What are you doing here?"

"I have a meeting with King. Every now and then we get together and argue for fun. Today seemed like a good time to do that again."

The inner workings of Donovan's security company never interested Rachel, and she had no knowledge of any meetings Donovan previously held with Jonathan. "What are you arguing about today?"

"Same thing we've been arguing about for over ten years. He wants to buy me out."

"And you don't want to sell," Rachel finished for him. "Men and their toys."

"Normally, we do this at my office, but we're both tired of our lawyers doing the arguing for us. Plus, I've always wanted to see where King lives and now I'm glad I came. Lots of interesting things happening on his grounds."

"Jonathan," she said, but then changed her mind before she said anything more. Arguing would only succeed in irritating her while deepening her attraction toward him.

"What?" he asked, a childlike grin plastered on his face.

She lightened her tone. "Mr. Thomas, if you'll please follow me." She turned and moved toward the conference room.

The meeting didn't last long. Rachel stood in the corner of the room across from Donovan and tried to ignore both men. She resented Jonathan for being there, and she resented Donovan for forcing her to be there.

The competitive relationship of the two men magnified her discomfort. She suspected something else was being discussed below the surface of every spoken word, a hidden agenda she knew nothing about.

For over thirty minutes, Donovan highlighted his latest proposal for purchasing Jonathan's company. Ten more minutes of heated argument ensued before Jonathan decided he had enough.

He stood to leave, then turned back around. "You know, King, I did a lot of thinking this morning before I came here. I've spent almost twenty years building my company, making it exactly what I've always envisioned. That company is my entire life. I have never had the slightest desire to sell to you because there's nothing you could offer me that is equal or superior to what my company means to me. This morning, I decided I would sell to you."

"You just rejected my offer," Donovan said.

"I didn't like your offer. I have a better one, and the terms are non-negotiable."

"Name it."

"I'll give you my company in exchange for the permanent employ of Ms. Pettis."

Rachel's mouth dropped and her mind raced. She didn't know whether to be flattered or appalled, though she leaned toward the latter.

Donovan's jaw set in anger and hatred flashed in his eyes. "We tend to frown upon slave trading in these parts, Thomas."

Jonathan shrugged. "Can't blame a man for trying."

"Get out of my home."

Rachel left the conference room and escorted Jonathan to the front door. She opened the door and turned to face him.

"Rachel—"

"Whatever it is, no. You need to leave now." She didn't like being so aware of him, of his eyes, his mouth, his hands. The unspoken emotion between them reared up again, a fire that shouldn't be there. If she could sense it, so could Donovan.

He smiled and gave her a wink. "I'll see you again soon." He walked outside before she could argue.

Shutting the door, her impulse was to go to Donovan. She wanted to reassure him that she loved him, wanted reassurance from him. She decided against the idea, knowing that he needed time to cool down from the exchange with Jonathan. She couldn't handle another violent outburst.

As she walked toward the basement stairs, she questioned if it was possible to still love Donovan while experiencing feelings for another man. The answer unnerved her and renewed her frustration with the situation.

She flew down the steps and almost ran over Paul as she turned the corner. "That was quick," he said. "Who was the meeting with?"

"Jonathan Thomas."

"You're kidding. Anything get accomplished?"

She stopped and faced him. "Hell, no. Next time they should just duke it out on the school playground like the snotty little rich brats they are." She stormed into her room, leaving Paul with his mouth open.

Chapter Fifty-four

Rachel emerged from her room later that afternoon, refreshed from a nap and ready for a workout so she could expel the rest of her frustration. As she walked to the gym, she decided she would erase Jonathan's visit from her mind. The guilt over the kiss consumed her and continuing to allow Jonathan to dominate her thoughts wasn't fair to either her or Donovan. She owed everything to Donovan and refused to betray him a moment longer.

She smiled at her decision to forget Jonathan, and the tension in her shoulders released its hold on her. She entered the gym and stopped walking. Eric laid on the bench press, lowering the barbell toward his chest. Her pleasant mood deflated. "I'll come back later," she said and turned to go.

"I don't understand something," Eric said.

Knowing he was baiting her, Rachel turned around to face him. "What's that?"

He grunted as he lifted the weights back up, and lowered the bar onto the rack. "How you can screw up everything you do."

Her eyes narrowed and she stepped toward him. All of the anger and frustration from the day flooded back into her muscles.

Eric pushed himself up into a sitting position. "Dancing with Jonathan Thomas in front of King?" His patronizing laugh filled the room. "How stupid can you get?"

Rachel moved further into the gym. "I've had enough of you, Eric. I think it's time we finish this."

He rose from the bench and picked up a nearby towel. "What are you rambling about?"

She gestured at the mat. "I may not be able to take care of you out there, but in here I have every right to spar with you."

Eric leered. "You're on." He wiped the towel across his flushed brow and stepped on the mat. Sweat glistened off the rough stubble on his head.

Paul walked into the gym. "Rachel, what do you think you're doing?"

Rachel shrugged. "Just practicing. Right, Eric?"

"Just practicing," Eric said.

"Damn it, Rach," Paul said.

Eric threw his fist at her. She dodged to the side and caught his hand. She whirled around, grabbed his wrist and arm, and flipped him over her shoulder, but he anticipated her move. He landed on his back and swept his arm under her legs, knocking her down.

He jumped to his feet seconds before she did. His wrist bounced off her arm as she blocked his punch. She misjudged the next one, and his knuckles crashed into the side of her face, landing on the existing bruise. Her neck whipped to the side, and she looked back at Eric in time to see his fist again. This time, it clipped her jaw.

Rachel backed away from Eric to give herself a moment to recuperate. She touched her cheek, stinging not from Eric's punch, but with the reminder of Donovan slamming her into the wall. She realized that Eric could only cause superficial pain; Donovan had secured all rights to really hurt her.

Eric held his fists in front of him with an arrogant grin, ready to strike again. She raised her fists and bent her knees in response to his challenge. He moved toward her, and she expected him to throw his fist again. His hand jerked, enough for her to raise her arm up to block, leaving her abdomen exposed.

His foot landed in her stomach, but she folded with it as Paul taught her years earlier. Though the pain was minimal, she covered her stomach with her arm and remained bent at the waist. Paul took a step toward them, but she held up her hand to stop him.

"Is that all you have for me, Rach?" Eric asked, laughing. "You can do better than that."

Seconds passed like minutes while Rachel stared at Eric. She kept her breathing uneven to maintain the pretense of an injury. His shoulders dropped and his facial muscles relaxed.

She whirled around and kicked the side of his face, stunning him. She drove her fist into his mouth, once, twice, three times. Blood flowed from his mouth in response to the sharp blows. Her foot connected once more with the side of his face and he hit the ground.

Rachel crouched beside him and thrust her knuckles into the hollow of his neck. She pushed against his windpipe to cut off his air supply. "Don't ever mess with me again," she said.

Paul picked her up from the mat. Eric rolled to his side and grasped at his neck, coughing and wheezing. Rachel stalled to watch Eric's temporary suffering, and Paul dragged her out of the gym. He pulled her into her bedroom, his anger apparent in his tone. "What is going on with you today? And don't pull that 'time-of-the-month' crap on me."

"Nothing's going on," she said. She rubbed her tender knuckles. "I'm perfectly fine."

"You're agitated as hell. I want to know why."

She didn't answer.

"Listen, I have to go with Donovan to check out this job we're doing in a couple weeks. We'll be back in an hour or so. I want you to go take a bath or stay in here and read, whatever it's going to take to keep you out of trouble. When we come back, you and I are going to talk and you're going to tell me everything. Promise me you'll stay away from everyone until we return, okay?"

"Alright," she said.

"One hour." He kissed her forehead. "By the way, you did great in there. Serves him right."

Chapter Fifty-five

Jonathan paced the floor of his office, as he had off and on all afternoon. He had stirred up trouble that morning at King's estate, and he didn't know if he should be worried about upsetting King or excited about the developments with Rachel.

Seeing Rachel brought back every feeling he had while dancing with her. He had no control over his emotions or actions when he was with her, so it had been no surprise he kissed her, even if he didn't know he would do it until it happened. Kissing her had been everything he expected, and he never wanted to stop.

When he did let her go, he saw the bruise on her cheek. The bruise was not the result of an accident, of falling down, or of being clumsy. The purposeful and angry discoloration was also recent.

As he snuck back to the house to wait for his meeting with King, he came to terms with the idea that he might have been the cause of the bruise. That dancing with her at the dinner pushed King over the edge and he had hurt her. Yet, he also knew that with a bruise like that, it was not the first time she had suffered at King's hands.

Seeing Rachel in the same room as King worried Jonathan, as he remembered her saying she lived in the house with him. The longer she lived with King, the more chances he would have to hurt her. The offer of giving up his company to get Rachel out of harm's way came out of Jonathan's mouth without thought.

After he had said it, he knew he meant it. This woman had infiltrated his heart to the point that he would give up everything he had to be with her and whisk her out of the hell she lived in. No man had the right to treat her like that, to put his hands on her in a hurtful way. Somehow, Jonathan had to get her out of there.

A knock on his office door told him that Walt had arrived with the information about Rachel. "Come in," he called.

Normally, Rita would conference him to tell him his guest was waiting for him, but Jonathan gave her the day off, much to her dismay. Rita had not taken a day off in a decade of working for Jonathan, and she had not accepted his offer to take one off now without a fight. He ended up giving her double time on her salary to get her away for the day. The expense was worth it. Having her around would raise questions as to why he had gone to King's estate that morning, and what Walt was digging up for him.

Walter Sykes strolled through the office door, clutching a briefcase at his side. As they shook hands, Jonathan noted Walt had lost more hair from his already frail comb-over.

"Thanks for getting this to me so soon, Walt," Jonathan said. He led Walt to the conference room on the other side of his office.

Walt took a seat opposite of Jonathan and set his briefcase on the table. "I'm not sure what you've gotten yourself into, but this has to be one of the strangest cases I've ever seen. And, I've seen some strange ones," he said.

Jonathan narrowed his eyes, curious why Walt would say that about a simple background check. "What do you mean? What about it is strange?"

Walt opened the briefcase and took out a thin manila file folder. He flipped open the cover of the folder. He picked up a single piece of paper from inside the folder and waved it in the air. "This is what I have on your girl."

"That's it?" Jonathan asked. "One page?"

"Not even half a page. Your girl is what you'd call 'off the grid.' In fact, she's so far off the grid, that she was quite difficult to find in the first place."

"What did you find on her?"

"She was born in San Diego and lived there until she was ten. Then her parents were killed in a drunk driving accident. They weren't drinking, someone else was. Her dad, Luke, had one brother named Paul. There was no other living family, so Paul retained custody of Rachel. That's where the trail ends." Walt leaned over the table in dramatic fashion. "There is no record of Rachel Pettis after age ten."

At first, Jonathan thought he might have misunderstood. "Age ten? How is that possible?"

Walt tossed the paper on top of the folder. "You got me. I've never heard of anything like this."

"Did you find out anything about this uncle that took custody of her?"

"Paul Pettis was actually a pretty prestigious doctor in Los Angeles at Cedars-Sinai until eighteen years ago. That's when his wife was raped and murdered."

"Let me guess. He fell off the grid soon after he lost his wife."

Walt cocked a finger at him. "You got it."

Jonathan rubbed his forehead and tried to put the pieces together. "So the uncle falls off the grid, then a few years later Rachel does the same after he takes custody of her. How does she get from San Diego to working for Donovan King, but remain invisible?"

"She must be working under the table. I would bet good money that the uncle works there also, and that's how she met King. If she's working in that capacity for King, she's not involved in anything good." Walt closed his briefcase and slid the report over to Jonathan. "You have a check for me?"

"No check. You get an envelope this time."

"Cash, huh? I like it, though it makes me feel a little shady. I take it you don't want Rita to know about this one."

"I don't want anyone to ever know about this case, but it's not like it matters. You gave me more questions than answers."

"I don't make up information to give you your money's worth," Walt said, as he rose from the table. "You get what you get and do with it what you want."

Jonathan smiled and walked toward his office desk to get the envelope for Walt. "You gave me a mystery, and I don't have the slightest clue what to do with it, but it was still worth the price."

Walt stopped walking and caught Jonathan's eyes. "This girl must be important for you to go through all this trouble." He did not wait for a response. "You'll take the mystery and you'll solve it. Figure out what you have to do to get the results you want. That's what you're best at."

"You're right," Jonathan said. He opened the top drawer of his desk and took out the envelope for Walt. "She is very important to me and she is worth the mystery."

Walt accepted the envelope. "Be careful," he said. "Something stinks about this, and if you keep poking around, you need to tread lighter than you ever have before. If you need anything else, give me a call."

Jonathan thanked him, and Walt walked out of the office. He scanned the report on Rachel. Everything Walt told him was in writing, so he put the page through the cross-cut shredder next to his desk. He couldn't risk Rita finding the document and questioning him about who Rachel was and why he paid Walt to run a background check on her.

Walt's report only added a layer of mystery to Rachel Pettis. A young woman, living off the grid at Donovan King's estate. She not only worked for him, but she was with him. In return, she had sustained at least one bruise at his hands.

Jonathan was sure of two things. One, he fell in love with her the moment they met. Two, he couldn't allow her to stay with that monster for one more minute. He had already made quite the mess at King's residence that morning. Treading lightly wasn't exactly an option at this point.

He picked up the phone to call his brother, Cory. He would need a bit more time off if he was going to figure out how to get Rachel away from King.

Chapter Fifty-six

A bath was exactly what Rachel needed. She relaxed beneath the bubbles, allowing the hot water to soothe her aching muscles and relieve her tired mind.

Shortly before she turned nineteen, Donovan suggested having both the bathroom and bedroom remodeled, as they had remained the same since she moved to the estate. Rachel declined his offer and wondered if he would ever understand that his money, which could buy her the world and all of its material possessions, meant nothing to her.

She simply wanted him. She wanted to wake up next to him every morning after sleeping beside him, something that had still never happened. She wanted him to whisk her away and marry her, announcing their love to the world. And, someday, she wanted to have children with him, raise a family, and be a family. Above all, she wanted a fairy tale with him.

But not long after he suggested the remodel, he struck her in the library. Then, what she thought would be an isolated incident, happened again. And again, and again.

Her whole world changed that night, she thought. With the bathwater cooling, she lifted her head from the pillow. A thin layer of dissolved bubbles and soap coated the top of the lukewarm water. Paul would be back soon, and then she could tell him everything that was happening and seek some much-needed words of wisdom.

Stepping out of the tub, Rachel heard her bedroom door open and shut. Paul always knocked first, but sometimes Donovan came in without announcing his presence. Smiling, she dried off and slipped on her silky, black bathrobe. Donovan most likely wanted to spend time with her after the tense morning with Jonathan. She welcomed having time to not only spend with him, but also open up to him.

Rachel opened the door to her room, expecting to see Donovan. Instead, Eric sat on her bed. Her eyes fell down to the knife he twirled in his hands. The blade glinted as he maneuvered the handle between his fingers.

"What are you doing in here?" she asked.

"Waiting for you," he slurred.

When he stood and started toward her, Rachel identified his telltale signs of ingesting too much alcohol. "I think you need to leave," she said.

"I think I'm gonna stay right here. I think you're gonna give me some of the same action you're giving King."

Rachel maintained her composure, despite the tense cords rising out of her neck. She glanced at her surroundings in preparation to defend herself against Eric. Wearing only a bathrobe was not ideal for the situation, but she still took several steps toward him. She kept her knees bent in case he attacked her. "This is your last warning, Eric. You better leave now before you get hurt."

She sensed movement behind her, coming from her closet. Before she could react, someone grabbed her arms and pulled them tight behind her back. "No, Rachel. This is your last warning." She recognized Aaron's dull voice, and he pushed her toward Eric.

Her mind raced, but it seemed an impossible situation. She tried to keep the fear out of her voice so she could reason with them. "Look, it doesn't have to happen like this. You've obviously been drinking and made a mistake. You guys can still go now, and I promise Donovan will never hear about this."

Eric grabbed a fistful of hair on the back of her head and pulled it tight to hold her head still. "He'll never hear about this anyway," he said.

As he moved his head toward hers, Rachel mashed her lips together. She squirmed, but she couldn't move her face away from him. He pressed his lips to her mouth, and she squealed and groaned in protest. When she continued fighting against him, he released her hair from his hand. "You need to loosen up a bit." He reached his hand down and untied her robe. "Or maybe it's better to keep you feisty."

Rachel gathered all the saliva she could into the front of her mouth and spit in his face. She clenched her teeth and said, "Donovan's going to kill you the second he comes back, and I'll make sure you suffer."

Eric laughed and stepped back. He lifted the bottom of his shirt and wiped his face. "King doesn't scare me."

"But I bet he scares you, Aaron," Rachel said, hoping to get through to the weaker member of the duo.

Aaron remained silent and kept his grip tight on her arms.

"That won't work," Eric said. "Aaron wants part of you as much as I do." Grabbing the back of her head again, he pulled her head back until her neck was taut. Eric positioned the knife against the front of her neck and whispered in her ear. "But you better watch yourself, Rach. I have no problem slicing your throat open before you have the chance to scream for help."

He applied pressure to the knife. Rachel winced, and a soft cry escaped her lips as the blade bit into her neck. Warm, thick blood trickled from the burning wound.

Eric pressed his fingers against the wound and coated his fingers with her blood. She cried out again with pain. He held his bloody fingertips up for her to see, then turned them around toward his mouth. His tongue snaked out and licked the blood off his index finger. He grinned and grabbed her face. Pinching her cheeks, he kissed her again.

Rachel tasted her blood as he invaded her mouth. Reminding herself of the knife on her throat, she restrained herself from biting off his tongue.

After he broke away from her, he said, "That's much better. I knew you'd warm up to me eventually." He kept the knife close to her neck and took a step away from her. He peeled back her robe, and Rachel's insides curled away from her skin.

"What have we got here?" He touched the tip of the blade to the nape of her neck. He swirled the knife in an S pattern down to her navel, his eyes swallowing every inch of her exposed skin. "Look at what King's been keeping to himself."

If she could get Eric to back away from her, she could try to kick the knife away from him. Aaron would probably break her arm before she wrestled free, but that was an acceptable outcome to her when faced with the alternative.

Eric used his free hand to unfasten the button on his jeans. "On your knees."

Bile rose in her throat and she stiffened her legs to stop Aaron from forcing her down.

"Before you decide to try anything," Eric said, "remember I'd love the chance to use this knife on you."

She struggled against him, but Aaron's grasp was too strong for her to break free.

"Get her down to where she belongs," Eric said. "Just kick out the backs of her knees."

An idea rushed into her mind. She made eye contact with Eric. "You must be pissed off that I hurt you today."

Anger flashed across his face. "You got lucky."

"Think so? Then why don't we fight again, right now? If I take you down, you and Aaron walk out of here and no one says a word."

"And if I win?"

"You get what you came for."

"I'm already going to get what I came for."

She raised an eyebrow and showed him traces of a seductive smile. "Not willingly."

The corners of his mouth turned upward and his tongue flicked across his lips.

"Damn it, Eric!" Aaron sounded panicked. "You said this would be quick!"

Rachel kept her eyes locked on Eric's while he considered her proposal. Having taken control of the situation, some tension flowed out of her body. There was no way he could beat her in a fight.

"Let her go," Eric said.

"Are you crazy?" Aaron asked.

Eric shifted his drunk, lustful gaze toward Aaron and narrowed his eyes. "I said, let her go."

Aaron released her. The moment she was free, she closed her robe.

Her bedroom door burst open. Rachel turned her head and crouched on the ground. Paul aimed his gun at Aaron and fired two shots.

Donovan shot Eric in his left kneecap. Eric fell to the ground, and the knife tumbled out of his hand. Donovan watched Eric writhe in pain, and then fired a second shot into his right kneecap.

Eric's screams pierced the air, and Rachel's hands flew up to cover her ears. He thrashed about on the ground, and Rachel couldn't bring herself to look away. Donovan kicked the knife away from Eric before smashing the butt of his gun repeatedly on his head.

Rachel crumpled to the ground with exhaustion, and Paul ran to her. He examined her neck, and his fingers probed the wound. "Are you okay?"

Relief seeped from every part of her. "How did you know?"

"I had a bad feeling about Eric after we left. When we got back, Tony told me Aaron didn't show for rounds and Eric was drunk. I wasn't sure where they were, and then I heard Eric's voice in here so I got Donovan." He touched her neck again. "How bad does it hurt?"

Rachel didn't realize how much the knife wound hurt until Paul asked. "It stings a lot."

"He didn't… did he?"

Rachel lowered her eyes and shook her head. "He would have if you hadn't come along."

Paul laid his hand on her shoulder. "It's okay, Rachel. He'll get what's coming to him, but I need to clean up your neck first. You need a few stitches, and probably something for the pain. I'm going to get my bag and—"

"Paul," Donovan said with a cold voice. He pointed to Eric. "Get him out of here and throw him in the trunk. We're not done with him."

Paul stood and faced him. "Rachel's seriously hurt and needs stitches right away."

"I'm sure she can take care of that herself. You and I have work to do."

Paul paused for a moment, but then took Eric's arms and dragged him out of the room.

Donovan stood over Rachel, and she hung her head low. He indicated Aaron's body. "Tony and Joe will be down soon to help you clean up this mess. You are not to leave this room until this is all straightened out."

Rachel stared after him, long after he slammed the door shut. She didn't ask for any of this, and she needed a chance to explain what happened.

She retreated to the bathroom and washed off the blood Eric smeared across her face. She cleaned up the wound on her neck the best she could. The cut wasn't as deep as she expected, but she did need some stitches. The pain started to set in as well. Paul would have to stitch her up and give her something for pain when they returned from dealing with Eric.

From the way Donovan had shot out his kneecaps one at a time, whatever they did to Eric would not be quick. For the first time, the thought of killing someone failed to bring her guilt. The blood tracks across her carpet from where Paul dragged him out brought her some comfort in knowing how much he would suffer before he died. Eric deserved every ounce of pain he was about to experience. She just wished she was there to savor it.

After she dressed, she sat on her bed and stared at the hole in the back of Aaron's head, grateful he had fallen face first. She tried to ignore the puddle of blood beneath him. She expected him to move, to come alive and start talking to her, but he remained motionless.

How many times had she seen death before, actually pulled the trigger herself? This time was different, having known Aaron. She was sure what happened was Eric's idea alone. Aaron was never anything more than Eric's little follower, and he followed Eric right into death.

Her bedroom door opened and Tony came in, with Joe right behind him. "Let's get this cleaned up," Joe said. He pointed to Aaron's legs. "Rach, you take that end."

Rachel moved over to Aaron's legs, with Tony right beside her. Every instinct screamed for her to stop what she was doing and run, but she kneeled at the end of Aaron's body and slipped her hands under his stiff ankles. Movement flickered in the corner of her eye. She turned her head in time to see Tony's gun descending.

Chapter Fifty-seven

Rachel's first thought was she needed to take some aspirin. Her second thought was the jackhammer in her head was the least of her worries. Her blood ran cold, and she realized her nightmare was just beginning.

Lying on her stomach and wearing only a pair of shorts, the air kissed goosebumps on the bare skin of her back. She tried to move her arms to push herself up, but an unseen restraint stopped her.

She raised her head and looked toward the front of her bed. Rope secured her hands to the posts on her bed frame. She tugged against her binds, but the rope tightened around her wrists. She tried to move her legs to get into a better position to pull her hands free, but she was met with the same resistance as with her hands. Panic set in, but no matter how hard she tried, she could not free her hands or feet.

Rachel rotated her head to the left, to the other side of her room. Donovan sat in a chair, his face almost unrecognizable beneath his anger. "You have lived here for thirteen years," he said. "In that time, I have given you everything. Shelter, food, clothes, whatever you needed and so much more. I gave you me, Rachel, *all* of me. I love you, more than anyone or anything in my entire life."

Rachel's face bunched up and tears stung her eyes. "Donovan, please, let me explain—"

"Your recent behavior has been unacceptable, and the way you handled this situation tonight was inappropriate. I've lost two men over this incident. But, what bothers me most is how informative Eric was before he died. He had a lot to say about Jonathan Thomas." He spoke the name as if it contained poison.

He knew about Jonathan, about the kiss that morning. Rachel's chest tightened and fear seized her heart. Her breaths came in short bursts. She tried to speak, but couldn't form any words.

Donovan stood up and moved toward the closet, where she could no longer see him. "Apparently, I've not made myself clear before now, and you've left me with no choice. I don't think there is any other way to impress upon you that you are mine, Rachel. You always will be mine."

When he came back into view, Rachel's eyes widened and fixed on his hands. One held a red rag. The other held a coiled whip, one she recognized from a case in the waiting room. Tears spilled across her face and onto the bed. "No, Donovan, no, no, no." The words came out between sharp breaths, and her entire body ached in anticipation of the whip touching her back.

She jerked against the rope to break free, but it only tightened more and cut into her wrists and ankles. Blood ran down her skin, but she kept tugging as hard as she could. Donovan watched her try to free herself without a word.

Her muscles slacked from exhaustion. "Donovan, please, don't do this," she said. "I love you, Donovan. You don't have to do this. Please, Donovan."

Donovan walked over to the bed and knelt down. He stroked her hair. "I love you, too, Rachel, and that's why I have to do this."

The smell of liquor overwhelmed her as he spoke, and his glassy eyes reflected his intoxication. Rachel lost all hope of reasoning with him. In all her years at the estate, she rarely knew him to indulge in liquor. With alcohol and jealousy driving his rage, he wouldn't listen to any rationale, nor would he be stopped.

He kissed her cheek, and his lips lingered on her tear-soaked skin. He lowered his head and grazed her mouth with his. As his lips moved over hers, the tears flowed down her face, but she returned his kiss. She willed him to realize how wrong he was, to untie her, and just love her.

When he parted from her, he stood up and his fingers traced the bare skin on her back with light touches. She usually enjoyed his fingers fluttering across her skin, but now it only served to set her pain receptors on high alert, as if he lit small fires on every inch of her back.

"Please, Donovan," she cried. "Don't you know how much I love you and I'd never betray you? I love you so much, Donovan. Please don't do this to me."

"But you've already betrayed me, Rachel," he said. Anger flooded his voice and spilled out from his eyes. "That won't ever happen again, not after I've branded you as mine. When you see my marks on you, you'll be reminded that you belong to me and only me. No one else will ever want you, not after tonight."

He forced the rag into her mouth. Her teeth clamped down on the material, and she screamed as loud as she could for him to stop, but no discernible words came out of her mouth.

Donovan stepped back, and the whip rolled down from his hand. "Don't worry, Rachel. It will be over soon."

She squeezed her eyes shut and her body stiffened. *It's a dream*, she thought. *It's only a dream.*

Chapter Fifty-eight

Pain. There was so much pain. Every breath she took intensified the burning until it was almost more than Rachel could stand.

The first time the whip had cracked across her skin, goosebumps covered her entire body in an instant and her eyes bulged with the force of the pain. It had taken some time before her voice reacted, and she screamed louder than she ever believed possible. Her binds had cut into her skin around her wrists and ankles, and numbness claimed her back.

When the whip didn't immediately connect with her back again, she thought Donovan had realized he crossed the line. Then he had stepped over to her and touched her back with his fingers, running them along each side of the wound. He wasn't rethinking his actions, but admiring his work. Then the whip had come down again, over and over and over.

At some point, she had passed out, but she wasn't sure for how long. When she woke up, Donovan had spoken to her, and then the whip had its say. She had screamed until there was nothing left, and then her absent voice scraped like razor blades against her raw throat. Every so often, he would stop and watch her, half-naked and bound to the bed with her skin ripped open. Whenever he stopped to examine her back, she thought the pain would finally end, and then he unleashed his fury on her again.

After he had released the binds from her hands and feet, he raised her limp head from the mattress and kissed her like never before. He left the room with the bloodied whip, and she passed out again with the pain.

When she woke, Paul tended to her wounds. He gave her antibiotics and a shot of morphine. He tried to cover her body with a sheet, but she cried out in protest, the pain too much to have something touching her back. Day after day, he changed the dressings on her skin and gave her the maximum amount of morphine he could without her overdosing. For Rachel, it was never enough.

At the end of the first day, she pleaded with him to accidentally leave a bottle of pain pills in her room. Though he refused, she continued to beg him for it when he came to see her. She wanted nothing more than to die. She willed her body to shut down on its own, but she continued to wake from every sleep.

Still breathing, still burning.

Despite the overwhelming desire to die, she would never kill herself. Even if Paul gave into her requests to leave the pills in her room, she would only take the amount he dictated. She was not coward enough to take her own life, no matter what Donovan did to her. The pain would end, and this period of time would be nothing more than a horrible memory, a nightmare she could pretend never happened.

During the lucid times, the painful times, her thoughts alternated between suicide and killing Donovan. He had hurt her like never before. His temper was never welcome, but she always tolerated the random beatings. This time, he reached an inexcusable level. She had to ensure it would never happen again.

Murder was not a foreign action to her, but there was a difference between killing a stranger and killing the man she had loved for so many years. She knew that when the time came, she would never be able to go through with it.

When she was medicated, her thoughts incoherent and jumbled, she blamed herself for his actions. She had done something wrong, and she deserved every crack of the whip. All he ever asked of her was love and devotion and she had betrayed him. She allowed another man to kiss her and she enjoyed it, an unforgivable act.

She chastised herself and thought of all the things she should have done differently. She wished she could return to the place where she had strayed from Donovan's arms. She told herself he was right to punish her, and he had only done so because he loved her like he told her. He couldn't bear the thought of losing her, so he exercised control over her to keep her with him. He branded her so no other man would ever want her and she would never forget where she belonged.

After six days of drifting in and out of consciousness, six days of listening to the dueling voices in her head, she found the middle ground that silenced them both.

She would leave.

It wasn't an easy option. She couldn't pack her bags and walk out the front door, promising to send a postcard. No one left the estate on their own accord, especially not her. As soon as her parents died, she was sentenced to spend her life at the estate. Donovan would never allow her to walk away.

A few days later, the solution presented itself when Paul told her to come to the conference room for a meeting. He helped her up despite her protests that she was fine. It had only been a day since she could put clothing on over her wounds, but the healing process seemed to be well underway.

She went into her bathroom, pulled her hair back, and splashed water on her face. As she dabbed it dry with a towel, she studied her reflection. Her face appeared worn, like a child had used her skin for modeling clay. Lines appeared around her eyes and mouth, ones that had not been there before. It seemed ridiculous, as no one aged in a matter of days. She ran her fingers over her cheek and tried to brush the lines off like dirt, but the lines clung to her skin.

Rachel threw the towel at the mirror and walked upstairs to the conference room, where the others waited for her. She stood by the wall behind Paul's chair. If she sat down, the back of the chair would press too hard against her still raw wounds.

Donovan sat across the room from her, yet she couldn't bring herself to look at him. Vague memories came to mind of him coming in and out of her room while she was heavily drugged. The first time he came to see her, he knelt beside the bed, took her hand, and cried. He cursed himself for hurting her, for losing control and punishing her like that. Between the alcohol and what Eric told him, he fell victim to his own temper.

After his tears stopped, he pulled a sheet over her back to hide the evidence of his abuse, stroked her hair while talking to her, and told her how much he loved her. He visited her several times a day, sometimes talking, sometimes crying and begging her forgiveness. That he hadn't abandoned her after that night comforted her, but she still could not look directly at him. Not yet.

"We have two jobs tomorrow night," Donovan said at the start of the meeting.

Rachel was taken aback. She knew about the Pierson job, but had not heard about a second one.

"Paul, Rachel, and I will take Pierson. It's pretty standard, quick in and out with only the security alarm to bypass. We'll leave at eleven-thirty for that one. Tony and Joe, I want you to leave by ten o'clock for the Thomas job." Donovan's eyes burned through her, and she held still, not daring to blink. She didn't want to give a reaction of any kind.

"It shouldn't take long to get into the house," he continued. "Tony will go in and do it. I want you on the grounds no longer than forty-five minutes."

He spoke for another fifteen minutes, further detailing the Pierson job, but Rachel stopped listening. Jonathan was going to die because of her. There had to be a way to help him.

Everyone stood to leave the room, the meeting over. She turned to go when Donovan called her back. She shut the doors to the conference room and braced herself to face him.

He looked as he always did, the same enchanting amber eyes and smooth, handsome face, but there was a difference when she looked at him. During recent years, he had pushed her to the point where she was slightly afraid of him, afraid of his temper, of his lashing out at her. Now, she was no longer afraid. She was terrified.

He moved over to her and touched her arm. She recoiled at his touch, and her heart raced. He put his hand on her face and she trembled beneath the heat of his palm. "I'm sorry, Rachel. I never meant to hurt you like I did. I don't know what came over me. There's no excuse for my actions, and I can't express how sorry I am that I hurt you that much. I love you more than anything else in this world."

She met his eyes and could see his words were true. Had he lied about his remorse, leaving would be much easier, but the tears welling in his eyes mirrored her own. Though his apology was sincere, from his actions that night she knew he was excited by the idea that he had branded her. As long as those wounds remained visible, she belonged only to him. No one else would want her, which was his desired outcome.

Donovan kissed her and his fingers tickled the skin around her mouth. She didn't know if she was upset because the man who savagely beat her kissed her, or because her body responded to his touch. Her love for him had not died as she thought it would, but instead, she loved him as much as she always had.

Rachel broke the kiss. "I love you, Donovan," she said. Despite her mind crying out for her to retain sanity, she meant the words. She couldn't rid herself of such a strong emotion overnight, and part of her wanted to stay with him forever. There had to be a way to make him not want to punish her anymore.

She wanted to tell him about her plan to leave him and promise to stay if he stopped hurting her. The pain in her back flared, and she stopped herself from saying a word. If she stayed, there would be nothing holding him back from using a whip on her again, if not doing much worse things to her. She had no choice but to leave.

When the idea came to her, she almost didn't recognize it, but when she did, she acted on it. She pulled off his jacket and kissed his face and neck, ignoring the severe pain that shot across her back every time she moved.

"I love you so much," she said, reinforcing her feelings in both his mind and hers. Nothing she said was a lie, and she was determined to prove it to him. Her mouth teased his with light kisses, and she tugged his shirt out of his pants. While she worked on unbuckling his belt, Donovan raised her shirt over her head and tossed it to the floor.

She unbuttoned his shirt and pushed it over his shoulders. His mouth found her neck, and his hands wrapped around her waist. Pain mixed with desire and Rachel bit her bottom lip. Her hands traveled across his chest, while his mouth nuzzled the crook of her neck and his fingers fiddled with the button of her jeans. Her eyelids fell and, for a few minutes, she enjoyed being close to him.

"I've really messed up lately," Rachel said. "I want to make it up to you."

"What do you mean?" he asked, the words escaping with shallow breaths.

"I want the Thomas job. I want to kill him for you."

He stopped kissing her. "You would do that for me?"

She stared into his eyes and touched his face. "Of course I would. I love you, Donovan. I'm yours, and I want to show you that I know where I belong."

He smiled and put his hands under her arms. Being careful not to touch her back too much, he lifted her onto the table. He slid his hands under her thighs and pulled her hips toward his. His mouth landed on hers and she put her body on automatic pilot, her mind in another place, focused on the task of killing Jonathan.

She opened her eyes and glanced over Donovan's shoulder at the clock on the wall. She had a little over twenty-four hours to make this work.

Chapter Fifty-nine

Twenty-four hours later, Paul barged into her room. "What the hell do you think you're doing?"

Rachel continued lacing her boots and avoided looking up at him. She didn't want to see Paul before she left the estate, knowing it would make it harder to go through with her plan. "I'm going on the job."

"You're doing the Thomas job?"

"Yes."

"Rachel, that's insane," Paul said. "Your back isn't even close to being healed. You're in no condition to do this. I even objected to the idea of you going with us for Pierson."

She finished tying her boots and rested her hands on her knees. "Donovan thinks I'm capable of handling Thomas."

"Of course he does, Rach," he said. "Sending you is the perfect revenge on Thomas."

She lifted her eyes to look at him. "It wasn't Donovan's idea. I requested this job."

"What?" Paul took a step back. "Why would you volunteer to kill Jonathan Thomas?"

"Because it's easy. A hell of a lot easier than the Pierson job will be. If I do this one, I don't have to do the other."

"Who's going to do your part for Pierson?"

"Tony." She stood up and met his gaze. "Are you done lecturing me? Can I go now?"

His expression softened. "Rachel, that day when I left with Donovan to check out the job…" He paused as he formed his words. "Were you going to tell me about Thomas? Was that why you were so upset after your rounds?"

"Yes."

"Tell me now what happened."

"I don't know, Paul. It all happened so fast. He came to the estate to meet with Donovan. He must have snuck out the back because he found me while I was on rounds. I tried to get him to leave, but then he kissed me. I guess I kind of let him do that. I shouldn't have, but things were so confusing and then Eric saw us kiss and—"

"Wait." Paul held his hand up in the air. "Thomas kissed you? That's all?"

Lead pulled her heart down into her stomach, and the realization came over her that something was terribly wrong. "Yes, he kissed me. That's all."

Paul covered his face with his hands.

Already knowing what his response would be, she asked, "What is it, Paul?"

He dropped his hands in front of him. "That's not what Eric told Donovan. He made it sound like a longstanding affair. He said he saw you in the woods with Thomas, and that he watched everything. The things he said about you and Thomas were…" Paul hesitated. "I told Donovan we shouldn't believe Eric, that after being tortured for so long, he was saying those things to get out of his own mess. In the end, Eric was so convincing that I even started to believe what he said."

Rachel bowed her head and closed her eyes, her mind spinning. Eric had won. He knew he was going down and he succeeded in dragging her as far into hell with him as he could. She opened her eyes when she heard Paul speaking again.

"Eric's story destroyed Donovan. We came back and he hit the bottle hard. I've never seen him like that, drinking straight out of the bottle. I left him alone, thinking he would pass out from how fast he was drinking. I didn't know—"

Rachel touched his hand. "Don't go there, Paul. It's not your fault. You couldn't have known."

Paul lowered his head for a moment. "When you and Joe return from the Thomas job, the rest of us will still be gone for Pierson. We'll be on that job for quite a few hours."

She blinked. "It had crossed my mind."

"I brought some part-timers in from the security company to patrol the grounds tonight. George and his crew were inexplicably unavailable to cover for us. Tonight's crew has never been here before, and I don't think they're competent."

Her eyes darted around the room, digesting the meaning behind Paul's words. "That's too bad about George," she said, despite her elation. She had been concerned with getting around George and his sharp-eyed crew when the time came to leave. "Anything else I should know?"

"Joe has a couple beers every night."

Rachel looked at Paul. "I know this."

"If you decide to drink a beer with him, I sure wouldn't take any pain medication. Taking three or four of those with alcohol would probably knock you out good."

"I bet it would." She smiled, grateful to have Paul in her corner.

Paul reached into his pocket. He took her hand and pressed a bag of pain pills against her palm. "I trust you to do the right thing with these."

Her hand tightened around the bag. "I promise," she said. She shoved the small bag into her front pocket.

"Good luck with Thomas," he said. He planted a kiss her cheek.

She fought the tears that threatened to fall. "Thank you, Paul," she whispered.

Chapter Sixty

Rachel crept down the hallway, her boots making no sound on the marble floor. Her heart pounded in her throat and her breathing echoed in her ears, magnified by the silence.

As she neared the door at the end of the hall, the subdued melody of a piano filled the air. She placed her ear against the door and strained to hear the music. She recognized the beautiful and complicated meshing of tones, could follow them exactly in her mind, yet she struggled with how she knew the song.

She gripped the doorknob and turned it with the greatest of care. Holding her breath, she eased open the door, alert for any creaks the hinges might utter.

The marble floor continued past the door. To her left, a circular staircase rose from the floor and reached for the second floor below a dome ceiling. Any other time, she would have appreciated the beauty of the intricately detailed railing, but she didn't care about the staircase.

Across the room, Jonathan was seated at a white grand piano with his eyes closed. His head moved in time to the music he created, his face rich with emotion. As soon as she saw him, she remembered the origin of the song, and her hand covered her mouth. She wondered why she didn't identify it sooner.

They had danced to it.

No distractions.

Donovan's instructions from her first kill forced her to move forward. She walked across the floor, her gloved hand leveling her gun in front of her. The long sleeves of her black shirt concealed her chafed wrists.

She didn't bother keeping her footfalls silent, and Jonathan's fingers ceased dancing across the keys. As he stood up and walked toward her, his casual dress astonished her, given the tuxedo and business attire she had previously seen him wear. His unkempt hair topped off blue jeans and a plain, cotton shirt. Rachel's thoughts wavered, her attraction to him rekindled, and she almost forgot the reason for breaking into his home.

His eyes moved from her face to the gun and back again. "I knew you were an angel, but I didn't realize you were a dark one," he said, showing no indication that he was surprised by her presence. "I take it you do little more than security work for King."

"It's true I came here to kill you."

"Sent by King, no doubt."

"You won't sell to him, but those who will take over your company upon your death will be easier to persuade." The hollow words sounded rehearsed, and she hated having to force the unconvincing charade.

"That's funny. I didn't realize my company was worth so much to him. Are you sure that's the real reason?"

Rachel remained silent, her well-practiced script falling apart before her eyes.

"I just wish my life was worth more than that to you," he said.

"If it weren't, you'd be slumped over your piano right now. I'd like to make you a deal. A business proposition."

"And what would that be?"

"You pay me one million dollars, and you get to keep breathing."

Jonathan didn't blink. "One million? I take it King doesn't know about this."

"I don't suppose he does."

"How long do I have to come up with the money?"

Rachel glanced at the wristwatch she wore over her long sleeve. "Twenty-seven minutes."

"You're expecting a miracle."

"Not necessarily. I also need you to create an account for it to go into, one that can't be traced back to me.

"And you're awfully trusting in that request. My computer is in there," he said, pointing to a door behind him.

She followed him into his den, where his laptop rested on an oak desk next to a towering houseplant. Rachel focused on the wall to her left. Pictures of children with their parents covered the top half of the wall, and Rachel found herself drawn to the photographs.

"That's my family," Jonathan said. "Brothers and sisters, nieces and nephews."

She noticed a black and white photograph in the center of the pictures. An older house was in the background, but the focus of the picture was a toddler standing barefoot on a gravel driveway. His too-small pants had holes over both knees, his shirt looked stained, and he had a smudge of dirt next to his unsmiling mouth. She stroked the glass over the boy.

"I was two years old in that picture. I keep it up there to remind myself where I came from."

It was an interesting glimpse into the world of Jonathan Thomas. She wanted to know more, but there was no time for that.

Rachel spun around at his presence behind her. Her breathing rattled in her lungs, and she let him take the gun from her hands.

He placed the gun on the desk behind him and turned back toward her. "Do you have any concept of how beautiful you are?" he asked. He lifted her chin and touched his lips to hers. His fingers moved through her hair and the other hand traveled around to her back. His hand tightened on her back and he pulled her closer to him.

Pain zapped her out of her blissful state. She broke away from him and tried not to cry out. The blood drained from her face and her muscles tightened.

"What is it?" Jonathan asked, his brow creased.

"This is wrong. We shouldn't be doing this."

"That's not it. You look like you're in pain. Are you hurt?"

"Nothing happened," she said.

His expression became suspicious. "I didn't ask you what happened. I asked if you were hurt."

She wanted him to stop probing. She couldn't let him find out what Donovan had done. "I'm not hurt."

His eyes searched hers. "I don't understand. Why are you lying to me?" His frown deepened when she didn't reply. "You were okay until I touched your back. Did you hurt yourself?"

"I'm fine."

"Stop lying to me."

Rachel folded her arms and scratched at an invisible itch under her sleeve. "I'm fine," she repeated.

Jonathan took her arm and pulled it toward him. Her right sleeve had shifted when she crossed her arms, exposing her chafed wrist. Jonathan pushed up her sleeve and examined the healing red circle around her wrist. "What in the—"

She snatched her arm back from him and pushed her sleeve down over her wrist.

"Rachel, turn around."

"No."

He took her arm again, but didn't tighten his grip so as to hurt her. He stressed each word he spoke. "Turn around."

Rachel bit her bottom lip and rotated. She closed her eyes and bowed her head. He took the sides of her shirt and raised it. He held the material up for a moment and then lowered it back down. She turned around.

His eyes shifted away from her, and rage boiled beneath the surface of his wavering voice. "Why?" he asked.

"It doesn't matter anymore. It's over."

"Why?" he yelled.

"It's over!"

"It's because of me, isn't it? Because of what I told King? Or did someone see us together on the estate? Is that what happened?"

His words made her uncomfortable, and she wished she had never come. "It doesn't matter now."

"It does too matter. A person cannot… he cannot do that to you." He took his cell phone out of his front pocket. "I'm calling the police."

"No!" She grabbed his arm. "You can't do that. Promise me you won't do that."

"Give me one reason why I shouldn't." As soon as the words left his lips, understanding crossed his face, and he glanced at the gun on the desk. "Exactly what kind of work do you do for King?"

"I am security at the estate. I didn't lie about that." She ran her tongue over her dry lips, and guilt consumed her. "I'm also a thief. I can pick any lock and crack any safe."

He returned his phone to his pocket. "You didn't break in here tonight to steal something. Have you killed many people?"

"Too many."

"I see." He took a deep breath. "How long have you worked for King?"

"About ten years now, since I was thirteen."

"You started picking locks when you were thirteen?"

"That's when I was taught how to do it. I moved to the estate when I was ten, after my parents died. My uncle works for Donovan."

"Let me see if I understand. After your parents died, you went to live with your uncle who happens to work for King. And, King took advantage of that and trained you as a thief and a killer. Then he what, trained you as his mistress, too?"

"It was never like that," she said. "There's love."

Sadness claimed his eyes. "What he did to you, Rachel, that's not love. There's nothing even remotely similar to love in what he did."

"Jonathan, I'm a professional thief and a contract killer. Maybe I don't deserve love."

He brushed the tears from her cheeks. "Yes, you do. You deserve it more than anyone I've ever known." He cupped her face in his hands and kissed her again. Breaking away from her, he lowered his head. "How long has he been hurting you?"

Everything Jonathan said confused her, and heartache sliced through her chest. She didn't want to talk about any of this, didn't want to admit that everything Donovan did to her was wrong. She had explained away his actions for so long that she believed it was okay for him to do those things, that she deserved all of it.

Her eyes moved around the room in search of something to focus on to avoid looking at Jonathan. "Over four years now," she said. "Since I was nineteen."

Jonathan's eyes dampened, but his body remained tense with anger. "Is this the first time that he… that he did…" He gestured toward her.

"Yes," she said. "That was the first time, and it's the last time."

Jonathan clamped his hands together in front of his waist. "Well, you're leaving him. That's the most important thing. I guess I'll work on getting you that money." He sat behind the desk and worked on his computer.

Rachel kept her eyes lowered, not wanting to see the anger in his hard eyes and clenched jaw. She consulted her watch every few minutes to keep track of the time.

"What name do you want this under?" he asked.

"I don't care. Make something up."

"Make something up," he repeated. He lifted his eyes and studied her face. "Of course." He started typing again.

"What?"

"Angel Thomas."

"Interesting."

"I think it's perfect." After several more minutes of rushed typing, Jonathan clicked the mouse and the printer beside his desk responded. He leaned back in his chair and examined her, his face now expressionless.

Rachel tried to ignore his inspection of her. So many things he said made sense to her, and she questioned what she thought she had with Donovan. Part of her wanted to scream at Jonathan for trying to open her eyes to the truth, for shredding her life apart within minutes. The rest of her wanted to collapse in his arms for protection.

The printer stopped, and he removed the pages it ejected. Standing up, he said, "I created two accounts. One is overseas and has the bulk of the money. The other is in the States and has five thousand in it. When you transfer money from one account to the other, always make the transfers less than ten thousand and make them at least a month apart. As long as you're not transferring large amounts of money day after day, the government won't trace it."

Rachel stored away the information in the back of her mind. She had never considered that taking large amounts out at once could call attention to her movements. Once she left, Donovan would do everything he could to find her and get her back, and she needed to stay off his radar.

Jonathan handed the pages to her. "Here is all the information you need to get the money."

The first page showed the account with five thousand dollars as the balance. She turned to the second page, and her lips parted with surprise. The balance of the overseas account was five thousand short of five million dollars. "Five million dollars?" she asked. She read the balance again to make sure it was right. She raised her eyes to his. "I don't understand."

"I want to make sure you'll be taken care of."

"Why are you doing this?"

"You demanded one million dollars so I could live to see another day. The way I see it, I bought myself five days. But, according to my accountant, I made an anonymous donation to a private battered women's shelter. He'll have a coronary working out the details." He shrugged. "Or maybe I won't tell him about this at all. That might be best."

Battered woman. Is that what she was? She had never heard the term before, but she knew exactly what it meant. In that instant, every bruise, every punch, every backhand, and every crack of the whip came alive on her body at once.

With trembling hands, she folded the pages Jonathan gave her and shoved them into her pocket. "That's very generous of you," Rachel said.

"It's not generous," he said. "It's the only thing that's right, the only thing that will let me sleep at night. Knowing you're safe and he can never touch you again."

He handed her a business card and pointed to a phone number he wrote on the back. "If you need me for anything, you can reach me directly at this number, twenty-four hours a day. It doesn't matter what I'm doing or how late it is, I will always answer your call."

Rachel took the card from him. "Thank you." She grew uneasy as he moved closer to her. "I have to go," she said.

"You don't have to leave, Rachel. You can stay here with me. I can help you and I can take care of you."

"I can't stay."

"It's King, isn't it? Please don't tell me you still feel anything for him."

"It has nothing to do with him," she said.

"I know you must be experiencing a lot of confused emotions right now. I'm sure he told you he loved you before and after he did those terrible things to you, and I'm sure you believed him. Because you've been there so long, you probably don't know any better. You also must be terrified of him after what he's done to you, but I can make it so he will never hurt you again. I can protect you from him."

Her lips tightened. "No, you can't. No one can protect me from him."

Jonathan held his hands up in resignation. "Go then. If that's what you have to do."

"It is." Relief flowed through her, and she realized she had been holding her breath. He was allowing her to leave much easier than she had anticipated. "I have to do this on my own. Well, as much as possible, that is. I, uh…" She swallowed hard. "I wish things were different."

"I understand." He moistened his lips and placed his hands on her shoulders. "Rachel, be smart about your moves. Don't stay in one place too long, and don't put yourself in a position where he can find you."

"Okay," she said.

"This money comes with the condition that you will keep me updated on where you are. When you settle in somewhere, call that number and tell me. When you leave a city, call me before you go and let me know where you're headed. If you are even slightly tempted to go back to him, call me and we'll talk about it."

He was doing far more to help her than she ever dreamed. "I will, Jonathan. I swear to you that I will."

"Good," he said. "It's important that you keep me updated. Since you've lived at his estate for so long, no one knows that you exist. Outside of him, I'm the only one who knows you're out there. But, unlike him, I'm the only one who cares, and I'm the only one who can help keep you safe."

Rachel believed his words, that he did care about her and would help her however he could to ensure her safety.

"When you've had a bit of time to yourself to sort through some of this, I'll come get you and take you far away from everything. If it's too dangerous for you here, we'll go somewhere else. We'll leave the country if need be, but as long as I'm around, he will never touch you again."

Her watch beeped, reminding her to leave, but she couldn't stop herself from leaning into him and kissing him again. He put his hands on her arms and avoided touching her back, much as Donovan had done the day before. His kiss was much softer than Donovan's, and she found it near impossible to stop kissing him.

She realized there was more waiting for her out in the world. Here she stood, kissing a man who promised to take care of her and to never hurt her. She didn't know that was an option before tonight. She had been taught to believe that love and pain were synonymous.

Jonathan was right. She needed some time to sort through what she was feeling, but she would still do everything he asked of her, and make sure that he always knew where she was. When he did come to find her, she would go with him and trust him to keep her safe. She wanted to stay with him now, but Donovan would soon find out what she had done. This would be the first place he looked for her.

She ended their kiss, knowing she had to leave before Joe came in after her. “Listen to me, Jonathan. He wants you dead, and when he finds out you’re still alive, he’s going to come after you.”

“Don’t worry about me,” Jonathan said. “Only worry about yourself and getting somewhere safe.”

She thought about giving herself so freely to Donovan yesterday in the conference room for the purpose of convincing him to give her this job. “You don’t understand. I sold my soul to come here tonight.” Tears formed in her eyes, and she whispered, “Please don’t let him kill you. I don’t want you to die.”

“I’m not going anywhere, and I’m not going to die, not when there is so much to live for.” He touched her cheek. “It’s not too late for you to stay with me.”

“I’m sorry.” She picked up her gun from the desk. She gave him one more kiss before saying, “I’ll call you soon.” It took all her strength to turn and leave the room.

Chapter Sixty-one

I'm going to get a beer. Want one?" Rachel asked Joe once they were back in the basement of the estate.

"You're in good mood," Joe said.

She was in the worst mood of her life, stressed she had gone too far to turn back, and anxious to finish her plan. Her thoughts rested with Jonathan, and she prayed he had enough sense to run before Donovan found out he was still alive.

Instead of displaying her real feelings, she smiled at Joe and said, "Of course I'm in a good mood. Donovan will be happy with our work tonight."

"You're right," Joe said. "He's wanted to eliminate Thomas for some time now."

"So how about that beer?"

"Might as well." He followed her into the kitchen.

Rachel took two beer bottles out of the stainless steel refrigerator and handed one to Joe. She opened the bottle and leaned forward on the island countertop. "One of us should check in with security and make sure they're okay."

He regarded her with suspicion. "You know I'm not supposed to leave you alone."

"Come on, you left me alone at the Thomas house for almost an hour. If I was going to do anything, don't you think it would have been then?"

"I don't know," he said.

"All you have to do is go grab your radio and call them. You're going to leave me standing here by myself for five minutes, max. If I were going anywhere, I'd have to go all the way upstairs and right past you to get there. Besides, what can I possibly do in the time you're gone? Finish this beer?"

Joe relaxed and laughed at his paranoia. "I guess you're right. I'll check in with security since it is their first time out here. Need to make sure the estate is secure." He left his beer on the counter and walked out of the kitchen.

Rachel reached into her pocket and removed five of the oval pills Paul gave her, saving the rest for her to take later as needed. She took a butcher's knife out of a drawer and rested the blade on top of the pills. She pressed the palm of her hand against the blade and smashed the medicine into a fine dust.

She gathered as much of the dust as she could and shoved it into his beer bottle. The liquid fizzed with the addition of the pills. "Dissolve, damn it," she whispered to the bottle. She wiped the knife clean on her jeans and put it back in the drawer.

The last bubble floated to the top as the door opened and Joe came in. She was leaning against the counter again, smiling with her beer bottle next to her lips.

"Everything's okay with security," Joe said. "I think I'm going to finish this beer and then see if I can help outside."

"Good idea."

They stood in silence for a few minutes. Rachel tried to focus on her escape, but she could only think about Jonathan. She shouldn't have left him behind unprotected. Donovan would go to him first to look for her, and he would not allow Jonathan to live. As soon as she made it away from the estate and found her way to a phone, she would have to call him and convince him to leave.

"You know, Rach," Joe said, "I'm sorry about that whole thing. I didn't want any of that to happen to you."

She waved her hand. "It's okay. You were doing your job."

"I feel bad," he said. "I've always considered you a friend, even when you were an obnoxious little rug rat. Well, maybe you weren't that little."

Racked by guilt over drugging him, she faltered. Joe was not responsible for Donovan's actions, yet he stood between her and freedom. She recovered before he detected anything was wrong. "Don't worry about it. It's over now." She looked at the level of his beer. Three-quarters gone. He was drinking much faster than she could have hoped.

Joe put a hand on his head. "Man, this is something else."

"What's wrong?"

"This beer is starting to hit me. I probably should have eaten more today."

"Shouldn't drink on an empty stomach. Do you want something to eat?"

"No, I should be okay." Joe tilted the bottle and finished it. He walked to the other side of the kitchen to throw the bottle away.

She decided the drugs weren't working fast enough and she needed to take further action if she was going to get away. She gulped down the rest of her beer. Her eyes watered from the bitterness on her tongue and she shivered. "Do you mind getting me another one?" she asked, as she started toward him.

Joe shrugged and opened the refrigerator. When he leaned over to grab another bottle, Rachel walked up behind him and broke the empty bottle over his head. He fell to the floor, unconscious. Kneeling beside him, she checked his pulse, and then kissed his cheek. "I'm so sorry, Joe," she said, as if he could hear her. "I hope you understand that I had to do this."

Rachel removed two bottled waters out of the fridge and ran down the hall to her room. She pulled a few sets of fresh clothes out of her dresser and threw them into her black duffel bag along with the bottled water. On top of the clothes, she laid down wire cutters and the baseball cap her dad bought her before he died.

She rushed into her bathroom and grabbed some personal items to add to the bag. From her closet, she removed a small compass and a penlight, and put both into her pocket. She also took her stethoscope that she used for safecracking.

Rachel checked the safety on her gun and laid it down on her bed. That was a part of this life she was not taking with her. She would have to pick up a different gun for protection somewhere along the way.

With everything she needed to survive for a couple of days in her duffel bag, she raced upstairs to Donovan's room with the bag slung over her shoulder and her stethoscope in her hand. She would need money until she could retrieve what Jonathan had given her, and Donovan kept money and valuables from recent jobs in a safe in his bedroom.

Rachel hesitated in front of his door. In over thirteen years, she had never set foot inside this room. She opened the door and flipped the light switch. It was a typical bedroom. She let out the breath she was holding. "What were you expecting?" she asked herself. "A coffin instead of a bed?"

As she looked around, the similarity to her own bedroom struck her. Both of their rooms had no more furniture than required. No paintings or photographs hung on the walls, no rugs or plants sat on the hardwood floor. It was as if he didn't want the distractions of material possessions when he retired at night, and he longed for the same peace Rachel did when she retreated to her room to gather her thoughts.

There were three closed doors in his room, and she found his safe behind the first door she tried. On impulse, she pulled down the safe's handle, smiling as the door opened to reveal money. He had forgotten to spin the dial the last time he closed the safe.

She put her stethoscope in her bag and grabbed as many banded stacks of bills as her bag would hold. She closed the safe door, but didn't spin the dial in case he left it open on purpose. She didn't want him to know right away that she had taken anything.

On her way out of his room, she glanced back at his bed. On it laid the jacket he had worn before he changed clothes for the Pierson job. She moved to the bed and lifted the jacket, despite the screaming objections inside of her.

She closed her eyes and pressed the material to her face, inhaling the warm, inviting scent that was distinctly him. It filled her heart as well as her lungs and placed tantalizing thoughts in her head.

She didn't have to leave. She could stay and it would be okay in the end. She could easily explain her actions to him and he would forgive her, as she had forgiven him so many times before. After all, he loved her and he was sorry this time for the way he had hurt her. He would change and it would never happen again. Maybe things could go back to the way they were in the beginning. Or maybe they would be better than ever before.

She opened her eyes and put the jacket back down, eyeing it as if it was the embodiment of evil. As good as it sounded, she knew it would never happen and there was still the matter of Jonathan. She had left him alive and Donovan wanted him dead. Donovan would be furious to know she hadn't completed the job. Then there were those pesky feelings she had for Jonathan. It was better for her to leave and start her life over. No more rounds, no more jobs, no more guilt.

No more pain.

At the bottom of the stairs, she stopped to consider which exit to use: the front door, the back door, or a side window. She decided on a side window, knowing there would be security near the back entrance of the house, and the front lights were much too bright.

Without thinking, she entered the waiting room. As she moved toward the nearest window, she forced herself to not look at the cases on the wall. One of them contained the whip that marred her back. She pushed the curtain aside and unlocked the window. She threw her bag outside and followed it, closing the window behind her.

Rachel crept toward the back of the house. A security guard stood in front of her and another paced fifty feet to her left, ignoring the normal patrol patterns. Their incompetence outraged her because it impeded her plan. There was nothing she could do but wait for one of them to move.

The guard in front of her surprised her by walking over to the other security guard and starting a conversation. She ducked behind a tree next to where he had been standing. A branch broke beneath her feet. She held still, ready to fight anyone who came near her tree. After an agonizing moment, she peeked around the tree, but the two men had not budged.

Rachel used the shadows and darkness to transport her to the back of the property. When she reached the fence, she dug the wire cutters out of her bag and went to work, cutting several slits large enough for her to fit through.

She put the cutters back in her bag and climbed through the fence. Already exhausted, her muscles ached with tension. She glanced back at the estate through the fence and battled the strong impulse to turn around and go back to the world she knew. She could still change her mind, no matter what consequences she would face when Donovan returned. No punishment could be worse than what he had already inflicted on her.

But she couldn't go back. Despite her fatigue, exhilaration flowed through her veins. She was free.

She pulled the compass and penlight out of her pocket and turned east. She looked ahead at the woods in front of her. The sound of Jonathan's piano played in her head.

She ran.

Part Three

Chapter Sixty-two

It was impossible.

Maybe Paul was mistaken. Maybe he was talking about someone else, but not Rachel.

How many people did Paul say she had killed?

Mark closed his eyes. He thought of Rachel's slender fingers, and the ability they had to send electricity through his body every time she touched him. He found it difficult to believe those same fingers could pull the trigger of a gun and end the life of another human being.

But as much as he tried to deny it, he knew it was true. Everything Paul said was consistent with the Rachel he knew. The pieces of the puzzle blended and completed the picture. He hated what he saw and was disgusted by his reaction to it. Something shifted within him, and for the first time in his life, rage filled him.

Rachel was not the target of his anger. He told her nothing could change his love for her and he meant it. He couldn't hold her responsible. Raised a criminal, she had no chance at a normal life. She had been manipulated and broken by a man who controlled her with the slightest jerk of her strings.

Mark couldn't understand how one man could have so much influence and control over other people. He thought of Paul's seeming inability to interfere and help Rachel. He had been powerless to do anything but turn his back and ignore her muffled screams. Mark wished he could travel back in time and rip her out of that world.

And now she was back in it.

He looked up as Paul entered the room. Paul offered a stressed smile. "You don't look so good," he said.

Mark lifted his hand to his forehead. His eyes glassed over, and exhaustion tugged on every part of his body. "You just told me the woman I love killed people because that's what she was raised to do. How the hell am I supposed to look?"

"I know it's a lot to sort through," Paul said. "I wish I could have told you a different story."

Mark thought the tension in his neck would snap his spine in two. He snaked a hand around the back of his neck and rubbed his muscles. The memory of touching Rachel's scarred back flashed through his mind and his eyes flew open at the image. "She has scars on her back," he said, not knowing where the words came from. "I don't think she knew they were there until I asked her about them."

Paul crossed his arms. "She probably did know, but didn't want to, so she never checked. I lied and told her she wouldn't have any scars. I thought it might help her heal emotionally if she didn't think she would have them forever."

He lifted his gaze to Paul and stared at him with reddened eyes. "Help her?" he asked. "You thought it would help her? You didn't stop him."

"If I had known what he was going to do," Paul said, "I'd have killed him and buried him next to Eric."

Anger boiled in Mark's gut. "But you knew he was hurting her when he was doing it. You may not have known to what degree, but you said you could hear her scream while he—"

Paul didn't let him finish. "And don't you think it eats me alive every time I think about it? I hate him for what he did to her. I hate myself for not doing anything about it."

"Then why didn't you stop him? She's your niece, your own blood! You could have stopped him."

"And get us both killed? Or worse yet, get myself killed and leave no one for Rachel?"

"She might as well have had no one. I mean, what good did you do her?" Mark asked. "You were in a position to help her all those years and you didn't."

"If I could go back and do things differently, then I would without hesitation."

"That didn't help her then and it's not helping her now. It never should have gotten to that point. You should have gotten her out when you saw what was happening."

"I know, Mark. I know how wrong I was."

"You're more than wrong," Mark said, his voice filled with contempt. "You're as guilty as he is."

Paul tightened his lips and looked away. "You're right. I have no defense. I didn't tell you about her life because I'm seeking forgiveness for what I've done wrong. I don't deserve that in the least, not from God, not from her, and not from you or anyone else who cares about her. But, I also didn't come in here to try and defend myself. I've sent Sean out on an errand. We only have about ten minutes, but I can sneak you in to see her, if you want."

Mark snapped to attention. "Of course I do." He followed Paul down a long, narrow hallway and around a corner.

Paul stopped in front of a white door and faced Mark. "I haven't seen her yet, so be prepared for anything." He pushed open the door.

Mark looked down and ran a hand through his hair. His mind and body were both spent. He wasn't sure how much more he could handle, but he forced himself to move into her room.

Rachel's eyes were closed, her body tucked under a white comforter with random splashes of red on it. Swelling, cuts, and bruises interrupted the serenity of her face. Her shallow, irregular breathing troubled Mark almost as much as the blood on the floor and on the blanket that covered her. His throat tightened and his hand reached for his hollowed-out stomach.

At Paul's prompting, Mark stood away from the bed, next to the door. Paul sat on the bed beside her and uncovered her halfway. She stirred into consciousness. "Rachel? Come on, it's time to wake up."

She moaned and her eyelids rose to half-mast. "Paul?"

He smiled. "I'm here. Are you feeling okay?"

"I'm so tired," she whispered. She grimaced, and rubbed her eyes.

"Why are you tired, honey?"

"The needles."

"He drugged you?" Paul swore under his breath. "How much did he give you?"

Rachel's eyelids fell shut again. "I wanna go back to sleep," she mumbled.

"You need to stay awake for a little bit. Can you do that for me?"

She gave him a weak smile. "Did you miss me, old man?"

"Not enough for you to be back here. You know you almost killed Joe when you left."

"Is that why he's so mad at me?"

"I imagine that would do it."

"Who's the guy with the mustache?" Rachel asked.

"Sean. He's a real shady private investigator. Donovan brought him on to find you."

"Should've seen that one coming. There was a cop, back in Wichita. I can't remember her name."

"Officer Shelly Duncan," Paul said. "She worked for Wilkes and called in when she saw you."

"I thought something was off with her."

"Sit up, Rach." He took her arm and eased her into a sitting position.

She shifted a couple times, her eyes lowered to the blanket. Her fingers reached for her mouth and she pushed on the swelling on the side of her mouth. Her tongue ran over the split in her bottom lip. Mark's heart ached as he wondered how many times in the past she had tasted her own blood.

Rachel raised her head and her eyes fell on Mark for the first time. Her surprised expression hardened. "What are you doing here?"

Mark started toward her. "Rachel—"

"Stop." She looked at Paul. "What is he doing here?"

"Donovan is holding him here," Paul said. "I brought him in here to see you. He needed to see that you're alive."

"Get him out of here, off the estate."

"I'm going to get you both out of here tonight. For good."

"No. I'm not going anywhere."

Mark's brow knitted and he stepped forward to the bed. "Rachel, you can't stay here. You need to come with me."

"I don't need to do anything. I'm staying here."

Anger rose inside Mark. "What are you saying? Why would you want to stay here?"

"Paul will get you out of here," she said. "You don't belong here."

"Neither do you!"

"Yes, I do. This is my home."

"Rachel," Paul said, "you both need to leave. I'm not letting you stay here any longer."

"No," she said. "I'm tired, Paul. I'm not running anymore."

Mark looked at Paul to intervene further, but Paul remained silent. He turned back to Rachel. "You have to come with me. I'm not leaving here without you."

She dropped her head and stared at her hands twisting in her lap.

"Please, Rachel," he said. "I love you."

"I'm sorry, Mark," she said, lifting her eyes, "but I don't love you."

Her words paralyzed him with a greater sting than he could have ever imagined. "I don't understand."

"It's simple. I'm staying here, with Donovan. I love him. I should have never left to begin with. This is where I belong."

Mark searched her face, but found it impossible to read her expression. "How can you say that? Have you seen yourself? Your face is bruised and swollen. He did that to you, and he's done far worse in the past."

"I screwed up, okay? I stole a lot of money from him and then I took off. It's my fault—"

"Is what he did to your back your fault also? I've seen the scars, Rachel, remember? He used a whip on you. He tore your skin open, dozens of times. You can't possibly think that you did anything worthy of that kind of abuse."

Rachel's eyes avoided Mark, and she stumbled over her words. "I deserved all of it. I made a lot of mistakes. I'm lucky I'm not dead."

"Yeah, well, Danielle wasn't so lucky. Did she deserve to be shot like she was nothing?"

Rachel stared at him. "What do you mean?"

"Exactly what it sounds like. Donovan had her killed. She died right next to me. She died protecting you."

Her hand shook as it moved to her mouth, and tears fell from her weary eyes.

Mark kneeled beside the bed. He looked up at Rachel, finding her eyes. "I'm not sure what's going on here, but I know that you aren't yourself. I don't know if it's the drugs he gave you or what, but you don't mean any of what you're saying. You can't love him, not after what he's done to Danielle and to you. And, I know you love me. I know you do, the same as I love you. There's no doubt in my mind."

"You don't get it. You have no understanding of what this place is or what is going on. You don't even know who I am so there's no way you can love me."

"I do know who you are, Rachel," Mark said. "I know and I love you, even more than before. Nothing will change that for me, ever."

"I don't love you, Mark. I made a mistake, and I'm sorry, but you're going to have to leave without me. I love Donovan. I belong to him, I always have, and I am not leaving him again."

Mark pushed himself up from the floor and away from the bed. She spoke as if she had been brainwashed. He didn't know if her words were true, and he failed to understand the change in her. The shell in front of him was nothing like the strong woman he loved. Although he knew that part of her had to be in there somewhere, he didn't know how to reach her.

"Can you get him out tonight?" Rachel asked Paul.

"Yes, I can," Paul said. "Are you sure you don't want me to get you out as well?"

"I'm sure."

Mark couldn't look at her. He knew what they had was real, knew without hesitation that they loved each other, but he didn't know how to combat the influence that controlled her.

Rachel's eyes started closing again while her complexion drained of color. "I'm so tired."

"I know you are. Lie back down and close your eyes." She slipped down into the bed, and Paul covered her with the blanket.

"Wait." She grabbed his arm. "I have to know something. Who did he send to kill Jonathan?"

"Me. I made sure it was quick."

"Thank you for not letting him suffer," she whispered.

"Before he died, he asked me if his angel was free."

She smiled and let go of Paul's arm. She glanced at Mark and said, "Paul, please get him out. He shouldn't be in this house."

Mark crossed his arms. She didn't belong here any more than he did, yet she refused to leave. Her voice sounded convinced that she needed to stay, that everything Donovan did to her was justified.

Paul came up beside him, and they walked back to the Mark's room. Closing the door, Paul said, "I need to leave you alone for a bit so I can work on getting you out of here."

"I'm not going anywhere without her."

"You have no choice. She isn't leaving."

"Then I'm not leaving either."

"I get that you want to help her, but you don't appreciate the severity of the situation. Donovan fully intends on killing you due to your relationship with Rachel. If you stay here, you will die, just as Thomas died, except this time I won't have the control to make it quick and painless."

Paul's firm words broke through Mark's stubbornness, but he still had no intention of leaving Rachel behind. "I understand all that, but why didn't he kill me back in Kansas, when he killed Danielle? Why bring me here at all?"

"I stopped speculating about Donovan's motives for anything he does a long time ago, but you're a threat to Donovan. No matter what he's done, he does love Rachel and the knowledge that she ever gave you a second glance tears him up inside. He can't stand the thought that you might have meant anything to her and he can't risk that she would still have feelings for you. He needs to eliminate any and all competition."

"I can't leave her here so she can suffer even more than she already has," Mark said. "He's going to end up killing her one of these days. I can't sit back and let that happen."

"Do I need to describe to you how Eric died? It was the slowest, most painful death I've ever seen and it was all Donovan. The only thing I did was put the bullet in his head that ended his agony."

Paul's words should have scared him, but instead Mark mulled over what Paul had told him about Eric. "Did it feel good?"

"Killing Eric?" Paul cracked a smile. "Yeah, it did. After what he did to Rachel, it felt great. If you had it in you, you would have enjoyed it, too."

Mark believed him.

"Now," Paul continued, "I'm going to see what I can do for Rachel. I'll try to change her mind, but I don't know if it will do any good. I'll come back for you tonight and somehow I'll get you out of here. I know you don't want to leave without her, but neither of us can force her to go. As soon as you're out, go to whatever authorities you can and get her out of here. But, to do that, you have to leave her here. You won't be able to help her if you're dead."

Mark agreed, and he studied Paul's face. Through the hardness, his eyes were weary, even guilty. Mark had felt so much anger toward Paul for allowing Rachel to live in such appalling circumstances.

Rachel, however, did not blame Paul, and Mark doubted that she ever once thought to. When they had been in Rachel's room, he could tell she loved this man. She had come alive, and even glowed in his presence. If Rachel still loved Paul, then maybe Mark could forgive him.

A thought entered his mind. "I don't understand something," he said. "If you get me out of here, but you and Rachel stay, won't Donovan know that you let me go and kill you?"

Paul started for the door, pausing before he left. "Like I said, you can't help her if you're dead, which is what you will be if you stay here much longer." He turned around and faced Mark. "I'm counting on you to help her."

A chill traveled through Mark's body. Paul was putting his life on the line for him and Rachel. The ultimate sacrifice and Paul was willing to make it for them.

After Paul exited the room, Mark slumped down to the floor. He wanted to help Rachel. He wanted to get her out of this nightmare forever, but who was he kidding? He was an average, ordinary guy who only left the state of Kansas because he had been kidnapped. He had never been in a fight, had never even fired a gun. He was exhausted, overwhelmed and in a world he knew nothing about. He couldn't be more ill-equipped to save her.

Rachel needed her Prince Charming. He was nothing more than the court jester.

Chapter Sixty-three

Mark wasn't sure how much time had passed when his door opened again. Expecting Paul to come in with a master plan to help him escape, Mark stood up, only to see Donovan walk through the door.

"I'm glad we have an opportunity to talk," Donovan said. He held a gun near his waist and raised it to make sure Mark saw it pointed at him.

Thick air filled Mark's lungs with every step Donovan took toward him. The walls closed in around him, though he had never been claustrophobic in his life. He saw what Donovan did to Rachel, and he claimed to love her. He also witnessed how callously he snapped his fingers and extinguished Danielle's life. What was the man willing to do to Mark, someone who had dared to love Rachel?

Despite his panic at seeing Donovan, Mark had to pretend he'd never seen Rachel and that Paul had never spoken to him. Paul was their only chance of getting out, and saying the wrong thing could prove fatal for both him and Paul. "Where's Rachel?"

Donovan stopped walking in the center of the room. "She's here. She's fine, now that she's back home with me."

Mark was incredulous. Rachel had been beaten and drugged and he thought she was fine. "This isn't her home," he said. "If it were, you wouldn't have had to force her to return."

"Rachel made a mistake and she's learned from it. She knows where she belongs and who she belongs with."

Mark's jaw tightened. "The only mistake she made was not leaving sooner than she did." He narrowed his eyes. "She told me all about you.

You're under the delusion that it doesn't matter what you do to her or how far you push her, she's always going to love you. You're wrong. She's been running away from you for three years, and she never wanted to come back. Rachel doesn't love you."

Donovan smirked and moved toward Mark. "Rachel would never sleep with someone she doesn't love."

Mark recoiled and the blood drained from his face. It wasn't true. Rachel would not be intimate with this monster, not now, not after all he had done. At least not willingly. If she had indeed slept with him, it wouldn't be because she loved him, but because she had been forced to, or beaten into submission.

Mark snapped when Donovan reached him. Ignoring the gun, Mark tried to hit him, but Donovan evaded his fist. The gun caught the side of Mark's head and knocked him to the ground. Mark rolled over on his side and tried to get up, but a loud ringing in his ears kept him down. Vertigo washed over him, moving the room around him like the ocean's waves.

"Why would you do that?" Donovan said. He kicked Mark in the stomach. "Why would you try to come after me when I have a gun? Your friend died right in front of you, so you must know I'm more than willing to kill you right here. You can't possibly think you can hurt me." His foot flew into Mark's stomach again.

Nausea overcame Mark as he clutched his abdomen. Fighting for breath and consciousness, he rolled onto his back to stem the assault, but Donovan kicked the side of his ribs several times. When he stepped back, he straightened out his jacket and regained his composure.

A fit of coughs racked his body and Mark gritted his teeth against the pain. His head lolled to the side. Risking another kick to the ribs or worse, Mark managed to speak through his gasps for air. "Rachel doesn't love you. She never loved you."

"I understand your reluctance to accept the situation," Donovan said. "I can tell you love her and you desire her love in return. Rachel is not only a beautiful woman, but she's astonishing."

The ringing in his ears began to subside. Mark caught his breath, but his side flared with pain when he dared to pull air into his lungs. "Yes, she is," Mark said, as he sat up.

"It's impossible to know her and not love her, so I suppose I shouldn't blame you for falling in love with her. Except that I do." Donovan smirked and his eyebrows shot up. "Blame you, that is. Your downfall in life is that you believe someone like her would fall in love with someone like you."

"I know she loves me."

"No," Donovan said. "She's much smarter than that. She wants someone who can take care of her, all of her needs, her desires. You can't seem to take care of yourself. At first, I thought I would kill you right away, but maybe I should keep you around so you can find out how things really are with Rachel." He glanced around the empty room. "This would be a good place for you to sit and think about how you shouldn't have fallen for Rachel, not when she's mine."

"She's not yours," Mark said. "She's not a piece of property. You can't do whatever you want to her."

"But she is mine," Donovan said. "She always has been and always will be. She's agreed to marry me, to have children with me. We've already gotten started on that. Maybe you would be more understanding if you saw it for yourself. I could put a camera in our room so you can watch how much she doesn't give you a second thought when she's in bed with me. She sure didn't think about you when she was touching me, calling my name, begging for more."

Mark looked away from Donovan. Tears spilled out from his eyes and his stomach bottomed out.

"You can sit here and watch us together, while you barely hold on to what's left of your pathetic, worthless life. While you're struggling to take just one more breath, you can see how much she loves me." Donovan crouched beside Mark and put his gun next to Mark's head. "You can watch, day after day, month after month, as her belly grows with my child inside of her. How does that make you feel, Mark? To know that as we speak, Rachel might already be pregnant?"

Mark closed his eyes, his trembling lips unable to utter a single word. Donovan's words were far more torturous than the pain in his side, far worse than any physical pain Donovan could inflict on him.

Donovan rose to his feet. "Of course, I'd have to keep you alive for quite some time. A little food and water here and there, just enough to keep you breathing while our lives unfold in front of you. How long do you want to live for, Mark? How long do you want to see Rachel love me? At what point will you break and beg for me to kill you?"

"You're sick," Mark said. "Rachel will never love you, no matter how much you beat her into thinking she does."

"As much fun as it would be to keep you around, it might be a bit arduous with you in constant denial. Maybe we should just ask Rachel who she loves. She'll let you know you're wrong."

Chapter Sixty-four

Sleep cradled Rachel in a warm blanket and enticed her to stay tucked beneath its comforting covers. Her eyelids stayed shut most of the time, but she fought against sleep's beckoning darkness. She had already slept so much since coming back to the estate, with only fleeting moments of consciousness, usually filled with the sight of Tony.

The two times Tony came into her room, stoic-faced and armed with a syringe, he didn't speak a single word to her, as if she was a complete stranger. The shots he gave her were in different locations on her arm, and she thought she would soon look like a pincushion.

She didn't battle Tony when it came to the shots. Donovan wanted her to be sedated most of the time. It was his way to retain control over her until he could trust her again, and she complied the best she could with his wishes. She had a long way to go until they got back to where they were before she left.

The door to her room swung open, and Mark came through the door, followed by Donovan. Her eyelids struggled to stay open, and she forced herself to slide out of bed. She struggled to take full breaths, and her eyes seemed out of focus. Despite her body crying out, begging for more sleep, she remained standing.

Mark walked to the center of her room, and Donovan went straight to her. He removed his jacket and laid it on her bed. He then turned his attention to her and kissed her with more passion than ever before. It was no doubt an attempt to demonstrate to Mark his vast power and control over her.

Though Rachel had no desire to hurt Mark any more than she already had, she didn't dare break away from Donovan. She ignored Mark's presence and gave every part of herself to Donovan in that kiss, so he wouldn't know how much Mark affected her.

It wasn't until his mouth pressed down on hers that she realized Donovan had something in his hand, something he transferred to her before releasing her from the kiss. From the cold shape of the object in her hand, she knew without looking it was a gun.

Donovan moved away from her and leaned against the wall. He crossed his arms and said, "Mr. Jacobson seems to have a problem understanding you are no longer part of his life. I would like you to clarify that for him."

Rachel lowered her eyes to the gun. Her old gun, the third one she had owned. The last time she saw it was when she left it on her bed before fleeing the estate three years ago. Her hand operated the slide without thinking about her actions and she caressed the familiar contours of the gun, her fingertips cold and numb against the steel.

Her mind traveled back to the day when Donovan gave her the gun, and a smile tweaked the corners of her mouth as the past intertwined with the present. Memories of better times flooded her mind, and she remembered Donovan watching with excitement while she untied the ribbon and tore apart the wrapping paper.

When she saw the gun, she had placed the package down on her dresser and wrapped her arms around him. She forgot about the gun and concentrated on him. That night he fell asleep beside her, though he woke long before morning and left to return to his own room. She had enjoyed those few hours of him holding her, like she had always wanted.

Now, her smile vanished as she relived the empty feeling of him leaving her that night. She no longer wanted to touch the gun, afraid of the other memories it would bring.

Brought back to the present, her immediate predicament confronted her. Two different worlds had collided, and she needed to eliminate one of them.

She glanced at Donovan. Her life revolved around him for so long that his presence dominated her. As long as he lived, she would belong to him. The scars on her back proved that to her.

The gun she held could end that possession, but she knew she could not end his life. Nor did she want to. Being with him hadn't always been a bad thing. He could be gentle, wonderful, loving. She could learn to love him again, as she had before. She could change herself to be more acceptable for him so he wouldn't want to hurt her again.

Sensing Mark's stare, Rachel shifted her gaze to him. Pain drenched his face and his eyes pleaded with her. She hated that he was here at the estate. What had she done? Why had she included him in her life when she knew that it could only end like this? The love she had for him, what they had together, was real, just as he said earlier.

But that was in a different time, a different place. She was home now, the only place she ever truly belonged. She had left once and Donovan found her. Jonathan and Danielle, the two people who did everything in their power to help her, had both died because of her. Mark was next on that list. This was her home, and it was where she needed to stay so she couldn't destroy anyone else's life.

As she stared at all the might-have-beens in Mark's eyes, she knew there was only one answer to solve the dilemma in front of her.

Before she lost the courage, Rachel raised the unusually heavy gun and pointed it in Mark's direction. The walls pulsed in her vision, blurred with tears at what she had to do. The carpet floated beneath her bare feet, and her finger twitched against the trigger. "I'm sorry, Mark," she whispered. "I really do love you."

Don't think, just act.

Rachel turned the barrel of the gun toward herself.

Chapter Sixty-five

Rachel, no!" Mark leapt forward and stumbled. His hand flew toward the weapon. The gunshot deafened his ears, and the back of his hand smacked against hers. The gun jerked out of Rachel's hand, bounced off the side of her bed, and thudded to the carpet.

Rachel's expressionless face remained unchanged, as if she did not know, nor did she care that the gun left her hand. Her large, glazed eyes remained fastened on Mark. Her lips parted, but no words emerged.

Fear tightened Mark's throat, and the sound of his racing heart roared in his ears. "Rachel?"

Rachel fell, and Mark's arms barely reached her before she hit the ground. Donovan ran up on the other side of her and slid his arms underneath her body. They lowered her to the floor and she curled up on her side.

Glancing over Rachel's body, Mark saw no blood pouring from a gunshot wound. His eyes scanned the room until he saw the bullet hole in the plaster above her bed. In his peripheral vision, Donovan rose to his feet and ran for the door, calling Paul's name.

Satisfied she did not shoot herself, Mark rolled her over onto her back. She was unresponsive to his questions, and he couldn't figure out what was wrong with her. Mark placed his index and middle fingers on her neck and tried to find a pulse.

Mark moved his fingers to various areas on her neck. Panic swelled in his chest when he could not feel her heartbeat under his fingertips. He gave up on her neck and lowered his right ear to her mouth and nose. Shallow puffs of warm air touched his skin, and tears sprang to his eyes.

Mark brushed back the hair from her eyes. He cupped the sides of her face and willed her to be okay. "Open your eyes, Rachel," he said. "Just open your eyes for me."

Rachel lay unmoving on the ground. Mark rubbed his hands over hers, but couldn't warm her chilled skin.

Paul ran into the room, with Donovan right behind him. Mark let out the breath he was holding. "She's cold, but she's still breathing," he said.

Paul knelt on the other side of Rachel. "That's a good sign, but we need to watch her closely in case she needs CPR," he said. He checked her pulse and looked up at Donovan. "Get me what's left of the sedative you gave her along with the syringe you used. I need you to calculate exactly how much you gave her."

Donovan jumped up and started for the door.

"I also need my medical bag," Paul called after him.

As soon as Donovan left the room, Mark asked, "Paul, what's wrong with her?"

"I suspect she overdosed on the sedative that he gave her." He motioned to the bruises smeared across her face. "With all she's been through, I imagine her body couldn't take anything else."

Mark's mind flashed on the image of Rachel turning the gun on herself. She had taken all the abuse she could stand, and the sedatives Donovan gave her wanted to finish the job.

"I know you want to be with her, Mark," Paul said, "but you're the last person Donovan will want to see near her when he gets back. Go stand against that wall, and don't move a muscle unless I tell you to."

"I don't care what anyone wants. I'm staying with Rachel," he said. He returned his attention to Rachel.

Paul glanced over his shoulder at the doorway. "There's not a whole lot we can do for her here but keep her breathing. I don't have anything that can help with an overdose, so we need to get her to a hospital and fast. Donovan won't allow that to happen. If you're determined to see this through, I need your help. Do exactly what I say, when I say, no questions."

Mark's forehead creased. "Whatever helps Rachel."

"Get the blanket from her bed. We need to keep her warm."

Mark complied, and helped Paul cover Rachel's body with the comforter from her bed. The sight of her blood against the white of the comforter did not make him feel any better about her condition.

Donovan came back into the room with a large medical bag. He set the supplies down between himself and Paul. He handed Paul a bottle half-filled with liquid and a syringe. On the syringe, he showed Paul how much of the sedative he had given Rachel and told him she'd had three injections since being back at the estate, in addition to the one at her house.

"That's way too much," Paul said. "She's overdosing." He rummaged through his medical bag. He pulled out a packaged syringe and a small vial of medicine, and handed both to Mark. "Fill the syringe up to the top."

Distracted by Donovan's presence, Mark fumbled with opening the package around the syringe.

Donovan reached for Rachel's hand. "Don't die on me, Rachel," Donovan said, with a strained voice. "I love you more than anything. Please don't die on me."

Agony ripped through Mark when Donovan spoke those words to Rachel. It wasn't right that Donovan was next to her, holding her hand, coaxing her to live when he was guilty of drugging her and causing her overdose. Hatred radiated from every part of Mark, driven by the strong conviction that if Rachel weren't unconscious, he would kill Donovan with his bare hands.

"Mark," Paul said. "I need that syringe now."

Mark tore his eyes away from Donovan and stuck the needle in the vial. After the liquid filled the syringe, Mark pulled the needle out of the vial. He held the syringe out over Rachel's body for Paul to take.

Paul did not take the syringe. Instead he said, "Bring it over here to me." He rubbed an alcohol swab over the crook of Rachel's elbow.

Confused by Paul's direction, but remembering his admonishment not to ask questions, Mark got to his feet and walked around Rachel's body until he stood beside Paul. He held the syringe down to Paul, but again, he did not take it from Mark's hands.

"Donovan, I need more blankets," Paul said. "I don't think this one will keep her warm enough."

"Anything else?" Donovan asked.

"No, but please hurry."

As Donovan stood, Paul rose to his feet as well. Donovan took two steps toward the door and Paul pounced, tackling him from behind. Donovan landed face down on the floor, and Paul covered him with his body. "Mark!" Paul shouted.

Mark understood. He rushed over to Paul, who struggled to keep the thrashing man below him subdued. "Where do I use it?"

"In his arm," he said. Paul shifted his weight and pressed Donovan's head into the floor with his forearm. He used his free hand to pin Donovan's arm to the ground.

Mark closed the needle in on the upper part of Donovan's arm. Paul moved again to keep Donovan's arm from jerking. Mark jammed the needle into Donovan's arm through his shirt and pushed down on the plunger. Donovan groaned, and Mark pulled the needle out.

"The gun," Paul said. "Get the gun."

Mark went to where Rachel's gun had landed near the bed and grabbed it. He raced back to Paul.

"His head!" Paul said.

Mark panicked. "I… I can't shoot him."

"Not shoot him. Hit him. Check the safety to make sure the gun won't fire." At Mark's confused look, he added, "Red is dead."

Mark found the safety on the side of the gun and flipped it so the red dot no longer showed. He looked at Donovan's crimson face, and anger rushed through Mark's veins, giving him strength to raise the gun and smash the grip against the side of Donovan's head. When Donovan did not stop moving, hatred drove Mark's arm to bring the gun down on Donovan's skull three more times, without thought as to the consequences of his actions.

Donovan ceased movement, and his body slumped to the floor. Paul wriggled off Donovan and stood up.

Mark stepped back. Blood flowed from an open wound above Donovan's ear. "I didn't… did I?"

"Kill him?" Paul asked. He looked down at Donovan. "Nah. You did knock him out pretty good and that sedative you administered will keep him out for a while." He walked back over to Rachel and checked her pulse. "Donovan's cell phone is in the inside pocket of his jacket. Get it, quick."

Donovan's suit jacket was on the floor near Rachel's bed. Mark found the cell phone right where Paul said it was, and took it to Paul.

"Thanks," Paul said. He pushed some buttons on the phone and put it to his ear. "You did good, Mark. Real good."

Mark crouched next to Rachel. She seemed the same, shallow breathing and pallid skin in the few spots that weren't covered with a bruise. Mark put his hand on her face. Her cold, clammy skin struck Mark's heart. "Stay with me, Rach. We're going to get you out of this place for good, but you have to stay with me, baby."

Paul spoke to a 911 operator, saying Rachel was unconscious from an overdose of sedatives, and her pulse was weak. Mark also heard the words, "kidnap victims."

Paul pressed a button on the phone, disconnecting the operator. "Now, we wait. Keep her warm, and keep checking her pulse and breathing. Do you know CPR?"

Mark had taken a class several years ago, but didn't remember anything from it except push on the chest and breathe in the mouth. Guessing how to do CPR wouldn't help Rachel, though. "I don't remember how to."

"It's okay, Mark." Paul tossed Mark his radio. "If her condition changes, call me on this. If she stops breathing or her breathing slows at all, let me know and I'll come right away to give her CPR. I'm going to meet the ambulance and police to make sure they get let in. The last thing we need are overzealous security guards getting into a shootout with police."

After Paul left, Mark crossed his legs and settled down next to Rachel.

He held her hand, and kept his eyes glued on her face. He didn't know what else to do but talk to her. Every so often, he stopped talking to her to check her breathing.

He told her everything he had ever wanted to say to her, everything she needed to hear. Most importantly, he assured her that he wouldn't let anything bad ever happen to her again. He didn't know if she could hear him, but he hoped by telling her she still had something worth living for, it would help her survive.

Mark leaned over to get a closer look at Rachel. Her lips took on a bluish tint that stood out against her pale skin. He knew that meant she wasn't getting enough oxygen, but he didn't know how to help her.

As Mark reached for the radio to call Paul, the pounding of footfalls grew louder in the hallway outside her door. Paul rushed into Rachel's room followed by paramedics. Mark forced himself to move away from Rachel. The paramedics went to work, checking her vital signs and asking Paul questions about her overdose and medical history. Two other paramedics simultaneously worked on Donovan. Mark wanted to tell them not to bother.

Five police officers filed into the room. They honed in on Mark and Paul with guns drawn. Mark lifted his hands in response to the guns pointed at him.

One of the officers hovered over the paramedics. "What's the situation here?" he asked.

A paramedic stood up and faced the officer. "She's overdosed, apparently on sedatives. She's also taken quite a beating." He pointed at Paul. "That one says she was kidnapped."

"This is a medical emergency," one of the paramedics kneeling over Rachel said. "There are too many people in this room. You need to take this outside, now."

One of the officers in front of Mark held his gun steady on Mark's chest. "Turn around and get against the wall, now. Put your hands high up on the wall."

Mark raised his hands above his head. When he finished turning toward the wall, one of the officers ran his hands over his body to search for weapons, while the other officer recited the Miranda warning. The officer pulled down Mark's arms one at a time. Cold steel clamped down on his wrists, and shock waves rippled through his body.

As the officer rotated Mark back around, Paul protested, "You don't have to arrest him. He was kidnapped with the girl."

Mark ignored the rest of the argument between Paul and the officers. He focused instead on the paramedics. Frustration bubbled inside him as he tried to translate the terms and lingo they threw around.

The officer gripping Mark's arm tugged him in the direction of the door. As they neared the door, a paramedic announced Rachel stopped breathing and they were starting CPR.

Mark struggled against the officer that led him away. "Rachel!" Mark continued fighting against the policeman to watch the paramedics work to revive Rachel. Another officer grabbed Mark and helped the first officer drag Mark from the room.

Chapter Sixty-six

Mark jerked awake. Though his eyes were open, the images from the final scene at the estate continued playing on a screen behind his eyes. It had been another sleepless night, having drifted off two or three times, only to be woken by nightmares.

His reluctant body climbed out of bed, and he wished he could grab one more hour of sleep. He knew it would do no good to close his eyes again. Sleep would continue eluding him, as it had ever since he left the estate in the back of a police car five days ago.

He stretched and tried to shake away the drowsiness, but ended up moaning with pain. His hand reached for the bruise that covered most of his left side. The doctor at the hospital said he was lucky none of the three broken ribs punctured his lung, although the x-rays showed two of them came close.

Mark shook off the pain and picked up the remote control to mute the television he left on all night. He showered and dressed, every mundane movement now arduous and insignificant. After he tied his tennis shoes, he went to the small table by the window and used the motel phone to call a taxi.

He sat back down on the edge of the bed and stared at the silent pictures of the morning news broadcast. His obstinate body resisted movement, exhaustion reaching into his joints and gripping them like a vise.

A picture of Jonathan Thomas flashed in the upper right-hand corner of the screen. Mark picked up the remote from the bedside table and pressed the up arrow for the volume.

"...story we have been following very closely. We recently reported on the three year anniversary of the unsolved murder of prominent businessman

Jonathan Thomas…"

Another name Mark never wanted to hear again. Why couldn't the media give it a rest? The man was dead and they acted like he was a saint.

Mark turned off the television and tossed the remote on the bed. He stifled his thoughts, knowing that being jealous of a dead man was more than ridiculous. Jonathan had done nothing but try to help Rachel when he was alive. His conflicting thoughts about Jonathan originated from his own personal desire to keep her safe, something he was unable to do.

At the table, he picked up the telephone receiver again and dialed. Greg answered on the first ring. "Hello?"

"It's me," Mark said.

"How are you? Anna's worried about you."

"Tell her to stop worrying."

"I'm worried, too, and so is James and everyone else here. Did you finally sleep last night?"

"Not much."

"You're going to make yourself sick. With those broken ribs, you need to take it easy so you can heal. You should take something to help you sleep."

The last thing Mark wanted was a sedative, at least not while the image of paramedics working on Rachel still lingered in his mind. He even refused a prescription for pain medication, despite his broken ribs making every breath and every movement a painful chore.

"I'll be fine," Mark said into the phone. "Stop being so overprotective."

"It's my job. Do you have enough clothes? Do you need me to wire you more money? You should probably get one of those disposable cell phones to use until you get home."

Even though Greg meant well, his words reminded Mark of his helpless state. "I have plenty of clothes, and no need for more money or a disposable cell phone. You wired more than enough for food and clothes, and you're already paying for the motel room. You and Anna have done way too much, and I'll pay you back every dime as soon as I get home."

"The only way you're paying us back is by coming home safe," Greg said. "When is the memorial service?"

Mark bowed his head and covered his eyes with his hand. "Tuesday morning."

"So you'll be back in Wichita by then?"

"Yeah," he replied. He pulled back the dusty, motel colored curtain and peered outside. His taxi waited by the curb in front of the motel's lobby. "I have to go."

"Call me later tonight and we can talk some more. If there's anything you need in the meantime, let Anna and I know. We're here for you."

"Thanks, Greg." Mark replaced the handset in the cradle and shoved the keycard to his motel room in his front pocket. He picked up a small gift bag from the table and left the room. He double-checked the door to make sure it was locked.

Mark slid into the backseat of the taxi. Pulling the door shut took more strength than he had. He melted into a seat laced with the scent of too many passengers and not enough cleanings. Sunlight streamed through the window and a small rainbow appeared by his hand, but he was uninterested in anything nature had to offer. The sun was a distraction, a disturbance. It tried to make him appreciate the warmth that could heat his skin, but could never reach his soul.

The taxi reached its predetermined destination. Mark handed cash to the driver and told him to keep the change. He maneuvered through the rotating door and walked a short distance to the elevators. Mark punched the up arrow and waited, grateful no one else wanted a ride. He studied the scuff marks on his tennis shoes until he heard the ding of the arriving transport.

Mark held his breath with apprehension, and the elevator doors creaked shut after him. The tight confines of elevators never bothered him before he was locked in the room at the estate. To help stop the walls from closing in while the elevator shuddered up five floors, he kept his eyes glued to the inspection certificate.

The sudden halt of the cab jolted him. The doors opened, revealing a small group of people waiting to get in the elevator. Realizing his luck at not having to share the elevator with so many people, Mark promised himself he would take the stairs on the way back down.

An older woman in navy blue scrubs greeted Mark when he neared the nurses' station. He recognized her kind face, but couldn't seem to remember her name. "There you are," she said with a smile. "She asked about you earlier, but I think she's sleeping now. Such a sweet girl."

"She is," he said. "Thank you." A second wind surged through his body, and he picked up his speed down the tiled hallway toward room 527. He acknowledged the FBI agent sitting outside the hospital room door, the same one who had worked the morning shift for the past three days. Mark closed the door behind him and crept over to the bed. As the nurse said, Rachel was sleeping.

The quiet beeps of the machines attached to her reminded him that she would be fine. Even the overwhelming odor of antiseptic comforted him. A clear bandage on the back of her hand held in the needle of an IV, and he glanced at it to make sure the needle was still in place, the same as he did every morning.

His eyes followed the tubing up to three bags hanging from the IV pole. Each bag dripped at various speeds, delivering measured doses of medication to her broken body. They would soon be removed one by one, as the hospital staff prepared to discharge her from their care.

Mark lifted a visitor's chair and situated it next to the bed at an angle where he could best see her. He set the gift bag on the floor next to the bed and collapsed in the chair. Ignoring the sharp pain in his side, he leaned forward and brushed a stray hair out of her face.

After five days, he finally saw an improvement in her appearance. Multiple bruises were still scattered across her face, but the blues and purples were fading into greens and yellows. The swelling appeared to be reduced on the right side of her mouth, and the split in her bottom lip had almost healed.

To Mark, she never looked more beautiful.

She was alive.

Having watched her sleep so much over the past few days, Mark had more than enough time to run what happened to them through his mind. More than once, he was left with the harrowing thought that Rachel tried to kill herself. If he had been the slightest bit slower in reaching her and the gun, she would have succeeded. The only thing that helped was knowing she was drugged at the time, and not in complete control of her thoughts and actions.

When Rachel's physical condition stabilized after two days in the ICU, she moved into a private room in the oncology unit. Agent Eli Jackson, the FBI agent in charge of their case, determined it was best to keep her in an area where no one would think to find her. There was a short list of nurses and doctors allowed in her room, and deviation from that list was not tolerated for any reason.

Agent Jackson didn't anticipate any problems, but he made it clear he would not take chances. Besides the constant FBI presence outside her room, two FBI agents stayed in the motel room next to Mark's. His room was wired so they could listen in around the clock, and he was monitored from afar by another two agents at all times. Other plainclothes agents took turns wandering the main floor and parking structure of the hospital, watching for anything out of the ordinary.

Mark ignored the FBI's necessary intrusion on their lives. He spent every waking hour with Rachel and stayed with her well beyond visiting hours. Had he been able to spend each night in her room on a cot, he would have done so, but her doctors advised against it. They wanted her to get lots of rest so she could heal.

As her body started bouncing back, the deep emotional damage surfaced. Because she was drugged at the time she tried to kill herself, her primary doctor did not require her to stay in the psychiatric unit. Instead, he insisted she speak to a psychologist during her hospital stay. Rachel refused to talk to anyone alone, and Mark listened for hours as she reluctantly described years of abuse to the psychologist.

The stories of what she went through devastated Mark. He never allowed himself to break down in front of her, but after she talked about the whip for the first time, he retreated to his motel room and cried. As she relayed those four years of her life, he thought about what he had been doing with his own life while she was suffering. He wished he knew she was out there so he could have saved her back then.

Having known nothing different, Rachel struggled with thinking of herself as a victim. From working at domestic violence shelters, she knew all the terminology, yet she never applied any of it to herself. Until the time she met Mark, she believed she deserved everything that had happened to her. Their relationship gave her a different perspective on what love was supposed to be, but to a certain extent, she still thought she received just punishment.

The scars on her back were the most difficult for her to discuss. Learning the scars would never disappear was a source of great anguish, and she expressed that Mark wouldn't want her since she had been branded by another man. While the psychologist worked to help her understand the scars were not a symbol of ownership, all Mark could do was hold her hand and assure her that he wasn't leaving, no matter what scars she had.

After several hours of talking to the psychologist over the course of two days, the psychologist walked with Mark to get some coffee. She explained Rachel would quite possibly need years of counseling to help her sort through both what had been done to her and the things she had done. That Rachel didn't want to talk to anyone without Mark present made the psychologist believe that he was the most important part of her recovery. Rachel already associated him with a healthy relationship, with love and happiness.

The road ahead would be more than difficult, but as Mark listened to her controlled breathing while she peacefully slept, he knew he would do whatever it took to save her. He kissed her forehead, held her hand, and waited for her to wake up.

Chapter Sixty-seven

Rachel smiled before she was fully awake. Another night had come and gone without dreaming, the fourth night in a row. She never wanted to dream again, and prayed all of her nightmares were gone for good.

Aware of Mark holding her hand, she opened her eyes. The smile remained despite her fear for him. He should have left the second both the police and FBI released him from questioning, yet he kept coming back. Didn't he understand the danger he was in? Was he not aware that every second he spent with her, he put himself at risk?

Of course Mark knew. He knew and he understood, just as Danielle and Jonathan both had. The risks hadn't stopped either of them from being a part of her life, and they were both gone.

She'd had ample time to mourn Jonathan in the three years since his murder, but the familiar pain that accompanied thoughts of Danielle pierced Rachel's heart. She couldn't keep Danielle safe, and even with the constant presence of the FBI, there were no guarantees of Mark's safety. Though she wanted him to run far away from her so he would be out of Donovan's crosshairs, she couldn't deny she loved knowing he was there with her. If he chose to stay, she wasn't about to push him out of her life.

Mark smiled at her and brushed her hair away from her forehead. "Are you feeling better?" he asked, his voice filled with strain and exhaustion.

"Much better," she said. "I'm ready to get out of this place for good."

"Not quite yet," he said. "Maybe a couple more days, and then we'll go home." He gestured toward her almost full tray of cold breakfast food. "We'll need to fatten you back up when we get you there since you seem to have labeled everything they serve you as inedible."

Rachel laughed. "I could definitely use some of your cooking about now," she said. She appreciated that he still tried to cheer her up every day. In those moments, he looked like ordinary Mark, but no amount of showering, shaving, or scrubbing could erase the haggard edge in his eyes, and the jaded gleam they projected. His eyes reflected everything she couldn't see, the things that caused her heart to break.

"Danielle's memorial service is on Tuesday morning," he said. "We shouldn't have any problems making it back to Kansas in time."

"Thank you for taking care of the arrangements for me," she said. Minutes passed as they sat in silence. There were so many subjects they avoided over the past few days. After her condition had stabilized, she bared her soul to the psychologist with Mark in the room. He provided the safety net of support that she needed to open up about her life.

Yet as soon as the buffer of the psychologist disappeared, they stopped talking about what happened. There were a lot of other things to keep their minds busy, and it was easy to avoid what needed to be said.

The events at the estate gnawed at her insides, and Rachel could no longer internalize her thoughts and emotions. There was one topic they mutually avoided from the start. "Mark," she said, "I know you don't want to talk about it."

"We agreed not to discuss it."

"I don't care. I have to tell you. Those things I said to you at the estate weren't true. I didn't mean it when I said I didn't love you and that I wanted to stay there."

"I know, Rachel," he said. "I don't want you to feel like you have to explain yourself."

"But I do have to explain myself. It killed me, and it still does now, but I had to say all those horrible things to you. I was scared if I didn't, he would know. If he found out how important you were to me, I don't know what he would have done to you. And, I just… just couldn't…" Her eyes stung and she blinked away the forming tears. The words flowed from her lips unchecked. "I couldn't go through what he did to me before. I can't do that again and—"

Mark jumped up from his chair and sat on the bed, facing her. "Rachel, stop, please." He placed his hand over hers and caressed her skin. "Don't think about that now. You're safe. He can't hurt you." He drew her into his arms and held her until her tears stopped.

She pulled away from him and wiped her face with her fingers. Shame crept over her cheeks. She had broken down in front of him so much in the past few days, and she hated herself for burdening him. "I'm sorry, Mark. I didn't mean to—"

"Don't apologize, Rach. You don't ever have to apologize for anything ever again. I understand why you said what you did, and I don't want you to worry about it anymore. You only did what you thought was necessary to help us both."

Though he fell silent, she could tell there was more he wanted to say, more he wanted to know. Over the past few days, he always stopped speaking before the question left his tongue, but she knew what he was thinking.

She moistened her lips and tucked her hair behind her ear with a shaky hand. "I know you think I should have killed Donovan, but I can't kill anyone, no matter who it is. That's not who I am now and I never want to be that person again."

"I never asked you to be, but I can still wish he was dead."

She looked away, knowing that if it were up to Mark, they would skip an investigation and trial, and go straight for the death penalty. Rachel changed the subject. "The prosecutor is coming by this afternoon."

"He called me in the middle of the night." His hand tightened around her hand and he locked his eyes on hers. "Rachel, they're handing everything over to the FBI."

Rachel's brow furrowed. "I thought Paul was talking to the prosecutor and they were moving forward with charges."

Mark paused, and his expression became solemn. "Apparently Paul changed his mind. The prosecutor said he's pleading guilty to Jonathan's murder, but he's not talking about King at all."

The news unnerved her. Though she knew Paul had his reasons, the prosecutor said that if he didn't testify against Donovan, they wouldn't afford him any leniency on Jonathan's murder. Paul would spend the rest of his life behind bars.

"The only thing they have now is you, but the FBI wants both King and Graham Wilkes. Once they have all the evidence, they'll talk about throwing in what happened to you as well."

Rachel knew what he trying to tell her. "They let him go?"

"He was released right after midnight," Mark said. "But the FBI will be watching him and us at all times. They won't let him get near either one of us."

Despite having FBI protection to help keep them both safe, Rachel's flesh turned cold. The knowledge of Donovan's freedom made her anxiety climb. Though Donovan's methodical, logical side would keep him in check and wouldn't allow him to try something while the FBI was investigating him, unless he were in prison, they weren't safe. "What happened to the kidnapping charges?"

"He has witnesses. Twelve people, including Graham Wilkes, say he was in a meeting in Los Angeles that evening."

She placed her hand over her mouth. With Donovan running around and his connections to Wilkes, they may never be safe no matter how much protection the FBI provided. The feds had to get him on something so he would be locked away. "I take it they haven't found Danielle yet," Rachel said.

"Rach, the police back home don't believe there was a murder. Your house is clean. No bloodstains, fingerprints, nothing. Not even evidence of bleach being used to clean up. Agent Jackson believes me, but he had techs go over the house twice and couldn't find any evidence. With no body and no evidence, there's nothing he can do. I don't know how King did it, but it makes me doubt what I saw."

Rachel grimaced. "Graham Wilkes, that's how he did it. Between him and Donovan, anything can be accomplished. I'm sure they had everything planned out well in advance. They probably replaced the carpeting and all of the furniture to be sure no evidence was left behind." She hesitated, unsure how Mark would react to her next statement. "I want to see Paul."

"I know you do," he said, "but I don't know if they will let you right now. We can ask the prosecutor this afternoon. As far as everything else goes, the FBI is on our side, so don't dwell on it."

Rachel had tried for days not to dwell on it, to no avail.

Mark lifted her chin. "Rachel, ever since I've known you he's been there in the back of your mind. You were always wondering where he was and if he knew where you were and if he was going to find you. He's controlled your thoughts, your actions, your feelings. I want to be with you and know it's just you and me."

The accuracy of his words frightened her and she tried to shut them out of her mind. They were too much of a reminder that Mark deserved better. She pulled her hands into her lap and scratched at the bandage around her IV. "I know the FBI will do everything they can, but I'm still afraid."

"Don't be afraid." Mark put his hands over hers. "You don't have to do this alone anymore, Rachel. I'll be with you every second, doing everything I can to make it easy for you. We're going home in a few days, and you and I are going to live a normal life. We'll ignore the FBI watching us and we'll forget about the bruises and broken bones. Maybe together we can make this nightmare end."

Rachel met his eyes. The determination in his voice told her he meant every word he said. She relaxed a bit, knowing that in his arms, she would finally find sanctuary.

"Agent Jackson also called last night," Mark said.

Agent Eli Jackson had taken a personal interest in their case. He went above and beyond his duties as an FBI agent, swearing to them both that he would keep them safe and find a way to put Donovan in prison for life. Every time she spoke to him, Rachel felt a little better about their situation.

"What did he call about?" Rachel asked.

"He spoke to Cory Thomas, and the family won't accept your offer to give the money back."

"No, he has to convince them," she said. The one thing she wanted out of the whole ordeal was to return the remaining money to Jonathan's family where it belonged. "Cory has to take it. I never felt right about having it in the first place."

"Cory refuses to take it. He considers it one of Jonathan's last wishes. But, he does want to come to the hospital tomorrow so he can meet you. He's driving down in the morning."

Rachel knew a visit from Cory could prove too much for Mark. He already struggled with Jonathan's role in her escape from the estate three years ago. "I don't think that's a good idea," she said. "That might be difficult for you and—"

"Rachel, you don't have to protect me," he said. "Jonathan did nothing but try to help you. Honestly, I..." He took a deep breath. "I wish I could thank him for that. As for Cory, he wants closure."

"We all want that," Rachel said.

"It's a good idea for him to come, for all of us. I'm sure the psychologist will agree. Cory deserves to hear directly from you how much Jonathan helped, and I think you need to meet him so you'll stop blaming yourself for Jonathan's death. Agent Jackson also said that as far as the money goes, you don't have to worry about the IRS knocking on your door," Mark said. "Apparently Cory is influential about these things."

"Mark, thank you for taking care of all of this. I don't know what I would do without you."

"I'm just relaying the messages," Mark said. He snapped his fingers. "I almost forgot. I brought you something." Mark picked up a gift bag from the floor and set it on his lap.

Rachel eyed the bag suspiciously. "What is that?"

"A couple of little things Agent Jackson helped me get for you." With a large smile, he reached into the bag and pulled out a small, white box.

Rachel accepted the box and lifted the lid. Inside was a rectangular paper the size of a business card. She stared at the card and read it several times before comprehending what it was. She looked up at Mark. "It's a social security card," she said.

"Not any social security card. That's your social security card."

She looked back at the card. The name she was given at birth, Rachel Renee Pettis, was printed in the middle of the card in all uppercase letters, along with a social security number above it. "I don't know what to say," she said.

"You might not like it much once you have to start paying taxes like the rest of us," Mark said. "Agent Jackson is also getting your birth certificate. When we get home, one of our first trips will be to the DMV so you can get a real driver's license. There's no need to change names anymore, no need to pretend you're someone else. You have your own identity now."

Rachel wiped the tears from her eyes before they got too far down her face. To most, it was a card to number them among the masses. For Rachel, it was a return to the world. The card made her a real person, not a gust of wind blowing about and disappearing without anyone noticing. She wished Danielle was here to see it. "You have no idea what this means to me," she said.

"There's one more thing," he said and handed her the bag.

She reached underneath the tissue paper and pulled out a framed photograph. Behind the glass was an engagement announcement from an old newspaper. She didn't need to read the words underneath the photograph box to know who the people in the picture were.

"You told me you didn't remember what your parents look like." He pointed to the picture. "I know it's only a newspaper clipping, but it was all we could find."

Rachel touched the glass over the couple locking hands in front of an oak tree. Her dad could have been Paul's twin, only smaller in stature. Paul told her years ago that she looked like her mother, and he was right. Other than her father's eyes, her mother had passed on the rest of the genes to Rachel. They shared the same face and hair, the same crooked smile.

"Is it okay?"

Rachel lifted her eyes. "It's perfect, Mark. It's more than perfect." She laid the picture down in her lap. She grabbed his shoulder and pulled him to her. Her arms wrapped around him and she set her head down on his shoulder. "You're perfect," she whispered. "I love you so much, Mark."

He tightened his hold on her. "I love you, too." Mark let go of her and squeezed her hand. "Now, let's get you healthy again so we can go home," he said, giving her a tired smile.

Rachel leaned over and kissed him, a single thought dominating her mind.

Every fairy tale has a Prince Charming.

###

About Angie Martin

Angie Martin lives with her husband and pets in Overland Park, KS. She grew up in Wichita, Kansas and has lived all over the United States. Her work reflects not only her background and schooling in criminal justice, but her love of music.

False Security is her first novel, with a print edition published in 2004. The novel was put under heavy sedation and operated on for several months before becoming what you read today. Her second novel *Conduit*, an award-winning, bestselling psychological thriller with a paranormal twist, is about a private detective who is the target of a psychic serial killer. Her third novel, *The Boys Club*, is a fast-paced romantic suspense with lots of action and mystery. She also has a poetry collection published, and is hard at work on her next projects, including the sequel to *False Security*, titled *False Hope.*

Website: http://www.angiemartinbooks.com/

Fan Group: http://www.facebook.com/groups/angiesconduits

Facebook: http://www.facebook.com/authorangiemartin

Twitter: http://www.twitter.com/zmbchica

One Last Thing…

Thanks for reading! If you enjoyed this book, I'd be very grateful if you would post a short review on Amazon and/or Goodreads. Your support really does make a difference and I read all the reviews personally so I can get your feedback. Thank you again for your support!

Made in the
USA
Middletown, DE

76639351R10169